LIES WITH
MAN

MICHAEL
NAVA

AMBLE
PRESS
ANN ARBOR

2021

Amble Press

Copyright © 2021 Michael Nava

Print ISBN: 978-1-61294-197-4

Amble Press First Edition: April 2021

Printed in the United States of America on acid-free paper.

Cover designer: Ann McMan, TreeHouse Studio

Amble Press
PO Box 3671
Ann Arbor MI 48106-3671

www.amblepressbooks.com

This is a work of fiction. Names, characters, places, and
incidents are the product of the author's imagination, or,
in the case of Proposition 54 and historical persons,
are used fictitiously.

For Mike Lyons and Alan Heppel.

If a man lies with another man as with a woman,
both of them have committed an abomination.
They shall surely be put to death.
Their blood guilt shall be upon them.

Leviticus 20:13 (Modern English Version)

There is no fear in love,
but perfect love casts out fear.

1 John 4:18 (English Standard Version)

PROPOSITION 54
For the California Ballot, November 1986

I. Text

Acquired immune deficiency syndrome (AIDS) is an infectious, contagious and communicable disease and the condition of being a carrier of the HTLV-III virus is an infectious, contagious and communicable condition and both shall be placed and maintained by the director of the Department of Health Services on the list of reportable diseases and conditions mandated by Health and Safety Code Section 3123, and all personnel of the Department of Health Services and all health officers shall fulfill all of the duties and obligations specified in each and all of the sections of said statutory division in a manner consistent with the intent of this Act, as shall all other persons identified in said provisions.

II. Analysis

Declares that AIDS is an infectious, contagious and communicable disease and that the condition of being a carrier of the HTLV-III virus is an infectious, contagious and communicable condition. Requires both be placed on the list of reportable diseases and conditions maintained by the director of the Department of Health Services. *Provides that both are subject to quarantine and isolation statutes and regulations.* Provides that Department of Health Services personnel and all health officers shall fulfill the duties and obligations set forth in specified statutory provisions to preserve the public health from AIDS.

ONE

The boy's eyelids fluttered like butterfly wings as if restlessly scanning the dreamscape into which sleep had transported him. Keeping vigil beside the bed, Daniel thought people were wrong to describe death as sleeping; sleep was an activity of the living, filled, like Wyatt's, with squirms and fidgets, groans and sighs, frowns and smiles. He was pinned to the narrow bed by IVs and monitoring devices emitting beeps and buzzes above the rasp of his troubled breathing. Daniel drew a deep breath and slowly exhaled as if, by example, he could encourage Wyatt to clear the sickness from his lungs. He entwined his fingers with the boy's—the warm hand was limp and unresponsive to Daniel's touch. He should pray, he thought, but what more could he say to God that God had not already heard? Still, he whispered, *Father, please . . .*

The faint pressure of a hand on his shoulder silenced him. Gwen held out a foam cup of milky coffee to him. He took it, gratefully. She resumed her watch on the other side of the bed. Behind her, the windy San Francisco night growled faintly against the window. The brisk, jarring, urgent noises of the ward had subsided to a thrum, creating a peculiar intimacy in the small room, as if they were the only three people in the world.

"Did he wake up at all?"

He shook his head. "I think he's out for the night."

1

She smiled wanly. "He hasn't slept through the night since he was admitted, and he wakes up confused and scared."

Her shift had ended, but she was still in her nurse's scrubs. He wondered when she'd last slept.

"He's lucky he's here where you work instead of with strangers," Daniel said. "Your nurse friends have been dropping in all night to check on him."

"Everyone's rooting for him."

"It's hard to believe this is where we ended up," he said.

She lifted Wyatt's hand delicately and rubbed her thumb along his palm as if imparting her life force into him. The gesture sparked an old memory, and Daniel asked, "Did you ever read his fortune?"

She glanced at him in bewilderment.

"Don't you remember? The first time we met, you read my palm."

She smiled, and for a moment he saw in her tired face the beautiful Black girl who had taken his hand, turned it palm up, and studied it intently on a chilly day in Golden Gate Park almost twenty years earlier in the Summer of Love.

"This is your wisdom line," Gwen had told him, gravely, tracing a line in his palm. "You're a seeker."

The sun was a white disc in the gray sky, and a cold wind crackled through the tops of the eucalyptus trees, but the park was still crowded with the young. The swirling shapes of dancers, cacophony of drums, clouds of marijuana surrounded Daniel and Gwen on the poncho she'd spread on the ground with a hand-written sign on it that advertised "Free Palm Readings."

He closed his hand around hers and said with mock seriousness, "Seek and you shall find."

She laughed, stood up, playfully pulled him to his feet, and took him to her squat where they spent the rest of the afternoon on a mattress on the floor.

2

⍋ ⍋ ⍋

"You said I was a seeker," he reminded her now.

"I was right, wasn't I?"

"At the time I thought I'd found what I was looking for."

"We all did back then," she said with a trace of a smile.

At first, living in Haight-Asbury had been like living inside a kaleidoscope, all mirrors and flashing colors. The old Victorians had been reclaimed as communes and painted outrageous colors, purple and orange, red and yellow, pink and blue, and their doors left unlocked to welcome young refugees from what neighborhood graffiti called AmeriKKKa. AmeriKKKA was the death machine from which the young had escaped, following the directive spray-painted on the wall of the free clinic: *Turn On, Tune In, Drop Out.*

Daniel, a recent dropout from San Francisco State College, embraced the creed. If he panhandled tourists, he wasn't begging, he was giving them an opportunity to support a free life; if he dropped acid, it wasn't to escape his grubby circumstances, but to expand his consciousness; if he grabbed food from the supermarket without paying, he wasn't stealing it, he was liberating it. Every act that defied the laws and conventions of the squares was an act of revolution.

Gwen was as much a believer as he, but while his political ideas were a grab bag of voguish platitudes, hers were the fruit of a studious and methodical mind. She was not playing at revolution; she really wanted to dismantle the machinery of oppression, and her first step was to understand it. While he threw Frisbees in the park, she hunkered down with *The Wretched of the Earth, The Autobiography of Malcom X,* and *The Second Sex.*

Daniel spouted slogans; Gwen advanced arguments. Her clarity about the mechanism of oppression helped him convince himself that simply by being with her, a Black girl, he was engaged in the

3

struggle against it. When, however, her studies took her into women's consciousness-raising groups, and the oppression under discussion was male, her critical gaze fixed him in her sights. Their life together became a series of confrontations for which he was ill-prepared. He saw the logic of her arguments against male domination but protested, "Not me, Gwen," which only infuriated her. At the same time, the Summer of Love came to a chilly end. Darker colors seeped into his kaleidoscope. Lured by tales of the free-loving, drug-taking hippie Utopia in San Francisco, a more desperate crowd descended on the neighborhood: wounded kids, kids addicted to stronger drugs than pot and acid, kids with mental troubles, and ordinary criminals looking for easy marks.

When Gwen left him to live in a women's commune, he wandered the Haight without plan or purpose, hedged by anxiety, lost in fear. One day, hungry and tired, he went to a storefront coffeehouse he'd heard was serving free meals. In the window was a painting of an oxbow with the words "For my yoke is easy and my burden is light" in psychedelic script.

Remembering those days now, he said, "I was drowning without you."

She'd had no time for his self-pity then, when her feminist analysis of his behavior hurt his feelings, and she had no time for it now. "Is that why you jumped on the Jesus lifeboat? If you'd waited, a better one would have come for you. White boys aren't allowed to drown, not then or now."

"We both knew plenty of white boys who did," he replied brusquely. "The one who ended up on drugs. That could have been me, shooting up and overdosing in an alley. It wasn't an accident I found the Living Room. I was led there."

He had pushed open the door and was greeted by familiar smells—patchouli, pot, tobacco—but it was the aromas of coffee and soup that drew him and his rumbling stomach farther into the big, shabbily furnished room. Another quotation painted on the wall brought back a childhood memory of sitting in church: "For God so loved the world he gave his only begotten son so whoever believes in him shall not perish but have eternal life." A boy with curling hair that fell to his back, wearing a beat-up, fringed leather jacket, approached Daniel with a wide smile and gripped his hand in a soul shake.

"Hey man, I'm Ronnie; who are you?"

"I'm Daniel."

"You hungry, Daniel? The girls made chicken soup, and there's doughnuts and coffee. Come and help yourself."

Daniel was studying another quotation on the wall: "I am the way and the truth and the light. No one comes to the father except through me."

He looked at Ronnie and asked, "What's your trip, man?"

Ronnie's big smile got even bigger. "Jesus is my trip."

Jesus is my trip. Ronnie Carson, the wild-haired urchin who had brought him to Jesus, was still out there somewhere preaching in the streets. He would have been nineteen, the same age then as Wyatt was now. So young, both of them; Daniel himself only twenty-one when he had stumbled into the Living Room, as the coffeehouse was known. He returned day after day to eat soup and drink coffee and listen as Ronnie or one of the other men who ran the place read scripture and talked about Jesus.

Daniel was indifferent to Christianity. In his Lutheran family, religion was something reserved for the starchy hour they spent in church on Sunday, which otherwise did not impinge on their lives. What drew Daniel to the Jesus people wasn't their beliefs but their joy and their generosity which recaptured for him the original spirit of the Haight.

Almost without knowing it, Daniel had become part of the community, scrubbing the toilet in the Living Room's squalid little bathroom or going out on the daily dumpster-dives for food behind supermarkets or to negotiate with local bakeries for day-old bread and pastries. He faithfully read the little New Testament they gave him, donated by a local church and originally intended for missionaries in India, and joined in the Bible studies. The Jesus they believed in was nothing like the remote, ghostly presence he remembered from Sunday school. This Jesus was an earthy, long-haired, street-wise preacher who consorted with the lowly and took the powerful to task. Daniel loved this Jesus. But was he God? That was the precipice where Daniel found himself stalled.

One morning, as he was sweeping the sidewalk in front of the Living Room, Ronnie approached him with a sly smile. "Let's hitch to Ocean Beach and drop a tab of this fantastic acid I just scored."

It was a glittering December day; the surface of the ocean was like plates of glass slowly sliding one over the other. Gulls dipped and soared in the blue air. The sky was cloudless. They sat on a tree trunk someone had dragged onto the sand. The air was filled with the decaying smell of the kelp scattered on the beach. Ronnie put the tab of acid on Daniel's tongue as if it were a communion wafer and placed the other on his own. They swallowed and sat, waiting for the drug to kick in.

Daniel remembered how he had stared at the sand where, it seemed to him, he could see simultaneously the golden glint of each individual grain and the golden carpet of the entire beach. He remembered he had raised his eyes to the sky, and the dip and soar of the gulls was transformed from flight into script. The words they wrote across the sky he repeated aloud: "I come from the Father and have come into the world and now I am leaving the world and going to the Father."

Beside him, Ronnie said, "John sixteen twenty-five."

"What?"

"It's what Jesus said to the disciples before he left them to go home to his Father."

Daniel began to sob. "He's abandoned us," he stuttered. "He's left us here alone."

Ronnie put his arm around Daniel and said in a warm, urgent, intimate whisper, "No, Danny, listen to the rest of the verse. The disciples say, now we understand that we know all things and there's no need to question you. From this we can believe that you came from God. And then Jesus goes, do you now believe? He's asking, do you believe I'm God? That's the question every Christian has to answer, Danny. He's asking you. Do you believe Jesus is God? Do you accept him as your Lord and Savior so he can be with you always?"

Daniel wiped tears and snot on his shirtsleeve, and when he looked back at the sky the script had faded, and everything was light.

"Yes!" he shouted. "Yes!"

Ronnie had jumped up, hauled Daniel into the freezing ocean, and baptized him.

"Remember that moment," he told Gwen. "That Jesus boat wasn't just something to grab onto because you left me."

She relented. "I'm sorry I was disrespectful, Daniel. In my family Jesus was the strap they used to keep me in line whenever I did anything my mom didn't think was ladylike." She sipped her coffee. "That's what Jesus meant to me when you told me you were saved. I should have asked what it meant to you."

He remembered the glittering ocean, the pang of salt in the air, the cries of the gulls in the dizziness of blue above him, and how he had felt filled with light.

"It meant," he said, "for a moment, I was blinded by love and when that passed, nothing looked the same again."

But at the time, when she had come to see him at the Living Room, his conversion was still too fresh for him to have words for it. She looked around the room, read the scripture on the wall, listened to his story about how he'd been struck by the glory of the Lord, and said dismissively, "The Lord? You mean that old white man in the sky who told women to bow down to the men?"

"Paul said in God there is no male and female and all are one in Jesus Christ."

"Tell that to the girls washing dishes in the kitchen while you guys sit around out here smoking and drinking coffee and rapping." She got up. "This trip isn't for me and maybe, when the acid high wears off, it won't be for you, either."

He grabbed her hand. "Gwennie, don't go. I love you."

She pulled her hand away, looked at him and said, "I'm pregnant."

"What?"

"Don't worry, Danny, I'm going to take care of it."

"What do you mean, take care of it?" he asked in horror. "You don't mean an abortion."

"That's for me to decide," she said flatly.

"It's my child, too," Daniel protested. "You can't just kill it."

"You don't tell me what to do with my body."

"Marry me," he exclaimed.

Her eyes which had been angry, filled with sadness. "You don't mean that."

He drew in a breath. "I'm serious. Marry me. I'll do whatever you want me to do, even if it means leaving my friends here. Leaving the city, getting a straight job, starting over somewhere else."

She shook her head. "I don't want you to change your life for me anymore than I want to change my life for you. I won't marry you, Danny. Our thing is over. You go your way, and I'll go mine." And with that she had left.

Now, he said, "I went to the commune where you were living. A redheaded girl told me you'd gone hone and slammed the door in my face."

Gwen chuckled softly. "That would have been Alice."

He continued, "I realized I didn't even know where your family lived. I had no way to reach you." He shook his head. "I stood there and cried until another girl came up the steps and

8

saw me and told me I should leave." He shrugged. "At least she was nice about it."

The quiet of the hospital room was broken by the splash of rain against the window. They both looked over as water began to streak the glass. He remembered how he had wiped his eyes and nose on the sleeve of his dirty cowhide jacket and gone heavily down the stairs.

Six years later the Living Room had been shuttered, its people scattered, but Daniel's conversion stuck. He returned to school, a small Christian college in Orange County. There, the freewheeling faith he had learned on the streets of San Francisco was tempered by the corollary tenets of man's inherent sinfulness and the requirement of repentance. Daniel, having watched with dismay as what was left of the idealism of the sixties soured into consumption, materialism and licentiousness, accepted those teachings. If other principles, like the inerrancy of the Bible and the exclusivity of Christianity, gave him pause, he hammered out his doubts with his teachers until he arrived at a place of, if not blind, then working acceptance. As the years passed, the distinction evaporated.

He was ordained, became the youth pastor at a big, unaffiliated evangelical church in Los Angeles called Ekklesia. He thrived in the role, bringing dozens of young families into an aging congregation. He also discovered a gift for raising money that, more than his ministerial skills, brought him to the attention of Max Taggert, Ekklesia's founding pastor. Taggert's only child was a daughter, Jessica, who could not, of course, inherit his position, as women were barred from ordination. Taggert, eyeing a successor, began to call Daniel "son."

A church in San Francisco had invited him to help design its youth ministry. After six years, the city was at once familiar and unrecognizable. The streets were the same, but the feet that trod them belonged to strangers. One afternoon he strolled through the Haight, where no trace of the sixties remained except in fading graffiti and a couple of old hippie businesses. Moved by nostalgia, he stepped into a phone booth, opened the phone book, and looked up Gwen. He didn't really expect to find her since, as far as he knew, she'd never returned to the city. But there she was: Gwen Baker. Or, a Gwen Baker. Living in the Mission on Fair Oaks Street. Impulsively he called her. She knew him by his voice, even before he said his name, and invited him to dinner.

Daniel had stood at the front door of Gwen's flat—one half of a tall Victorian on a street of tall Victorians—and peered through the window at a steep flight of stairs. He rang the bell. A moment later the small figure of a boy came hurtling down the stairs and opened the door, breathless. He was seven, Daniel later learned. He had Gwen's frizzy hair, complexion, and elegant features but his eyes—blue and awash with curiosity—were Daniel's.

"Hello," Daniel said. "Is your mother home?"

"She's cooking," he said. "She said to let you in. I'm Wyatt."

"I'm Daniel."

Their conversation was limited by Wyatt's presence. Bright, inquisitive and bold, he had interrupted them when they attempted to speak in grown-up code and demanded to know what they were talking about. Eventually, they gave up and restricted themselves to pleasantries as they sipped coffee in Gwen's comfortable living room while Wyatt sprawled on his belly on the floor with crayons and paper, coloring with one hand and shooing away a plump gray cat with the other.

"What are you drawing?" Daniel asked.

"It's a stego—stego . . ."

"Saurus," Gwen said.

"Mom! I was going to say that."

"I'm sorry, Wyatt."

"My school went to the natural history museum, and we saw the dinosaur bones. When I grow up, I want to be a paleo— a paleo . . ." Now he glanced at Gwen for help.

"Paleontologist."

"And dig up dinosaur bones from millions of years ago."

"You know, Wyatt," Daniel said, "the Bible tells us God created the world and all the animals in it in seven days and seven nights."

He gawked at Daniel and exclaimed, "That's ridiculous!"

"Wyatt, don't be rude to our guest."

Wyatt grunted and went back to his drawing. A few minutes later, he got up with his picture and went to Daniel. He held out the drawing and said, "I'm sorry I was rude. You can have my picture."

Daniel studied the drawing of the lumpy, spiky-backed green blob with Wyatt's name in the corner. "Thank you, Wyatt. That's very nice."

"And now," Gwen said, "it's time for you to go to bed."

While Gwen put Wyatt to bed, Daniel walked around the living room. On the mantel over the fireplace there were framed photographs of Gwen's family—people Daniel had never met— and Gwen in a graduation robe and mortarboard. A banner on the wall behind her indicated the photograph had been taken at the nursing school of San Francisco State. There were a half-dozen photographs of Wyatt from infancy on, some with Gwen or other family members, some of Wyatt alone. But no men other than those he took to be her father or brothers. No boyfriend. No husband.

She came into the room and said, "I usually have a glass of wine after I get him into bed. You want one?"

He shook his head.

"You mind if I do?"

"Not at all."

She disappeared into the kitchen and emerged holding a large wine glass half-filled with dark liquid. Drinking was not proscribed by his church—even his future father-in-law enjoyed

11

his occasional tumbler of Scotch on the rocks—and many of his congregants drank, a few to excess. Daniel chose to set an example of sobriety for the younger people he worked with. Now, looking at her wine, he thought if ever there was a time for alcohol, this was it.

"You know," he said. "I think I will have a glass."

"Here," she said. "Take mine. You probably need it more than I do."

She sat beside him on the plush couch and handed him the wine.

"Why didn't you tell me about Wyatt?" Daniel asked, turning the glass in his hand.

She took a deep breath. "I didn't know until I went home that I couldn't go through with an abortion. After Wyatt was born, I had enough on my plate without tracking you down and adding that complication. I thought that maybe later I could find you, but by the time I came back to the city that place in the Haight was closed down and I didn't know where else to look for you."

"What changed your mind about the abortion?"

She took the glass from him for a sip, then handed it back. "Wyatt may not have been planned, but he was conceived in love. And you were—are—a good person. I'm sure you're a wonderful father to your other children."

"I'm not married," he said.

"Oh," she exclaimed. "Sorry. I'm surprised."

"I will have to, eventually," he said. "We're not Catholics. Unmarried pastors don't inspire a lot of confidence."

"Getting married is like a job requirement?"

"I want a family," he said and, after a moment, continued. "You aren't married, either. Why?"

"I didn't want a man who wasn't Wyatt's father to raise him."

"Will you write to me sometimes and let me know how he is?"

"He can write to you himself."

"You'll tell him who I am, then?"

"When he's a little older. Is that all right?"

12

"Yes, but, when the time comes, I'd like to be here."

"Of course. You are his father."

He gazed at her and thought she didn't want to marry a man who wasn't Wyatt's father and here he was, Wyatt's father, also unmarried. Shouldn't they at least consider . . . ? For Wyatt's sake? He looked at the glass in his hand as he imagined breaking the news to Pastor Taggert, the man who called him "son," and who had grown up a white man in the Jim Crow South with all the prejudices that implied.

She broke into his thoughts, observing, "We lead very different lives, Daniel. I'm happy with mine. I hope you're happy with yours."

"I am," he said.

"Good," she said, answering his unspoken question once and for all.

A few days later a letter arrived at the church addressed to him with the word *Personal* written on the envelope. When he opened it and unfolded the paper, there were four lines in green crayon:

> *Dear Daniel, today we went to the Golden Gate Park*
> *and had a fun time. I liked you. I hope you come*
> *back to see me again.*
>
> *Love, Wyatt*

A year later, Daniel married Taggert's daughter and when Taggert died, took his place as head of Ekklesia.

Daniel stroked Wyatt's forehead and said, "I've kept everything he ever sent me. Every drawing, every photo, every letter. Even the one where he told me about his—that he was gay."

Gwen said, "It took you weeks to answer him."

He frowned at her. "What did you expect? It was the last thing in the world I wanted to hear."

"He thought you hated him."

"I know," Daniel said. "He told me. I told him I could never hate him."

"I could never hate you, Wyatt." He had stared ahead as he spoke, at the turbid water on a cold, foggy August afternoon at Ocean Beach. Wyatt sat beside him on a blanket spread across the sand, his tension as palpable as an electric current, a cigarette burning between his long, slender fingers. "But I do wish you wouldn't smoke."

Wyatt made a noise, half-laugh, half-groan, and crushed the cigarette into the gray sand.

"Come on, Dad, at least it's not pot." Then he looked at his father. "I thought you'd be mad because, you know, your religion."

Daniel chose his words carefully. "I accept your decision, but that doesn't mean I approve."

Wyatt's eyes flared. "I didn't decide anything. It's who I am."

"And I'm who I am," Daniel replied. "If you want me to respect who you are, you have to respect who I am."

"That mean we never talk about it again?" Wyatt said sullenly.

"There's nothing we can't talk about, even the hard stuff, but that doesn't mean we won't disagree. That's what adults do."

Wyatt stared out at the ocean, thoughtfully. "Okay, Dad," he said, at last. "I guess I can live with that."

"We think there are different kinds of love," Daniel had once preached to his congregation, "and some are greater than others, but that's not true for Christians. For Christians, there is only one kind of love because there is only one God and John tells us God *is* love. Now, it's true that we have different obligations to the different people we love and some of those obligations are greater than others, but the love, that's the same. Don't forget that because once you go down the road of, oh I don't love this person as much as that person, it's not that much of a jump to start treating people you say you love differently, some better and some worse. When that happens, you've stopped loving."

Four times a year, his congregants knew Daniel went on a silent retreat at a Jesuit order house outside of San Francisco. He arrived on Friday and spent the first night and the following morning at the retreat house, but then he drove to San Francisco where he remained until Monday with Gwen and Wyatt. Wyatt grew from a cheerful child into a mostly cheerful teen who got C's in math and science and A's in English and art, played point guard on his high school basketball team, had been busted by his mother for smoking pot, was proud of his driver's license, and wrote monthly letters to Daniel that Daniel kept in a locked desk drawer in his office at the church. The love Daniel felt for his son was as unfiltered and uncomplicated as if it had traveled like a beam of light directly from God into Daniel's heart.

But then came the terrible call from Gwen. "Wyatt's sick," she said. "It's AIDS."

"You let him have sex with another man!"

"I didn't let him do anything. He's eighteen, Daniel. He made his own decision. It was a mistake, but kids make mistakes. Like we did when you got me pregnant."

"You can't possibly compare that with what he did. Oh my God. Wyatt," he had sobbed. "My boy."

"You should go back to the apartment, get some sleep," Gwen was saying. "You have an early flight."

"I can't go without saying good-bye to him."

Slowly, insistently, Gwen said, "He's going to recover from this, Daniel. There will be other times."

15

"This kind of pneumonia, though, isn't a sign that he'll get worse?"

"Not necessarily."

"I wish I could believe you."

Gwen started to reply but before she could, Wyatt's eyes flew open, confused and unfocused. He looked at his mother and then at Daniel, peering at him as if seeing him for the first time. Then he smiled and said, "Dad, you're here."

Daniel answered, "Where else would I be?"

TWO

The vehicle blocking the driveway as I backed out of my garage was so conspicuously nondescript it could only be a plainclothes cop car. I rolled down the window, cut the engine, and waited. A short-haired woman in a pantsuit the same dull, dark gray as her car got out of the driver's seat, followed a moment later by a buff young guy in a suit almost indistinguishable from hers. She approached my window. He stood a step behind her. The sunglasses hiding his eyes were a kid's idea of intimidation.

"Henry Rios," she not quite questioned.

"Who's asking?"

"Doris Whitcombe. Special agent, FBI. My partner, John Colby."

I glanced at him. "Trainee?" When neither responded, I asked, "What do you want?"

"The man who owns this house, Larry Ross, was involved in drug smuggling. We have reason to believe there are still drugs on the premises. We'd like to look around."

Doris Whitcombe looked less like a cop than a high school science teacher—the sensible haircut; utilitarian clothes; plain, intelligent face; unthreatening voice. The feds didn't go in for the stormtrooper bluster of LAPD, but behind their blankness was the same implied threat of menace.

"Larry Ross died six months ago. The drugs he allegedly smuggled were over-the-counter medications from Mexico to relieve the suffering of men infected with HIV. That's not a violation of any federal statute I'm aware of."

She replied, crisply. "Those drugs are not approved by the Federal Drug Administration for HIV."

"That's a regulatory issue, not a criminal offense. Doctors routinely prescribe off-label uses for drugs. Are you going to bust them?"

"These drugs were not prescribed by doctors."

"Because they're nonprescription drugs."

"In Mexico, not here. You could be charged with conspiracy to distribute illegal drugs."

I'd had it. "Go to hell. You and your boy should be ashamed of working for a government that would rather let my friends die than have access to drugs that might save their lives. If you have probable cause I've broken any law, arrest me. As for searching my house without a warrant, fuck you. Now move your goddamn car. I have to get to court. Or didn't you know I'm a criminal defense lawyer?"

Her face had gone red, but she maintained her bureaucratic monotone and said, "We will be back, sir."

I wanted to shout at her something about it being 1986 and not 1984, but I figured the George Orwell allusion would be wasted on her. I started the car. She and her partner walked down the driveway to their own car, got in, and drove away.

As soon as they were gone, I cut the engine again and pressed my forehead against the steering wheel. Grief and fury surged through my body like electrical shocks. It was moments like this that I most missed Larry Ross, my friend and AA sponsor.

It was a clear, mild day in May. The sun warmed my face. Birds chirped in the trees. A vine of deep red bougainvillea crept up the wall that enclosed the back yard of Larry's hillside house. Well, my house, technically. Without telling me Larry had put the place into joint tenancy with me. When six months earlier an aneurysm had burst in his brain in a hotel room in Mexico City, I became the owner of his fifteen-room, 1925 Spanish mission residence in a canyon above Franklin Avenue, at the edge of

Griffith Park. Far too much house for me, and I couldn't enter a room without expecting to find him there, but I couldn't bear to leave it yet, either. It was my last physical connection to him.

In his late forties, Larry'd been a hugely successful partner at the most successful entertainment law firm in LA. He was also an alcoholic, a coke addict, and a closeted gay man. Forced from the closet when a trick he'd picked up at a bathhouse tried to blackmail him, he'd come out to his law partners who had had no problem with his homosexuality but forced him into rehab. When he emerged, he had poured the same energy and tough-talking empathy that had made him a preeminent entertainment lawyer into helping other people get and stay sober. Two years earlier, he'd found me in a halfway house in San Francisco with three months of shaky sobriety, feeling hopeless and desperate, and had steered me back to sanity and a new life in Los Angeles where I was slowly rebuilding my criminal law practice.

He invited me to stay at his house until I got on my feet, but even after I could have found my own place, I stayed on. We got along as roommates and, by then, Larry had been diagnosed as HIV positive. He'd suffered a bout of PCP, the virulent strand of pneumonia that was often the first of the opportunistic diseases that attacked the compromised immune systems of people with the virus. After that, there was no question of my moving out.

The near-death experience of PCP changed his priorities. He had cashed out of his law practice and thrown himself into the battle against AIDS. He took as his motto Mother Jones's axiom: "Pray for the dead and fight like hell for the living." Not content to be a checkbook activist, he looked for a way to fight on the front lines. He heard about two drugs that, when used together, had bolstered the immune system of some people with HIV. The catch: the drugs weren't authorized for HIV treatment in the United States, and the Federal Drug Administration had rejected requests to begin trial of them for that purpose. They were, however, available over the counter in Mexico.

An underground already existed of people crossing the border, smuggling the drugs in bulk and distributing them at cost to anyone who wanted to try the regimen. But it wasn't enough to keep up with demand. Larry bought a Cessna, hired a gay pilot, and began flying all over Mexico to scour pharmacies for the drugs. I had once helped him unload the boxes in the big storage facility where he stored the drugs but only that one time.

"You need to keep your hands clean," he said, rejecting my further offer to help with the operation. "Because if I'm arrested, I'll need you to represent me."

So I knew little about the Mexican operation and nothing about the mysterious activities that had him flying to Israel, France and Japan except that he was pursuing leads about drugs and treatments that might be effective against the virus but which the FDA refused to consider. I worried that he was pushing himself too hard and would get sick. In the end, the brain aneurysm that killed him was a completely unexpected and yet, maybe merciful end considering the death he might otherwise have suffered from AIDS.

He'd left me a letter to open after he died. It contained the combination to a safe he had installed in his home office where I found a quarter-million dollars in cash. The letter provided detailed instructions about to whom and in what amounts I was to deliver the money. I visited a half-dozen cities across the country delivering bundles of cash to various people. I asked few questions, and they volunteered little information. Had I broken the law? Not as far as I knew. It was Larry's money, and he could give it to whomever he wanted. I was simply the courier. What they did with the funds was not my concern. Nonetheless, the appearance of the FBI agents had me rattled. I'd been a defense lawyer a long time and I knew that insulating myself through ignorance of possibly illegal activity went only so far.

I started up my car and headed off to court.

The Santa Monica courthouse was one of those ubiquitous institutional, International Style buildings of the 1960s—straight lines, square corners, glass fenestration, a gleaming white façade—

that could have been a bank, a school, or for that matter a church; all the architect would have had to do was add a cross. The hearing in *People v. Woods, et al.*, however, was not being conducted in one of the building's austere courtrooms but in a trailer behind the courthouse pressed into service to handle the court's overflow.

I was not an attorney of record in *Woods*. A friend had asked me to stand in for him because he was in trial elsewhere. *Woods* involved the arrests of some UCLA students at an anti-apartheid demonstration at the federal building for trespassing. A few of the demonstrators had scuffled with the cops and were then also charged with resisting arrest and with battery on a police officer. The kids said the cops started the fracas. I and the lawyers representing the other defendants were here on a *Pitchess* motion. *Pitchess* was a defense request to examine a cop's personnel records for prior citizen complaints of misconduct that could be used against the cop at trial. We wanted to know if any of the officers in this case had been subjects of prior complaints of excessive force to buttress the kids' claim that the cops started the fight and the protestors acted in self-defense.

Despite attempts to invest the trailer with some kind of judicial dignity—there were wooden benches in the gallery and an elevated dais for the judge—it was unmistakably a trailer, windowless, cramped, and poorly ventilated. My fellow defense counsel—six of us in all, for each of the six defendants, Lewis Woods being the lead defendant—were huddled around one of two counsel tables at the front of the room. As was typical of pretrial hearings, the defendants themselves were not present. At the other table sat the solitary DA assigned to the case, and in the gallery was another lawyer I recognized but was surprised to see here, Marc Unger.

Marc was an Assistant Los Angeles City Attorney. He ran the division of the office that represented the police departments in civil suits, defending cops from lawsuits that charged them

21

with misconduct up to and including the wrongful death of suspects in their custody. He had a cop's beefy build himself—three quarters muscle, one-quarter fat—and an easy but authoritative baritone. He exuded such unapologetic, traditional masculinity few people would have guessed he was gay. But he was gay, uncloseted, and comfortable in his skin.

I knew Marc from meetings of the gay and lesbian lawyers association where he flirted with me relentlessly. Not that I was special in that regard—he flirted with any attractive gay man who crossed his path. He saw me and smiled his charming, crooked smile. He was, as always, elegantly turned out in a bespoke suit, his handsome face smooth and glowing as if he'd just been shaved by his own personal barber who had also clipped and styled his hair to camera-ready, movie star perfection.

"Marc?" I queried, approaching him. "What are you doing here?"

"Hello, Henry," he said, shaking my hand. "You represent one of the defendants?"

I shook my head. "I'm standing in for Mitch Prynne. He's in trial. You didn't answer my question."

He smiled sunnily. "Just observing."

That was, as we both knew, a lie. Marc was far too busy and was too much of a big shot to waste a morning observing a pre-trial motion in a misdemeanor prosecution in a trailer courtroom on the far end of town from his posh office in City Hall East.

"Bullshit," I said.

Still smiling, he leered and rumbled, "You kiss with that mouth?"

When it was clear that was all I was going to get from him, I headed back to the counsel table and asked the same question of Ellen Lefkowitz, a tough, smart defense lawyer representing the lead defendant Woods.

"I don't know," she said, "but something's up. I saw him out in the parking lot arguing with the DA. Don't worry, I'll get to the bottom of it."

At that moment, the bailiff stood up and said, "All rise. Department 5 of the Santa Monica Superior Court is now in session, the Honorable Pauline Masanque-Brown presiding."

The judge came in unceremoniously through a door behind the clerk's desk and took her seat. She was a small, dark-skinned woman—the superior court's only Filipina—with graying hair, a frosty demeanor, and a stern, no-nonsense reputation. If you were prepared, she was an exemplary judge, efficient and fair, but if you weren't, God help you.

"Be seated," she said. "We're here on *People v. Woods, et al.* Counsel, state your appearances for the record and then we'll move on to the motion."

When I stated my appearance and explained that Mitch was in trial, she glared. I braced myself for an interrogation about why he hadn't moved heaven and earth to make his appearance, but instead she turned to her clerk and asked, sharply, "Did he call?"

"Yes, Your Honor. He called on Friday. The trial is in Lancaster and the judge denied his request for a continuance so he could be here today. He apologizes."

I's dotted and t's crossed, she said, "Fine. Welcome, Mr. Rios."

I smiled. "Always a pleasure, Your Honor."

"Now," she said, "I've read the motion and the opposition. I will allow each side five minutes if they wish to say anything further before I—"

"Your Honor," the DA said.

"What is it, Mr. Robinson?" she asked, displeased at the interruption.

"Your Honor, the People move to dismiss all charges against all defendants in the interests of justice."

At the defense table we exchanged baffled looks.

"Did you file a 1382 motion?"

"No, Your Honor. I'm making it verbally now."

This was exactly the kind of surprise she did not like. "Tell me,

23

counsel, what are the interests of justice that would be served by dismissing a case against these defendants after two months of taking up this court's time and resources?"

Robinson visibly paled but plunged on. "We have new information."

"What information?"

He took a deep breath. "I can't say in open court."

Before she could respond Marc Unger was on his feet. "Your Honor, Marc Unger, Assistant City Attorney. If I may approach."

"What's your interest in this case, Mr. Unger?" she asked, sharply.

"If Mr. Robinson and I could approach and speak to you privately, I will explain everything," he said suavely.

Ellen was on her feet. "The defense objects."

Unger glanced over at us and in the same dulcet tone said, "If Her Honor agrees, the case against your clients will be dismissed. How could you possibly object to that, Miss Lefkowitz?"

"Because," Ellen replied, "if she doesn't agree, we want to know why you asked for a dismissal."

Manasque-Brown said, "Counsel, talk to me, not each other." She scowled. "Mr. Unger, Mr. Robinson, I don't know what you're up to but this is no way to proceed. If you wanted to dismiss this case, you should have filed the appropriate motion."

"Your Honor," Unger said. "This is a matter of the utmost sensitivity."

After a tense moment of silence, she said, "Approach."

Unger and Robinson stepped to the bench, and for the next five minutes they and the judge conducted a conversation in fierce whispers. At the end of it, she said, "Step back."

Ellen said, "Your Honor, the defense—"

"Objects, I know," she said. "Your objection is noted, but it's also irrelevant because I'm granting the People's motion and dismissing all charges against all defendants. With prejudice."

"Why?" I blurted out.

"Ask Mr. Unger," she said. "We're adjourned."

I caught up with Marc in the parking lot.

"Hey," I said. "What was that all about?"

He blasted me with his smile. "You been working out, Henry? Because you are looking good. You know, if I weren't already taken—"

"Answer my question."

He shrugged. "Your guy got off. Take the win."

I thought for a moment. "You represent the police department. We were asking for personnel records. There was something in them you didn't want us to see. Something worse than excessive force complaints. Something so bad you forced Robinson to drop the charges to keep those records private."

"You're wasted in the defense bar. You really should come and work for me."

"But what," I asked, "could be more damaging to a cop's reputation than excessive force complaints?"

He responded with a Cheshire cat grin.

"Come on, Marc, the case is over. Who am I going to tell?"

"You promise to keep this between us?"

"I swear on my gay card."

He smirked. "Fine. The department had an undercover cop in the anti-apartheid group the defendants belonged to. When the defense filed the *Pitchess* motion, some idiot police clerk included his name and records with the response. The DA had no idea who he was and called the department and they called me. We couldn't have the judge turn his name over to you guys and blow his cover. We need to protect our people."

"Even if it means dismissing the case?"

"What case? Misdemeanor trespass for a bunch of kids protesting apartheid? Hell, I agree with them."

"Is the undercover cop still in the group?"

"Nah, he's been reassigned."

"Why did the department plant an undercover cop there in the first place?"

"Objection. Beyond the scope of cross-examination. I've got to run, Henry. Call me for lunch sometime."

He got into his Beemer—the higher-ups in the city attorney's office were notoriously well paid—and drove off, leaving my question unanswered.

But I didn't have time to worry about it. I had a full day of court appearances ahead of me and a meeting at the end of it with a group of gay activists fighting Proposition 54, a ballot initiative to quarantine people infected with the HIV virus.

Proposition 54 was spawned by an alliance between a right-wing Congressman named Schultz and an evangelical preacher named Shelby who led an outfit he called the Alliance for Traditional Family Values. Both had long and ignominious records as gay-bashers. Even their fellow bigots—the politer ones anyway—found their views too extreme, but then AIDS emerged, and Schultz and Shelby were no longer voices crying in the wilderness. The theoretical threat posed by men having sex with each other had now, in the mind of many straights, become the actual threat of a lethal disease, no matter how often they were told the virus could not be casually transmitted. People still believed AIDS could be contracted through casual touch or even breathing the same air as an infected person. Schultz and Shelby, riding these waves of ignorance and fear, had put together Proposition 54 for the November ballot. If passed, it would allow county health officials to identify and round up people who were HIV positive and force them into quarantine camps. At the moment, seven months before the election, the polls showed Proposition 54 winning by twelve points.

I turned off Highland into the parking lot of the Gay and Lesbian Community Center and nosed my car into a narrow space. I always suspected, from its long L-shape, that in a previous life the center had been a hot sheet motel. Painted industrial gray, it was an unimposing building that, nonetheless, was constantly being vandalized with graffiti like the phrase I saw now in red spray-paint: "AIDS = Anally Inserted Death Serum." It looked pretty fresh, so I guessed the center's employees hadn't yet had a chance to paint over it. A couple of dozen people were milling around the entrance, smoking, laughing and, as usual wherever there are more than two gay men together, discreetly cruising. Though mostly a male and white crowd, there was also a sprinkling of women and of Black and brown faces. There wasn't much mixing among the groups, though, and that was a problem. Defeating Proposition 54 would require the community to unite but the community consisted of people whose difficult, private struggles to come out had left them mistrustful of all authority and strongly averse to being told what to do.

Fortunately, I didn't have to herd the cats. My job was to talk to would-be demonstrators about their legal rights and how to respond to the cops. I made my way into the community room, pausing in front of racks of pamphlets and brochures from the city's various AIDS organizations pushing safe sex and offering counseling and medical and social services. It never ceased to amaze me how quickly gay men and lesbians, aided by straight friends, had shaken off their terror of AIDS and organized themselves to take care of their own. The despair I had witnessed in San Francisco in 1984 had only two years later ripened into resistance.

In the main community room, a pudgy, white-haired man in black-rimmed glasses and a herringbone sports coat banged a gavel on the table at the front where he and a half-dozen other men and women were sitting. All the folding chairs that had been set out in the big space were occupied, and dozens of other people were standing against the walls or sitting on the floor. It was a pretty young crowd: there were a lot of black leather jackets, wallet chains, and hemmed jean shorts—the activists' wardrobe. T-shirts were emblazoned with the names of AIDS activist groups or slogans like, "How dare you presume I'm straight!" A dozen or so of the crowd, men and women, wore black T-shirts with a single word written across their chests: QUEER. I knew one of them—Laura Acosta. She taught a gay studies course at Los Angeles Community College. At her invitation I had spoken to a couple of her classes about the developments in the law regarding gay rights. Not much to report there.

Laura was a self-described butch dyke, her stockiness a product of power weight lifting, her hair cut and gelled into a flat-top, invariably dressed in men's khakis and a guayabera shirt. She was brash and loud and formidably smart. An anthropologist by training, with a PhD from the University of Arizona, she was overqualified to be teaching at a community college, but her efforts to find a tenure-track job at a four-year institution had been unsuccessful because, as she once told me, "I go in with three strikes against me. Woman, Chicana, dyke." I told her if she ever wanted to sue, I'd find her the best gay rights lawyer I could but, as it turned out, she liked teaching at LACC where her students were like herself, brown and Black kids who were the first in their families to go to any kind of college and who found in her a warm and generous mentor and an aggressive advocate.

I caught her eye as the meeting started and nodded. She grinned and mouthed, "Talk later."

The white-haired man at the front of the room, an old-school activist, pounded his gavel again and declared, "I call this meeting to order."

A tall, thin boy in a QUEER T-shirt jumped to his feet and shouted, "Who the fuck are you to be up there running things? Who put you in charge? We didn't elect you."

The old veteran replied calmly, "I'm not in charge of anything. No decisions are going to be made here this afternoon. This is purely an informational meeting. The people up here have been tracking Proposition 54 and they want to share what they've learned. How the community responds to 54 is up to everyone in this room."

"But you set up the room like you're the head honcho," the boy shouted back. "Like you got authority."

There was a hurried, hushed deliberation among the people at the head table, and then the older man said, "Point taken. Why don't we get rid of the table and form a circle? That way, no one's at the head of the room."

I groaned. This was precisely the kind of bickering that wasted time and energy better spent in organizing against the quarantine. But like everyone else I helped rearrange the room, shuffling chairs and bodies until we had achieved a semblance of a circle.

The older man, who introduced himself as Madison Knight, again called us to order and introduced the first speaker, a young lawyer named Wendell Thorne. Thorne gave us the background of the initiative, its potential effect—quarantine camps to which people with HIV would be forcibly removed— and the worrying poll numbers and concluded: "We have seven months to put together a statewide coalition to defeat the proposition, and I got to tell you, right now it looks like an uphill fight."

"That's impossible!" some shouted in disbelief.

"We have to make it happen," Thorne replied.

Another panelist, also a lawyer, a flame-haired woman who introduced herself as Kate Cassells from the Lesbian and Gay Legal Defense Fund, broke in. "We're also taking the fight to the courts. The LGLDF is about to file a lawsuit in the state supreme court trying to knock 54 off the ballot because it violates the state constitutional right to privacy by forcing people to disclose their HIV status."

It was a decent argument, but the state supreme court had an entrenched conservative majority. There was no way those ancient white men were going to side with people they doubtless considered deviants. Proposition 54 would have to be defeated at the ballot, or not at all.

Knight was saying, ". . . want to present some possible—and I emphasize possible—strategies to defeat 54. Like Wen said, the Christian right's all over this, but we are not without our allies in the church. Reverend Hester Price from St. George Episcopal has some ideas for mobilizing the Christian left—"

"Fuck that!" The tall QUEER T-shirted man who had disrupted

the proceedings earlier was on his feet again. "Who invited her? Christians are the enemy. They're all bigots and homophobes."

The man sitting in front of me stood up and shouted back, "I'm gay and I'm a Christian!"

The tall man strode toward us, got in the second man's face, and screamed, "Then you're an asshole and a traitor."

He shoved the second man, who slammed into me with such force I went over in my flimsy folding chair, smacked the back of my head on the concrete floor, and saw stars. I rolled away from the chair, touched the back of my head, and came away with blood on my fingers. Meanwhile, the meeting had dissolved into screaming voices and flailing arms.

A young man's face swam into my line of vision. A moment later he was kneeling on the floor beside me and saying, "Are you all right?"

"Help me up."

He pulled me to my feet. "Are you bleeding?" he asked, the blood from my fingers now staining his.

"A little, from my head. I need some air."

Still dazed, I staggered out of the room and slumped down on a bench outside the building. The young man reappeared, a wad of damp paper towels in his hand.

"Let me look at you."

I rested my chin on my chest and felt his fingers gently part my hair, then dab my skull with the paper towels. "It's not deep. There's a first aid kit inside. Don't move. I'll be right back."

He returned with a metal first aid kit, again parted my hair, applied a stinging antiseptic and then a Band-Aid to the cut.

"There," he said. "Good as new."

I smiled. "Are you a doctor?"

He smiled back. "Ex-Eagle scout. My name is Josh."

"I'm Henry. Thanks for coming to my rescue."

He glanced down at his feet, then up at me, and said shyly, "Um, it was my chance to meet you. Not," he added quickly, "that I wanted you to get hurt."

I guessed he was in his early twenties. His hair was a mass of black curls restrained by a shiny mousse. He had a delicate, bony face; a long nose; a wide, strong mouth; and a dimpled chin. Behind the lenses of his tortoise-shell framed glasses his eyes were the color of honey, the same tone as his skin.

"It was worth the blow to my head," I replied. He was wearing a QUEER T-shirt. "You're with that group."

He smiled. "For today anyway. My roommate drafted me. He said—"

The tall man from QUEER stomped out of the center accompanied by a shorter but more muscular Latino, also in a QUEER T-shirt. He regarded me with cool, confiding eyes, as if to say, *Can you believe these gringos?*

The taller man said to Josh, "Come on, we're leaving." He glared at me. "These people are losers."

Josh said, "He's the roommate I was—"

"Come on, Josh," he interrupted. "Let's go."

"I'm the one with the car," he said to me, apologetically. He took a pen from his pants pocket, lifted my hand, and carefully wrote a phone number on the back of it. "Call me?"

"Yeah."

"Promise?"

"I promise."

He smiled, said, "Okay, talk to you later," and went off with the QUEER cohort. At the edge of the parking lot, he turned back, smiled, and waved.

"Queers United to End Erasure and Repression."

Madison Knight—"a pseudonym, my dear, adopted back in the '50s when you could get locked up for daring to suggest homosexuals were human"—pronounced each word with slightly disdainful precision.

We were sitting in the now nearly empty community room, the town hall having ended. A few people still milled around, plotting, planning, despairing.

"That's quite a mouthful," I said.

Madison laughed. "The whole point is the acronym. *Queer*. A hate word for people our age. These boys and girls fling it in our faces, reclaim it, they say, to show us what old fuddy-duddies we are. Sellouts. And worst of all, the ultimate curse word, *assimilationists*."

"As opposed to what? Separatists?"

He shook his head. "No, my dear. Revolutionaries." He laid a liver-spotted hand on my arm. "It's part of an old, ongoing quarrel in the community between people willing to work in the system and people who want to bring it down. It started with Harry Hay and his Mattachine Society in the '50s. Hay had been a Communist. When they tossed him out of the party for sucking cock, he transferred his ideals from overthrowing the capitalists to overthrowing the straights. But most of us," he said, glancing around the room, "aren't revolutionaries. We just want what other people have—"

"'The most comprehensive of the rights,'" I quoted. "'The right to be let alone.'"

"Ah, I recognize that. Justice Brandeis." His glasses had begun to slip down his nose. He pushed them up and said, "Yes, the right to a truly private life. One where the government and the church aren't down on their knees outside the bedroom door peering through the keyhole and clucking in disgust. Within a few years Hay had been tossed out of Mattachine and it was taken over by what our QUEER comrades would call assimilationists." He smiled, showing cigarette smoke-stained teeth. "The irony, of course, is that we need both groups. The bomb throwers and compromisers. But they rarely see it that way." He sighed. "Sadly."

I imagined when the QUEER kids looked at him all they saw was a musty old man with a big heavy body, a lined face, and a crepe-y neck and thinning white hair. They had no idea of how he had put his life on the line for them long before they were born and what he had sacrificed to do it.

"Those kids owe you," I said, bitter on his behalf.

He laughed. "Oh, darling, nothing exists for the young but each other."

"Narcissists," I said, dismissively.

He shook his head. "Biological imperative, but thank you. What was I saying? Oh, yes. AIDS has only sharpened the division among us. With our lives now literally at stake, some of us see that the only solution is to cooperate with the politicians and the medical people to find a cure while groups like QUEER are convinced the pols and the doctors are bent on genocide. When something like 54 comes up, it's harder to write those views off as paranoia."

A deep voice boomed, "Is this *viejo* filling your head with stories about the good old days?"

I looked up and extended my hand. "Hello, Laura."

Laura Acosta casually crunched my hand. "Hey, Henry, how's your head?"

"I'll live. Madison was telling me about QUEER."

She smirked. "I bet. Listen, whatever he says, he's wrong. We're committed to peaceful civil disobedience. That's what I need to talk to you about."

Madison got up. "I'll excuse myself now. Henry, Laura."

She gave him a bear hug. "You know I love you, *viejo*. Thanks for organizing this."

"Try to stay out of jail."

She laughed. "I wouldn't be doing my job right if I did. Anyway, that's why we need Henry."

"Need me for what?" I asked, after Madison departed.

She sat down and spoke urgently. "Everyone's got to fight this *pinche* proposition in their own way. The lawyers in the courts, the political consultants with their ad campaigns. We're going to fight it in the streets. We're planning a bunch of demos and protests between now and November, and some of them," she grinned, "might cross a legal line or two. We need lawyers to observe the cops during the demos and to get us out of jail and represent us in court, if need be. What about it, Henry?" She leaned forward urgently in her chair. "Will you help?"

"No violence."

"Not from us," she replied. "Cross my heart."

"Do you run QUEER?"

She laughed loudly. "No one runs QUEER, *hombre*. We're a collective made up of smaller affinity groups. The affinities propose the actions and we talk about them. Endlessly. Then we reach a consensus whether or not to support the action as a group."

"What if the consensus goes against the action?"

She shrugged. "We can't stop it if that's what you're asking. All we can do is issue a statement saying it doesn't represent the group."

"So, if someone wants to throw a bomb or two, you can't prevent it?"

"We're angry, not stupid. No one's going to be throwing any bombs."

"What about the guy who started the ruckus where I ended up with a head wound?"

"Theo? Ah, he's a speed freak, that's all. Was probably high tonight. Gets aggressive when he's high."

"There a lot of drug use in QUEER?"

"Who am I, the DEA? Look, Theo's loud but harmless. Freddy keeps him in line."

"Freddy?"

"His boyfriend. The Chicano dude." She got up. "Can we count on you?"

"Yes."

"Cool. Come to our meeting on Monday at Plummer Park and you can see how we operate. It starts at eight and goes until—well, plan on a late night."

I turned the doorknob to let myself into the house from the garage and saw the phone number Josh had written on the back of my hand. It was a sweet, childlike gesture, as if we were little boys and he'd grabbed my hand to tug me to the playground. I hadn't been on the playground for a long time. The numbers were starting to blur. I dropped my keys into the bowl where I kept them, went into the kitchen, and wrote his name and phone number on a message pad. *I'll give him a call sometime*, I thought. Sometime? What was I waiting for? I picked up the phone and dialed.

THREE

Max Taggert had built his church on a drab, industrial section of South La Brea Boulevard, buying up warehouses and vacant lots and converting them to the landscaped grounds and the glass-and-concrete structures that made up the Ekklesia compound. Taggert was not a man for subtlety or nuance and the compound reflected his personality.

The sanctuary, built for up to 800 worshippers, was a jutting, soaring edifice that looked like an immense grouping of stalagmites. The entrance was plate-glass windows and doors that looked into a foyer paved with marble. A second set of doors led into a chapel paneled in mahogany, carpeted in plush gold wall-to-wall, and illuminated by stained-glass windows and dripping crystal chandeliers. The rows of well-padded, red-upholstered seats descended in a semi-circle to the raised platform of the altar. Throne-like chairs for the church elders made a semicircle behind the raised pulpit. Hidden in the rafters, TV cameras recorded and broadcast Sunday services on a Christian network to tens of thousands throughout California.

Behind the sanctuary was a courtyard bounded north and south by two long buildings. The north building held meeting places and administrative offices; the south building was a K to sixth-grade school. The courtyard between the buildings was divided in two. Half of it was a grassy playground, and the other half a rose garden in the center of which was a sculpture of a weeping angel in Carrera marble that marked the tomb of Max Taggert. The eastern boundary of the courtyard was marked by an ivy-covered wall and behind it was the church's parking lot. The entire compound was surrounded by immaculately kept lawns and flower beds. Over the entrance were enormous letters spelling out "Ekklesia," which at night blazed the name in blue neon, like a road sign to Heaven.

Daniel pulled into his parking space in the lot behind the church, noting that his wife's car was already in the spot reserved for the pastor's wife. Those were the words painted on her spot: "Reserved for the pastor's wife." His read: "Reserved for Pastor Herron." He was always more keenly aware of these tiny affronts to her dignity after he'd returned from seeing Gwen who would not have suffered them in silence. Jessica never mentioned it, but that didn't mean she hadn't noticed. He had learned early on in their marriage that Jessica noticed everything that affected her status as founder's daughter and pastor's wife, but she chose her battles carefully. Chose them not only for their significance to her, but whether the terrain was favorable to her particular battle techniques.

Jessica was coaxing, adaptable, and deferential. Her arguments often began with references to "my father," a reminder she was, after all, his only child, the last direct link to him. She never claimed this entitled her to special privileges. Rather, she would suggest her participation in this or that committee or initiative especially if controversy would help legitimize it. She was also thinking of the women of the church, she would say. If they had questions about a position or policy the men adopted, wouldn't it be better for them to direct those questions to her than for them to trouble the men?

When, inevitably, the men turned to Daniel for his thoughts, he almost always backed his wife. "Almost always" because there were times when he vetoed one of her requests, not so much because he disagreed with it, but because his position required him to occasionally assert his dominance over her as her pastor and her husband. He was well aware the other male leaders of the church believed women were, if not a different species entirely, then certainly, as scripture said, "the weaker vessel."

Max Taggert's teaching on this point was very clear. His standard texts on the status of women in the church were Timothy's admonition: "I do not permit a woman to teach or exercise authority over a man; she is to remain quiet." And Paul: "Wives submit to your husbands as to the Lord." Daniel, with his pre-conversion exposure to women like Gwen, found these references antiquated and condescending. But when, early on as youth minister, he had suggested as much, the blowback was immediate, fierce and, surprising to him, led by the women. He never raised the subject again.

In the same passage in Timothy that forbade women from exercising authority over men and directed them to keep quiet, the apostle offered women a single path to salvation: "Yet she will be saved through childbearing—if they continue in faith and love and holiness, with self-control." That path was closed to his wife.

Jessica was seven years older than him, thirty-five when they married. Why she had remained unmarried so long was the subject of speculation in the church, some kind, some not. The kind explanation was that she had forfeited marriage to care for her own mother—a frail, nervous woman who suffered a litany of health problems before cancer carried her off. The unkind explanation alluded to her appearance—short, stocky, and plain. The unkind whispered that marriage to Taggert's unprepossessing, aging daughter was forced on Daniel as a condition of succeeding Taggert as head of the church.

It was true that Taggert had told Daniel if he wished to succeed him he would have to marry. He made the comment in Jessica's presence, leaving no room for doubt as to his meaning. But what drew them together wasn't Taggert's unspoken directive, but a shared secret. Taggert had begun to slip into dementia

38

in the last years of his life. Between them, Daniel and Jessica concealed his condition until his death. In that work, Daniel saw firsthand her intelligence, discretion, and shrewdness. He also knew she was worried that when her father died, she would lose her standing in a community that was all she had ever known. For his part, Daniel knew a faction of the leadership opposed Taggert's choice of him as his successor. For these men, who'd been with Taggert from the start, Daniel was an interloper, too young, not born into the faith, and his preaching lacked the hard edge their fanaticism demanded. They wouldn't challenge him while Taggert was alive, but once he was gone, they would come for him.

A marriage to Jessica would consolidate his position and hers. When he proposed, her reply startled him.

"I can't have children." Before he could ask, she continued, "I have a condition called endometriosis. You can ask your doctor to explain it, if you're interested. I don't want to talk about it."

"Is that why you haven't married before?"

"Do you think I've had this conversation with other men?" she said, sharply. "With anyone outside my doctor? I'll marry you because it's what Dad wants, but if you marry me, you won't have children."

But Daniel had a child, Wyatt, so her news, while shocking, also came as a relief; he wouldn't have to create a second family while concealing his first. Still, because he did not want her to sense his relief, he asked, "What about adoption?"

She glared at him. "Do you think all children are alike, one as good as another? I could never be a mother to a stranger's child. It would only remind me of my—burden."

It was then he knew he could never tell her about his son.

He told her, "We'll carry the burden together."

Despite his good intentions, the burden had lain most heavily on her. In their family-centered, family-driven community, her childlessness was thrown into high relief, and because her body was the vessel, its failure was attributed to her. Jessica was, depending on temperament, faulted or pitied by the members of the congregation. The whispers and gossip withered her spirit even as it enraged her. Of course, she could show neither grief nor rage to the community. She hid her grief even from him, except when, once or twice, it emerged in a comment or quiet tears. She did not, however, conceal her anger.

"Do you want a divorce?" she demanded after recounting gossip in the church that he was planning to leave her and marry a woman who could give him children.

"Of course not, Jess. I don't know how those rumors got started."

"Because I won't give you one," she said, ignoring him.

"I don't want a divorce."

"I won't be set aside," she said. "Not by you, not by anyone."

"I would never do that to you."

She only repeated, "I won't be set aside, Daniel. I won't."

At such moments, when her composed mask slipped and she revealed the wounded woman beneath it, he wanted to tell her he loved her. He wished he could tell her everything—about Wyatt and Gwen—and share with her his doubts and fears about his ability to counsel the injured people who came to him for help. He wanted a real marriage, not the business arrangement they had agreed to, but after so many years of that, and with his secret creating an abyss between them, he did not know where to begin.

Daniel took his place at the head of the table in the executive conference room. Around the long rosewood table were a dozen comfortably padded seats. His own seat, inherited from his father-in-law, had a higher back and scrolled armrests—a throne, in effect, that he disliked but that Jessica insisted he maintain in her father's memory. Behind him a large arched window looked out on the courtyard where children shrieked in the playground, their voices muffled by triple-paned glass. Plates of doughnuts were arranged on the table along with coffee and water carafes; the air had a sweet, yeasty smell.

Jessica sat quietly in a corner of the room, knitting. It seemed to him it was always the same bit of work she busied herself with but never finished. She was not, of course, an Overseer—women were barred from the office—but no one begrudged her presence. Indeed, most of the men appeared not to notice her in the room at all.

Daniel poured himself a glass of water and smiled gamely at the twelve Overseers, all but one white, and more than half well over sixty. All wore dark business suits, white shirts, and subdued ties—they were lawyers, businessmen, bankers, developers. Rich men, mostly, and men of status and power in their professions; not exactly, Daniel had often thought, the fishermen and laborers Jesus had assembled around himself, nor even the men Daniel would have chosen had he had a free hand.

Most of the Overseers had been chosen by Taggert who, Daniel knew, had had his reservations about Daniel's orthodoxy at times. It wasn't that Daniel had ever expressed the slightest doubt about any of the tenets of their faith; Taggert was skeptical of his style. The old man had expressed this skepticism succinctly when, once after hearing Daniel preach, he had growled, "A little less love and a lot more brimstone next time. These people have to be scared into salvation." The men Taggert had appointed as Overseers—led by his old friend and lawyer, Bob Metzger— shared his hard-bitten theology and were not reluctant to try to rein Daniel in when they thought he strayed too far afield from it. He resisted, and relations between him and Metzger's faction ranged from tense to hostile. Over the years Daniel had been able to appoint a few Overseers of his own. He looked forward to the day when the deaths or resignations of his father-in-law's men would give him control of the board. He was playing a waiting game, and he and Metzger knew it. Since he could be removed as pastor only by a unanimous vote of the Overseers—

41

a provision Taggert had written into the church's charter to protect himself from deposition—they also knew that Daniel would ultimately win.

"Shall we begin?" Daniel said. "Bob, I think you had something to say."

Craggy-faced, silver-haired Metzger flashed a tight smile at him and uttered a curt "Thank you, Pastor." He turned to his colleagues. "You all probably know by now that our friend Congressman Schultz has qualified a measure for the November ballot that would give health officials the right to identify people who have this AIDS virus and quarantine them so they can't spread their horrible disease. He's asked us to endorse and support Proposition 54." He paused. "And by support, I mean raise money, recruit volunteers to campaign for the initiative and to publicly lend our name to the Yes on 54 effort. I, for one, am completely in favor of joining his godly campaign."

Caleb Cowell asked, "Won't getting involved in a political campaign endanger our tax-exempt status?"

Disapproval soured the faces of some other Overseers. Cowell taught mathematics at LA State and was as precise in his appearance, thought, and manner as might be expected from someone whose world was numeric and logical. Dan had noticed the older Overseers regarded him with a combination of curiosity and low-grade hostility. This could have been due to his cool, detached personality or, more problematically, the fact that he was the only Black Overseer, controversially appointed by Daniel.

Metzger, ever the lawyer, replied, "The law bars us from supporting specific candidates for office, not from taking stands on issues of public morality or public health."

"Well," Joe Barton declared, wiping doughnut glaze from his thick fingers on his napkin, "it's about time we took a stand against these deviants. God has. AIDS is his judgment on their immorality. Romans 1 clearly says the homosexuals will receive in their bodies the penalties of their behavior. This law would protect decent people—"

John Wilson, a thin, jittery man who seemed always on the verge of exploding, broke in, "And let the queers go off and die."

Metzger grimaced. "That's not the kind of thing we want to say in public."

Wilson snorted. "We're not in public, brother, so don't get politically correct on me."

"All I mean," Metzger said, smoothly, "is we got to be careful how this thing is presented to the unbelievers because we need their votes to pass it."

Before his silence became conspicuous, Daniel forced himself to speak. "What's the strategy?"

Metzger sat back in his chair. "We know the homosexuals will play the martyr card and say 54 is singling them out because of what they are," he began. "Our side will argue that all we're doing is treating AIDS like any other communicable disease that threatens public health. We quarantine people with TB, for example, and no one says those people are being persecuted. It's even more urgent to protect normal people from AIDS because we don't know how it's spread."

Cowell interjected in his mild voice, "My understanding is that the virus can only be transmitted through blood or semen."

An uncomfortable silence followed this incursion of science, broken finally when Barton said, loudly, "That's what the homosexuals want us to believe, but they're lying to us. We know there are other ways to get it."

"We do?" Dan asked.

Barton nodded. "There's a surgeon up in San Francisco, good Christian woman, who refused to operate on people with AIDS because so many doctors and nurses are coming down with it after they get that tainted blood into their systems. The hospital fired her so she went and wrote a book that proved you can catch it through, what's it called, casual transmission."

Metzger, nodding approval, chimed in. "She writes about two teenage brothers living in the same house. One got the virus from a blood transfusion and then passed it on to his brother who was clean. Those boys were obviously not having sex with each other. Then there was a case up in Connecticut where a homosexual bit a police officer during a demonstration and the officer became infected. Of course, the homosexuals want to suppress those cases and the medical establishment goes along because it doesn't want to create panic. Me, I wouldn't shake hands with a homosexual or breathe the same air."

Barton added, "They've found the virus in spit, in tears."

Cowell removed his wire-rimmed spectacles, cleaned them on a snowy white handkerchief, and observed, "If the virus was transmitted by casual contact, a lot more people would be infected."

"Even the loss of one innocent life is one too many," Metzger snapped.

Barton chimed in, "Hear, hear."

Wilson said, "You ask me, we should lock up all the homosexuals. My God, they eat each other's feces."

"John," Metzger snapped. "There's a lady in the room."

Daniel glanced at his wife whose head was bent over her knitting, seemingly oblivious to the discussion.

Barton said, "John has a point. It's the filthy habits of these men that unleashed this disease on the rest of us. It's time to draw a line in the sand, and hopefully once this passes, we can push them back where they belong."

"Into the closet," Metzger said with a smile. "Then lock the door and throw away the key." He looked around the table. "I move we formally endorse Proposition 54 and coordinate with Congressman Schultz's campaign."

"Second," Wilson said.

They looked at Dan. "Yes, uh, there's a motion on the floor. All in favor?"

The vote was unanimous.

Metzger gave Dan a sharp look and said, "We're expecting you to take the lead in this, Pastor."

Daniel nodded. "Of course."

The meeting ended and the Overseers filed out. Daniel called to Cowell, "Caleb, a minute."

Cowell resumed his seat and looked at Daniel without expression. When the room had cleared and the door was closed, Daniel asked, "What did you mean by what you said about casual contact?"

"I meant what I said." Cowell spoke slowly as if to a not very bright student. "If you could be infected with HIV by shaking someone's hand or breathing the same air, we'd have millions of cases, but we don't, so we have to infer that the virus isn't transmitted by that kind of exposure."

"What about those cases Brother Metzger mentioned? The surgeon, the teenage brothers, the police officer?"

Impatiently, Cowell said, "They don't prove anything without all the facts. Maybe the brothers shared a razor or a toothbrush and exchanged blood that way. And the police officer and the demonstrator? What actually happened there? Maybe the bite broke the officer's skin and the demonstrator's gums were bleeding. Who knows? Maybe the officer had been exposed to the virus before."

"A quarantine won't stop the spread of the disease?"

"Of course not," Cowell said, firmly. "The latency period for HIV is years. Lots of people walking around now don't know they're infected. How are you going to catch them all except by forcing every man, woman and child to take the test? And even then you'd miss some people."

"What's the solution?"

"Educating people about how the virus passes and how they can protect themselves while scientists look for a cure."

"You seem to know a lot about the subject," Dan remarked.

"My nephew," Cowell said briskly. "Homosexual, but a good boy. When he got sick, my sister came to me because I'm the educated one. Read up on it. Couldn't give her any good news, but I learned a lot."

45

"There are no treatments?"

He sat back in his chair and thought. "You know, I read about these drugs. One was ribavirin and the other one was . . . I forget, starts with an *i*. Some people report a good result with them. Not approved for treating AIDS in the US but available over the counter in Mexico. Some of the gays have been going down there, buying them in big quantities and smuggling them across the border. Apparently, there's a whole underground network."

"That sounds illegal."

"Probably is but if it were your life, you'd break some laws, too, I imagine. I called around the AIDS organizations and asked about those drugs for my sister's boy. They were pretty cagey, but I got a couple of names. Gave them to her. Don't know if she followed up."

"You didn't follow up yourself?"

"I have my tenure to protect," he said. "Can't get involved in breaking the law."

"Caleb, if you know all this, why did you vote to support endorsing the proposition?"

"I've learned to pick my battles," Cowell replied. "This isn't one I want to fight."

"Do you think AIDS is the judgment of God on homosexuals?"

Cowell squinted at him. "You're asking me? You're the pastor."

Jessica was waiting in his office when he came in, sitting on a sofa in a corner of the spacious room with her little bit of knitting abandoned at her side. On the low table before her was a thermos of coffee, two cups, cream and sugar. He joined her. Across the room the big bulk of his father-in-law's nineteenth-century partner's desk was flanked by an American flag. On the wall above it was a reproduction of the painting by Heinrich Hofmann of *Christ in the Garden of Gethsemane.*

It was the kind of painting the young convert Daniel and his Jesus People friends might have gently mocked back in the day for the spotlessness of the Savior's robe, his beautifully groomed hair and beard and stately look of sanctity. Their Jesus back then looked like them: holes in their clothes, unkempt hair and untrimmed beards, filled with laughing, joshing energy. Someone who, as Daniel had at the beginning of his ministry, would have baptized the young by dunking them into the ocean at Venice Beach. Would have slapped together cheese and baloney sandwiches to pass out on LA's Skid Row where Daniel had preached in the shadow of St. Vibiana, the Catholic cathedral. Sometimes a couple of Franciscan monks had joined him in feeding the homeless or Mormon missionaries had wandered by and stopped to listen and compare notes on conversion techniques. There was always singing. Someone had a guitar, and everyone had a voice and they sang the old songs in a van decorated with flowers and the words "Jesus Saves" in psychedelic script.

"Coffee?"

"Thank you, Jess," he replied.

He watched her pour him a cup, mixing sugar and milk in the exact proportions he preferred.

"I thought the meeting went well," she said, pouring her cup, black with two teaspoons of sugar.

She wore a peach-colored pantsuit over a white blouse with a big bow tied at her neck. Stiff wings of hair, once naturally blond, now discreetly dyed, framed her face. She wore lipstick and a touch of blush. The mask was on. She sipped her coffee, put the cup into its saucer, and said, "I'm so gratified we're going on record supporting Proposition 54. Those people need to be stopped, Dan. We're not safe with them around."

"Caleb Cowell says people can walk around for years without knowing they're infected. That quarantines won't catch them."

A slight frown creased her face. "Caleb spends so much time around those young college students, I don't wonder that their permissive attitudes rub off on him."

"He makes a good point. How is the proposition going to catch people who don't know they have the virus?"

"Bob says the next step will be mandatory testing," she replied.

"You talked to Bob about this?"

"For a minute or two before you came into the room," she said, hackles rising.

He suspected from her defensiveness the conversation had been private and longer but asked, "How would mandatory testing work?"

She took another temporizing sip of coffee, as if reluctant to impose herself. "We'll make getting tested a condition of renewing a driver's license, entering a public school, receiving medical services, or applying for a marriage certificate," she said. "Anything that people need from the government or for medical care, they'll have to give a blood sample first."

He shook his head. "You want the government invading people's lives like that? It's a bad precedent."

"It's a public health emergency, like Bob said. Emergency measures are needed."

"It'll never pass the legislature, not with the Democrats in charge."

"If we fail in Sacramento, Bob says we'll put it on the ballot in 1988. After Proposition 54 passes, it should be no problem to convince the voters to take the next step."

"Are you so sure Proposition 54 will pass?"

She looked at him quizzically. "Of course it will pass. The polls give the yes vote a twelve-point lead. Do you have doubts, Dan?"

"I remember reading about the last time we took a position on a ballot measure, when your father supported the one that banned school desegregation back in the '60s. We got called bigots and—"

"Daddy was not a bigot," she said sharply. "Daddy was from the South, where the races don't mix."

"I'm not saying he was," Daniel replied, soothingly. "It's about appearances, Jess. We don't want to appear to be intolerant."

"There are worse things," she replied. "'Blessed are you when they revile and persecute you and say all kinds of evil against you for my sake. Rejoice and be glad, for great is your reward in Heaven, for so they persecuted the prophets who were before you.' These are the kinds of enemies we want, Dan."

They drank their coffee in silence for a minute; then he said, "You know, Jess, if Bob Metzger has something to say to me, he can say it directly. He doesn't have to use you as the middleman."

"I've known Bob since I was a little girl," she replied. "Of course we talk. That's what old friends do."

"Sure," he said. He stood up. "Thank you for the coffee, Jess. I better get to work."

She gathered up the coffee things on a tray and left.

He settled himself behind his father-in-law's ostentatious desk and thought about what Caleb Cowell had told him of the smuggling of drugs for AIDS. He had wanted to ask him who he had called and the names he had been given but that, of course, was out of the question. He opened a heavy drawer and removed the phone book. He started at the A's for AIDS and there he found it: AIDS Project Los Angeles. He buzzed his secretary and instructed him that he would be in prayer for the next hour and was to be completely undisturbed. Then he dialed the number.

FOUR

Judge Ipswich peered over her half-glasses and said, "I'm ready to deliver my ruling."

That didn't take long, I thought glumly. The seat of the chair on the witness stand was still warm from the tight-assed arresting cop who'd just finished filling the air with lies about how he'd entered my client's apartment and discovered the crack that had assembled us here for a suppression hearing. My client, Jaime Mendez, perched beside me at the edge of his chair nervously tapping his foot. He'd testified that the cop had pounded on the door, pushed his way in with gun drawn, and ransacked the place until he found the drugs where they'd been hidden, in an empty lard bucket beneath the sink. The cop testified my client had let him into the apartment voluntarily and that the drugs were in plain sight on the kitchen counter.

I'd grilled the cop for an hour, but he hadn't even bothered to conceal his smirk as he calmly repeated his lies.

Still, I'd felt encouraged by the judge's body language, the impatient shifting as the cop went on and on, and the drawing together of dubious eyebrows, but the speed of her decision was bad news. Joan Ipswich was a decent judge but, in the end, there was no way she was going to go on record taking a drug dealer's word over a cop's, whatever her private reservations about the cop's truthfulness.

"The motion is denied," she said.

"Aw shit," my client said. "Judge, I want a new lawyer. This one don't know what he's doing because that cop was lying."

"Mr. Mendez, your lawyer did an excellent job, but that's my ruling."

"Then I want a new judge," Mendez shouted across the well of the court. The bailiff's hand went down to his gun. "I want a new fucking system."

She turned her attention sharply to me. "Mr. Rios, control your client."

"I don't know, Your Honor, I wouldn't mind a new system myself. One that doesn't automatically defer to police officers no matter how clear it is they're committing perjury."

"That's enough, counsel. Your motion's denied. Your client's remanded and we are adjourned."

She hurried off the bench, and the sheriffs came to take my client back to county, but before he left he said with grudging respect, "Thanks for telling off the bitch."

And as he left, the cop muttered to me, "Asshole."

I remained at the counsel table, gathering up my papers and stuffing them into my briefcase. Another day at the office. I shook off my frustration. There was no time to indulge it. I had a meeting in a few minutes with a desperate stranger trying to save the life of his son.

The call had come a few evenings earlier. The caller, who had declined to identify himself, asked for Larry. I knew from the anxiety in his voice he was calling about the drugs Larry smuggled in to treat HIV. There had been a few other such calls since Larry's death. I told the callers Larry had died, gave them the names of some other people to call, and wished them well. When I told this man Larry was gone, he began to sob.

"Hey," I said, "it's okay."

"No," he said, "it's not okay. My son is—he's sick. Can't you help me? Please."

"You're calling about the drugs."

51

He pulled himself together. "From Mexico, yes. I heard Mr. Ross was helping people get them."

"He was," I said. "There are other people involved. I could give you their names and numbers."

"Do they really help? The drugs, I mean."

"In some cases, I'm told there's been improvement, but I don't know the details. I wasn't involved with Larry's project."

"Did he die from AIDS? Did the drugs fail him?"

"Larry was killed by a brain aneurysm," I said. "Not AIDS. Do you want those other numbers?"

"Look, sir," he said, "it took all my nerve to call you. Please, help me. Please."

"It's your son?"

"He's my only child. He's still a boy." The caller broke down again. "He's only nineteen. Please, help us."

The rawness of his plea made it impossible for me to turn him down. I told him to meet me in the courthouse cafeteria two days hence.

"I'm Henry," I said. "What's your name?"

After a long pause, he said, "Call me Dan."

"Okay, Dan, I'm going to bring another guy with me named Jim. He and Larry worked together. Jim will be able to answer your questions about the drugs far better than I can. Is that all right with you?"

"Yes," he said. "God bless you, Henry."

Later, it occurred to me that maybe I was being set up by the FBI but if Dan was a federal agent, he deserved an Oscar. I called Jim Mulvaney, explained the situation to him, and he agreed to join us.

Jim was waiting outside the cafeteria when I came down from the courtroom. He was a tall, shambling, long-haired man with a ready smile and the soothing manner of a nurse, which he was. Jim was gay, but HIV-negative. He'd become an AIDS activist after watching a couple of dozen men, including his best friend, die from the diseases that preyed on them after the virus had knocked out their immune systems.

"The docs kept saying there's no cure," he had told me once, "and I said, what do you mean, no cure? This is a public health emergency. If there's no cure, it's because someone doesn't want a cure. Then I watched that guy, Reagan's press secretary, Speakes? When someone asked him about AIDS, he turned it into a joke. I thought, aha, that's who doesn't want a cure. No one's going to help us here. We're on our own."

"Henry," he boomed, enveloping me in a bear hug. "This is the saddest cafeteria I've ever been in, and I've worked at hospitals."

I glanced around the room—scuffed-up walls and linoleum, over-bright fluorescent lights that flattered no one, chafing dishes filled with dispiriting displays of overcooked scrambled eggs and greasy bacon.

"Yeah, it's not the Ritz," I allowed.

He grinned. "How are you, handsome? The last time I saw you was when you dropped off that bag of money from Larry."

"Which I assume you accounted for in your tax returns," I said, extracting myself.

"It wasn't income to me," he said. "It was a charitable contribution to start up a new AIDS organization that's running trials on ribavirin."

"Private drug trials? Can you do that?"

"We are," he said, "since the feds refuse to. We're setting them up here and in San Francisco. So far, no one's tried to stop us."

I mentioned my visit from the FBI agents looking for drugs.

He shrugged. "That's different. Technically, it is drug smuggling, which is, technically, illegal. Nothing illegal about drug trials as long as they follow established guidelines, which we do." He glanced around the room. "So, this guy, Dan. How will we know who he is?"

I consulted my watch. "We're a few minutes early, so he may not be here yet. Let's go in and sit somewhere conspicuous and let him find us."

We got coffee and settled at a table in the center of the room. As Jim told me more about the ribavirin drug trials, a man entered the cafeteria and paused, as if searching. He was medium height, dressed in khakis and a gray V-neck sweater over a light blue shirt. Fortyish, good-looking white guy in a suburban dad sort of way, the edges of his nicely barbered hair beginning to gray, crinkles appearing at the corners of his eyes. Those eyes—blue I saw once he was near enough to tell—fell on us questioningly. I motioned him over.

"Dan?"

"Henry?"

"Yes. This is Jim. Have a seat. You want some coffee? I'll get it for you."

"No thank you," he replied, sitting. He looked around at the shabby cafeteria and asked, "Why are we meeting here?"

"I'm a criminal defense lawyer," I explained. "I had an appearance this morning upstairs, and I have another in an hour in the same courtroom."

"Ah," he said. He gave us a searching look. "Are you both homosexuals?"

Jim laughed. "Are we what?"

"Homo—"

"Yeah," Jim said, "I heard you the first time. It was the way you said it, like you wanted to know if we're unicorns. We're both gay, Dan. I'm guessing you're not."

He shook his head. "No." Then a moment later. "I think I will have a cup of coffee."

As he stepped away from us, Jim asked, "Think he's going to make a run for it?"

"He does seem a little spooked."

But Dan returned, foam cup in hand, and sat down. Whatever doubts or reservations he had had about us he had resolved on his coffee run. He asked, decisively, "What are these drugs you're bringing in from Mexico? Are they a cure?"

Jim answered. "There is no cure, not yet, but these two drugs have helped some PWAs get better."

"PWAs?"

"People with AIDS," Jim replied. "Not victims, not patients, but people."

This drew a puzzled, "I don't understand the difference." from Dan.

"Victims and patients," Jim explained, "are passive recipients of whatever treatments the medical establishment decides are in their best interests. We're not passive anything. We're fighting for our lives here. That means challenging the doctors, the drug companies, and a government that would just as soon let all the queers go off and die."

The force of his words pushed Dan back in his chair a bit. "Oh, okay. People with AIDs. What about the drugs?"

"Ribavirin is a broad-spectrum antiviral agent. That means it belongs to a class of drugs used to treat various diseases caused by a virus. It's an over-the-counter drug in Mexico that people take when they get colds, but it's not approved by the FDA for us in the US."

"The FDA?" Dan asked.

"Food and Drug Administration," I said. "The federal agency that approves all drugs in this country."

"Why hasn't it approved—" Dan began.

Jim cut him off. "Because the drug companies don't think they can make money off it, so they're not going to spend their money to do the testing the FDA requires before it okays a drug." With a sour grin, he added, "Look, Dan, you got to understand something. The big drug companies aren't in the business of curing disease; they're in the business of making money."

"Don't they want to help sick people get well?"

"That's what they say but it takes millions of dollars and years for the drug companies to run the kinds of trials the FDA demands before it signs off on a drug as being safe for human consumption," Jim said. "The drug companies want that money back in sales and then some."

"But," Dan said, "if ribavirin is already being used in Mexico, then hasn't it already been found safe for people to take?"

"Fair point," Jim said, "but the FDA has its own protocols for drug safety, and the fact that some other country says a drug is safe doesn't carry any weight with it. Plus, the FDA is heavily influenced by whoever's running the federal government. The guy currently in charge isn't a friend of gay people." He sipped his coffee. "Okay, back to the drugs. The other drug we've been bringing in is called Isoprinosine. It's what's called an immune modulator that may boost the body's immune system. What we've seen is that some PWAs using the drugs individually or in combination have seen some real improvements in their condition."

"What kind of improvements?" Dan asked, cautiously.

"People report it's helped relieve the major symptoms of AIDS, wasting, fevers, sweats, loss of energy. That might be evidence the drugs are helping boost the immune system to fight off the virus. How sick is your son?"

Clutching his untouched coffee, Dan said, "He had the pneumonia."

"PCP?" Jim asked.

"Yes."

"That's good," Jim said. "And bad."

"What does that mean?"

"It means he's at an early stage of the disease, but it also means his immune system is very compromised, and he may now become susceptible to other infections."

"Can these drugs help him?"

"There haven't been any formal studies on whether the drugs work," Jim said. "The anecdotal evidence is mixed. Some people say they helped; some say they didn't. I can't tell you whether they'll do your son any good."

"Will they hurt him?" Dan asked.

Jim shook his head. "The one thing I can say is that no one's reported any kind of serious side effects."

"Is there anything else?" he asked. "Any other drugs?"

"There's only one drug that's currently being tested as a treatment for HIV," Jim answered. "It's called AZT. The FDA recently approved Phase II trials."

"What does that mean?"

"That means the drug worked in the lab and on animals and now it's being tried on people. There are trials in San Francisco and LA, though as far as I know all the slots are taken."

"Slots?"

"People volunteer to be enrolled in the study," Jim told Dan. "There are only so many slots."

He absorbed the information. "Who decides how many people can enroll?"

"The people conducting the trial," Jim said. "Here it's at UCLA, and up in San Francisco I think it's at the University of California, San Francisco Medical Center."

"Does the government have any say?" he asked.

"What do you mean, the government?"

"If someone in the government wanted to get someone into the study, could he?"

Jim narrowed his eyes disapprovingly. "Are you asking if someone with juice can pull strings? That's the way of the world, but it's not fair."

"I can't worry about what's fair," Dan replied. "Not if it means keeping my son alive."

"What do you do for a living, Dan?" I asked, curious about his implication that he had friends in high places.

"I'd rather not say," he replied. He stood up and extended his hand. "Thank you, gentlemen. God bless you and the work you're doing."

Surprised at the abrupt termination of our conversation, Jim said, "Don't you want to know how you can get the drugs we've been talking about?"

Dan said, "As I understand it, bringing those drugs in is illegal, but this other study with AZT, that's government approved. I can't—well, I'd prefer not to break the law if I can avoid it."

"What if you can't get your son into the AZT study?" I asked.

"Then you'll be hearing from me again."

Jim pulled a business card out of his pocket. "Call me directly," he told Dan. "We can cut out Henry." He grinned. "We're saving him for when the feds bust us and throw us into jail."

Dan looked alarmed, but took the card and tucked it into his pocket. We shook his hand. He had the firm handshake of a man used to shaking many hands, a politician's handshake.

"So," Jim said as Dan disappeared. "Who was that masked man?"

"No idea," I said, "but he carried himself like he's someone who matters."

Josh's last name was Mandel. He was twenty-three years old, the youngest child of three, the only boy. He'd grown up in Encino, dropped out of UCLA halfway through his sophomore year, worked as a waiter at a trendy restaurant on Robertson, and lived in Hollywood on a street named after a flower.

Those were the bare biographical facts of the young man who had doctored my head at the Gay and Lesbian Center. He had revealed them in our late-night conversations—while he lay in his bed and I lay in mine. Tonight, I was heading to a bar at the edge of West Hollywood to meet him after his shift.

"I'm not much of a drinker, either," he hastened to add when I said I didn't drink, "but sometimes I'm too wired to go straight home from work, so I stop for a beer. We could meet somewhere else if bars make you, um, uncomfortable."

"I'll see you there at ten," I replied.

Although we had talked almost every night, I hadn't seen him in the flesh since we'd first met, ten days earlier. Our schedules were incompatible. He went to work about the same time I was calling it a day, and during the day, when he was home, I was rarely in one place long enough to call. Two years after relocating from San Francisco, I was still putting together my practice. My bread and butter were 987.2 appointments. That provision in the penal code authorized judges to appoint a private lawyer for indigent defendants when, for whatever reason, the Public Defender's office declared a conflict and couldn't take the case. The appointed lawyer was paid by the county. The rate was considerably less than I would have charged a private client, but it was a steady source of income while I built up my private practice. Each of the forty-seven courthouses in Los Angeles County kept its own 987.2 panel of lawyers and I was on half a dozen panels, so I spent a lot of time running from one courthouse to another.

All that travel was exhausting but useful. Armed with my five-hundred-page Thomas's Guide—the city's comprehensive street map—I learned the geography of the city, not simply the physical layout but the economic and racial layout, too. LA was an east/west and hills/flats town. The farther west and higher into the hills you went, the richer and whiter the city got. The air was better the closer you got to the ocean; the hills offered privacy. The intangible benefits of wealth. The flat neighborhoods of the east side were crammed with working-class and poor people, most of them Black or brown. Their disadvantages—from potholed streets to overcrowded schools, gangs, and drug dealers—were all too tangible.

My physical office, in a small, three-story run-down building on Sunset near Highland put me dead center in this geography, in a kind of no man's land. In the city's complicated schema, I was neither fish nor fowl. My fancy law degree, nice suits, and inherited house in the hills assigned me to the professional classes, but my brown skin and *mestizo* features marked me as an outsider in those almost entirely white precincts. Plus, I was gay. In 1986 Los Angeles, no one, rich or poor, white, brown or Black, eastsider or west, threw out the welcoming mat for queers. So, I belonged . . . to myself. The insider as outsider or the outsider as insider. I belonged to a world that had not yet come into being but was struggling to emerge. A world where people were not deformed by baseless hatred and fear because they were variations on the human theme.

I told some of this to Josh as night lapped at our windows and our conversations drifted from shallow into deeper waters. Larry's house was on a cul-de-sac perched at the edge of a canyon carpeted with chaparral, the native low-lying, thorny, fragrant gray-green woodland of Southern California. The nights were so quiet at Larry's I could hear not only bird song but the whirl of their wings as they swooshed though the air. The dusty smell of sage and manzanita seeped into the bedroom through the open door. On the other end of the line I heard police sirens and car alarms and the neighbors' music blasting through the thin walls of Josh's Hollywood apartment. Two entirely different landscapes. Two very different lives. Two men, each lying in his bed, talking, voices light with laughter or serious, silences that were comfortable or pendent, the stories sometimes linear but often not as we wound our way toward each other.

"I love your voice," he told me one night, suddenly. "The way it sounds."

"I love your voice, too."

He laughed. "No, I have a gay voice."

"You have a soft voice, if that's what you mean. It's soothing and—sexy."

"Um, sometimes I get hard just listening to you. I don't even have to touch myself . . . . Henry, are you still there?"

"Yeah," I said roughly. "I'm still wearing my boxers. I had to adjust myself."

He whispered, "Take them off and I'll tell you how to adjust yourself."

On another night, when we'd both had long, wearying days, the conversation was forced and was punctuated by awkward pauses. I was about to end the call when he asked me, "When you were first coming out, to yourself I mean, when you first knew you were," a soft chuckle, "not like the other boys, did you wonder or worry that maybe you would never . . . find someone?"

I had closed my eyes and thought for a moment. "You mean, was I afraid I'd never be in love?"

"With someone who loved you back."

I was sitting up in bed. I smoothed the sheet covering my legs and remembered how it had felt to be a sixteen-year-old with a secret.

"I thought about it a lot. I wondered if I was the only boy like me and if I wasn't, I wondered where the other boys were and how I would find them."

"Me, too," he said. A pause and then a tentative, "Have you ever been in love?"

"Once," I said. "It didn't last long."

"You broke up?"

"He died."

"AIDS?"

"No, he was killed." I tipped my head against the pillow and pictured Hugh, my beautiful, fucked-up lover. I realized he and Josh were physically similar, same height, same build, but Hugh had been a golden blond whereas Josh was olive-skinned and dark-haired. "That's a long story for another time. What about you? Have you been in love?"

"No," he replied. "I'm still trying to work through everything that's happened to me since I came out."

"Like what?"

After a moment, he said, "That's also a long story for another time."

The sadness in his voice when he spoke moved me and, in that moment, he became real to me—not simply a good-looking guy I flirted with over the phone but someone substantial enough to cast a shadow.

"Will you tell me that story someday?"

"If you'll tell me yours."

"I'll tell you anything you want to know about me, Josh, and I'll never lie to you."

There was a long silence. "Thank you, Henry," he said. "Good night."

The inflection in his voice when he said good night made me think I'd said something wrong.

When Josh told me the name of the bar, I thought he was joking but painted on the blue canopy over the entrance were the words "Bar None." It was wedged between a deli and a manicurist, on an unglamorous block of Santa Monica Boulevard. I stepped past a couple of collegiate-looking guys standing outside the entrance smoking a joint and went inside.

The front room was a long rectangle with the bar running the length of it. In the center of the room was a narrow table with barstools on either side. Along the far wall was a shelf and beneath it cases of beer. The bar, counter, shelf, and floors were made of the same dark, varnished wood that showed signs of age and wear. Above the bar and along the center of the ceiling were rows of small recessed lights, white above the bar, red above the ceiling. The air smelled of cigarettes, beer, cologne, and the hopeful musk of men on the prowl. From overhead speakers Dolly Parton sang "Jolene," and in every corner mouths moved, singing along with her.

There were guys in suits and guys in flannel shirts and jeans, guys in glittering unisex tops and guys in crew neck sweaters, most of them probably between twenty-five and forty but with a scattering of gray-haired daddies and barely legal twinks, not necessarily together. Guys with biceps like grapefruits and thighs stretching the seams of their 501s and skinny guys who looked like they never lifted anything heavier than a cocktail and all shapes and sizes in between. Like the sign outside said: Bar none. The vibe was friendly and familiar. Nothing like the desperate dives where I'd spent the final days of my drinking career with a handful of other drunks, grimly drinking ourselves into early graves. I had a clear and visceral enough recollection of those days that, even here, in these relaxed surroundings, I hadn't even the faintest impulse to drink.

I wandered through the bar into a poolroom where I spotted Josh on a barstool next to a chalkboard that listed the order of players. He wore jeans and a white button-down shirt. His glasses dangled from his shirt pocket; a red sweater was spread across his lap. One hand held a cigarette, and the other grasped a long-necked bottle of beer. He was watching the game, a slight smile curving his lips and revealing the gleam of straight, white teeth. His gelled hair had come undone in the humidity of the bar and fell in curls around his neck and across his forehead. His olive skin, illuminated by the green-shaded light above the pool table, had the sheen of a light sweat. He pressed his slender body forward to watch the bearish, bearded player set up his shot.

I want you, I thought, and as if I had spoken the words aloud above the din of the music and the male chatter and the click of one ball striking another on the felt, he looked up and our eyes met. His smile faded, and he drew a breath so deep the fabric of his shirt moved as his chest expanded. He exhaled and so did I, not aware until that moment that I had been holding my breath. The smile returned. I crossed the room and put myself in front of him.

"Hey there," I said and, with a second's hesitation, kissed him lightly on the lips.

"Hello, Henry," he said.

"Is there somewhere quiet we can talk?"

He hopped off the barstool, crushed his cigarette into a plastic ashtray, took my hand, and said, "There's a patio. June gloom makes it too cold for most people. We'll probably have it to ourselves."

He led me out to a small fenced-in courtyard. In the center was a firepit where a low gas fire burned; the fire and the exit light above the door provided the only illumination. We sat on a bench beneath the feathery leaves of a jacaranda tree. Josh tugged his sweater over his head, made a valiant attempt to smooth his hair, and put on his glasses.

"Let me see your head," he told me. I lowered my head and felt his fingers gently probe the spot where I had been cut. "It's all healed."

"I had a good doctor."

"My dad would love hearing that."

63

"He wanted you to go to med school?"

"As far as he's concerned, if you're a smart Jewish boy you got three options for work: doctor, lawyer or accountant. I went premed at UCLA to make him happy, but it wasn't what I wanted and then . . ." His voice trailed off.

"And then?" I prompted.

"And then I couldn't lie to myself anymore about who I was. What I was."

"Gay?"

"Mmm," he said. He thumbed the damp label on his beer bottle. "I knew for as long as I can remember, but with my parents, especially my dad, coming out wasn't an option."

The fire wasn't enough to dispel the chill in the air. He leaned into me for warmth and I put my arm around him.

"I told them I was depressed," he continued, "which, believe me, I was and dropped out of school. I moved to West Hollywood and went crazy." He laid his hand on my leg. "This is the part of my story I couldn't tell you on the phone."

"Why?"

"I needed to see your face while I told it."

"Because?"

He squeezed my leg. "Because people can hide their feelings in their voices, but not in their eyes."

I nodded, locked eyes with him. "What happened after you dropped out of school?"

He slipped his hand into mine.

"I discovered sex and drugs, and I couldn't get enough of either. I partied very, very hard and in places that . . . well, when I think of them now, they were no place for a nice Jewish boy from Encino. They were . . . degrading. I did things I don't think I'll ever be able to tell anyone."

"Do you still use drugs?"

Wide-eyed he exclaimed, "Oh, God, no! No. I kicked."

"On your own?"

"Theo helped me."

"The tall guy from QUEER who started the fight?"

64

"Yeah, Theo Latour. We ran with the same crowd. I'd see him at bars and parties and in back rooms. He was protective of me, like my gay big brother. One night I was coked out of my head and about to head out of a bar with some very bad guys. He grabbed me and took me home and stayed with me until I came down. He told me, 'You know, Josh, most guys party to feel good, but you party because you hate yourself. You keep it up and you'll party yourself to death.' I guess I was ready to hear it because after that I stopped. Started to pull myself together. Theo was there for me the whole time. Knew the guy who owns the restaurant and helped get me my job."

"That doesn't sound like the angry guy I saw at the center," I observed.

Josh took a slug from his beer and delicately wiped his mouth with the back of his hand. "He tested positive, and it blew up his world. Theo does—well, he did—porn. He was making a lot of money at it. Once he tested positive, the studios dropped him; his boyfriend dumped him and threw him out of their apartment. His party friends treated him like he was poison. He showed up at my place with nowhere else to go and asked if he could stay with me. I had to think about it. I was afraid, too."

"Afraid of what?"

"That I'd catch it from him," Josh said. He peeled the paper label from his beer as he continued. "But I couldn't say no, not after what he'd done for me." Guiltily, he added, "I still wouldn't drink from the same glass, though, and when I used the toilet after him, I wiped down the seat with rubbing alcohol. Stupid, huh?"

"In the beginning no one knew how the virus was spread."

"Still," he insisted, tearing off the label. "I was worrying about accidentally using his toothbrush when I should have been worried about what I'd done in the orgy room at the Melrose Baths."

"Is Theo still living with you?"

He nodded. "Off and on. I told him he couldn't stay with me if he was high, so when he's on a run, he'll disappear, but he always comes back."

65

"What kind of drugs is he on?"

He set the bottle down beside him. "Amphetamines, mostly, Crack when he can get it. And something called crystal. I think it's like super-meth. That's the worst one."

"Why doesn't he move in with his boyfriend? The Latino guy."

"Freddy? He lives with his family and he's not out to them."

"Is Freddy an addict, too?"

"No," Josh said. "Freddy's not into drugs. He's good for Theo. Stable. When Theo goes off at a QUEER meeting, Freddy calms him down, and he keeps an eye on him when I'm not around. Theo would be in a lot worse shape without us. I worry that he's going to end up killing himself."

"He took his diagnosis hard," I said.

"The doctor told him he had eighteen months to live."

"How long ago was that?"

"That's not the point," Josh said. "Eighteen months, two years, it's a death sentence." He took a deep breath, met my eyes and said, "I haven't taken the test. I don't know my status. Do you?"

"I'm negative."

"I'm afraid to find out."

"Not knowing what your status is doesn't change it," I said. "My friend Larry said it's better to deal with reality than to deny it."

"Your friend who died," he said, remembering that I'd spoken of Larry in our phone calls.

"Yeah, him."

"I'm twenty-three years old," he said. "I don't want to be worrying about whether I'll live to see thirty."

I put my arm around his shoulder and drew him close. "Whatever your status is won't make a difference to how I feel about you."

He looked at me, about to reply, but before he could I kissed him. He hesitated a second when my tongue touched his lips, but then he parted them, and I tasted beer and nicotine and beneath that, wet warmth and flesh. I dropped my arm to the small of his back, lifted his sweater, tugged his shirt tail out of his jeans and slipped my hand beneath his shirt to touch bare, smooth skin. We half-turned to hold each other even closer, my free hand grazed his crotch, and I felt his cock pushing hard against the rough denim. He threw his arms around me, kissed me with increasing depth and passion, and a tiny spot of wetness stained his crotch. I felt a primal animal comfort in the weight of his body pressed against mine that I had not felt in a long time, my separateness dissolving as we seemed to breathe a single breath.

"Do you want to get out of here?" I asked, when we stopped kissing.

"Is it okay if we take this kind of slow?" he replied, a little breathlessly.

"As slow as you want," I said.

"I mean," he stuttered. "I want to go home with you. A lot. But—"

"You don't have to explain."

"I want to be sure," he said. "You know what I mean?"

I nodded. I wanted to tell him I was already pretty sure about him, but I knew it wasn't me he doubted. He wasn't sure about himself.

FIVE

She set down her glass and took another look at the photograph of the woman named Gwen. Now that she was over her first shock—Daniel's lover was Black—she studied her carefully. Was it worse that Daniel had chosen a Black woman over her? She wasn't racist, of course, but she was her father's daughter and he considered miscegenation as much a perversion of God's order as homosexuality. No, she assured herself, it wasn't the woman's race that wounded her. It was everything. Gwen. Even her name, blunt and astringent, pained her. Full-figured and, there was no way around it, rather beautiful even in hospital scrubs. She looked thirty but was, according to the investigator's report, forty-two. Younger than Jess, but definitely not a girl.

The investigator had photographed her at a table outside the hospital where she worked, eating lunch out of a Tupperware container. Her eyes were sad and thoughtful, as if her mind was far away from the forkful of salad she was lifting to her mouth. Beneath that photograph was another, this one of Gwen and a teenage boy she was assisting down the steps of the building where they lived in San Francisco. His name, the report informed her, was Wyatt. He was nineteen years old and on his birth certificate, on the space for "Name of Father," was the notation "Daniel Herron."

◌ ◌ ◌

It had started with a phone call from Congressman Schultz's wife, Marie.

After the initial courtesies were exchanged, Marie said, "I wanted to call you and personally tell you how sorry I am that John couldn't help get Dan's nephew into that drug study."

There was something in the way she said this, a slight breathlessness, that put Jessica on her guard; the woman was fishing for scandal.

"That's very kind of you," Jessica replied neutrally.

"And how awful," Marie persisted. "I mean, having AIDS in your own family even if it was caused by a blood transfusion."

She tamped down the shock and panic and managed a curt, "Yes, it's terrible."

"I'm afraid we're going to start seeing more and more of these innocent victims like your nephew," she said, pronouncing "innocent" with a touch of doubt. "I do hope he'll be all right."

Jessica's mind went blank. Without another word, she hung up the phone, went to the bar and poured herself a double. As she drank, she realized that by hanging up on her she had given the woman what she wanted, confirmed there was something scandalous afoot. Something to dine out on with the other twittering ladies in their common circle of acquaintances. Still, providing fodder for the gossip mill was the least of it.

There was no nephew with AIDS. There was no nephew at all. Dan's two sisters—whom, in any event, they rarely saw—only had daughters. Perhaps, she thought, he had called the congressman on behalf of a church member, but if that was the case, why invent the nephew, why bring it so close to home? It. AIDS. For one horrifying moment she wondered if Dan had been calling for himself. She quickly rejected the possibility. It was too monstrous. Only slightly less monstrous was the possibility that the private investigator's report now confirmed. The boy in the photograph, leaning against his handsome mother and looking tired and ill, stared at her with her husband's eyes.

Bob Metzger tidily stacked the pages of the report, aligning the corners perfectly, slipped them into the folder, and said, calmly, "This is very bad, Jessica."

The windows of his Spring Street office framed City Hall, invariably reminding her of the police officer's badge in the opening sequence of *Dragnet*, which had been one of her father's favorite television shows. Her sense of her father's presence was always powerful when she was with Bob, "Uncle Bob" as she had known him when she was a child. The lawyer had been her father's closest confidant, and they had had in common troubled marriages with unstable women. Regarding their wives, both had adhered to a strict policy of denial—her father to his wife's alcoholism, Uncle Bob to the profound depression that ultimately had led his wife to take a fatal dose of sleeping pills. Indeed, he had kept the manner of her death secret to all but her father in a conversation Jessica had happened to overhear.

After her father's death, Metzger had cultivated her, counseled her and supported her as she tried to stake her small claim in the church's leadership. In this, ironically, he was aided by Daniel who in all other respects was Metzger's nemesis on the Board of Overseers. Both had their reasons to help her, and she was well aware that few of those reasons involved her ability. Metzger wanted her as an ally against her husband, a marital spy, although he was excruciatingly careful to conceal his motives beneath his professed concern for her well-being. And Daniel? She had always suspected his support for her was motivated by guilt, and now, investigator's report in hand, she knew the source of that guilt.

Metzger was indirectly responsible for the revelation. She had told him about her suspicions Daniel was concealing something—perhaps an affair—and it was he who had encouraged

70

her to hire a private investigator. When she demurred, he had pressed the point, fueling her insecurities until she finally agreed to hire a man he found for her. Now, Uncle Bob raised his eyes to hers, a glint of disapproval in them as if she were responsible for Daniel's secret life.

"I had no idea," she said.

"Come now, Jessica," he replied, as if to a child. "You had to have had some idea. Those mysterious trips to San Francisco. Retreats at a Catholic monastery? I never believed that for a minute. You must have suspected he was doing something up there he didn't want you to know about."

"I never imagined it was something like this," she said. "Not a family."

"A Negro mistress and a half-breed son with AIDS," he said dismissively. "I wouldn't call that a family. I'd call it a potential scandal, especially now. If our enemies discover this, it could destroy our campaign to pass Proposition 54. You must know that."

"Yes," she murmured, again feeling the sting of his implied judgment on her failings as a wife. "What should I do?"

"You? You should do nothing. Keep this to yourself. I'll take care of it."

She looked at him anxiously. "What will you do?"

"I," he repeated, "will take care of it."

I must pray, she told herself, as she drove home slowly, blinded by tears, but even as the words formed in her head, they were ritualistic and empty. God was her father's business, not hers. Her faith had leaked out as she sat at her mother's bedside year after year and watched her drink herself to death. Not only was God missing in action, so was her father. He had surrendered his life to bringing Jesus to everyone trapped by sin in the web of the world. Nothing took precedence over his ministry, certainly not wife or daughter. Her father had been faithful to a fault to Jesus's command, "You must love me more than your father, mother, wife, children, brothers, and sisters—even more than your own life."

She had loved him anyway; he was powerful, charismatic and on those rare occasions when he turned his attention to her, it was like basking in the sun. At the same time he had made clear to her the pettiness of her demands for his attention. Not cruelly, for he was never cruel, but briskly and firmly. She learned early on that, while she mattered to him, she would always matter less than his work because who could compete with God?

After life with her father, Daniel's consideration caught her off guard. In the close quarters of early marriage, she was seen and heard but, instead of bringing her happiness, she felt exposed. Daniel was intelligent, educated, articulate, dynamic, and kind. She was the girl who had watered her mother's vodka, had been homeschooled by a series of tutors chosen by her father more for their discretion than their ability, and was isolated from other kids by her status as the founder's child. She had brought nothing to the marriage but her father's name. She couldn't even give him children.

Daniel had to know this, which ultimately made his attentiveness seem like a taunt. She withdrew, creating in her marriage the same deep, unbridgeable silences that had defined her father's home. Courteous silences, resentful silences, painful silences, convenient silences—their marriage was like a house filled with shadows that, over time, had become more solid than the objects that cast them. Now and then he would throw a line across a chasm. Once he even said he loved her and that was the most shameful thing of all, not because she didn't believe him, but because she did.

Or so she had believed until the investigator had brought her the folder filled with photographs of her husband's family.

Tommy Jones blinked back tears from already reddened eyes and in a rough whisper pleaded, "Tell me what to do, Pastor?"

"You've prayed to be relieved of the temptation since we last talked?"

"So hard," he said. "I prayed so hard."

They were in his office, chairs pulled close, the building silent and only a single, small lamp burning. Tommy was a big man, owned a landscaping business, was married to Lois, and was father to two preteen boys and a sixteen-year-old girl, Mindy, for whom he had developed a frightening lust. Daniel had been counseling him for the past two months. Tonight he'd revealed that three nights earlier, after everyone was asleep, he had slipped out of bed, gone to his daughter's room, stood over her sleeping form, and touched himself.

This was the kind of confession that nothing in Daniel's training had prepared him for. Far from it. His training had turned a condemnatory eye toward all things sexual that took place outside the marital bed, raining down on them the ancient proscriptions from Leviticus and Deuteronomy. But proscribing conduct was useless when the conduct had already occurred or seemed likely to occur. To say to Tommy Jones that the Bible says incest is an abomination punishable by death, so don't do it, might fulfill Daniel's pastoral obligations but it was hardly an answer to Tommy's anguish or solved the issue of his daughter's safety.

"You have to send her away."

Tommy looked at him uncomprehendingly. "What do you mean?"

"I mean," he said, "Mindy can't be in your house while you're trying to get these feelings under control. It's not safe for either one of you."

"Where would I send her? What would I tell Lois?"

"There's a private Christian boarding school for girls up in Washington state where I have some contacts," Daniel said. "I can arrange for them to admit Mindy. I'll explain to Lois what a great opportunity it is for her. Lois trusts me. I think I can convince her."

"You won't tell her . . . about me?"

Daniel shook his head. "No."

"Will I have to tell her? I mean, you can't keep that kind of secret from your wife, can you? Isn't that lying?"

"Sometimes in a marriage God requires us to carry our guilt alone instead of inflicting it on our spouse when it would only cause them greater sorrow." He patted Tommy's hand. "This is one of those times."

"Thank you, Pastor Dan."

"We're not done, Tommy. After Mindy leaves, I want you to see a therapist to help you get to the bottom of these feelings."

"A shrink? But—Pastor Taggert said those people are ungodly. He said they make excuses for our evil by blaming it on our parents and the way we were raised."

"Pastor Taggert was a man of his time," Dan said, choosing his words carefully so as not to contradict the still-revered founder. "Back then it may have been true that psychiatry and psychology didn't take account of religious beliefs. Times change. There are many, many Christian therapists who no longer believe faith and psychology are incompatible. I have a couple in mind I think could help you. Of course we'll continue our counseling sessions. Sound good?"

Tommy nodded. "Yeah, if you say so, Pastor Dan. Thank you."

He walked Tommy to the door. "I'll call that school tomorrow. In the meantime, if you feel the urge to enter your daughter's bedroom again, I want you to call me. Any time, you understand, no matter how late it is. You call me."

The man nodded.

"I'll see you next Thursday."

Daniel closed the door behind the man and slumped in the big chair behind his desk. He could feel the disapproving stare from the portrait of his father-in-law that hung on the far side of the room, directly in his line of vision. He was intimately familiar with Max Taggert's views on psychotherapy. Any suggestion that human nature might be more complicated than sin and repentance was met first with derision and then fury. "Man is evil because he has a sinful nature, not because his daddy hit him when he was a little boy, or his mommy stopped breast-feeding him too soon." And that was that.

Daniel had learned to keep to himself any opinion that might inspire his father-in-law's ire. Was evolution only a theory? Maybe so, but it was a pretty convincing one. Did God condemn all unbelievers to hell regardless of their individual merit? Possibly, though a God who couldn't distinguish between a Hitler and a Gandhi wasn't the God Daniel had embraced upon his conversion. Doubts about theology were not doubts about God, but this was a distinction he didn't dare propose to Max Taggert. And over time, his doubts had been submerged beneath his day-to-day responsibilities. He was grateful for that and for the advice one of the Jesuits had given him. "God is action, not belief." Besides, doubt might be natural—even Jesus on the cross had his moment—but as Jesus also showed, it wasn't necessarily a door to deeper and greater truths. Most of the time doubt was a dead end where the mind, cornered and frantic, simply lost itself in fear. Daniel had his work and he had his doubts but, of the two, only the work truly mattered.

He thought about the advice he'd given Tommy about whether he should tell his wife about his feelings for their daughter. Some secrets you keep to yourself because to disclose them will only cause greater, irreparable injury. Of course, keeping the secret required building a house of evasions where you lived alone with your guilt. He glanced at his watch. Nine o'clock.

It was time for his weekly call. He picked up the phone, dialed the familiar number, and on the first ring Wyatt picked up and greeted him with a cheerful, "Hi, Dad!"

The two-story half-timbered faux Tudor country house was dark except for the porch light and lights that burned in the library where the Bible study convened. Outside, gracious old oaks spread their canopies over the dark lawns and flower beds of the other mansions that lined the quiet Hancock Park street. The men had rolled up in luxury late-model cars, had been welcomed into the house by a uniformed Mexican maid and ushered into the library where their host waited for them amid the scent of leather bindings and percolating coffee. They arranged themselves on comfortable couches and armchairs upholstered in leather and brocade. Though it was early summer and the weather was warm, the host had had a fire set in the massive fireplace and turned down the thermostat to a chilly sixty degrees.

The text for their study had been chosen by their host, who called himself Zenas, after the lawyer mentioned in Paul's letter to Titus. Romans 1:18-32: "For the wrath of God is revealed from heaven against all ungodliness and wickedness of men who by their wickedness suppress the truth. For what can be known about God is plain to them, because God has shown it to them. So they are without excuse; for although they knew God they did not honor him as God or give thanks to him, but they became futile in their thinking and their senseless minds were darkened. For this reason, God gave them up to dishonorable passions. Their women exchanged natural relations for unnatural, and the men likewise gave up unnatural passions and were consumed with passion for one another, men committing shameless acts with men and receiving in their own persons the due penalty for their error."

"I chose this," Zenas said, "not for the obvious reason, the strong affirmation of God's condemnation of the homosexual but, if you will pardon me, to discuss its legal implications."

One of the others, a judge who called himself Thomas because he had converted late in life warned playfully, "Careful, Zenas. I can't correct your theology, but I'll be listening for misstatements of law."

"I'm forewarned, Your Honor," Zenas replied. The other men around the room chuckled at the exchange.

"Continue, brother," said the police chief who called himself Eleazer, after one of King David's generals.

"Criminal law distinguishes between crimes committed on impulse and crimes that are planned and intentional; those crimes we punish much more harshly. Killing, for instance. Not all killing is murder. A killing committed unintentionally is manslaughter. Even an intentional killing is punished less harshly than a killing both intentional and planned."

"You're speaking of a premeditated murder," Thomas said.

"Yes, Thomas. Premeditated murder is a crime we punish with the death penalty." He paused. "When Paul speaks of wickedness in this passage in Romans, he is speaking of premeditated wickedness. What does he say? 'For what can be known about God is plain to them, because God has shown it to them.' Shown it to them, brothers. They know God's way and yet Paul tells us 'they are without excuse; for although they knew God they did not honor him as God or give thanks to him.' So I submit, brothers, these homosexuals, these 'men committing shameless acts with men' are like the killer who acts with premeditation. They deserve the harshest punishment, for their rebellion against God is nothing less than demonic."

Eleazer said, "That's why God has sent AIDS as a judgment upon them and an example of his anger toward sinners like them."

Zenas nodded. "Yes, but unfortunately, they have powerful friends who want the world to see homosexuals as pitiable victims, and I'm afraid they are succeeding. That brings me to my other legal analogy. These people who are helping the homosexuals advance their agenda would in legal terms be called aiders and abettors. Am I correct, Your Honor?"

"You are," Thomas replied.

"And in the law," Zenas continued, "one who knows that a crime is planned and intentional and who aids and abets in its commission is as guilty of the crime itself as the one who actually carries it out. So, the punishment for one who aids and abets a premeditated murder must be the same as it is for the one who carries it out."

"That would seem to indict the American Medical Association," said the chief of staff of a county supervisor, who called himself Titus, after Paul's disciple. "They've just come out against Proposition 54."

"Yes," Zenas said, "excellent example. Our effort to quarantine the homosexuals who are spreading this vile disease is being opposed by the AMA, the American Bar Association, the ACLU—"

"Speaking of demonic," said the millionaire industrialist who called himself Zacchaeus, the small man who climbed a tree to get a glimpse of Jesus. The other men laughed again.

"The state Democratic party," Zenas continued, to groans, "and even, I am sorry to say, some prominent Republican officeholders."

"Not mine!" Titus exclaimed, to more laughter.

"No, not yours," Zenas said, "and we are grateful for the supervisor's continuing support. The homosexuals have even enlisted as aiders and abettors the Episcopal bishop of California and others who call themselves Christian."

"Pharisees!" someone exclaimed.

"Indeed," Zenas said. "We know them for what they are—those tombs Jesus spoke of that appear outwardly white and beautiful but inwardly are filled with all manner of uncleanness. The public, however, does not know them as we do. The effect of the opposition to Prop 54 of the bishops and the doctors and the politicians is that we are once again being portrayed as bigots. I have here," he continued, reaching into his suit coat, "the results of our latest internal polling. Two months ago the yes vote was ahead by twelve points. As of yesterday we're only six points ahead. Our lead has been cut in half."

"Tell me the amount you need," Zacchaeus said, "and I'll write the check here and now."

"Thank you, brother," Zenas said, "but money alone will not win this campaign. We need something to unmask the homosexuals for the violent and wicked men they are. The public needs to know the truth." He leveled his eyes at Eleazer. "An action."

Later, when the study group had adjourned and the men had helped themselves to coffee and cake, Eleazer approached Zenas.

"The chief sends his regards," he said.

"How is Chief Gates?"

"Holding the line. You saw how the press went after him for his defense of choke holds."

Zenas nodded. Earlier that month, Gates had defended the use of choke holds after a Black suspect died when he was placed in one, saying, "We may be finding that in some Blacks, when the choke hold is applied, the veins or arteries do not open up like in normal people."

Eleazar continued. "One dirtbag dies and now we're supposed to stop using choke holds completely. What are we supposed to do? Start shooting Black suspects instead? We'd never hear the end of that."

"He's a good man in a tight spot," Zenas agreed. "This city . . . sometimes I feel it's America's cesspool for every kind of filth and depravity." He sighed. "Still, we do what we can. You and me and people like the chief. We're all trying to hold the line."

"Your lead in our discussion was inspirational. What you said about the homosexuals being guilty of premeditated evil. Maybe we need to get back to Leviticus."

Zenas quoted, "'If a man lies with a male as with a woman, both of them have committed an abomination; they shall surely be put to death, their blood is upon them.'"

"Yeah, the old Jews got some things right."

"They did indeed," Zenas said. "Brother, can you stay after the others leave?"

Eleazer smiled. "Of course."

With a shit-eating grin on his face, the one that deepened the dimples in his cheeks, Freddy stood in the middle of the living room like he owned the place. "So where's your pussy roommate?"

"Josh had a date," Theo replied.

Freddy stripped off his black leather jacket and tossed it on the couch. He looked, as usual, like a fucking god in his cut-off jeans, Doc Martens, and a form-fitting black QUEER T-shirt that clung to his heroic chest, flat belly, and big round biceps. A tattooed snake wrapped itself around his right arm, green and black and red, the flame-like tongue darting from its mouth just above his wrist. In the corner of his right eye was a tiny blue tattooed tear; "for the sadness of life," he had told Theo in a rare, intimate moment. The snake? What did it symbolize? "My hard nine inches." And just like that, the fleeting memory of Freddy's cock in his mouth got Theo hard enough to cut glass.

Freddy smirked and asked, "A date? With who?" Before Theo could tell him about the lawyer Josh had been seeing, Freddy sprawled on the couch and said, "Get me a beer, babe."

Theo went into the tiny kitchen and rooted through the fridge. There was only one Dos Equis left from Josh's six-pack. For a moment, Theo hesitated. Whatever, he thought, grabbing the bottle. Josh *was* kind of a pussy so the worst he would do was bitch a little and let it go. Maybe he'd finally let the lawyer fuck him and come home in a forgiving mood. God knows, the lawyer was hot—old, but hot—though not as hot as Freddy. Why Josh hadn't given it up to him yet Theo did not understand. He'd been ready to drop his pants for Freddy the first minute he set eyes on him. But that hadn't happened. Not yet anyway. All Freddy'd let him do so far were hand jobs and a little cock sucking. God, he wanted Freddy's dick up his ass, big time. But Freddy said, "Sorry, babe, you got the bug. Can't take any chances." That hurt. A lot. But he couldn't exactly argue the point. The virus was like the snake on Freddy's arm, slithering in his veins, filled with venom. He was lucky Freddy let him touch him at all. Maybe today Freddy'd let him go down on him again. He was so horny he felt like crawling out of his skin.

Back in the living room, on the sofa, Freddy's legs were spread wide open and he was rubbing his dick through the worn fabric of the Levi's cutoffs. Mesmerized, Theo handed him the beer.

"Thanks, babe," Freddy said. He nodded at the glass pipe on the coffee table that Theo had forgotten to hide. "You high?"

"A little."

"That crystal shit again? That stuff's gonna kill you, *m'ijo*. Where do you even get it?"

He shivered with pleasure; he loved it when Freddy called him that. Freddy had told him it meant "my little boy." "And I'm your *papi*," Freddy had continued. "Your daddy."

"It's, you know, around. I need the lift some days."

Freddy patted the sofa cushion and said, "Sit down, baby."

Theo flopped down beside him. Freddy put a muscled arm around his shoulders and pulled him in close enough that Theo could swear he felt the heat of Freddy's flesh rising from the collar of his T-shirt.

"You need a lift, huh? You feeling sick?"

"No, nothing like that, I swear. But you know some days it's hard to think of a reason to get out of bed."

"You should hit the gym, babe. That'll get the endorphins going. Plus, you'd have a nice body if you worked at it."

"Yeah, I used to. I look like shit now, though."

Freddy took a slug from the bottle. "You're okay. A little skinny maybe. Don't lose any more weight. You don't want to look like you're wasting."

Why did Freddy have to say that? Remind him of the spectral figures haunting Boystown, so wasted by AIDS they looked like x-rays of themselves? The look of death. It would happen to him, he knew that. Only a matter of time before he was one of the walking dead, and Freddy, who was negative, would still have his juicy body, those arms, that cock, that ass. He buried his face in the other man's neck and breathed deeply.

"What are you doing?" Freddy asked, amused.

"Smelling you."

"Do I stink?"

"No, you smell . . ." and words failed him. Theo had grown up in Riverside County, east of LA, and he remembered walking to school along a road lined with orange trees on spring mornings when the dew was still on the ground and the trees were in bloom. The sweet fragrance of the orange blossoms mingled with the musky smell of the damp earth and spilled through the air, thick as honey. Freddy smelled like that, sharply sweet and earthy but mixed with an animal swelter. He smelled like life. Theo's own odor was thin and stale and chemical, a sickroom smell.

He felt like such a loser! Maybe he'd always been one though it hadn't seemed so, back when he was so hot strangers would come up to him on the street, press little pieces of paper scrawled with their phone numbers into his hand and beg him to call them. Offer to pay. He'd enter a bar and people would whisper, *that's Brock Tanner*—his porn name—recognizing him from his picture on the DVD cases. He felt like he was king of the world, but looking back, spreading his legs on camera didn't feel like much of an achievement. Dancing on a platform in a smoky bar while strangers shoved dollars into his jockstrap, selling himself to some rich old fag, getting high with B-list actors at parties in hillside mansions he would never afford turned out not to be so glamorous after all when all the smoke and tinsel had cleared.

In the cold light of day, it turned out he'd just been another pretty boy thrown out by his family, with low self-esteem and something to prove. Because beneath the glitz was raw need. He'd fuck almost anyone, not for the sex, but for the scraps of attention they gave him, for the feeling of being wanted, for the voice calling him baby and the strong arms that held him after the sex. For a few minutes in that sentient darkness he felt—what? Loved? Yeah. Loved. But there was always the morning after. Putting on the party clothes from the night before that looked ridiculous in the light of day, smelling like sweat and cum, and stumbling out into the street, clutching, if he was lucky, the guy's phone number but more often not even sure of the guy's name.

God, he wanted another hit of meth. Freddy slapped his hand away.

"I told you that shit will kill you."

"I'm going to die anyway."

Freddy scoffed. "Is this how you want to go? Sitting in a room with the curtains closed, getting high and feeling sorry for yourself? Letting them win?"

"Letting who win?"

"You know who," Freddy said. "The fuckers who are doing this to us. The fucking politicians and doctors who would as soon let the queers die as find a cure. Those asshole Christians who want to lock us up. The fags who think marching around with signs is going to save us. No one is going to save us except us. If we're going to die, let's take some of those fuckers with us!"

People in QUEER thought Theo was a loudmouth, but everything he said, he learned from Freddy. Freddy couldn't be bothered to talk to those losers, but he encouraged Theo to speak out because someone had to remind them what was at stake when they descended into endless bickering about their so-called "actions." The only action the situation called for was war; that's what Freddy said: "If I could, I'd strap a couple of bombs to my body and walk into the White House and blow it up. Take a baseball bat to that fucker Jesse Helms and bash his head like a piñata. Take an Uzi into Falwell's church and let loose. Let them suffer like we suffer. Let them bury their dead for a change."

Theo loved Freddy's passion—it got him higher than a bump of meth. He faithfully repeated in public what Freddy told him in private.

Now, as Freddy raged, "We should kidnap their kids and infect them. Turn their lives into graveyards for a change," he rubbed his crotch in agitation. Gingerly, Theo extended a finger and touched Freddy's dick. Freddy stopped talking, looked at him, smirked and unzipped his fly.

"This what you looking for?" he asked, pulling his hard dick out of his briefs.

"Can I . . . suck you off?"

Freddy responded by grabbing the back of Theo's head and smashing his face into his crotch. Theo managed to get his mouth around Freddy's dick.

"Yeah, fuck," Freddy groaned. "Oh, yeah baby, just like that. Deep throat it." He thrust his cock down Theo's throat, holding down his head as he did, choking him. Slobber poured from the corners of Theo's mouth, and he was gasping, his body twitching, but Freddy wouldn't let go.

"Oh fuck, I'm going to come."

He pulled Theo's head back and splattered his face with semen. It ran down his chin with his spit and snot.

"Shit—go clean yourself up," Freddy said, wincing with disgust.

In the bathroom, Theo beat off and shot a geyser of cum.

SIX

The courtroom was filling up. The judge had allowed TV cameras at the hearing, so the camera operators were setting up at the back of the room while the TV reporters touched up their hair and makeup and tested their mics. The print reporters squatted in the first couple of rows, notebooks out, eyes prowling the room for potential interviewees to supply provocative quotes. There would be no shortage of them after the judge announced his ruling.

For once, I was only a courtroom spectator, not a participant in the proceedings. The lawyers on the case were seated at their tables in front of the courtroom: plaintiffs' counsel on the left, defendants' counsel on the right. Their backs were turned to us in the gallery, but Kate Cassells' bright red hair was instantly recognizable. Beside her, Wendell Thorne's head was bent over a stack of papers. Across from them at the defendant's table sat three white-haired white guys in impressive suits, staring directly ahead to the bench as though they'd been carved in granite.

The question before the court involved the interpretation of an obscure Election Code statute—not the sort of thing that ordinarily filled courtrooms. Six weeks before any election the secretary of state was required to mail to all registered California voters an official voter information pamphlet. Among other items in it the pamphlet contained the text of any initiative on the ballot and arguments for and against the initiative written by its proponents and opponents. The relevant statute said the arguments should not be either false or misleading.

In their argument in favor of Proposition 54, the proponents claimed: "AIDS is not 'hard to get'; it is easy to get"; "Potential insect and respiratory transmission has been established by numerous studies"; and "There is no evidence for the assertion that AIDS cannot be transmitted by casual contact." In other words, the supporters of the quarantine wanted 20 million California voters to believe you could catch the HIV virus from mosquito bites, shaking hands, or even breathing the same air as someone infected with the virus.

I was part of a roundtable of lawyers who'd met occasionally to discuss legal strategies to fight the initiative. The day Wen Thorne got wind of the casual transmission claims he called an emergency meeting.

"If they get this crap in the pamphlet," he said, "we lose. What are we going to do about it?"

Our solution: an emergency lawsuit to have the statements declared false and the secretary of state ordered to strike them from the ballot pamphlet. That had led to this four-day hearing in front of Judge Leonidas Byrnes. Over the course of the proceeding a half-dozen experts, five on our side and one on theirs, gave the mild-mannered, seventy-something-year-old jurist an education in the sexual practices of gay men that often left him quite literally speechless.

"I'm sorry," he said, after one exchange between a defense lawyer and one of our experts. "Did you say fishing?"

"No, Your Honor," the witness replied. "Fisting."

"And that means what?"

"The insertion of a fist into the anus," defense counsel, playing to the media, said loudly.

For a moment Judge Byrne simply stared at him and then mumbled, "Is that even possible?"

"Oh, yes, Your Honor," defense counsel continued helpfully, "it's quite common among homosexuals."

Wen Thorne jumped to his feet. "Objection to the characterization. There's no evidence the practice is common or that it's restricted to gay men. Moreover, Judge, there's no evidence this practice transmits the virus. It's completely irrelevant."

"That's true, Your Honor," the witness said. "There are no reported cases of transmission through fisting. Given what we know about transmission, it would be, at best, a very low-risk activity."

The judge looked at Thorne. "Mr. Thorne, are you asserting that heterosexuals also engage in this practice?"

The witness spoke up. "Yes, but it's generally vaginal fisting, Your Honor."

The judge nodded, then said, "Objection sustained. I think I need a recess. Ten minutes."

And so it went, the defense attempting to drag out every ugly stereotype about gay men it could get into the record—child molesters, sexual predators, debauched sex fiends—while Kate and Wen tried to redirect the hearing to the actual subject matter of how people got HIV. The defense expert was a prim middle-aged orthopedic surgeon who had become famous when she refused to operate on HIV positive men because, she claimed, she was at risk of "aerosol" infection, that the mist of blood and air caused by surgical tools during orthopedic operations could transmit the virus.

Her claims were debunked, and she had been fired from the San Diego hospital where she worked. Now she made her living pushing a conspiracy theory that the medical establishment under pressure from the powerful "gay lobby" was lying about HIV transmission. According to her, HIV could be transmitted by any contact with an infected person. Wen and Kate had challenged her expert credentials—she had no experience as an HIV researcher—and had moved to have her testimony stricken, but the judge had allowed it, which seemed to me to be a very bad sign.

We had assembled this morning to hear Judge Byrne's ruling.

From my seat in the last row of the gallery I watched people continue to file into the courtroom. Congressman Schultz, the author of the proposition, entered the room with a retinue that included a man who looked familiar to me. I saw him only in profile at first but when he turned in my direction, I recognized him as "Dan," the man who had been looking for alternative treatments for his AIDS-stricken son. He saw me. Panic flashed across his face and he quickly turned away and burrowed into a seat on the other side of Schultz. I remembered how he had asked if someone in government could get his son into the AZT trials. A Congressman? Schultz? Who was this guy?

There was a commotion at the entrance to the courtroom as a group of QUEER activists flooded in, holding up cardboard pink triangles inscribed with the names of people who had died of AIDS-related disease, including Rock Hudson. The bailiff rushed them. Sensing trouble, I followed.

"You can't have those in here," the bailiff was telling Laura Acosta.

"Why not?" she asked. "This is public property."

"Hello, Laura," I said and then said to the bailiff, "I'm Henry Rios. I'm a lawyer and I represent this group."

"Then you explain why they can't be waving these signs around."

The disturbance had attracted the attention of the media, and the TV cameras swung in our direction; the reporters began to circle like sharks.

"As long as they don't pose a security threat or disrupt the proceedings, I don't see why they can't hold up their signs."

"Holding up the signs does disrupt the proceedings," he said.

"Come on," I said. "I've tried murder cases where the families of the victims come in holding photographs of the victims. No one says anything about that. This is no different. The names on these signs are people who died of AIDS."

"Sir," he said, in the voice cops use before they arrest you. "I'm telling you they can't hold up their signs."

Wen Thorne approached us. "What's going on, Henry?"

I explained the situation to him.

"Look," he said to Laura, "I appreciate the support but I'm asking you to keep the signs down until after Judge Byrne makes his ruling. Then you can do whatever you want. If he comes out here and sees there's a demonstration, he could clear the courtroom or, worse, adjourn. It's been a tough case. The last thing we need now is to piss him off. Please."

Laura said, "We'll caucus."

They huddled in the corner for a few minutes of loud back-and-forth whispering and then returned.

"Okay," she said. "We'll keep them in our laps for now."

"Thank you," Thorne said, relieved but pissed off, too.

The bailiff returned to his post and I to my seat. A moment later, the buzzer sounded on the clerk's desk, which was the sign the judge was about to take the bench.

"Please rise," the bailiff said. "Department 33 of the Los Angeles Superior Court is now in session, the Honorable Leonidas Byrne presiding."

Byrne sat down, looked mildly surprised at the mobbed courtroom, and began to read from a paper on the bench. "This is an action for declaratory and injunctive relief by which plaintiffs seek to enjoin the secretary of state from publishing certain statements in support of Proposition 54, commonly known as the AIDS quarantine initiative in the voter's information pamphlet for the November 1986 election. Those three statements involve whether the HIV virus can be casually transmitted by means other than by blood or semen. The relevant statute is Elections Code section 3576. Pursuant to that section, any statement that is shown by clear and convincing evidence to be false and misleading shall be deleted from the pamphlet."

He looked up and paused, showing a keener sense of theater than I would have credited him with. "After listening to all the testimony, and considering the points and authorities filed by both sides, I conclude that the plaintiffs have sustained their burden and shown by clear and convincing proof that the three statements in question here are false or mislead—"

The rest of his words were drowned out by applause and hoots of approval from the QUEER activists.

"Congratulations," I said to Wen and Kate when I finally made my way through the crowd.

"Now all we have to do is win the election," Kate said.

"The last polls show us down five points from twelve," I observed. "Things seem to be moving in our direction."

"It's only July. Four more months. That's forever in politics," she said. "They have a lot of money, and losing this fight will only make them double down. We got their lies stricken from the pamphlet, but we can't do anything about their ads claiming you can get HIV from toilet seats."

"Not to mention keeping them in line," Wen said, indicating the QUEER activists who were waving their signs for the cameras while Laura Acosta was interviewed by a poufy-haired reporter. "The last thing we need is for them to do something stupid."

"QUEER isn't a violent organization," I said.

"It's not an organization at all," he replied. "It's a collection of angry people who don't answer to anything but their own rage."

"You can hardly blame them for being angry."

"That's not the point," he said with exasperation. "I'm angry, too. We all are, but we can't afford to alienate straight voters. You're their lawyer. Can't you keep them in line?"

"Like I said, Wen, they aren't violent and like you said, they're not a conventional organization. They're not centralized; they don't have a single leader. Everything gets talked to death."

Kate laughed. "Reminds me of the dyke commune I lived on back in the day. Even the smallest, tiniest issue got processed until the cows came in. Literally. We had cows."

I saw Dan slipping out of the room and asked them, "Do you know who that guy is? The one at the door?"

90

They both looked.

"Daniel Herron," Kate said. "He's the pastor at Ekklesia, a big evangelical church on La Brea. They just gave twenty-five grand to the Yes on 54 campaign."

"And he signed that open letter from right-wing religious leaders endorsing it," Wen added. "The pro-54 people bought space for it in every major paper in the state."

"Longtime bigot?" I asked.

Kate said, "Before now, he hadn't been on our radar, but it looks like he's going all in on 54."

Daniel scuttled out of the courtroom as quickly as he could. The lawyer—what was his name? Henry—had recognized him. He was sure of it. He hurried to the elevator, jabbed at the button impatiently and panicked when he felt a hand clutch his shoulder.

"Pastor? Are you leaving?"

He turned and saw it was only one of Shultz's aides, a pale, moon-faced young man in a blue blazer and red tie with an American flag pinned to his lapel.

"The Congressman thought you might want to make a statement to the press," the young man said.

"I can't imagine I could say anything better than he already has, and I do have some pressing personal business to attend to."

"Oh," the boy said, momentarily flummoxed. He was apparently unused to people turning down a summons from his boss. "I'll tell the Congressman you had an emergency."

"Yes, thank you." Behind him the elevator door slid open. "Well," he said, awkwardly, "good-bye then."

He stepped into the elevator. The door framed the boy's puzzled face as it closed. Dan wondered what he was thinking, what he would tell Schultz. Clearly, he'd felt it was necessary to upgrade Dan's "personal business" to "emergency" to excuse his abrupt departure from the scene of battle. What had Schultz been telling his aides about Dan? He thought Schultz had been treating him differently since he had asked the Congressman for his help in getting Wyatt into the AZT study in San Francisco.

He'd thought long and hard before calling Schultz. The Congressman was an avowed enemy of what he called "the homosexual agenda" and he expected his allies to embrace his crusade against it. Dan feared that raising the subject of AIDS in the context of helping someone infected with the virus would earn him Schultz's suspicion as not being sufficiently on-board against the homosexuals. He'd considered other options—any number of politicians turned up at the church around election time. None except Schultz, however, was a federal official who could intervene with the FDA so, in the end, Dan had taken the plunge.

Schultz hadn't had the faintest idea there was a drug study, much less the disease for which the drug was being tested. Dan had sensed the disapproval in Schultz's silence on the other end of the line as he explained the nature and purpose of the study. When he finished, Schultz had asked, "Is your nephew a homosexual?"

"I didn't ask how he had contracted the virus," Dan had replied, "but I believe it was a blood transfusion."

"You believe," Schultz had repeated skeptically.

"Congressman, what does it matter? He's my nephew."

"If he is a homosexual," Schultz said, "then he chose that diseased lifestyle over his family and he must accept the consequences."

"No one is beyond redemption."

"Are you saying if he gets on this drug and it cures him, he'll repent of his sin?"

"He won't have the chance if he dies."

"His best hope is to repent now, accept Christ into his heart, and face death as a Christian." There was a long pause. "I don't understand why I have to explain this to you, Dan. You, of all people."

Dan, his chance to save his son slipping away, had said, desperately, "He's nineteen, John. A boy."

"My thoughts and prayers go out to his parents. And to you. I'm sorry, I can't help. Even if I wanted to, once the press got wind of it, they'd be calling me all kinds of hypocrite. We don't need that kind of press when we're in the fight of our lives against the homosexuals and their friends. This battle, Dan, it's more important than a single life. Don't you agree?"

That last was less a question than a threat.

"I understand," Dan said.

"Good," Schultz said, ignoring the ambiguity of Dan's response. "I'm glad you see it my way. May I also suggest, Pastor, that you keep your family situation to yourself until the election is over. You're also vulnerable to attack. Let's not give the homosexuals any ammunition."

"Of course," Dan replied.

He had put the phone in its cradle and thought about Schultz's children. The daughter was a drug addict with whom Schultz had no contact; the older son had been disowned when he moved in with his girlfriend without marrying her. The younger son, a lawyer following in his father's political footsteps, was pictured on Schultz's Christmas cards with his wife and their three children.

By the strictures of their faith, Schultz could not be faulted for the way he had treated his three children. The two older children, having fallen into sin, had to earn their way back into the family by forsaking their sinfulness and repenting. Their father could point the way by the example of his life, but the children had to find their own path to Christ. Until then, not only was Schultz justified in keeping them at arm's length, but that distance was necessary for his own salvation lest he become their enabler and an accessory to their sin. That was the economy of faith, and if to outsiders it seemed cruel, that was because they did not understand the stakes.

Outsiders called them fundamentalists as an insult without making any effort to understand what was fundamental to their beliefs—that Satan exists, that he is ceaselessly at work in the world, and that hell is a place, an actual, physical location where those who have rejected Christ will suffer the consequences of their rebelliousness. The soul hung by a thread above that fire, and only Christ could pull it up and only if it had not been frayed or weighted down by sin. The Christian must be constant in his vigilance, militant in his condemnation of evil, and forceful in his evangelism.

Dan had believed he believed all this until the moment Wyatt had asked him, "Dad, do you think I'm going to hell because I'm gay?"

They'd been walking along Ocean Beach in San Francisco at the tail end of a glittering autumn afternoon. Wyatt had come out to Dan in a letter. In response, Dan had flown to the city to talk to him. And he did talk to him. Talked and talked and talked. Explained the unnaturalness and moral danger of homosexuality, offered to pay for therapy to change him, and urged him to consider the spiritual costs of fleeting sensual satisfaction.

"We're not just our bodies, son," he told him. "They aren't even the most important part of us. The body is only the vessel for the soul, like a glass of water. The water is sacred. It comes down from heaven in the form of the rain and ends up in the glass, but the glass is just a container that will one day break and be discarded. We have to keep the glass clean, so the water stays clean because one day the water will evaporate and return to the sky. On that day, you want it to be as pure as the day it fell to the earth."

Dan was proud of that analogy, had used it effectively in his preaching.

Wyatt considered it, looked puzzled, and said hesitantly, "But, Dad, if the stuff that's making the water dirty is heavier than the water, it won't evaporate when the water does. It says behind, like a ring around the glass. The water will always be pure."

"Well," Dan said, thinking quickly, "but you're responsible for the glass, too. You don't want to leave a ring around it."

"But our bodies don't go to heaven, Dad. What difference does it make if they're a little dirty when we leave them behind?"

"It will make a difference on Judgment Day, when you are bodily resurrected from the grave and God calls you to account for how you lived your life, including how you used His gift of your body."

It was then his son had stopped and asked the question about whether Dan thought he would go to hell.

The fading light illuminated Wyatt's hair and glimmered in eyes that were the same blue as Dan's. His round, young face was guileless. Behind them, the ocean thudded on the bright shore and children ran laughing along the tide while gulls dove and shrieked in the blue air.

Dan knew the answer to Wyatt's question was, yes, if he persisted in his homosexuality, eternal torments awaited him that he could not begin to imagine. Suffering beyond any suffering experienced on Earth. Gruesome, endless, and with no hope for reprieve or even momentary relief. That was the theologically correct response but as he studied the little vein beating anxiously in his son's throat, the anxiety in Wyatt's eyes, he simply could not bring himself to say it. He could not bring himself to hurt his son.

"Dad?" came Wyatt's worried voice. "Are you all right?"

"You will have to account to God," Dan said, finally. "I don't know for certain what his judgment will be; no one can know that. But I love you and I will always love you."

Josh was waiting near the entrance of Griffith Park with a blanket slung over his shoulder and a basket made of woven wood in his hand. He wore a loose blue tank top, a faded pair of red shorts, Converse sneakers without socks, and a Dodgers baseball cap. He grinned when he saw me, and I broke into a smile. Larry had once told me, if you're lucky enough to feel joy, don't question it, just be grateful. He knew my skeptical and overactive brain could tug at the thread of happiness until I had completely unraveled it and turned it into a problem. At this moment all I felt was simple joy that Josh was in the world. The questions and complications could wait.

"Hi," Josh said. "Did you bring the drinks?"

95

"The ice chest is in my car. Are we staying here?"

He shook his head. "Too crowded. There are quieter spots around Crystal Springs Drive. Let's take your car."

"Sure."

As I drove us east on Los Feliz, he slipped his hand into mine. I glanced at him. Our bodies pulled together like two magnets, but often I sensed his resistance and thought I knew its reason—that wanting to be sure—so I held back. I was surprised when he pressed our hands together, stroking my palm with his fingertip as if he was sending a message. We talked about his week and mine, and I mentioned that Laura and the other QUEER folk had turned up in court for Judge Byrne's ruling.

"They're doing an action at Grauman's this afternoon," he said.

The famous movie palace had been purchased and renamed Mann's Chinese Theater, but no one called it by its new name.

"What kind of action?"

"You know how in the courtyard there are those cements slabs where movie stars have left their hand and footprints? QUEER is going to cover them up with pink triangles and the names of people who've died of AIDS."

"Your roommate didn't conscript you this time?"

He frowned. "I haven't seen much of Theo lately, and when I do he's kind of scary."

"Scary how?"

"He's really hitting the speed. This meth stuff. He left his pipe out on the coffee table."

"Didn't you say you told him he couldn't use while he was staying with you?"

"Yeah, but . . ." He looked at me helplessly. "I can't kick him out. He doesn't have anywhere else to go."

"If he's using drugs in your apartment, it's time for you to tell him to clear out. You have your own sobriety to think of."

Josh sighed. "I know. I will. But I worry about him ending up on the streets."

"There are drug programs," I pointed out. "I could help get him into one."

"Park there," Josh said, directing me to a lot beside a patch of park. "Thanks. I'll talk to Freddy, and maybe between the two of us we can convince Theo to get some help."

I pulled into a parking space. We unloaded our picnic supplies and headed into the park. This side was less crowded. We found a stretch of lawn between two massive oak trees, laid out the blanket, food, and drink, and settled in. We stripped off our shirts and lay on our bellies facing each other, the sun warming our skin.

"You're almost as dark as I am," I said.

"That's the nice thing about working nights," he said. "I can go to the beach during the day and work on my tan. Plus, my family's Sephardic so we start out a little darker. Our ancestors probably both came from Spain before your Queen Isabella ran us off."

"Not my queen," I said. "She's the one who started the Spanish invasions that ended up wiping out most of my other ancestors in Mexico."

"History is just one long bloodbath, isn't it, Henry?"

I breathed in the warm air, the scent of skin. "Well, there's the official history, the one that gets written down, which is mostly a history of cruelty and destruction and then there's the unwritten history, the secret history of kindness."

He smiled. "If it's not written down, how do you know about it?"

"By inference. If humans were only cruel and destructive, we would have gone out of business a long time ago. Therefore, the reason we've survived is because the cruelty has been tempered with kindness. It's not as dramatic and the people involved aren't usually the ones in charge, so no one bothers to record it. Human history is basically a contest between our better instincts and our worst ones."

"Which one will win?" he asked.

"I don't know," I replied. "All I know is you've got to choose a side."

"You chose kindness."

I touched his face with my fingertips. "So did you."

He scoffed. "What am I doing that makes the world a better place?"

"It's not what you do; it's who you are. You're a good person, Josh," I said, my hand dropping to his chest, the beat of his heart beneath my fingers. "A kind person."

He said quietly, "That's not true. I'm not even an honest person."

"What are you talking about?"

He rolled over on his belly, buried his face in his arms, and murmured in a voice so low I almost couldn't hear him. "I lied when I told you I didn't get tested." He raised his head, looked at me, and said, "I did. I'm HIV positive. I couldn't tell you. I was afraid you'd . . ." His voice trailed off.

The words should have surprised me, but I'd always suspected the truth about his status. If he really hadn't been tested, it was because he was pretty sure the test would come back positive— and if he had, and wasn't telling me because he was positive, I believed he was too honest to conceal it indefinitely.

I threaded my fingers through his sun-warmed hair and said, "I already told you it doesn't make any difference in how I feel about you."

Abruptly he pulled himself up into a seated position. "I don't believe you."

"I told you I would never lie to you, and I'm not lying now."

He shook his head. "You just feel sorry for me."

"Oh my God, Josh," I said impatiently. "Pity is the last thing in the world I feel for you." I reached out, pressed my hand over his heart and said, "I love you."

In a small voice, he asked, "Do you?"

"Yes," I said.

He took an audible breath, exhaled, and said, "I love you, too."

I got to my feet and pulled him up. "Come on then," I said.

"Where are we going?"

"Back to my place."

We kissed. His skin felt like summer; his mouth tasted like life.

The late afternoon light filtered into the bedroom through the soft weave of the curtains illuminating the peaks and valleys of the tangled sheets we'd kicked to the bottom of the bed. A most curious thing had occurred when we got into bed; we didn't have sex. We undressed, we kissed, and naked skin touched naked skin. We looked into each other's eyes. Some ancients believed eyes emit beams of light and this is how we see, each eye a little sun illuminating the world. Others postulated that eyes are windows into the soul—the lamp of the body—illuminating not what is outside us but what is inside. At that moment, it seemed our eyes were illuminating both. I saw Josh and I felt seen—seen, accepted, accepting as our bodies, cast from the same mold, engaged from foot to forehead so that, for a moment, I could not tell where mine left off and his began.

"Is it all right if we just hold each other like this for a while?" he asked.

"Yes," I said.

After a few minutes, he turned his back to me and curled against my body. I slipped one arm beneath his neck and the other across his chest. I pulled him tight, kissed his neck, and we fell asleep.

A series of beeps sounded from our pile of clothes on the floor. I knew he carried a pager in case the restaurant called because someone had flaked on their shift. I carried one for business.

"Is that your pager or mine?"

Before he could answer, another pager beeped.

"It sounds like they're both going off."

He climbed out of bed, poked through his clothes for his pager, pulled it out and said, "This isn't the restaurant. I don't recognize the number."

I was looking at my own pager. I didn't recognize the number either, but that wasn't unusual—it could have been a client calling from any number of police stations.

"You take the phone in the kitchen. I'll use the line in Larry's office."

A few minutes later, we met back up in the bedroom.

"That was Laura Acosta," I said. "It was about that demo at Grauman's. She and several other QUEER people were arrested—"

"And they want you to come and get them out of jail," he said. "I know. My call was from Theo. He's one of the ones who were arrested." He sighed. "You can drop me off at my car on your way to the jail." After a moment, he asked, "Are you disappointed we didn't do anything?"

"We slept together."

"You know what I mean."

"It was better than any sex I've ever had."

He laughed. "You said you would never lie to me."

I kissed his forehead. "I'm not."

SEVEN

At the top of the sheet of the first page of his sermon was the title: *Salvation Not Tolerance.* He silently reread the opening paragraph: "We hear so much about tolerance these days, don't we? How we must tolerate those we disagree with and even those whose lifestyles are plainly unbiblical. We're told these people have a right to use their bodies any way they see fit, and we must respect their right and tolerate them. But what does the Bible say about this tolerance? Where is the verse that commands Christians to accept the presence of sin in their community? Where did Jesus, who healed the lepers, tell us we must accept their right to contract leprosy and spread it among the innocent? Nowhere! That verse, that teaching, isn't in the Gospel! When it comes to sin, the Bible is crystal clear—the sinner must repent and be saved or condemn himself to the everlasting torments of Hell. You may be asking yourselves who and what are you talking about, Pastor? You know who I am talking about. The men who lie with men, the women who give their bodies up to unnatural uses. The so-called gay and lesbian community."

The sermon was not his idea. The Yes on 54 committee had approached every clergyman who had signed the open letter endorsing the measure and had asked them to preach on the issue on the same Sunday. The political consultant explained in a conference call to the signatories, "We want a clear and ringing statement of support from a hundred pulpits on the same day. A call to arms that cannot be ignored by anyone calling himself a Christian." A committee of ministers had written the text that lay on the podium before him—not his words, but theirs.

He'd been trapped. There was no acceptable excuse or equivocation. He'd signed the letter and the church had made a substantial contribution to the campaign. At the time he had assumed nothing more would be asked of him. As the measure continued to lose ground in the opinion polls, however, the pressure on the clergy to speak out more forcefully had grown, culminating at last in what the campaign was calling the Day of Reckoning.

He felt the impatience rising like a mist from the congregation as he stood silent at the pulpit. Behind him on the stage were the Overseers. Metzger's eyes bored into the back of his head. Metzger, the most vociferous proponent of the measure, who had helped organize the statewide event. The coughs and throat clearings, low at first, now became an audible chorus of anxiety joined by whispers of concern.

He raised his head from the text and looked out at his congregation. Almost a thousand souls, most of them white and well-dressed, who had never known hunger or homelessness or the desperation of finding a way to get from one day to the next. Who had never had to look over their shoulders in fear of the fist or the rock or the epithet hurled in hatred with the force of law or custom or scripture. God's Chosen. Ordinary people who, for the first time in human history, lived lives untouched by pestilence, famine, or war, who had enough and more than enough.

Why were they so fearful?

His flock, these well-fed, prosperous people lived in constant and nameless anxiety, the lurking fear that something, someone somewhere was scheming to rob them of what they had and destroy their way of life. They had spoken to him of this fear in a thousand conversations over the years, the dread that infected their lives so that every setback, every difficulty—the lost job, the drug-addicted child, the failed marriage—was the result, not of life's uncertainty or human frailty, but of a dark power being wielded against them.

There was evil in the world. That was indisputable, but to live in constant fear of Satan was to concede that his power was greater than the Lord's, and that was faithlessness. No evil was greater than God. God was the cure for every ill, the path out of every place of darkness, the strong arm that reached out to the imperiled and pulled them to safety. That had always been Daniel's message, that was his faith; it was a message of hope and joy. But now he was told he had to exploit their fear. He was asked to terrify them into voting for a law that, if passed, might force his own child into a quarantine camp.

Just as he could not bring himself to tell Wyatt he was going to Hell, he could not bring himself to say the words on the page in front of him.

He unhooked his microphone from its stand, stepped away from the pulpit, strolled to the edge of the stage, and began to speak. "John tells us, 'There is no fear in love, but perfect love drives out fear, because fear has to do with punishment. The one who fears is not made perfect in love.'"

Caleb Cowell came through the receiving line, shook Daniel's hand, and said, "I liked your preaching, Dan, but it seems like you didn't quite get to what you wanted to say."

"What makes you think that?" Dan replied. He was conscious of Jessica at his side, listening to the exchange.

"You didn't get around to telling us exactly who you think we're afraid of."

"But I did," Dan said. "I said we shouldn't be afraid of people who are different or assume that because they are different God loves them any less or that they were not also made in His image."

Cowell nodded. "Yes, I heard that, and I was waiting for you to tell us exactly who you were talking about."

"It applies to a lot of people. You should know that."

Cowell said. "You mean you were talking about Black folk?"

"There are all kinds of prejudice," he said, growing uncomfortable.

"But you were thinking of a particular kind of prejudice. Weren't you?" There was a glint of a smile in Cowell's eyes.

Daniel shook his head. "Not really. Sorry, Caleb we've got to keep the line moving."

"Sure, Pastor. Jessica."

He moved away and Dan reached out his hand to the next congregant, but no hand was offered in response. Instead, Bob Metzger stood before him and said, stiffly, "I'm very disappointed in you, Pastor."

"Why is that, Bob?"

"You departed from the text we had agreed on."

"I was moved by the spirit in a different direction."

Metzger face was stony. "You agreed to participate in the Day of Reckoning."

Dan forced a smile. "As I said, the spirit moved me to speak on another text. There will be a time and a place to address . . . the proposition."

"Are you so sure it was the holy spirit that moved you?" Metzger asked, coldly. "Are you so sure, Pastor, that that was the voice speaking into your ear when you betrayed your promise?"

"Good to see you, Bob, "Daniel replied and reached for the next hand. "Tommy, Lois, how are you? How's Mindy doing at her new school?"

Josh fell into the habit of coming over after his shift at the restaurant a couple of nights a week and staying overnight, but all we did was sleep together. Then, one night, we started kissing, lightly at first, but then with greater intensity and purpose until we tangled up in each other's bodies, hands restlessly stroking and probing. My mouth moved down his chest, his belly, and then, just as I was about to take him in my mouth, he gasped, "Wait!"

"What, Josh?"

He ran his fingers through my hair. "I'm afraid of infecting you."

I pulled myself up on the bed so that we were face to face. "There's almost no risk with, uh, oral sex."

"Almost no risk isn't no risk."

"We don't have do anything you don't want to," I said, "but I take responsibility for myself."

He sighed. "I'm like an apple with a worm eating away at its insides. I feel so . . . unclean."

I pulled him into my arms. "It's a virus, not the judgment of God."

"Try telling that to my dad."

"Did he say that to you?"

He relaxed against my body. "No, but only because I haven't told him. Or my mom. Not about HIV. Not even that I'm gay."

"Maybe you should think about coming out to them."

He shook his head. "I've been enough of a disappointment to them already. Dropping out of school, disappearing. I'm the only son. My dad's counting on me to carry on the family name."

"Is that so important?"

"For a conservative Jew like my father, who sees history as one long pogrom, yes, it's very important. Each new generation of Mandels represents survival. If he knew the name would end with me, it would—well, I don't want to think what it would do to him and I'm afraid to find out."

I held him quietly for a moment and then said, "You can't keep it a secret forever."

"Don't you think I know that?" he said roughly. "You think I want him to find out from some doctor when I get sick? I know I have to tell my parents. I know I do. I just don't know how."

I understood then that his shame, as much as his fear of infecting me, was what kept him from letting me make love to him.

I kissed him. "Why don't we get some sleep?"

"I'm sorry, Henry," he said.

105

"You shouldn't be. I'm not. I'm glad you're here."

"But I'm such a mess."

"The circumstances are messy. You're fine."

He grinned. "God, you're such a lawyer. You have an answer for everything."

I kissed him again and spooned him, listening to his breath deepen as he drifted into sleep. I wished I could remove his shame and guilt. I knew he thought his behavior was responsible for his infection but, despite what he believed, he hadn't been uniquely promiscuous. I'd had as much sex in my twenties as he had, all of which was now considered "unsafe," and undoubtedly some of my partners had carried the virus. I hadn't avoided the infection through any special virtue of mine any more than he'd become infected because he was especially debauched. It was a crapshoot, a lottery, a game of chance. Guilt and shame were wastes of emotional energy.

When I'd staggered into AA filled with those emotions and a hefty dose of self-loathing, people told me, let us love you until you learn to love yourself. What bullshit, I thought, but I was wrong. If the people you love refuse to treat you with the contempt you feel for yourself, you eventually have only two choices: hang onto your self-hatred and lose those people or let go of the self-hatred and begin to see yourself as they see you—as someone worth loving. Whether he knew it or not, Josh was about to reach that fork in the road.

Sitting at his father-in-law's desk, Daniel reread the proposed agenda for the following day's meeting of the Overseers. All routine, except for the final item under New Business where five words—vote of confidence in Pastor Herron—were followed by the notation "Proposed by Brother Metzger." He'd been expecting an assault after his sermon the previous Sunday but not that the attack on him would be so direct or so clumsy.

Metzger's preferred tactics against him were subtle and spidery, like the man himself. A vote of confidence? It was meaningless.

Even if Metzger could muster a majority to disapprove of Dan's stewardship, Dan could not be removed except by a unanimous vote of the Overseers. Max Taggert had inserted the provision into the church's constitution to ensure his rule would be perpetual, and now Dan reaped the benefit. The old man, he thought, must be turning over in his very tomb on the grounds of the church. For surely, after Dan's performance on the Day of Reckoning, Max would have sided with Metzger.

He sighed. This pointless vote must be the opening shot of some larger scheme by Metzger to depose Dan. But what could it be? A lawsuit? On what grounds? A claim of financial impropriety? On what basis? And then a thought flashed through his head and his heart raced, *Does he know about Wyatt?* No, that couldn't be it. If Metzger had had that weapon in his arsenal, he would have deployed it before now. There was nothing to do but wait to hear what the man had to say.

With a start he realized it was almost nine. He picked up the phone to call Wyatt, but then an explosion at the front of the church rocked his office. His first panicked thought was earthquake. That explained the shaking but not the noise. A car crash on La Brea? No, the explosion was too loud and too near. He hurried to the window and looked toward the sanctuary where smoke was rising from the entrance. He dashed to his desk to call 911 but as he dialed the last digit, the world dissolved into chaos: shards of glass flew through the air, walls collapsed, an eardrum-splitting roar bellowed up from the floor, and the portrait of Max Taggert was incinerated by a visible wave of heat that seared Dan's flesh from his bone but not before he uttered, "Wyatt . . ."

The key turned in the front door, followed by footsteps, and then Josh hopped over the back of the couch and settled in beside me. I lowered the volume on the eleven o'clock news.

"Hey," he said, kissing me.

"Hey. How was work?"

107

"I waited on a famous person," he said, dropping the name of an actor I vaguely recognized as part of what the media called the Brat Pack. "He's even better looking in person, but he was also kind of a bitch." He glanced at the TV. "Turn the volume up."

On the screen, a reporter stood in front of the darkened façade of a weird-looking building. Behind him, a floodlight illuminated blown-out doors and windows as if the building had had its teeth knocked out. Wisps of smoke drifted out from within the building; there was some lettering over what appeared to be the entrance: An *E* and two *K*s and an *A*. Firefighters and police officers dashed around him.

". . . two blasts just moments ago, one at the entrance to the chapel, where I'm standing, and one in a building behind the chapel . . ."

"That's the church on South La Brea," Josh said. "I drove past there like, a half-hour ago."

"Police and the fire department are still arriving," the reporter said. "Police confirmed there were two explosions. We don't know what caused them or if anyone was in the building when it happened but as you can see behind me there's a lot of damage." The reporter paused, listening to his headphone. "Okay, we've just been told we have to clear the area because police now believe the explosions were caused by bombs and there may still be unexploded bombs in the area. Back to you, Bill."

In the studio, the avuncular anchor put on his gravest expression. "Bombs in churches," he said, shaking his head. "I haven't seen anything like that since Black churches were bombed in the South in the early days of the civil rights movement. We will keep you posted about this breaking story as we learn more."

"You drove past there?"

"Yeah, I didn't see anything, but I wasn't really looking. It's called Ekklesia, one of those big evangelical places that preaches God hates fags. It was on the list of churches for a QUEER action next month."

"What action? Laura didn't tell me anything about an action against churches."

Josh smiled. "Probably because she didn't want you to try to talk them out of it. I think the idea is everyone would dress up in their Sunday best, get into the church, and then stage a die-in in the aisles and stay there until the cops came."

I shook my head. "Trespassing on church property, disrupting a religious service. Talk about walking into the lion's den."

"Just like the first Christians," he replied with a smirk.

"It's no joking matter, Josh. There's a real potential for violence there."

"Are you kidding? They're behind the quarantine. They want to put me in a concentration camp! That's already pretty violent. Plus, the whole 'God hates fags' crap. You don't think some poor gay kid in one of those families hears that and doesn't think about killing himself?"

I'd never seen him so angry, so I waited a moment for him to compose himself before I asked, "Did you ever think about killing yourself?"

He deflated. "That's not the point."

"It is for me. I want to understand you."

He put his hands behind his head and shrugged. "Yeah, I thought about it when I first understood what I was. That was just before my bar mitzvah. Before I became a man." He smiled bitterly. "My dad, my uncles, the rabbi, everyone going on and on about what that meant. None of them said God hates fags— the idea I might be a fag never crossed their minds—but they didn't have to. The world they were sending me into as a man had no room for a queer boy. I looked and looked, but I couldn't see a future where I wouldn't have to hide and lie. I didn't think I could do it, not for a lifetime, so yeah, I considered suicide."

"Something made you decide against it."

"There was the practical problem of how I was going to do it, and then there was my mom. I thought about how much it would hurt her and how she would blame herself. And my sisters—even my dad." He shifted away from me on the couch, drew a breath, and said, "I thought about it again when I got my diagnosis."

109

"About killing yourself?"

"Yeah. For about a minute. Well, maybe five minutes. It was the same thing as when I was a kid, seeing a future filled with suffering. I didn't know if I would be strong enough to take it."

"You're not alone anymore."

"You say that like you mean it."

"I do mean it."

"Will you mean it when things get ugly? When I look like— you know. One of those walking skeletons you see all over Boystown?"

I reached for him, but he shook me off.

"Josh, we don't know what the future holds."

"We know you'll be alive in ten years and I—" he slumped against the back of the couch.

"You don't have to torture yourself this way," I said. "It's a choice."

"What's a choice?" he snapped.

"Your attitude about being infected. With all the uncertainty of what might happen, that's really all you have any control over. You can choose to live in fear or to live in hope. You can choose to isolate yourself from the people who love you or let them love you. Learn, even under these circumstances, to love yourself."

His serious expression dissolved into a grin. "That's pretty woo-woo coming from you."

I reached for him again, and this time he let me pull him toward me, stretched out on the couch, and laid his head in my lap.

"I learned it from Larry," I said, "who was the least woo-woo person I ever met. But he was right," I continued, stroking Josh's face. "Our minds want to take us to dark places, but we don't have to go. We can stay right here. And if we are going to fanta-size about the future, why not fantasize about a happy one?"

Josh smirked. "That's called wishful thinking."

"I prefer to call it hopeful thinking." Our eyes met and I said, "If you could see yourself the way I see you. . ."

"What would I see?"

"You'd see why I love you so much."

He looked into my eyes as if he was looking for a glimmer of his own image. Whatever he saw satisfied him because he said, "Let's go to bed."

I lay on the bed, naked, watching him undress. He quietly removed his shirt, pants, and T-shirt, and draped them over a chair until he stood wearing only a pair of black briefs banded with the inevitable Calvin Klein logo. His body was lovely, slender, smooth, leanly muscled—the body of a young man who gave no more thought to his body than a bird gave to its wings. He stepped to the edge of the bed within my arm's reach and asked, "Are you sure you want to do this with me?"

"Never been surer of anything."

He reached his fingers into the waistband, pulled down his underwear, and kicked it off.

I woke up the next morning alone in the bed. Josh's clothes were still draped on the chair, but my bathrobe was missing from the hook on the door where I hung it. Images of the night drifted though my head—his shudder of pleasure when I took him in my mouth, the taste of him, how, lying on his belly, he had looked over his shoulder, eyes clouded with want, and how his flesh yielded as I slowly entered him. Afterward, as he lay with his head on my chest, he said, "When I got my diagnosis, I didn't think I'd ever be able to have sex again."

"Why would you think that?"

"This is how I got infected, doing this. I didn't think I'd be able to stop thinking about that when I was in bed with a guy and it would freak me out. But I didn't feel that with you. I mean, I did a little, when you went down on me but then the way you touched me . . ." His voice trailed off.

"Yeah?"

"I'm trying to think of how to say it. I mean, it was hot, and you clearly wanted me but there was something else. It was . . . healing."

"I felt it, too."

"You did?"

"Mm-hmm." I threaded my fingers through his hair. "I haven't been with anyone since I moved down here from San Francisco two years ago."

He tipped his head up. "Come on, really?"

"Really," I said. "At first, I was too busy setting up my practice and then Larry died and that knocked the wind out of me and then with everything else going on—this quarantine thing, people getting sick—sex seemed trivial." I kissed the top of his head. "But sex isn't trivial. It's kind of the whole point. I'm not talking about an anonymous blow job in a bathhouse—that's its own thing and not what I'm looking for anymore. But this kind of sex, it opens a door to something deeper . . ."

I ran out of words and kissed him, and we again sank to each other's bodies.

The sun was shining in my eyes as I awakened alone in the bed. I got up, pulled on my boxers, and went out to find Josh. I followed the smell of brewing coffee to the kitchen where he sat at the table with the *Times* spread out before him.

"Morning, baby," I said, pouring myself a cup of coffee.

He lifted his head. "You should read this. It's about the church bombing. Someone was killed. One of the priests or whatever they call them."

I stepped to the table and looked over his shoulder. There were pictures of the church—the front entrance blown out, a second building shattered, the wall blown out to expose a burned-out room—and then a photograph of the victim, the senior pastor of Ekklesia, a man named Daniel Herron.

I sat down. "I know him."

"The priest?"

"Pastor," I said. "Yeah, him."

I told Josh about the Dan who had called me seeking alternative treatments for his son with AIDS and how Jack Mulvany and I had met with him.

"I had no idea who he was; all he would tell us was his first name. Then, I saw him at the hearing where the judge struck the casual transmission language from the pro-54 ballot statement. He was sitting with Schultz. Wen and Katie told me who he was."

Josh said, "You mean, this guy who runs a church that's supporting the quarantine has a son who has AIDS?"

"Yes. He wanted to get him into the AZT trials. Said he had a powerful friend. I'm pretty sure he meant Schultz." I scanned the article. "Two bombs. No suspects. No motive. Very strange."

Josh folded the paper. "I guess QUEER can cross that church off their list."

"Josh, a man died. A father who loved his son enough to cross enemy lines to try to help him."

"Sorry," Josh replied. "You're right, it's terrible. His poor son. Was he at least able to get him into the AZT trials?"

"I don't know. I hope so. You know, once it's approved, you'll have access to it too."

"Sure," he said, in a clipped voice.

"Did I say something wrong?"

"No, it's just—after last night, I don't want to think about it."

"I understand."

"I'm not in denial," he said.

"I know you're not. Will I see you again tonight?"

With a slight shake of his head, he replied, "I need to deal with Theo."

"What do you mean?"

"I mean," he said decisively, "that I'm going to tell him to move out. Now he's smoking meth right in front of me. He laughed when I suggested rehab. Plus, Freddy's practically living with us. I've let them run me out of my apartment. I've had enough."

113

"Do you want me to come as backup?"

"I can handle it myself," he replied. "I need to handle it myself."

"Will you call me and let me know how it goes?"

"Sure," he said. He picked up the paper and said, "You know, if this fundie preacher could accept his gay son, maybe my dad will accept me someday."

That evening after a sandwich dinner I was working on some long overdue billing when I heard the front door open and then Josh saying, "Henry? Where are you?"

I got up from the dining table and met him in the foyer.

"Hey, I wasn't expecting you." He set down the backpack that carried his toiletries and change of clothes. "You're staying? Is everything okay? You have a fight with Theo?"

He embraced me, kissed my cheek and said, "Yes, yes and no."

I released him. "You evicted your roommate?"

"I didn't have to," Josh said. He unzipped his backpack, removing a foil-covered package. "I brought you dinner."

"I ate," I said.

He scoffed. "What, peanut butter and jelly again? Come on," he said, heading into the kitchen. "It's pasta in cream sauce with prosciutto and zucchini blossoms. One of the chef's best dishes."

I followed him into the kitchen. He removed the foil, and the fragrance of garlic, cheese, and cream filled the room. He pulled a bowl out of the cupboard, filled it with pasta, slipped it into the microwave, and set it for ninety seconds.

"Theo was gone when I got to the apartment," he said, leaning against the counter. "His house key was on the kitchen table and he's taken all his stuff, clothes, toothbrush, everything."

"No explanation?"

"He left a note." He dug into his pocket, pulled out a scrap of lined paper, and handed it to me.

Josh, I'm taking off. Thanks for everything. I didn't mean to get you into trouble. Love, Theo

"Got you into trouble? What's that about?"

"His comings and goings late at night disturbed my next-door neighbor who complained about him to the manager, who reminded me I was the only person on the lease," he replied. "I'm a little worried about where he's gone."

"With Freddy?"

"Could be, but he told me Freddy lives with his folks and isn't out to them."

"It's not your problem anymore."

"No, I guess not." The microwave dinged. "Sit down and eat this. It's amazing and afterward . . ."

"Afterward, what?"

"You can take a shower with me."

EIGHT

I followed the story of the church bombing in the *Times*, feeling personally invested because I'd met Dan Herron. After a week, the story dropped from the front section to the Metro section and the articles were shorter and repetitive. I took that as a sign either that there were no new developments or that the cops were keeping quiet because they were closing in on a suspect and didn't want him to know how far the investigation had gone.

There had been two bombs. The first, planted at the entrance to the chapel, had a showier impact because of all the glass it shattered, but was less powerful than the second one, which had been planted in a doorway at the administrative building behind the chapel. The second explosion brought down a wall, killed Dan Herron, and blasted the garden where the founder of the church was buried, damaging his grave. The cops said the bombs were homemade pipe bombs set with timers. No other details were given, but I figured bombs that powerful were probably made by someone who knew what he was doing. The cops were also silent as to motive while stunned church members were at a complete loss as to why their church or leader should be the target of a bombing.

I stereotyped all evangelicals as fanatical Bible-thumping religious bigots, but Daniel Herron's obit, published five days after the explosion, revealed a more complicated character. He wasn't raised in a religious family but had converted in the late '60s in

116

San Francisco during the Jesus People movement, an odd amalgam of hippie counterculture and evangelical Christianity. Afterward, while attending Bible college in LA, he had run a street mission in Skid Row that not only proselytized but also fed and clothed the destitute. He'd joined Ekklesia as its youth minister where he apparently rejuvenated the congregation by bringing in young families and had raised a lot of money that went into expanding its facilities to include a school and various charitable programs. The founder had designated Herron as his successor, and he assumed leadership when the founder died.

Unlike other evangelical leaders, he tended to stay out of politics. His message, read the obit, "was always one of uplift, hope and God's love." Also unlike other evangelicals, he was something of an ecumenicalist. Hester Prince said he was the only evangelical clergyman to call and congratulate her on her ordination as the first woman Episcopalian priest in Southern California. Titus Jones, a bishop in the AME church, remembered that Herron had given the invocation at Mayor Bradley's third inauguration and had always maintained a bond with LA's Black clergy. Nonetheless, the obit continued, he fully subscribed to the tenets of his church's fundamentalist theology, was vocally opposed to *Roe versus Wade* and abortion for any reason, and favored the return of prayer in school. The biggest surprise for me came at the end of the obit, which listed his survivors: wife, two sisters, both parents. But no children, no son.

On a whim, I called Jim Mulvaney with whom I'd met with Herron when he came pleading for help for his son.

After some catching up, I asked him, "You remember Dan, the guy we met at the court cafeteria that day with the infected son."

"Sure," Jim said. "The mysterious stranger."

"Did you ever hear from him again?"

Jim ruminated for a moment. "As a matter of fact I did. He called me a few weeks after we talked and asked me about getting ribavirin and Isoprinosine for his boy up in San Francisco. I gave him a name and a number."

"That was that?"

"He was just as tightly wound over the phone as he was in the flesh."

"I guess he wasn't able to get his son into the AZT trial."

"I guess not," Jim replied. "Why are you asking about him?"

"You read about the church that was bombed on La Brea? He was the pastor there. He was killed in the explosion."

"No shit," he said, astounded. "Isn't that a fundie church?"

"Yeah, apparently."

"Wow, that's really strange, but I guess it explains why he was so cagey with us. Really sorry to hear he was killed. Whatever else he may have been, seems like he was a good dad."

To a son he had apparently never acknowledged, I thought, as we said our good-byes.

I'd been expecting Josh for an hour and had ordered a big takeout dinner from a local Lebanese restaurant to thank him for all the meals he'd made for me when the phone rang.

"Hello."

I heard a shaky, "Henry?"

"Josh. Are you okay?"

"I'm at the Hollywood police station," he said. "The police are saying they're going to arrest me."

"Arrest you?" I said, trying to make sense of the conversation. "For what?"

"Bombing that church," he said.

"What!"

"They're serious, Henry. They came with a warrant and searched my apartment and dragged me down here."

"Have you answered any questions?"

"I told them I wanted to talk to my lawyer."

"Good boy. Sit tight. If the cops try to question you again, tell them you won't talk until your lawyer arrives. I'll be there in fifteen minutes."

I hung up, ran to my car, and sped down the hill to the police station.

At the station I had a testy exchange with the beleaguered desk officer about Josh's whereabouts and his status; the cop conceded he wasn't under formal arrest.

"Detained," the cop growled, "as a person of interest."

"But not arrested."

"That's what I said, counsel."

"Then he's free to leave," I pointed out. "I want him released. Now."

The cop gave me a feral look, but I was used to that tactic; mad-dogging it was called on the streets when gangbangers used it to intimidate each other. I wasn't sure if the cops got it from the gangs or the gangs got it from the cops.

"My client has invoked the right to counsel. I'm his counsel. You are preventing me from talking to him in violation of his constitutional rights. You might not care about that, Officer . . ." I glanced at his name tag ". . . Healy, but I can promise you a judge will. If he's not under arrest, I want him released. Every moment you delay is an unlawful detention."

The words *constitutional*, *judge*, and *unlawful detention* seemed finally to register.

"Wait here," he barked and disappeared into the back.

A few minutes later he emerged with Josh and practically pushed him through the doorway into the waiting room. Josh looked disheveled and exhausted but managed a weak smile when he saw me. As soon as we were outside, though, out of eyesight of the cop at the counter, he threw himself into my arms, sobbing.

"Hey, hey, hey," I said, holding him. "Are you okay? Did the cops do anything to you?"

He pulled away a bit. "No, not physically, but I've never been so scared in all my life." He wiped his nose on his sleeve. "They said I helped Theo blow up the church."

"Let's go home. You can tell me the whole story there."

He slumped silently in the passenger seat. I had a hundred

questions, but he was still shaken by whatever had happened at the station, so I let him be. We stopped for a light on Sunset. On the left side of the street a billboard featured a diminutive, sweet-faced middle-aged woman in a house dress and frilly apron pointing a wooden spoon at a shirtless hunk. Above them were the words, "Mother says, Play safe."

Josh glanced at it and murmured, "The police officer called me a faggot. Faggot. Queer. Pervert. Every name he could think of. He said, 'don't worry, punk, where you're going, you'll have all the dick your ass can handle.' He pushed me against the wall and was screaming in my face. Accusing me of murder. I almost pissed myself, Henry. I thought he was going to beat me up. If you hadn't come when you did, I would have confessed just to get him to stop."

Fucking LAPD! There was nothing they wouldn't do to squeeze a confession out of whatever unfortunate they'd zeroed in on as a suspect, whether or not that person had committed a crime. Sure, there were some decent cops, but they were the exception, not the so-called bad apples I heard about every time one of them got caught committing some egregious act of misconduct. The bad apples ran the goddammed place.

"That's what they count on," I said when I'd calmed down. The light changed and I turned toward home. "You did well."

"Was it an act, or do the cops really hate us that much?"

"It's both." We drove up the hill to Larry's house. I pulled into the garage, cut the engine. "Why do the cops think Theo blew up the church? And why do they think you helped him?"

"Let me take a shower. I need to wash the smell of that room off of me."

I put out the food though I suspected neither of us would feel like eating and made a pot of coffee. Darkness pressed against the windows and a chill slithered through the shadowy rooms. Josh came into the kitchen in a pair of my sweatpants and an old T-shirt emblazoned with the name of my law school. They hung on his smaller frame, emphasizing his fragility. He looked at the spread.

"This for me?"

"Yeah, I figured I'd feed you for once."

He gripped me in a bear hug and muttered, "Thanks," and I knew it wasn't for the food. He let go, poured a cup of coffee, dumped what seemed like half a bowl of sugar into it, and sat down. Tension came off his body like steam.

"Can you tell me what happened?"

He blew out a breath. "I got home from work around five, grabbed a beer from the fridge, and turned on the TV to decompress before I came over. I heard a knock at the door. I looked through the peephole and it was Mike, the building manager. When I opened the door to see what he wanted, a police officer pulled me outside and slammed me against the wall. He shouted at me, asking if there was anyone else inside. I said no; then he handcuffed me and a bunch of guys in bomb suits went inside. I asked, 'what are you doing?' And the cop who handcuffed me said they had a search warrant." He lifted his cup with both hands and drank.

"Did you see the warrant?"

He shook his head. "The cop marched me downstairs to the sidewalk. The street was blocked off, and there was a crowd of people at the end of the road behind a police barricade. The cop pushed me toward the crowd—I recognized my neighbor, I guess they had evacuated the building—and then into the back seat of a police car."

He took a deep breath, picked up the coffee again, and put it down without drinking.

"Do you have any idea what they were looking for?" I asked him.

"They think Theo made bombs that blew up the church in my apartment."

"Why?" I asked, softly.

He gripped the mug. "They said they found fragments of one of the bombs at the church with Theo's fingerprints on it. They said they knew he was living with me. They accused me of helping him make the bombs. Is that even possible, Henry? Don't you need special equipment to make a bomb?"

"I had a client who blew up his ex-wife's house with a pipe bomb he made at his kitchen table," I replied. "The ingredients are simple and easy to obtain. Batteries, wires, a section of pipe, some kind of explosive—gunpowder, fertilizer or even match heads. Once you got the ingredients, all you need is *The Anarchist Cookbook* to give you step by step instructions on how to put them together. Theo's fingerprints . . ." I mused. "Could he have done it?"

"I don't—" he began, raked his hair with his fingers. "You've met Theo. He's a mess. I can't see how he'd get it together to build a bomb."

"Could Freddy have done it?"

"Freddy?" he said incredulously. "Freddy's the sane one."

"Did you get any idea from the cops about a motive?"

He came back to the table and sat down. "They showed me pictures of the church. Someone spray-painted 'Bash the Church' and 'Queer Revolt' on the walkway outside the entrance. Bash the Church is the name of the action I was telling you about yesterday, and Queer Revolt is one of QUEER's slogans. They asked me about QUEER. Was I a member, and who's in charge?" He shivered. "I'm cold. Is it cold in here?"

I got up, went to the foyer, and took a sweatshirt off the coat-rack. When I returned to the kitchen, he was mechanically scooping food from the takeout boxes onto two plates.

"Put this on," I said, handing him the sweatshirt.

He put down the serving spoon and pulled the sweatshirt over his head. He gave me a frightened look and said, "I guess I know now what Theo meant when he apologized for getting me into trouble."

"Did you have anything to do with the bombing?"

"How could you even ask me that?"

"I have to if I'm going to represent you."

"I didn't do anything!"

"Doesn't matter. The cops are like a dog with a bone when they get an idea in their head. Theo's fingerprint connects the bombs to him. The fact that he was staying at your apartment connects him to you. If the search uncovers any evidence the bombs were put together at your place, that's another connection to you. Unless they've found Theo and beaten a confession out of him, you're all they've got."

"Oh, my God," he moaned. "What am I going to do?"

"You're not going to do anything. I'll handle this. Those connections between you and the bombing are circumstantial and weak. Plus, you were at work the night of the bombing. There's not enough to arrest you and certainly not enough to charge you. What the cops are probably doing is putting the squeeze on you to get to Theo. Do you know where he is?"

He shook his head. "I haven't seen him since he moved out."

His stomach growled.

"You should eat something."

He managed a lopsided grin. "That's my line." He'd filled his plate with hummus, chicken shawarma, tabbouleh, and stuffed grape leaves. "It looks good," he said lamely, took a forkful of tabbouleh, and then put it down. "Maybe later."

"Eat," I said, and ate a forkful of chicken to encourage him.

He dipped a bit of pita into the hummus and ate it. He reached across the table and took my hand. "Thanks for rescuing me."

I couldn't bring myself to tell him the rescuing had just begun.

Jessica was embarrassed by the dust on the artificial flowers in the silver bowl on the dining-room table, but the room had seldom been used, either by her parents or by Daniel and her. Her mother had been in no condition to entertain, and she and Daniel were oddly friendless. Though he resisted it, the fact was that Daniel's status as head of the church made him socially unapproachable to his congregants—who invited the pope to a barbecue?—and the congregation was basically all the community they had. So the big formal room with its sea-green wallpaper; tall lace-curtained row of windows; antique china cabinet stocked with a Spode service and Christofle silver for twelve; and the long rosewood table was like an empty theater set waiting for the curtains to open on a play that never began. Until today. Today, there was drama.

The police detective—McCann—squeaked against the plastic-covered chair and attempted a look of solicitude but his eyes wouldn't cooperate; they remained hard and skeptical.

"Why was Reverend Herron at the church that night? I understand the church wasn't in use on Thursday nights."

Jessica glanced at the other men around her dining table—men, always men—a second detective whose name she hadn't bothered to catch and Bob Metzger.

"Thursday nights were his counseling nights," she said. "He chose it because he would be alone with—whoever he was counseling."

"Do you know who he saw?"

She shook her head. "No, you see, Thursday wasn't for regular appointments. He kept that night for congregants who had—special issues—that required some discretion. The appointments were private. He made them himself and kept them to himself."

"So," the detective said, "you don't know who he was meeting that night."

"Isn't that what I just said?" she replied, meeting his cold eyes with equal coldness.

She felt the collective disapproval of the men around the table at her tone. What did they want from her? Tears? Hysteria? She was tired of this. Her husband had been blown to bits, her father nearly dislodged from his grave. What did she feel? Shock, horror, exhaustion, remorse, and maybe the tiniest drop of relief—emotions she did not care to share with these emotionless men feigning sympathy. All she wanted was to be alone and a drink. She really needed a drink.

She managed a strangled, "Bob, can we stop?" Uncle Bob, she almost said, but knew that would be laying it on too thick.

Bob Metzger said, "I think that's enough for today, Detective McCann. My client is obviously under considerable stress."

My client, she thought. Since when did she need a lawyer?

"Of course," McCann said. He and the other detective got up to go. "Mrs. Herron, I am sorry for your loss."

She looked at him and murmured, "Thank you."

"But," he added, "we will have to talk again. When you're up to it."

Her polite nod concealed a "screw you."

When the detectives were gone Metzger reproached her. "I realize this is difficult for you, Jessica, but we have to cooperate fully with the police to find Daniel's killers."

"By asking me the same questions over and over?" she replied. "My answers aren't going to change."

"You're upset," he said soothingly. "You should get some rest."

"I do need to lie down," she said. "But I suppose—the funeral arrangements. I have to—"

"I'll handle them," Metzger replied. "Closed casket, I'm afraid."

She had a flashing, horrifying memory of the body bag into which the coroner had gathered what was left of Daniel; he'd been identified by dental records.

She thought she would be sick. "Whatever you think best. I'll walk you out."

"No need," he said. "I know the way."

He got up, arranged his face into what she imagined he thought was a sympathetic smile, and left the room. She heard his footsteps grow fainter as he walked through the other uninhabited rooms of the house. Her father had built his mansion in Baldwin Hills for its proximity to the church only later to realize he'd moved his family into what was known as the Black Beverly Hills.

When she heard the front door close, she got to her feet, smoothed her skirt, and forced herself to walk slowly into the entrance foyer and up the grand stairs to her second-floor bedroom. There she bolted the door and reached beneath the bed for the bottle. Hands shaking, she filled the water glass and took a hard, sharp swallow, then shuddered. She set the glass down as the warmth spread through her chest. She undressed, drew the curtains closed, and climbed into bed. *Pray,* she told herself. *Pray.* But for what? Dan was dead. The scandal of his secret life was averted. Her prayers had been answered.

Marc Unger met me in the reception area outside his sixth-floor office in City Hall East dressed, as usual, in a beautifully tailored suit that emphasized his broad shoulders while minimizing his thickening waistline. This one was a gray, pin-striped number he wore with a starched white shirt and red and blue regimental tie, the very picture of lawyerly propriety.

"Counsel," he said, extending his hand. "Are you lost? I think you want the criminal division on the sixteenth floor."

"No," I said. "I have business with you."

He lifted an eyebrow. "Well, then, let's get to this . . . business."

I followed him into the suite that housed the police litigation unit and into his capacious office. There were the usual framed diplomas—UCLA undergrad and law—certificates of admission to practice in various courts, including the United States Supreme Court, and photographs with dignitaries: the governor, the current and former mayor and the chief of police. Big desk, comfortable chairs, and a round conference table piled high with files, transcripts, and *US Reports*—the bound volumes of Supreme Court opinions. Bland and conventional but not quite believable; it was like a movie set of a lawyer's office. Or a disguise.

There was not a hint of the lewd and funny-verging-on-campy gay man I knew. I suppose he had to save that for his off-hours, when he wasn't defending cops in federal court in wrongful death actions. When I had once asked him how he had come to work for the cops, given who he was and who they were, he said he liked a good fight and he liked cops, and did I like the rapists and murderers I represented? The conversation ended in a draw.

126

"So," he said, ensconcing himself in his chair, "Henry. Am I going to have to chase you around my desk or will you just bend over it?"

"I'm here about a case."

He furrowed his brow. "What case? This is the civil side of the law, not the gutter where you practice."

"I wouldn't take the word civil too seriously. I've seen you at work. Civility's not your strong suit."

He grinned. "While I'd love to sit here all day and trade insults with a gorgeous guy, I do have a deposition to prepare for. What do you need?"

"It's about the church bombing."

He was instantly serious. "What about it?"

"The cops have identified a person of interest. I'm representing him."

He groaned. "Oy, of course you are." He shook his head. "How did you come to tilt at this particular windmill?"

"The cops think a gay group called QUEER is behind it. I'm their lawyer. My client is associated with them."

"These people make all of us look bad. Not," he added, "that I don't get why they want to blow things up. My friends are dropping like flies, and fucking Ronald Reagan—okay, that's a conversation for another day. Continue."

"They didn't blow up anything. Their thing is civil disobedience, political theater, not explosions."

He sank back into his chair, looked at me skeptically. "Evidently LAPD disagrees. Still don't understand what any of this has to do with me."

"The cops are going to hold a press conference this afternoon to discuss developments in the case. I want to keep my client's name out of it."

"Why?"

"He's a kid, Marc, only twenty-three, not even out to his family. It would be shitty if the way they found out he's gay is as part of a felony murder investigation. He's not a suspect. He just had the misfortune to be roommates with the guy the cops think planted the bombs. They questioned him and let him go. His name doesn't need to be disclosed."

He looked dubious. "If they questioned him and let him go, why is he still a person of interest?"

"He's the only connection the cops have to their actual suspect."

"The roommate," he said. "Off the record, Henry, and just between us girls, is your guy involved?"

"Absolutely not."

"Absolutely, positively," he said, with mild mockery. "And you know this how? Because he whispered it into your ear across the pillow?"

I knew he was joking, but it hit too close to home for comfort. I deadpanned, "There's no physical evidence connecting Josh to the bombing, and a roomful of people can swear he was working the dinner shift at Chez Richard's on Robertson when the bombs went off."

"Jacob's been wanting to eat there," he said absently. "Excuse me if I need to check with my people before I buy your story, but let's assume what you say is true. You don't want the kid outed. I get that." He closed his eyes and ruminated. "If he was falsely identified by name as a suspect, and he was later cleared, an enterprising lawyer might be tempted to sue the city and the police department for what? Slander? Defamation?"

"Don't forget false arrest," I added, catching his drift, "and intentional and/or negligent infliction of emotional distress."

He opened his eyes, leaned forward, grinned and said, "We can't have that. The city's broke as it is. What's the kid's name?"

"Joshua Mandel."

"A fellow Jew? Now I am insulted! Okay, if everything checks out, I can spin a tale about avoiding potentially costly litigation to keep his name out of it, but you better not be bullshitting me about his involvement because if he ends up in an orange jumpsuit that will be the end of our beautiful friendship."

"I swear I'm not, Marc. I come in good faith."

"Is he dishy?"

"What?"

"The kid," he said, with a lewd smile. "Is he a hunk?"

Since he was doing me a huge favor, I humored him. "He's a good-looking young man."

"Have you sampled the wares?"

Okay, time to cut this short. I got up. "Thanks, Marc. I owe you."

"Remember that next time I pinch your ass and ask you to come home with me."

"Does Jacob know you talk like this?"

He laughed. "Everyone knows I talk like this."

"Including the chief of police?"

"Scoot now. I have work to do."

Where the fuck was Freddy?

Theo jumped off the bed and went to the window for the fourth time that hour, parting the curtains just enough to get a view of the motel's parking lot. The same three cars he'd seen ten minutes ago were still parked there. The sun was sinking into the distant ocean, and a golden light shimmered behind the buildings that formed the Hollywood skyline—the old hotels and movie palaces, the Capitol Records tower, the T-shirt shops and falafel stands. Almost imperceptibly the street noises had begun to shift from day to night, the purposeful movement of cars and trucks and pedestrians, the urgent squalls and shrieks of the working day, fading into something more aimless, undirected, and covert.

They'd been on the move since the explosion almost two weeks earlier, going from one shabby motel to another while Freddy got the money together for them to head to Mexico. But Freddy'd been gone for a day and a half without any word and Theo was detoxing. Freddy had warned him not to call his dealer. "The cops will be looking for us," he'd told Theo. "I heard on the news they found fingerprints on pieces of one of the bombs. Didn't I say wear gloves?"

"What! No, you didn't—My fingerprints? You sure?"

"They weren't mine," Freddy said. "I wore gloves."

"You didn't say anything about gloves," Theo whined.

"The hell I didn't," Freddy snapped. "I gave you a fucking pair when you got out of the car and told you to put them on."

Theo was confused now. Maybe Freddy *had* told him to wear gloves. The days leading up to the night of the explosion and the night itself were a blur and not only because he'd been high most of the time. When he'd realized Freddy was serious about blowing up the church, he'd freaked. But through a combination of bullying and seduction, Freddy gradually wore down his resistance. He sealed the deal when he finally took Theo to bed and gave him what he'd wanted since they'd first met, his big cock and the words "I love you."

"If you love me," Freddy said as Theo lay in his arms. "If you want more of this," he grabbed Theo's hand and rubbed it against his big cock, "you'll help me."

"But what if someone gets hurt?" Theo said, taking the heft of Freddy's cock in his fingers.

"I told you, baby, I checked it out. There's no one at the church on Thursday nights. No one to get hurt."

Freddy slid his hand beneath Theo's ass and drove a finger into him. Theo squirmed with pleasure. "You like that, *m'ijo?*"

"Yes, *papi.*"

"Are you going to do what Daddy tells you?"

"If you promise no one will get hurt," he said in a small voice.

Freddy moved his finger inside him. "Baby, trust me."

He was amazed when they went to the hardware store how ordinary the stuff for the bombs was—pipes, caps, wires, alarm clocks.

"Is that all you need?" he asked Freddy as they pulled out of the Home Depot lot.

Freddy laughed. "No, babe, I still have to get the fairy dust."

He didn't understand what he meant until Freddy showed up at the apartment one evening while Josh was at work with a container of gunpowder. He shooed Theo out of the kitchen. Theo paced the living room anxiously. A couple of times, he peeked into the kitchen, worried that Freddy would blow them up, but Freddy worked with delicate intensity as he put the explosives together.

"When did you learn that?" Theo asked him when he'd finished.

Freddy replied in a voice that ended all further questions, "Someone taught me."

They went to the church the Sunday before to scout it out. Freddy'd brought a camera and took pictures until a couple of guys approached them. Seeing them, Freddy sent him to the car and later, when he asked why, said he didn't want both of them to be recognized.

"One of them was security. They know my face now," he told Theo. "You have to plant the bombs."

"What? You said all I'd have to do is be the lookout."

"Change of plans," Freddy replied curtly.

On the day of the bombing, Freddy spread a group of Polaroids on the kitchen table, marked with black X's where the bombs were to be planted. They went over them again and again until Freddy was satisfied Theo knew exactly where to place them.

But, as they were getting ready to leave, Theo said, "Can't you wear a mask or something?"

"What did you say?" Freddy asked dangerously.

"You could wear like a ski mask to hide your face and I could stay in the car and—"

Freddy's backhanded blow sent Theo sprawling to the floor.

"Listen, you little shit, we're in this together. You understand? You'll do what I say."

Theo, blood seeping into his mouth, stared at him in shock

and started to cry. Freddy pulled him to his feet, hugged him, kissed his cheek and said, "I'm sorry, *m'ijo*. I'm a little stressed. I just . . . I need you, Theo, you know. I need you."

His voice was soft, vulnerable. Theo wiped his face and nodded. "Okay, *papi*."

"Good boy. Look, we'll do this, we'll get a room tonight, and I'll fuck your brains out. Then we'll take off to Mexico for a while. I have friends in Puerto Vallarta. Right on the Pacific coast. We'll sit on the beach and drink margaritas. You'll love it there."

Theo managed a smile and asked, "Can I smoke a pipe before we go?"

Freddy frowned, shrugged. "Okay, but just a taste. We need your hands to be steady. I don't want you to blow yourself up."

At the church Freddy gave him the backpack with the bombs and a can of spray paint.

"Paint the slogans first to let them know who was here," he said. "Then plant the bombs and get the hell out of there."

Theo whispered, "Will you come with me?"

For a second he thought Freddy was going to hit him again, but instead he said gently, "You've come this far, *m'ijo*. You can do it. I'll be waiting here for you. Think about the beach, the waves, the margaritas."

Theo nodded. He got out of the car and crept onto the grounds of Ekklesia.

They were halfway to the underpass of the 10 when the bombs went off. Freddy grabbed Theo's leg and said, "You hear that?"

The sound was muffled by distance and the drone of traffic on the approaching freeway, but still audible. The blasts were unlike anything he had ever heard, concentrated, intense and sudden, the bellows of pure destruction. Later, he thought, if evil made a noise, it would be those explosions.

They spent the night in a motel in Boystown. Early the next morning Theo went out to get a newspaper and brought it back to the room. The bombing was on the front page with photos of the church and the man, the pastor, who had been killed in the explosion. He shook Freddy awake.

"What?" Freddy said sleepily, his back to Theo.

"You said no one would be there!"

Freddy rolled over in bed and said, "What are you talking about?"

Theo shook the front page at him. "There was a guy at the church, the pastor. We killed him."

Freddy grabbed the paper from him, scanned it, tossed it aside and said, "Accidents happen. Anyway, the guy was a fundamentalist asshole. World's better off without him. Now come back to bed and take care of this." He stroked his dick beneath the sheet.

"I killed someone," Theo mumbled, still shocked. "We killed someone."

"I said it was an accident. The place was supposed to be deserted."

"What are we going to do?"

Freddy sat up, the sheet falling from a body plated in muscle like armor, and said coldly, "What are you talking about, what are we going to do?"

"We could turn ourselves in to the police," Theo said, weakly. "Tell them it was an accident."

"You think the pigs will believe it was an accident? Do you think it will matter to them? We turn ourselves in and we'll die in prison." He reached for Theo's hand, gripped it. "Hey, you have to trust me. I have friends. I can get us out of this."

Theo felt the creep of emotional paralysis, mind and body sinking into numbness. All he could think was, *I need to get high.*

Freddy, watching him intently, said, "Call your dealer, but stock up because this is the last time."

Now, in another motel room, with twenty dollars to his name, no car, no speed, and no way of reaching Freddy, the walls closed in.

NINE

The chief of police stood at a lectern emblazoned with LAPD's seal—a complicated device involving the scales of justice, what looked like a family of aliens, city hall, laurel branches, and the ironic motto "To Protect and Serve"—and said grimly, "We have a suspect in the bombing and we're closing in on him. We also believe, however, that he did not act alone. We think he was part of a homosexual terrorist network, and we can't be certain they won't strike again so we are taking measures to provide extra security for the city's churches. We will be going after all of these people very aggressively." When a reporter asked for names Gates brushed her off. "We'll be releasing names when our investigation is at a point where we're ready to submit the case to the district attorney for prosecution."

The seven o'clock installment of the local evening news went to sports. I switched it off. Although the cops had questioned Josh about QUEER, they hadn't made any moves against the organization in the two weeks since the explosion. If they suspected Theo was part of a broader conspiracy, they weren't pursuing those suspicions, but seemed entirely focused on finding him. In fact, the department hadn't publicly released any information about Theo's possible connection to QUEER or the slogans painted at the site of the explosion, which, because the site had been off-limits to the media since the bombings, had not made it into press reports.

To be on the safe side, I'd let Laura Acosta in on what the cops had connecting Theo to QUEER and asked her to let me know if they started nosing around. She swore QUEER had had nothing to do with the bombing. I told her to keep our talks to herself unless and until the cops went public. Gates just had. It was clear to me who he meant by "homosexual terrorist network." I wondered if the police had been quietly investigating the organization after all and had discovered incriminating evidence I was unaware of. Not that I thought Laura would hold back on me, but the QUEERs were anarchists, and she wouldn't necessarily know what other people had been up to.

I got up from the couch, went into Larry's office, and dialed her number.

Skipping preliminaries, I asked her, "Did you see Gates's press conference?"

She laughed. "Hello to you, too, Henry. No, I had better things to do. What did he say?"

I recounted his remarks about the terrorists. "He meant QUEER."

"That's crazy," she said. "I told you we had nothing to do with that mess."

"Are you sure?"

"What do mean, am I sure?" she asked, hackles up.

I picked up a rubber band and threaded it through my fingers.

"Are you sure you know everything that everyone was doing? Can you be certain that no one in QUEER besides Theo was involved in the bombing? Because it sure sounds like the cops have done some digging and come up with something."

She took a nervous breath. "You know how we operate," she said. "People do their own thing."

The rubber band snapped.

"If anyone in QUEER knew in advance about the bombing and supported it in any way, you could all be charged with conspiracy, and from what Gates said at the press conference it sounds like that's the plan."

"Shit," she muttered. "What should we do?"

135

"I want to meet with everyone who was involved in planning the Bash the Church action. Sooner rather than later. Tonight."

"Okay, come to the Center at nine o'clock. I'll round up the people who need to be there."

I arrived at the Center just after nine and found Laura in a small meeting room off the big community room where I'd bashed my head the last time I was there. Everything was industrial gray, the furniture clearly secondhand, and the walls covered with posters and flyers advertising safe sex discussion groups, Twelve Step meetings, and a lesbian book club. Around the table with her were three young men—who identified themselves as Jack, Minh, and Bunny—and a gray-haired woman, Becca. Jack and Minh were dressed in revolutionary chic, black leather jackets festooned with political pins, shredded jeans and clunky boots. Bunny wore an embroidered denim work shirt over a leather kilt. Becca was in the flowing skirt and peasant blouse of an old hippie, her gray hair piled in braids on her head, her eyes sharp and humorous. Laura was in a white guayabera shirt and khakis.

I sat down. "You're the Bash the Church affinity group? Is this all of you?"

"Why do you want to know?" Becca asked neutrally.

"Didn't Laura explain?"

"I thought I'd leave it to you," Laura said.

"This is about the Ekklesia bombing," I said. "The police have a suspect, and though they haven't named him publicly I can tell you it's Theo Latour."

The shocked expressions all seemed genuine.

"His fingerprints were found on a fragment of one of the bombs," I continued. "There's also another detail the police haven't released to the public. The words 'Bash the Church' and 'Queer Revolt' were spray-painted at the site of the bombing."

Becca looked at Laura. "You knew this and didn't tell us?"

Laura shifted in her seat but before she could answer, I said, "I asked her not to tell anyone."

"Why?" Becca demanded.

"Because until today, I wasn't sure what the police were going to do with that information. If they didn't think they had enough to implicate the group, I didn't see the point of putting it out in public where it could be used to discredit you."

"Why are you telling us now, dude?" Minh asked suspiciously.

"Gates had a press conference this afternoon and said he was going after a homosexual terrorist network. That's you. If he's saying that publicly now, it makes me think the cops have evidence that implicates someone in the organization, other than Theo, in the bombing."

Minh tapped a clove cigarette out of a pack he extracted from his pocket, lit it and pronounced, "That's whack."

"Let me explain something to you," I replied, waving away the cloying smoke. "Under the law of conspiracy, one person can be liable for a crime another person commits if the first person conspired to commit that crime, and also for any other crime that was the foreseeable consequence of the crime that was the subject of the conspiracy."

Bunny said, "Uh, translation?"

"If Theo bombed the church and anyone else in QUEER knew about the plan in advance and supported it in any way, then they and maybe everyone else in the organization could be charged as co-conspirators with the bombing and the killing even if the killing wasn't originally part of the plan."

After a stunned moment, Becca said, "QUEER is committed to acts of peaceful civil disobedience."

"But was Theo part of this group? Did any of you know about the bombing in advance? Did any of you or anyone else in QUEER assist in the construction or the planting of the bombs? Even if you didn't, did you provide money to them or in any other way offer them assistance?" I looked around the table for the tiniest hint of guilt in anyone's expression, but all were stony-faced. "The cops will be asking you these same questions and your answers to them, unlike to me, won't be privileged."

"We have the right to remain silent," Jack said.

137

"Not to your lawyer," I replied. "Not if I'm going to defend you."

"Defend us?" Minh snapped. "We didn't do anything."

"Then answer my questions."

Minh took a drag of his cigarette, blew smoke across the table into my face, and said, "Theo came to some of our meetings. Freddy, too, sometimes."

"Were they involved in planning the action?" I asked.

Bunny said, "Minh, darling, put out that noxious cigarette before I jump over the table and shove it down your throat." Then to me, "Theo came to vent, like he always did. He told us how evil Christians are. Like that was news to us."

Becca broke in. "I've been an activist for a long time, and in my experience social justice movements attract two kinds of people. People ready to do the work and people who need a place to be angry. The angry people have been so wounded, so twisted by injustice they can't get past the trauma to take action. Theo was one of those broken people. Yes, he could be disruptive, but part of our work is to give people like him a safe space to be angry."

Minh rolled his eyes and muttered, "Hippie."

"You said Freddy came sometimes. Was he involved in the planning?"

Bunny laughed. "Freddy? No. I think Theo dragged him to our meetings. All he ever did was sit and spread his legs so we could all admire the size of his dick." He grinned. "A solid nine inches, I'd say."

Minh said, "At least. I stood next to him in the john when he was taking a leak. Uncut, too."

Laura rolled her eyes. "Boys."

"Don't forget he's a con," Jack said.

"Excuse me?" I said.

"Last year we zapped Barney's Beanery—that place on Santa Monica that had a sign that said 'Fagots Keep Out'—it wasn't spelled right—and a bunch of us were arrested for trespassing.

The cops cited us and let us go except for Freddy. They said he had an arrest warrant, so they took him downtown."

"Do you know what the warrant was for?"

Becca said, "I overheard the officer who arrested him say it was for ADW, but I don't know what that is."

"Assault with a deadly weapon," I said.

"Deadly weapon," Bunny exclaimed in mock horror. "You think they mean his dick?"

"He can assault me with it any time he wants," Minh said.

"What's Freddy's last name?"

"Saavedra," Laura said.

I jotted down his name. "If we're done discussing Freddy's penis, can we get back to my questions? Did any of you know anything about the bombing in advance?"

"No way, dude," Minh said, the crushed cigarette smoldering in an ashtray on the table in front of him.

"But," I said, "Ekklesia was on your list of churches for the Bash the Church action?"

"Sure," Bunny said, "along with the Catholic cathedral and the Mormon temple and some other places. We were planning to dress up in our Sunday best, sneak into the services and then, on the same day, at the same time, stand up and call out the church while other QUEER people ran in and staged a die-in in the aisles. That was the action. Not blowing up buildings and killing people."

"Why was Ekklesia on the list?" I asked.

Jack said, "They gave twenty-five thousand bucks to Yes on 54."

"And their pastor signed the letter in the *Times* endorsing it," Becca added.

"No other reason that it was particularly singled out?"

"Isn't that enough?" Minh said, disgustedly.

My beeper went off. I sneaked a look and saw that the call was coming from Larry's house. It must be Josh, home from work and wondering where I was.

139

I looked at each of the people sitting around the table, and I sensed, knew really, that one of them was holding back on me.

"Okay," I said. "We're done for now. If the cops try to question you, don't say a word to them. Call me. Day or night."

Becca smiled. "Thanks, Henry. We know the drill."

When I got home, Josh was at the kitchen table poking at a plate of pasta. As soon as he looked up at me, I knew something was wrong.

"Hey, baby," I said. "Are you okay? Something happen at work?"

"I didn't go to work," he said.

I sat down. "No? Are you sick?"

"I went to see my parents. I told them about me."

"What? Why?"

"I was getting ready to go to work when I got a page from a police detective. He asked me if I knew where Theo was. I told him I wasn't going to talk to him or any other police officer without my lawyer. He said if I didn't talk to him, he'd call my father and let him know his gay son was involved in a murder investigation." He rubbed his temples. "He knew my dad's name. He had our home phone number."

Shit, I thought. That had to have come from whoever Marc had spoken to in the department to keep Josh's name out of the press conference.

"What did you tell him?"

"I hung up on him."

"Why didn't you call me?"

"There was no time," he said, angrily. "For all I knew he called my folks as soon as I'd hung up on him. I drove to Encino as fast as I could. They were just sitting down to dinner when I arrived. I told them everything. Being gay. Being positive. The thing with Theo. You."

"What happened?"

He heaved a heavy sigh from deep in his body. "My mom freaked. My dad looked at me like he'd never seen me before in his life and told me to leave. That's all. But when he closed the door behind me, it felt like it was closing forever."

"I'm so sorry."

"I love my father," he said, looking up, but not at me. Seeing, instead, his father shutting the door on him. "He's tough, not like my mom, kissing my owies and spoiling me. Dad taught me the world's not fair to Jews, but we have the strength of our traditions and our families and our faith to rely on. When he closed the door, it was like he was taking all that away from me." Now he did look at me, his expression intense, almost angry. "How am I supposed to be strong without those things? How am I going to face AIDS? How am I supposed to live?"

"He loves you, too, Josh. Give him time."

"I don't have time," he snapped.

I stood up. "You don't know that."

Now he was angry. "You're right. I don't know anything. How much time I have. If my parents will forgive me. If you'll stick around when I start to get sick. I look at the future and see a black hole."

"I'm not going anywhere."

"You barely know me," he mumbled.

"I know myself. I know I love you."

"I'm such a mess," in a drained voice.

I pulled up a chair, sat, and took both his hands in mine. "You had to tell them sometime."

"Not like this."

"Josh, can you imagine any circumstance where they would have responded differently?"

After a moment, he shook his head slightly. "No, not really. I always knew they'd take it hard. I guess I can stop worrying about their reaction. What are you always telling me? Better to deal with reality than fantasy?"

"Something like that."

He managed a grin. "Reality sucks."

"It also changes," I reminded him. "Often, it gets better."

He got up, sat in my lap and laid his head on my shoulder. I put my arms around him and held him as if he were a tired child. The silence was broken only by the ticking of the kitchen clock. I remember asking Larry once, when I was having a day almost as lousy as Josh's, "Does time really heal everything?" Larry said, "Not if you mean does it make things right." "Then how?" I asked. "It puts tough things behind you and into perspective and they begin to lose their power to hurt you. They become features in the landscape of your life getting smaller and smaller as you move forward." This wasn't the moment to say it to Josh, but the terrible, immediate pain of his father's rejection would recede and he would see what he had to do next.

"Where were you when I got home?" he murmured.

I gave him the rundown of the day's events and my meeting at the center with the Bash the Church affinity group. When I said I thought one of them was holding back, he asked, "You think they helped Theo bomb the church?"

"I think one of them knows where Theo is."

He sat up straight. "Don't you think he's with Freddy?"

"There's no evidence Freddy was involved in the bombing, and from what people said about him, it seems like he tagged along to QUEER meetings because Theo made him. Everything points to Theo. He's the one the cops are after. He's the one on the run."

"Tell me again who was at the meeting," Josh said thoughtfully.

"Laura, Bunny, Jack, Minh, and Becca. Why?"

"It's Becca."

"What?"

"If anyone is protecting Theo, it's Becca."

"Why do you say that?"

He smiled. "She's like you, Henry. A rescuer."

She had never drank while her mother was alive. Her mother's pitiable existence was a cautionary tale about the evils of alcohol; her life shriveled until it did not extend past the confines of the bed where she spent the last years of her life, her legs atrophied from lack of use and her mind gone to mush. Jessica nursed her, a task that consisted mainly of cleaning her when she soiled herself and providing her with alcohol to prevent seizures and delirium.

Her father had confined himself to a single nightly Scotch, poured into a heavy-bottomed crystal tumbler filled with ice that he sipped while he watched the evening news. She didn't know whether he enjoyed the alcohol or if it was one of the habits he cultivated as part of his conception of being a powerful man—like the big black Lincoln Continental and the affairs. None of the affairs were women in the church. He probably thought he was being discreet but the occasional appearance in his life of a strange woman was more telling than if he had picked his girl-friends from among his eager female congregants. Jessica thought it was entirely likely that her childhood recollections of her father's odd, hushed phone calls followed by urgent, late-night pastoral emergencies had led her to suspect Daniel was having an affair.

Daniel did not drink as an example of abstinence to anyone who might be struggling with alcohol. Her abstinence lasted into the third year of her marriage when she moved into her mother's old room, leaving Daniel to sleep alone in their marital bed. Cleaning out a dresser drawer, she found hidden away among her mother's disused stockings and undergarments a pint of vodka wrapped in tissue paper. Unwrapping it, remembering her mother, she'd felt unbearable sadness, but then it seemed as if the discovery had been providential—a message from her mother. She emptied the water glass she kept beside her bed, poured two fingers of vodka into it, and drank it down in a single, shuddering gulp. She remembered how her entire body had seemed to exhale as if it had been holding a pent-up breath for years and years; everything went soft and warm.

She made rules for herself. She ever drank in public nor at home in front of Daniel. She bought her liquor at supermarkets far from their home and kept the empties hidden in the trunk of her car to dispose of in random dumpsters. During the day, while Daniel was at work, she allowed herself two or three drinks carefully spaced out to avoid the slightest hint of intoxication when he arrived home, choosing vodka because she believed it left the least trace of alcohol on her breath after she vigorously brushed her teeth. When they retired to their rooms, however, she poured her nightcaps with a heavy hand.

Her drunken mother had alternated between silent, sodden obliviousness and slurring, over-enunciated attempts at maintaining her propriety. But Jessica discovered there were intermediate states between sobriety and intoxication, some of them like a warm embrace while others left her crisp and clear-eyed. In the latter state, alcohol cleared her mind of all extraneous noise. Whatever moment of her life she turned her attention to, the insights and understandings flashed like lightning, illuminating areas that she had always sensed were present but had been unable to see.

Her father, for example, with his fine Scotch and big cars and mistresses. What were those things but the trappings of the successful men of his generation, the bankers, lawyers, businessmen, and politicians he liked to surround himself with? She understood that at bottom her father felt inferior to these men with his unshakable white-trash accent and little Bible college degree. He might preach the Kingdom of God but his stake in the world mattered to him, too, and it would never be as impressive, as important, as theirs. They made things happen while he could offer only commentary, judgment, criticisms, complaint. And wasn't that, after all, more a woman's power than a man's? Perhaps her father suspected that this was how those bankers and lawyers and businessmen and politicians regarded him and this lingering insecurity fueled his performance of their masculinity.

Max Taggert had cast himself as a great man, unlike Daniel who had only wanted to be a good one. Her father had carried himself as if he were a monument; Daniel's dimensions were human. Accustomed to her domineering father's grandiosity and harshness, she had mistaken Daniel's humility for weakness, his flexibility for indecision, his kindness for credulity. Now that he was gone, she saw she'd been all wrong about him.

144

Daniel was the true Christian, driven, however imperfectly, by love. And her father? He was a Pharisee, legalistic, intolerant, and proud. He had built the church in his image and she understood how unhappy Daniel must have been here, surrounded by her father's men who were intent on carrying out her father's legacy. Daniel was never supposed to have been more than a figurehead while men like Uncle Bob actually ran the church.

She had chosen the wrong side, her father over her husband. She and Daniel could have been allies, could have, in time perhaps, even come to have a real marriage. She should have gone to him when she learned about his other woman and his child. They might have achieved something like intimacy. Instead, she had betrayed Daniel by going to his enemy with his damning secret. At least, she thought, Daniel had died before he discovered her betrayal.

Becca—whose full name Laura told me was Rebecca Traynor, and who was a retired social worker—lived on a quiet Santa Monica street in a small 1920s bungalow painted bright yellow with a big, welcoming porch. I parked in front of her white picket fence and admired the little garden that filled her yard with flowers and herbs and—

"Are those pot plants?" Josh asked, pointing to the distinctive jagged, spindly leaves of a cannabis shrub. He had insisted on coming with me, arguing, reasonably enough, that if Theo was with Becca, he'd be less skittish if I brought a familiar, friendly face along.

"Over by the rosemary?" I asked. "I think so. Come on, let's see if she's home."

I pushed open the squeaky gate and clambered up the porch steps to a rainbow welcome mat laid out in in front of the door. I knocked. A moment later, Becca peered out of a side window. The doorknob turned and she opened the door just enough for us to see the light-filled interior behind her.

"I need to talk to Theo," I said.

She was in an old chambray work shirt and jeans, yellow garden gloves on her hands. She brushed a strand of white hair from her face and asked, "How did you figure it out?"

I indicated Josh. "Josh guessed if he'd gone to anyone for help, it would have been you."

A lithe white cat slipped out of the door and into the garden. Becca followed it out to the porch, closing the door behind her.

"What do you want with him?"

"I want to offer to represent him," I replied, "and to see if I can convince him to turn himself in."

"Sit down, you two," she said, indicating a porch swing. She peeled off the garden gloves and stuck them in her back pocket. "Theo's asleep."

"Wake him," I said. "This is important."

"After we talk," she replied. She leaned against the porch railing. "Why should he turn himself in?"

"For his safety, and yours. The cops are looking for him. They won't be too fastidious about how they catch him. If they figure out he's here, you'll have a SWAT team trampling your garden and shooting your door open. He could be hurt; you could be hurt. At minimum," I continued, "the pot plants will land you in jail, too. That and a charge of being an accessory after the fact to felony murder."

"He didn't mean to kill anyone. Freddy told him there wouldn't be anyone there."

"Freddy?" I said, surprised. "I thought Freddy was the reluctant boyfriend Theo dragged to QUEER meetings."

"So did I," she admitted, "but Theo says the bombing was Freddy's idea."

"It's Theo's fingerprint on the bomb," I pointed out, "which proves he was there, and if he was there, he's culpable, whoever planned the bombing."

"He admits he was there," she said, "and planted the bombs, but he says Freddy told him no one would be at the church."

"It doesn't matter whether the pastor's death was intentional. When someone is killed in the commission of a felony, it's still murder. And if you use an explosive, that's a capital crime."

"He could get the death penalty?" she asked, shocked.

"If the DA decides to seek it," I said. "That's the other reason he needs to turn himself in. If he's cooperative now, it gives me something to negotiate with. If they have to drag him in, they'll throw the book at him. There's also the organization to think about."

"QUEER? We had nothing to do with it."

"Gates's press conference was a declaration of war on QUEER. If they can't find Theo, they'll go after you. You should have told me last night he was here."

She leaned against the porch railing and sighed. "He was a wreck when he turned up, detoxing from drugs, terrified because Freddy had abandoned him. I had to take him in until he was at least well enough to make some rational decisions about what to do."

"I'm here to help him do that," I said.

"Come inside. I'll wake him."

Her sun-washed living room was sparsely furnished with what looked like heirloom pieces of Arts and Crafts furniture. On one table were two photographs, one a long-ago wedding portrait of a handsome young groom and a young bride who was, identifiably, Becca. Next to it was another photograph of the same couple much later in life. He wore a gray suit and she was in a flowered dress pinned with a corsage. They were standing in this room and behind them a banner tacked to the wall proclaimed "Happy 45th Anniversary."

She noticed me noticing the photographs.

"That was my husband, Roger. We were married for forty-five years until cancer killed him back in 1980."

Josh said, "Uh, you're not a . . ."

"Lesbian?" she said, smiling. "No. Roger was gay. Don't look so surprised, Josh. That's what gay men had to do in those days. Get married."

"Did you know?" Josh asked.

"Yes, he was the best of companions. Sit down. I'll get Theo."

After she left the room, Josh said, "Do you believe that Freddy was behind the bombings?"

"I haven't formed an opinion yet. What do you think?"

"From what I saw of them, Freddy was the only thing standing between Theo and complete self-destruction."

"If that's true, why didn't he stop Theo and where is he now?"

Before Josh could answer, a disheveled Theo shambled in with Becca on his heels.

"Hey, Josh," he mumbled, and greeted me with a sharp, unfriendly nod.

It had been a while since I'd seen Theo; mostly he existed for me as a topic of conversation with Josh. From those talks, I'd formed an image of him as a skinny, wired, erratic speed freak. The young man who entered the room was remarkably handsome in a fallen angel sort of way: black hair, blue eyes, lean, sculpted face. He was wearing a white T-shirt with a photograph of two young sailors kissing with the words "Read My Lips" printed across them, a pair of sky-blue cargo shorts, and flip-flops, as if he'd been strolling along the Venice boardwalk.

"Hello, Theo. I think you remember I'm a criminal defense lawyer. I'm prepared to represent you if you want me to."

"There wasn't supposed to be anyone in the church," he said in a flat voice.

I indicated Josh and Becca. "You two mind leaving?"

"I want them here," Theo said.

"They can't be here if our conversation is going to be protected by the lawyer-client privilege. Anything you say to me—anything at all—is confidential, but if someone else is in the room who isn't a lawyer, they can be compelled to testify."

"Come along, Josh," Becca said. "I could use a strong young back to spread fertilizer in the garden."

"Sit down, Theo. We're going to be here awhile." He sat. I continued. "The cops have your fingerprints on fragments of one of the bombs you planted at Ekklesia. They executed a search warrant at Josh's apartment looking for evidence of the construction materials used to make the bombs. If there was anything there, they found it." From the flicker of fear in his eyes I guessed he hadn't been too careful about cleaning up. "They know you were the bomber. The longer you run, the worse it's going to be when they eventually track you down. I'm advising you to turn yourself in. You'll save the cops the time and expense of a manhunt and give me leverage when I sit down with the DA to discuss how they're going to charge you."

He stared at me with his dark eyes as if I'd spoken in a language that he didn't speak, which, in a way, I had.

"I didn't mean to kill that man."

"You built and planted the bombs that did."

With a firm shake of his head, he said, "Freddy made the bombs. He told me where to put them. He told me there wasn't going to be anyone in the church. All I did was do what he said."

"Why would Freddy want to blow up a church?"

"He hates those fucking so-called Christians who want to lock us up. We——he——had to take the war to them."

"I was at the community meeting where you attacked the woman priest and got in a fight with a guy who said he was a Christian. Are you sure it was Freddy who hates Christians?"

"Okay, it's both of us," he replied defiantly. "But the bombing was his idea."

"Did you plant the bombs?"

"He told me to."

"Did he force you to help him?"

"I . . ." He faltered. "I don't know."

"You don't know if he forced you?"

He spread his hands in a gesture of helplessness. "It's complicated."

"Explain it, we have time."

"I love Freddy," he said. "I would do anything for him. And yeah, I hate the Christians. They say God hates fags and people believe them and we die. I had all this anger! Freddy did, too. He said we have to make them suffer the way we suffer, and it's not going to happen by waving signs and chanting slogans. He said we have to take the war to them. I thought it was all just talk but he was serious. I let him talk me into helping him, but I never meant to hurt anyone. We both thought the church would be deserted. That man's death was an accident."

"Where is Freddy now?"

He shook his head. "Mexico, I think. We were supposed to go there until things cooled down. I was waiting for him at a motel, but I started detoxing and was going crazy being there by myself. That's when I came here, to Becca's." He grasped the arm of his chair. "I didn't mean to hurt anyone. If I didn't mean it, is it still murder?"

"I'm afraid so," I said. "Everyone who participated in the bombing—the person who planned it, the person who made the bombs, and the person who planted them—is guilty of murder, and the use of an explosive automatically makes the murder punishable by death."

"What? I'm going to be executed?"

"That's up to the DA. It's not automatic, and he's required to consider mitigating factors."

"What are those?"

"Reasons not to execute a person," I said. "Age, for example. The law figures if you're young you might be rehabilitated. That works in your favor unless you have a long record. Do you?"

"I was busted for possession of coke, but I got diversion, and I was arrested at that demonstration at the Chinese Theater."

"No arrests or convictions for any kind of violent crime?"

"I'm not violent."

Except you just admitted that you helped blow up a church, I thought, but didn't say. Theo's capacity for dealing with reality seemed pretty limited at the moment. No need to overwhelm him.

"No prior record for violence is good. If, like you say, Freddy was the mastermind and you were following his instructions and you believed the church would be deserted, that might also count in your favor."

"Fuck," he wheezed. "I can't believe I'm sitting here checking boxes to decide if I live or die."

He was teetering at the edge of hysteria.

"Let's take a break," I said. "You want a glass of water?"

He nodded, still stunned. I went into the cheerful little kitchen, poured two glasses of water from the tap and went back into the living room where I handed him one. He finished it in a single long swallow.

"You have family, Theo? People who can help support you through this?"

He rolled the empty glass between his hands. "My stepdad kicked me out of the house when I was sixteen for being gay. I talk to my ma sometimes, but I haven't seen her in years."

"Friends?" I suggested.

"You watch porn?" he asked me. "Rent videos?"

"No," I said.

He made a derisive little noise in the back of his throat. "Figures." His eyes washed over me. "You seem pretty straight for a fag. I was a porn star. Worked for all the big studios. Drove around West Hollywood in my yellow Jeep Wrangler with the top down and the stereo blasting. Everyone knew who I was, and I had a million friends." He got up, went into the kitchen, and I heard the tap running. He stood at the doorway and sipped from his glass. "Then I tested positive, and it turns out I didn't have any friends at all. Except Josh. And Freddy." He sat down. "Can you save my life?"

"We need evidence besides your say-so that Freddy was behind the bombing."

"He bought all the stuff for the bombs," Theo replied. "I mean, I wouldn't have known what we needed or how to put them together. We bought some of it at that big Home Depot on Sunset. Pipes and wires and stuff. He packed the pipes with some kind of black powder. I think he said it was gunpowder, but I don't know where he got it. Does that help?"

"Yes. Anything else?"

He shrugged. "I don't know. I can't think now."

"I want you to write down everything you remember in the days that led up to and following the bombing in as much detail as you can."

"I'm not much of a writer," he said. He finished his water.

The drama, the tension had gone out of the room and it was just the two of us talking calmly, as if we were making banal conversation and not decisions that would potentially end with Theo on death row.

"I want to call the DA and negotiate your surrender, okay?"

"What do I have to do?"

"You need to prepare yourself for jail. I can get you into isolation, but it's still going to be a cell. Once you're in custody, remember the first, last and only rule: you don't talk to anyone, not the cops, the prosecutors, the press, or another inmate unless I'm with you."

In a resigned voice, as if he already knew the answer, he asked, "Will I ever get out?"

"My immediate goal is to keep you off death row," I replied. "After that, we'll see."

TEN

Everything about the woman who opened the door was practical—her tan slacks and blue blouse, efficient short hair, solid, stocky body—but a deep, feminine grace drew together her strong features. Her light brown eyes, even as they assessed the stranger before her, were doubtful but not unfriendly.

She was lighter-skinned in the flesh than she'd appeared in the photographs, but her Blackness still shocked Jessica because it represented a side of Daniel that remained fundamentally ungraspable to her. Jessica was not an overt racist like her Georgia-born father, and racial mixing had never seemed to her the abomination it did to him but only because it wasn't something she'd ever had to consider. Other than Caleb Cowell and his family, there were no Black people in her world, and she had no reason to think about them. Now, confronted with her husband's Black lover, the mother of his only child, she felt disoriented, speechless.

"Hello," the woman said. "May I help you?"

She managed to say, "I'm Jessica Herron. Daniel's wife."

Now it was Gwen who stared speechlessly at the woman on her doorstep. She cleared her throat and said, "Come in, Mrs. Herron."

Gwen offered tea, a diversion, Jess thought, to give them both time to absorb each other's presence. While she pottered in the kitchen, Jessica paced the cluttered, comfortable living room. A bay window framed the backs of the adjoining Victorians with long, complicated staircases leading down from the upper flats to small gardens just visible from where she stood. She wasn't sure what she'd expected but the quiet, pleasantly furnished room and shrill piping of a tea kettle in the kitchen—the ordinariness of her surroundings—calmed her apprehensions. Yet, as she ran her hand over the back of a wing chair, she thought, *Daniel might have sat here*, and a strange discomfort came over her, as if her presence violated, not Gwen's, but Daniel's privacy. *This was his real life*, she realized sadly, *and I have no right to be here.*

Her sense of having stumbled into a stranger's life grew as she studied the framed photographs on the mantel of the gas fireplace. Many were of the boy—Wyatt—taken from the time he was a toddler to his teens. Gwen was in some while in others were what she assumed were members of Gwen's family, solid, comfortable-looking Black men and women and children. Aunts, uncles, grandparents, cousins. In a photograph half-hidden among the others Wyatt was wedged between a smiling Gwen and a beaming Daniel in a high school graduation cap and gown. She lifted it from the mantel. Here was the conclusive evidence of paternity in the color of the boy's eyes, the curve of his nose, the shape of his face—all identical to his father's. As if discovering Daniel's secret life all over again, the photo left her nearly breathless with shock, then anger and then, to her surprise, a complicated sadness. Daniel's death had ended not only his life with her, but his life with them, his family.

Gwen came in with the tea things and set them down on the coffee table.

"That was Wyatt's graduation from Lowell," she said about the photograph in Jessica's hand.

Jess replaced it on the mantel. "He's a handsome boy. How is he? I understand he was—is ill?"

"Please, sit, have some tea." When they had arranged themselves in facing chairs, Gwen asked, "How did you know about Wyatt? Did Daniel tell you?"

Her voice was calm and candid, but she busied herself with the tea things nervously.

Jessica accepted the cup of tea Gwen had poured into a lovely, gold-rimmed china teacup—the cups she imagined Gwen brought out for guests.

"No, he never told me about you," she replied. "I hired a private investigator to follow him because I thought he was having an affair. He found you."

Gwen picked up her own cup. "Did he know you knew about us?"

She shook her head. "I never told him."

Gwen put her cup down, the tea untouched, and said, "Daniel and I were not having an affair. We were kids when we first met—not much older than Wyatt is now—and whatever we had was over a long time ago."

"But he kept in touch with you," Jessica said.

She shook her head. "No, after I told him I was pregnant we went our separate ways, and I didn't see him for another six years. Dan was in town for work and he looked me up. I suppose he was curious about me, the way you're curious about how people you knew when you were young turned out. He thought I'd had an abortion, so he certainly didn't expect to meet his son." She sighed. "Maybe I should have put him off, but I thought he deserved to know about Wyatt, and once Dan met him he wanted to be in his life. He was his father; it wouldn't have been right to shut him out, and Wyatt loved him, loved having a dad. So, you see Mrs. Herron, it was Wyatt he came to see, not me."

"Did Wyatt always know Daniel was his father?"

"Not at first," Gwen replied. With a slight smile, she said, "Neither one of us knew how to explain the situation to a six-year-old. He was just mom's old friend, but when Wyatt was nine, Dan took him out for ice cream, and he told me Wyatt looked at him and asked, 'Are you my dad?'"

Jessica, imagining the scene, could not suppress her own smile. "Why on earth would he ask that?"

"He has Dan's eyes. No one else in our family has blue eyes,"

Gwen replied. "One of Wyatt's cousins told him your daddy's a white man. Wyatt put two and two together. He's a very intelligent boy."

"He must be," she said.

"Daniel admitted he was Wyatt's dad. He said Wyatt just nodded and kept eating his ice cream. Later on, he was angry."

"Who was angry?"

"Wyatt didn't understand why he couldn't visit his father in Los Angeles," Gwen said. "He thought Dan was ashamed of him because he was Black. When we told him that wasn't the reason, he was even more confused. Frankly, so was I. I didn't understand why Dan was keeping Wyatt a secret. I confronted him, and he said it was to protect you."

"Me?" she said, startled.

"Dan said you were unable to have children, and knowing about Wyatt would have been very distressing to you."

"He told you about me?" Jessica said, bile rising in her throat.

"I cornered him," Gwen said, apologetically. "As soon as he said it, I was sorry I'd forced him to."

Jessica looked at the cup, tiny fragments of tea leaves settling at the bottom. Weren't tea leaves supposed to predict the future? What future was left for her?

"Did you tell your son about me?"

"All he knew was that his father was married," Gwen said softly.

"I suppose in his mind I turned into the wicked stepmother," Jessica said, "who kept his father away from him."

Gwen sipped her tea and set down the cup. "Wyatt's used to all kinds of families. Families with two parents, one parent, two dads, two moms. His favorite cousin is being raised by her grandmother, and some of his friends are adopted. After a while, he accepted our family's situation as what it was. The important thing was that he knew Dan loved him and wanted to be with him." She smiled. "Then he got to that age when he was more interested in being with his peers than his parents, and both Dan and I were just embarrassments to him."

"Well, I guess Dan didn't need children from me, did he?" Jessica said, bitterly.

Gwen waited a moment before she answered, softly, "He was a good father, Mrs. Herron. I imagine he would have loved having children from you."

She stared at her tea, wished it was alcohol. "He should have married you."

"We were very young," Gwen said, "and going in different directions. Dan had converted to his faith. I couldn't follow him there."

Jessica raised her head. "You're a nonbeliever?"

"I believe in kindness," she replied. "You were a much better match for Dan."

"Me? Do you think he married me out of love?"

"He spoke of you affectionately," Gwen replied.

"I think you mean pity," she said coolly. "My father founded our church and wanted to keep it in the family, but he had no sons, only me, a daughter. He chose Daniel to take over and married me off to him to keep the church in the family."

Gwen eyed her over the rim of her teacup. "That sounds more like Shakespeare than the Gospels."

"I'm sorry?"

"The old king without any sons to carry on the dynasty marries his only daughter to his hand-picked heir to keep the kingdom in the family."

The analogy struck a nerve. "I had a choice," she replied sharply. "I didn't have to marry Dan."

"I'm sorry. I didn't mean to be rude. Your marriage is none of my business."

"Then you should have stayed out of it!" Jessica said angrily.

Gwen's expression was both stung and sympathetic. After a moment, she said, "Dan wasn't married to you yet when he came back into our lives. If he had been, and I'd known, I wouldn't have let him in. After he married you, I should have—I don't know, told him to concentrate on his new family and stop coming around. I'm sorry for the pain I've caused you. I'm sorry that we interfered with your marriage."

Her apology knocked the air out of Jessica's anger, and she began to weep. She wept and wept in the cheerful cluttered room that had been her husband's second home, with the woman whom he must have once truly loved; she wept for the happy life he had given up and the barren life they had lived. Gwen reached across the little table, over the fancy tea service, and held her hand until the tears stopped. She fumbled in her purse for her handkerchief, wiped her eyes, and blew her nose.

"Dan's death must have been very hard on Wyatt," she said.

Now Gwen's face trembled with tears. "He was waiting for Dan's call the night Dan was killed."

"What?"

"They talked every Thursday evening. When Dan didn't call, Wyatt tried calling him but got a message the phone wasn't working. We didn't know what happened until the next day. Wyatt was devastated."

Jessica asked, "How is Wyatt doing?"

"He's . . . holding steady but Dan's death was a blow."

The room had darkened as the afternoon waned. Jessica read in Gwen's face the emotional exhaustion she herself felt.

"Thank you for the tea," she said. "For seeing me."

"I think—no, I know that I'm glad you came, Mrs. Herron," Gwen replied.

Jessica stood. "Call me Jessica. If there's anything I can do for Wyatt, please let me know. I'll leave you my number."

"Thank you," Gwen said. "Jessica, I am very sorry for your loss. I hope your faith is a comfort to you."

"Yes," Jessica lied. "It is. A very great comfort."

For once, I had a morning in my office instead of being on the road to some far-flung courthouse in a county the size of Rhode Island. The unusually efficient temp sent over by the agency that morning—a brisk woman named Emma Austin—was copy editing a motion for severance at her desk outside my office while I sat at my desk reading up on third-party culpability evidence or, as it was colloquially known in the defense bar, SODDI: Some Other Dude Did It.

In Theo's version of events, Freddy Saavedra planned the bombing and Theo's participation was minimal until Freddy made him plant the bombs. But even in this version, he completely incriminated himself.

Theo admitted: (1) he and Freddy had talked about bombing Ekklesia; (2) he had agreed to help Freddy carry out the bombing; (3) he'd gone with Freddy to the hardware store to purchase parts for the bombs; (4) he'd been in the apartment when Freddy made the bombs; (5) the Sunday before, he'd gone with Freddy to the church to scout locations to plant the bombs; (6) he'd agreed to plant the bombs; and (7) he'd planted the bombs. Objectively considered, Theo's own story implicated him as an accomplice to the bombing, and under the felony-murder rule, as guilty of the murder of Daniel Herron as Freddy.

If, in fact, he was even telling the truth about Freddy. I had only his word that Freddy was involved. Nothing from the police investigation—to the extent the cops had released details of it—pointed to any other suspect.

Theo also repeated his claim that Freddy had assured him the church would be deserted and that he'd been coerced by Freddy into helping him. Under the felony-murder rule, it was irrelevant whether Theo believed the church would be unoccupied. If someone is killed in the commission of a felony, you're still on the hook for murder. As for coercion, the law had its own definition—a threat or action taken by the perpetrator of the crime so intimidating that the person threatened lost the ability to refuse to assist in the crime. What Theo described, verbal abuse and being slapped around a couple of times, didn't cut it.

A potentially more promising defense was that Theo's emotional state was so compromised by drugs and his obsession with Freddy he lost the ability to make rational decisions: a kind of Stockholm Syndrome claim. But again, that was based only on Theo's word. He painted Freddy as a homicidal maniac, but no one who had ever seen them together supported that characterization. To the contrary, the people in QUEER thought Theo was the firebrand and that's what the evidence pointed to as well. I needed different evidence. It was time to call in my investigator.

Freeman Vidor's office was a short walk from the Criminal Courts Building on the second floor of an old brick building above a bail bondsman. I rapped at the door and he said, "Yeah, come in."

Behind a surplus sale metal desk, strewn with papers and fast-food bags, sat a thin Black man wearing a gold suit and a vintage Rolex. The dusty blinds were drawn over windows that fronted the noisy street; the only illumination in the room was the harsh light of a gooseneck desk lamp. Above a threadbare sofa was a license that attested to the legitimacy of his operation. Beneath it was a photograph of a much younger Vidor in an LAPD uniform.

At first glance, except for his graying hair, little seemed to have changed about Freeman Vidor since that picture had been taken. His face was still unlined, but he didn't look young. He looked like a man nothing had ever surprised. I'd been referred to him on another case by a public defender when I first started practicing in LA and had used him since then.

Freeman was the most thorough and tenacious investigator I'd ever worked with. He was also utterly without illusions about humans and human nature, a cynic to the bone. As such, he regarded his fellow humans and their behavior—however atrocious—without judgment. He brought intelligence and cunning to his work, but no emotional investment. As far as he was concerned, we were all specimens he regarded with clear-eyed curiosity and mordant humor. That included me: a gay, Mexican-American defense lawyer was the kind of oddity he enjoyed.

"Morning, Freeman," I said.

"Move that box off the chair and have a seat," he replied. "You want some coffee? I got a thermos here."

"No, I'm good."

160

He poured coffee into a mug, added a packet of Sweet 'n Low and stirred it with a pencil. "So, now you're defending church bombers. It's like you like being hated on."

"Everyone hates defense lawyers until they need us; then they expect us to pull rabbits out of hats."

"What rabbit are you trying to pull out of your hat for—" he glanced at the case file on his desk I'd sent over earlier, "Mr. Theo Latour?"

"I'm trying to keep him off death row."

In capital cases, once the defendant is convicted of the underlying murder, the jury chooses between two penalties: death, or life without the possibility of parole—LWOP. I was hoping to plead the case for a deal on the sentence. In my wilder dreams I even thought I could talk the DA into a life sentence with the possibility of parole.

"You want to offer up this Saavedra character to the electric chair instead of Latour?"

"You know California stopped using the electric chair decades ago."

He grinned. "I know, but it sounds scarier than lethal injection."

"I don't know about that," I replied. "Lethal is pretty scary."

"How are you going to do that?"

"We need to gather evidence that supports Theo's story that Freddy planned the bombings and made the bombs."

"You want me to find Saavedra."

"Actually," I said, "no. It's better for my defense if he stays disappeared because if he's found and arrested—"

"He'll pin the blame on your boy."

"Exactly. I don't want to fight a war on two fronts at trial, against the DA and Saavedra."

Freeman lit a Winston and said, "But if both boys point at each other, that will confuse the jury. Isn't that what you defense lawyers like? A confused jury?"

"Ordinarily, yes. A confused jury is at least a hung jury and maybe even an acquitting jury. But in felony murder, the jury doesn't have to decide exactly who did what to convict them as long as it's convinced they both did something. Theo did more than something. He planted the bomb that killed the victim. There's no possibility he won't be convicted of murder. It becomes a question of degree and punishment. If all he did was plant the bomb, not knowing someone was going to be at the church, and everything else was Saavedra's doing, maybe I can talk the DA into a deal or persuade a jury not to send him to San Quentin."

"Tell me again why these boys were blowing up churches."

"To protest the church's support for the quarantine initiative."

"You're not going to get much sympathy from a downtown jury for that," he said. "The Black folks you pull from south-central are likely going to be churchgoers, and your people from East LA are not big gay rights supporters."

He wasn't wrong. Downtown juries, largely drawn from the surrounding Black and Latino communities, were often better for the defense than the white suburban juries because they tended to be more skeptical of cops, but on the issue of homosexuality they were, if anything, likely to be more conservative than white jurors.

"I know," I said. "That's why I need hard evidence against Saavedra."

He tapped ash into an overflowing ashtray and asked, "Like what?"

"We need to prove he made the bombs. Theo told me he went with Saavedra to a Home Depot on Sunset where Freddy bought the components."

I reached into my briefcase and handed him a manila folder. "What's this?" he asked.

"It's a photograph of the two of them taken by a photographer for one of the gay papers at a demonstration. Take it to the Home Depot and see if anyone who works there recognizes them."

He was taking a long look at the photo, which showed Theo and Freddy standing in a crowd, shoulder to shoulder, fists pumping the air, screaming at a line of cops.

"These the bombers?" he asked, tapping the photo.

"Yeah."

"The Chicano dude I could see; the other guy—your client—he looks like an addict."

"He is," I said.

He slipped the photo back into the file. "What else do you want me to do?"

"Check out Saavedra's criminal history. Apparently, there was an arrest warrant out on him for an assault charge. Maybe there are other arrests and convictions for violence. When I get the police reports, I'll see if the cops got his prints in the apartment where the bombs were built. I know for a fact he spent a lot of time there. Theo's roommate could testify to that."

Freeman lifted an inquiring eyebrow. "He could testify he saw Saavedra making a bomb?"

"No, only that he was frequently in the apartment where the bomb was made."

"You talk to the roommate? Is he involved?"

"Yes and no," I said. "He's my, uh, boyfriend."

Freeman snorted with amusement. "You're dating a witness? Isn't that what you guys call a conflict of interest? I can already hear the DA asking him on cross, 'Isn't it true you're sleeping with Mr. Rios, the defense lawyer?'"

"The DA won't know unless someone tells him, and I'm not under any duty to disclose it," I said. "Besides, it's irrelevant."

He shook his head, still amused. "If you say so."

"Find me evidence connecting Saavedra to the bombing," I said, "and don't worry about my love life."

"I'm just surprised to hear you got one. I was starting to think you were one of those married-to-his-work types."

Freeman was right about Josh and me. If jurors knew I was sleeping with one of my witnesses, we'd both look sketchy. Plus, it would out me at trial as a gay man with all the negative associations that entailed. I couldn't see a way of keeping Josh off the stand, though. The bombs had been constructed at Josh's apartment. I needed to establish that Freddy had been a frequent visitor to the apartment, often while Josh was at work. Freddy's fingerprints—assuming the cops had lifted any—would only show he'd been at the apartment, not when or for how long. The only person other than Josh who could testify to Freddy's comings and goings was Theo, his accomplice. I needed untainted corroborating testimony: Josh.

Was Josh my boyfriend? At the moment, it wasn't at all clear to me what we were to each other. Since talking to his parents, he'd grown distant. He'd reached that fork in the road where he had to choose between fight or flight—fight through the shame and guilt to stay in our relationship, or run. The stress put him all over the emotional map. He still spent nights with me at Larry's house, but he came in later and later after his shift at the restaurant; he'd taken to going out with his coworkers for drinks. By the time he rolled in, I was usually asleep. Sometimes he woke me wanting to have sex and other times he kept to his side of the bed. If I asked him what was wrong, he'd say nothing, and if I pressed, he shut down completely. I knew I could do little but watch and wait. So I did, but I can't say it didn't hurt.

"You didn't have to wait up," he said that night after my meeting with Freeman. He tossed his leather jacket over the back of the sofa where I was reading a brief.

He went into the kitchen, poured himself a glass of water, came out, and sat down at the other end of the couch. I could smell the cigarettes and booze, but he seemed sober enough.

"We need to talk about Theo's case."

I explained why I might have to call him as a witness. I warned him that, to discredit him, the prosecutor would likely bring out the fact that the cops had questioned him as a suspect.

"Oh, that's great," he said sarcastically. "Now the whole world will know the police thought I was a terrorist and a murderer. Something to put on my resume because I'll be looking for another job."

"I'll have you testify that the police concluded you weren't involved and released you without charges."

"That's not what people will remember."

"People have very short memories. Anyway, your testimony will only be a minor part of the defense."

He flushed. "Minor! Maybe for you." He pulled a cigarette from the pack in his pocket and angrily lit it. "Will the prosecutor also ask me if you're fucking me? Wouldn't that also be—what did you call it? 'Relevant to my credibility'?"

His outburst solved my problem of how to broach the subject. "That could come out."

"Listen to you!" he shouted. "You sit there calmly telling me how I'm going to be humiliated in public like it's nothing to you. Why don't we let it all hang out? Tell the jury I've got AIDS, too. Or would that hurt the defense?"

"You don't have AIDS."

He stubbed out his cigarette and stood up. "I'm not in the mood for another pep talk from a guy who tested negative."

I took a breath. "Then maybe you should leave."

This got a shocked, "What?"

"If all you're going to do is treat me with contempt like I'm your enemy instead of the guy who loves you, I don't understand why you're here."

I couldn't read his expression and thought maybe I'd been wrong to put the challenge so bluntly, but even rejection was preferable to the loneliness we'd created for each other. "I'm sorry," he mumbled.

"We need to talk about what's going on with you, Josh," I said.

He huffed a sound between a laugh and a groan. "I wish I knew what was going on with me." He dropped back on the couch. "I feel trapped between the way things were before I got diagnosed and what might happen to me." He sank into the cushions. "I'm afraid, Henry."

"Fuck everything and run."

He furrowed his brow. "What?"

"It's an acronym for the word *fear*," I said.

165

He worked it out. "Oh, I get it. *F.E.A.R.* Fuck everything and run."

"It's one response to fear," I continued. "Deny it, try to escape it. Drown it with booze or silence it with drugs or, like I used to do, bury yourself in work."

He leaned forward. "What were you afraid of?"

"Some of the same fears that chase you," I said. "That I was broken, defective, dirty. It's hard to be hated for who you are, Josh. We can't help but absorb some of it. Work distracted me, but the booze took me to the place where I finally had to decide if I was going to live or die. You know what? It was a harder choice than you'd think."

"You got sober," he said.

"I stopped drinking," I replied. "I'm still getting sober. I'm still making that choice to face the things that scare me and work through them."

"I'm positive," he said quietly.

"Yeah, that's a fear you have to face that I don't, and it's not something you'll resolve once and for all. You'll have to face it again and again, but you don't have to do it alone. You'll have me beside you."

He sighed. "I'm sorry I've been such a prick."

"That's okay," I said. "Let's talk."

She saw the red light flashing in the rearview mirror, heard the siren, and jerked the steering wheel to move her car into the next lane and allow the patrol car to pass her. But the patrol car also switched lanes, closing the distance until it was almost on her bumper. Then she heard the voice over the loudspeaker: "White BMW, pull over to the shoulder. Now."

She flinched when the officer shined his flashlight in her face, and she fumbled for her driver's license and car registration. When he returned to his patrol car, in her panic she briefly considered driving off. Instead, she gulped air to calm herself. Cars slowed as they passed her, and she felt exposed and humiliated, but her overriding emotion was terror. In the back seat was a grocery bag containing a half-gallon of vodka; she'd roused herself and run out earlier to go to the liquor store.

As her drinking had increased, she went farther and farther from home to purchase her alcohol, reasoning vaguely that this way she could conceal her consumption. This liquor store had been in a neighborhood where the signs of the surrounding businesses were as much in Spanish as English. The clerk, a thick-waisted, dark-skinned man in black-rimmed glasses, bagged her purchase without comment, but she still felt judged and hurried out of the store without collecting her change. On the drive home she got lost and ended up on the wrong freeway. Spotting an exit ramp, she cut across two lanes of traffic so abruptly she nearly hit someone. That's when she saw the red light.

The officer was back at her window, her papers in hand. He was young enough to have been her son. For a moment, she thought he would simply return them and release her, but then he asked, "Do you know why I stopped you, ma'am?"

"No, officer, I'm sorry. Did I do something wrong?"

"You changed lanes without signaling and almost caused an accident."

"I'm terribly, terribly sorry. I will be more careful."

"Ma'am," he asked, leaning into the car, "have you been drinking?"

She stood at the window and watched the retreating back lights of Metzger's car. *Uncle Bob.* That had been her first thought when she was led from booking to the jail cell after her arrest. *I must call Uncle Bob.* Roused from sleep, he had appeared at the police station looking every moment of his seventy-six years, mouth curled in displeasure, eyes fogged with contempt. But he had secured her release and on driving her home had assured her he would personally resolve the issue with the sheriff before it proceeded any further.

She had hoped he would let her out and drive away, but he insisted on coming inside.

167

Once inside, he asked, bluntly, "How long has this been going on, Jessica?"

"I don't know what you mean."

He sat heavily, regarded her coldly, and continued, "Your mother was also an alcoholic, but your father protected her. He's not here to protect you and neither is Dan."

She went cold, then hot. "I am not an alcoholic."

"Cut the crap, Jess. I can arrange for you to go into rehab."

"I'm not going anywhere," she replied. "I'm not leaving my home."

"Technically, it's the pastor's residence, not your private home," he said. "The church owns it. There will be a new pastor soon. One with a family. We'll need the place back from you."

She stared at him. "I've lived here all my life."

"Of course, we'll help you resettle," he continued, as if he hadn't heard her. "But before any of that happens, you have to do something about your drinking. Do you understand, Jessica? What happened tonight can never happen again."

"I think you should leave, Bob."

He pulled himself to his feet. "We'll talk later."

"If Dan were here—" she began.

"But he's not," Metzger said. "No more of his hippie mumbo-jumbo. We're in the last days, Jessica. The enemies of the Lord are everywhere. We need soldiers, not sissies. Dan's death was—providential."

ELEVEN

Theo's arraignment drew a full house. The media were out in full force. Laura Acosta led a delegation from QUEER. There was also a cluster of conservatively dressed men and women I assumed were congregants from Ekklesia. The two groups made quite a contrast: one tatted and pierced, the other white-bread suburban. In the dark suit, white shirt, and striped tie I'd bought for him at the May Company, Theo would have fit in more easily with the Ekklesia crowd than QUEER's. He wasn't quite the all-American boy—there was an unconcealable drop of debauchery in his good looks—but the sedate clothes emphasized his youth, as if he were a boy trying on his dad's suit. No one would have taken him for a murderer.

His first words to me when they brought him out were, "My mom came to see me." He sounded surprised and happy.

"Is she here?" I asked. A mother in the court was always helpful to the defense.

He nodded, turned his head to scan the gallery, and turning back to me said, "That's her in the blue dress in the back row. I won't point to her because I don't want anyone to bother her."

"I'll talk to her when we're done here," I said. "Discreetly."

The bailiff intoned, "All rise. Division 59 is now in session. The Honorable Barry Mayeda presiding."

"Be seated," Judge Mayeda said when he took the bench. He was a slender, youngish man—formerly an assistant attorney general—with a reputation for indecision. He called the case, we lawyers stated our appearances, and then he said, "We're here today for arraignment. Mr. Latour, you are charged with one count of first-degree murder as to which it is further alleged as a special circumstance that the killing was committed by use of an explosive device. How do you plead to the charge and the special circumstance?"

"Not guilty," Theo said.

"Defendant denies the special allegation," I added.

From the gallery a man shouted, "Liar! That man, that deviant, murdered our pastor. How can you let him stand before God and deny it?"

Mayeda pounded his gavel. "Sit down, sir, or I'll have you removed."

"Perhaps you can remind that mob that Mr. Latour is presumed innocent," I said.

Now a woman shouted, "Man's law is not God's law! 'Your eye shall not pity; life shall be for life, eye for eye, tooth for tooth, hand for hand, foot for foot.'"

"What about our lives!" one of the QUEERs shouted back. "Our lives matter as much as yours."

The tooth-for-a-tooth woman hissed, "'If a man lies with a male as with a woman, both of them have committed an abomination; they shall surely be put to death; their blood is upon them.'"

Mayeda's attempts to gavel the court into order were lost in the ensuing screaming match between the two groups, who now approached each other with clenched fists and red faces. Out of the corner of my eye, I saw the bailiff speaking frantically into his phone. A moment later, a half-dozen sheriffs poured into the court and wedged themselves between QUEERs and Christians. One of the sheriffs shouted above the fray, "If you don't settle down, we're going to start arresting you!"

Over the fray, Mayeda shouted, "Clear the courtroom!"

Sometime later, in the now empty courtroom, Mayeda turned to the prosecutor. "Mr. Novotny, are the People seeking the death penalty?"

Novotny, a shambling bear of a man, pulled himself out of his seat and said, "The capital committee will meet later this week to decide, Your Honor."

Mayeda nodded. "Inform the court as soon as a decision is made. I need to know if we're going to have a penalty phase trial."

"Yes, Your Honor."

"I also want to know if we are going to continue to have outbursts like the one we had this morning," he continued, addressing both of us. Then, looking at me, he added, "Mr. Rios, I expect you to encourage your people to keep a lid on it."

"My people, Your Honor? The gay and lesbian spectators? It was that mob from the church that started the disturbance. Is there an issue of bias here, Your Honor?"

That struck home. "I assure you, Mr. Rios, I have no bias against the gay and lesbian community," he said, "and I apologize if I gave you that impression. I certainly intend to bend over backward to conduct a fair and impartial trial of this matter." Abruptly, he stood up and declared, "We're adjourned."

Theo said, "I don't want that judge on my case."

"No," I said, "it'll be fine. Mayeda doesn't want to look like a bigot. By calling him out just now, I've pretty much guaranteed that any close calls he has to make at trial will go our way."

"If you say so," Theo replied, skeptically. "What about the death penalty? You said you thought they wouldn't charge me with it."

"They haven't, yet," I said, "and I'm going to talk to Novotny. We'll talk later, okay?"

"Sure," he said, "and thanks for the suit."

After the bailiff escorted Theo into lockup, I strolled over to the prosecutor's table where Ralph Novotny was gathering up his papers.

"Ralph," I said, extending my hand. "You have some discovery for me?"

He pushed a couple of thick file folders toward me. "This is everything I got so far. You understand, the investigation is ongoing."

"Sure," I said, taking the files. "What are the chances your office will be asking for the death penalty?"

"Legally, pretty good. Morally, a little iffy, political, a toss-up."

"Let's start with legally," I said.

"Legally, it's a no-brainer. Your guy blew up a church and killed a preacher."

"He didn't mean to kill anyone."

"Two words: felony murder."

"I understand that," I said, "but we both know the felony murder rule was invented for crimes like robberies where the perp was face to face with his victim, had a split-second choice whether to pull the trigger, and went ahead and pulled it anyway. Not enough time to prove intent, much less premeditation, but still some degree of intentionality. In this case, the victim's death was accidental. There shouldn't be the same kind of culpability."

"We also both know the felony murder rule is a lot broader now than when it was created, and it's way broad enough to nail your guy. Culpability, that's a moral issue, not a legal one."

"Fine, let's talk about the moral dimension. Theo didn't think anyone would be in the church that night."

"And I should believe you, why?"

"Because I'm telling you."

"You're his lawyer; what else are you going to say?"

"It's the truth, Ralph. I've got the church's calendar for that week. There was nothing official scheduled for that night."

"Herron's wife told the cops he did counseling on Thursday nights in his office."

"Theo didn't know that."

"So you say."

"He also didn't plan the bombing or make the bombs. That was—someone else."

"Thanks for the preview of your defense, but the investigation hasn't implicated anyone except your client."

"Maybe the cops didn't look hard enough," I said.

"Maybe you're full of shit," he replied amiably.

"You said moral was iffy. Why?"

"The DA's a good Catholic. The church condemns capital punishment. He struggles with it."

"He's charged it before."

"Only where his conscience is completely satisfied it's the right thing to do." He dropped his files into his briefcase and snapped it shut. "I don't think charging someone who bombed a church is going to keep him awake at night."

"And the political issue?"

"Also the DA," Novotny said. "He wants to run for attorney general, and he sees himself as governor someday. He's a Democrat. He's got some big gay contributors, but he doesn't want to alienate religious voters." He grinned. "Not that many Democrats are churchgoers. Godless secular humanists, the whole lot of them."

"I take it you're a Republican."

"Card-carrying Dem," he said. "Anything else?"

"When will the capital committee be meeting?"

"Friday."

"I'd like you to postpone consideration of Theo's case for a couple of weeks."

"Why should we?"

"To give me a chance to gather evidence to persuade your boss not to charge him. Two weeks won't make any difference. This case won't be going to trial for months."

"It's high profile," Novotny said. "But I'll ask for the time. That's all I can do."

"Thanks, Ralph."

৯ ৯ ৯

173

Theo's mother was sitting on a bench outside in the corridor. Yellowish light poured in from a bank of grimy windows, and the other benches outside the other courtrooms were occupied by cops and civilian witnesses waiting to be called in to testify, some bored, some impatient, and some terrified. His mother's face was a mask of anxiety. When she saw me, she stood and said, "Excuse me, sir? Can I talk to you?"

"Of course," I said. "You're Mrs. Latour?"

"Mrs. Phillips," she replied. "I divorced Theo's dad when Theo was three and remarried. You're his lawyer, Mr.—"

"Rios. Henry Rios. Call me Henry. Thank you for coming to the arraignment, Mrs. Phillips."

"Kim," she said.

I guessed mid-forties, minimal makeup, unpolished nails, plain dress—a working-class woman—but remarkably attractive. I saw where Theo got his looks.

"This has all been a shock to me," she said. "After Theo left home, I didn't hear from him for a long time, and then it was just a phone call here and there. He called me. I never had his number. When I read about his arrest, I drove down from Lancaster where we live now to visit him in the jail. It's an awful place and—you know, he's sick."

"Sick?"

"AIDS," she said in a low voice. "Theo has AIDS."

"You mean he has the virus," I said. "Has he actually been sick? Had pneumonia or some other disease related to HIV?"

She looked puzzled. "I don't know about all that. All I know is he told me he had it."

"The virus is not itself a disease, but it does make him more susceptible to diseases. Serious ones."

"The jail's so dirty, there have to be a lot of germs there. Things that could make him sick."

She wasn't wrong. LA County Jail was a stink-hole, the worst place in the world to be HIV-positive.

"I promise I'll do what I can to protect his health while he's there."

174

The glimmer of a smile quickly faded. "That other lawyer, he said Theo could get the death penalty. I know what he did was terrible, but he didn't mean to kill that man. He told me he didn't know there would be anyone at the church."

"The thing to remember is that the DA doesn't have to seek the death penalty. I'm working on trying to get them to take it off the table."

"Even if you can," she said, "it sounds like he might never get out of jail."

"That may be true."

She gave a sad little cry. "This is my fault. I let Charlie, Theo's stepdad, throw him out of the house when he found out Theo was a homosexual. I sent him to live with my parents, but my dad wasn't much better with him than Charlie, and one day Theo ran away. He was only sixteen. Later he told me he lived on the streets here in LA, and, well, the life he described wasn't very pretty. I should have fought for him. If I'd stood up for him when he was sixteen, none of this would have happened."

"You're here for him now," I said.

She looked at me, eyes filling with tears. "Am I too late?"

"Theo's fighting for his life. You're just in time."

She wiped her eyes and smiled the hopeful, grateful, heart-breaking smile I'd seen on the faces of other mothers in other courthouses, the smile I had so often had to disappoint.

Downstairs in the courthouse cafeteria I got a cup of coffee and looked for a quiet table where I could do a preliminary review of the files Novotny had handed me in court. I picked up the discarded front page of the *LA Times* at an empty table and glanced at the headline: AIDS INITIATIVE IN DEAD HEAT 8 WEEKS BEFORE ELECTION, NEW POLL SAYS.

Outside, a yellow leaf fluttered in the air and scraped the window before sinking out of sight. Summer was ending. Eight weeks to November 6. The polls had been moving in our favor until the church bombing. After the bombing, the Yes campaign had released TV commercials showing burning churches and the LA chief of police talking about homosexual terrorists, and the numbers began to reverse.

I'd been fielding hate calls for representing Theo from both sides: the bigots who advised me I'd burn in hell, and gay people who called me a traitor for defending a terrorist. Wendell Thorne had apologetically dropped me from the lawyers' roundtable devising legal strategies to fight the initiative, saying some of the members objected to my presence.

I sorted through the investigative documents. Because the investigation was ongoing, what Novotny had given me wasn't the final case compilation that LAPD called the "Murder Book." I only had initial crime reports, the autopsy, the search warrant for Josh's apartment, the list of evidence recovered in the search, and some forensic analyses.

I skipped the crime reports for now and read the warrant. At first glance it seemed legit, but I'd give it a closer look later to see if I could find any basis to challenge it in a suppression motion. I read through the long list of items seized from Josh's apartment. The packaging from the double A batteries, wrappings for two electronic timers, electrician's tape, a length of copper piping, and traces of gunpowder confirmed that the bombs had been constructed in the apartment. The cops had also found a crumpled Polaroid of the entrance to the church with markings where the bomb had been planted. That confirmed the placement had been premeditated.

I paged through to the fingerprint analyses. I found the report that matched a single partial fingerprint found on a fragment of the bomb that blew up the building where Daniel Herron died to one of Theo's prints; they were in the system because of his earlier arrest for drug possession. It was only an eight-point match when the standard was ten to sixteen, leaving me room to challenge its reliability with my own fingerprint expert. But Theo's prints had also been solidly matched to prints found in the apartment and, especially damning, on the photograph. Thus, he could be placed at both locations—where the bombs were constructed and where they'd been planted. The inference drew itself.

Other unidentified prints had been lifted at the apartment, but none were matched to Freddy Saavedra. This was a surprise. It seemed likely that some of those prints were his. If they'd been lifted and run through the system there should have been a match from his assault arrest. Had the cops simply stopped looking once they zeroed in on Theo? I'd request all the prints in discovery, get a match to Freddy from my own expert to put him in the apartment, and rake the cops over the coals for conducting a sloppy investigation. That was something anyway, a tiny crack in the prosecution's strong circumstantial case. I already knew I wasn't going to drop some dramatic game-changing revelation at the trial. If we got to trial, it would be a war of attrition. I'd be chipping away at the prosecution's evidence, looking for the weak spots that might cumulatively amount to reasonable doubt in the mind of at least one juror.

"Nothing?" I said, disbelievingly.

Freeman shook his head. It was a quarter to two. The lunch crowd had left the Code Seven where my investigator and I were sharing a booth and a late lunch two days after the arraignment. The Code Seven was cop talk for meal break, and while it was both a bar and grill, the strong, cheap drinks were what attracted its cop clientele. The food was famously bad. I had confined myself to a grilled cheese sandwich, but Freeman had ordered the day's special: a big chunk of gray meatloaf and a mound of mashed potatoes covered with gray gravy with canned green beans on the side.

"Nada," he said, digging into his lunch.

He had just informed me he'd been unable to find any kind of criminal record for either Freddy Saavedra or any variation of his name: Frederick, Federico, Alfredo, Fico or Fede.

"Maybe he used an alias when he was arrested for ADW."

177

"The cops would have figured that out and listed it as an a.k.a," he replied through a mouthful of mashed potatoes. "Nothing came up. Are you sure about the arrest warrant?"

"I heard about it from the people who were with him when he was picked up," I said. "What about Home Depot? Anyone recognize him from the photo?"

Freeman shook his head. "It's a big store with a lot of workers. So far no bites, but I still have a few more to track down."

"Find Freddy," I instructed him.

"I thought you didn't want me to find him."

"At this point, I just want to be sure the guy exists."

From the Code Seven I headed to the county jail to see my client. Theo was housed in High Power, a bank of cells reserved for inmates deemed potentially dangerous or especially notorious. The unit bordered the main kitchen, subjecting the inmates to a massive cockroach infestation and regular blasts of hot, greasy, fetid air. The inmates were individually celled, with meals delivered by the guards. On the rare occasions when they were allowed on the roof for exercise time, they were not allowed to commingle. High Power was basically solitary confinement, but safer for Theo than general population where the charges against him might have made him a target for retribution and his looks and youth a target for rape.

We met in a small attorney conference room just outside the sally port that led into the unit, close enough that, when the doors rolled open to bring Theo out, I got a whiff of baked, rancid air. He sat down, his nice suit exchanged for the standard orange jumpsuit, his face more feral in the bleak, fluorescent jail light than in the softer light of the courtroom.

He took a couple of deep breaths. "Nice to get some fresh air," he said, although fresh was not how I would've described the stale jailhouse musk.

"I have to ask some questions about Freddy," I said. "Were you at the demo where he was picked up on an arrest warrant?"

178

"You mean at Barney's Beanery," he said. "Yeah."

I made a note. "Do you know what happened after he was arrested?"

He chewed the inside of his cheeks, a nervous tic I hadn't noticed before.

"The cops released him later that night," he said after a moment's thought. "He told me the warrant was for someone else with the same name."

"Another Freddy Saavedra?"

That would explain why his prints weren't in the system, but Freeman hadn't found any Freddy Saavedra with an outstanding arrest warrant for assault.

"Do you know if Freddy was ever arrested for anything?"

He shook his head, chewed his cheek and said, "No. Why are you asking?"

I explained about the fingerprint evidence, concluding, "We need to match prints taken from the apartment to his fingerprints to corroborate your story he built the bombs, but if his prints aren't in the system—"

"He wore gloves," Theo interjected.

I stared at him. "He what?"

"When he was making the bombs, he wore plastic gloves. Thin ones, like hospital gloves."

"You never said anything about gloves before."

He frowned. "I didn't remember until just now."

We sat in silence while I processed this new information. The light buzzed overhead, and just outside the door of the closet-sized conference room the indistinct but hard voices of men shouting directions and orders could be heard. Only one fingerprint on either of the bombs, Theo's. Because Freddy wore gloves or because Theo had constructed them?

"Nothing connects Freddy to the bombing except your word. All the evidence points to you and only to you. Did you make the bombs? Did you act alone?"

"No," he said, his voice rising, "it was all Freddy's idea."

"You're HIV positive," I said. "You have reason to be angry, but what about Freddy? What made him angry enough to want to blow up a church? Was he positive?"

Theo shook his head. "He tested negative."

"Did he lose someone to AIDS? A lover? A friend? A family member?"

"If he did, he never told me about it."

"Then what was his motive, Theo?"

Theo tapped his fingers on the table, tapped his foot on the floor, and chewed his cheeks, a compendium of jittery energy.

"You're asking me what he was thinking? I never knew what he was thinking. That's part of his appeal. That's what attracted me the first time I saw him at a QUEER meeting. The hot, mysterious bad boy. During the break I went up to talk to him. I was as nervous as I was turned on. He thought QUEER was a joke. Said they couldn't plan a brunch, much less a revolution. Asked me if I was a pussy like the rest of them. No way, I said, and he laughed and said, 'Yes, you are. You're just a little twinkie fuck boy trying to hit on me.' That's when I told him I was positive. I told him I wasn't there to hit on him, I was there to save my life. He said, 'you ain't going to do it with these people' and walked away. After the meeting, I followed him to his car and said, 'I am serious. Tell me what to do.'"

"And he told you he wanted you to plant bombs?"

"Not right away," Theo said. "At first, he just talked to me. Talked about how the system is rigged against people like us, and the only way to change it was to bring it down. Said HIV had been created in a government laboratory and was deliberately spread to gays to exterminate us."

I'd heard this conspiracy theory before. "You realize that's crazy."

He leaned forward, the flicker of fanaticism in his eyes. "Are you sure? Aren't they trying to put us in concentration camps?"

"That's not the government," I said. "It's a bunch of bigots."

He leaned back in his chair, shrugged. "Whatever. What Freddy said made sense to me."

"Are you saying Freddy brainwashed you?"

180

"I'm saying he was right about a lot of things."

"Eventually it moved from talk to planning."

He nodded. "We went to the meeting for the Bash the Church action. Freddy said the plan was lame. He said if we really wanted to make a statement, we should blow up one of the churches. Next thing I knew we 're buying stuff to make pipe bombs."

"How did he know how to make a bomb? Did he use a book?"

"I didn't watch the whole thing because it made me really nervous, but from what I saw, he knew what he was doing. I asked him where he learned it, and he said someone taught him. I didn't ask again."

"If he was the expert, why did you plant the bombs?"

"We went to the church the Sunday before to see where to plant them. Freddy had a camera and was taking pictures. He said the entrance would be a good place because all the glass would make a cool explosion. We were walking around in this courtyard where I guess the guy who started the church is buried. I said let's blow up his grave. Freddy said, no, it was better to blow up the building where they had their offices and kept their files and stuff. That would cause chaos. Anyway, these two dudes came toward us. One of them had a black T-shirt that said 'Security'; the other was an old guy. Freddy told me to go wait in the car. When he caught up with me, he said I'd have to plant the bombs because the security guy knew what he looked like."

The security guy had seen Freddy at the church a few days before the bombing, a potential witness if I could track him down.

"That's how I figured out that he'd set me up," he was saying.

"What?"

His jaw cracked when he opened his mouth, and his teeth were ground down. Speed freak dentition.

"Why would he be worried about the security guard seeing him if there wasn't going to be anyone at the church?" he asked. "Freddy knew there'd be people around. Maybe the guard, maybe someone else."

"The pastor?"

181

He massaged his cheeks. "I don't know, but someone. He meant for the explosion to kill someone, and he wanted me to plant the bombs so if there were witnesses, they'd see me."

We sat there for a moment. This version of events was clearer than any he'd given me before and less self-serving in a way—no claims of being abused or coerced—so it rang true, or at least, truer. And it gave me an idea about who Freddy Saavedra was, if that was even his name. Someone had taught him to make pipe bombs. That was a skill I associated with terrorists.

"Did Freddy ever say anything to you that suggested he might belong to some kind of politically radical group?"

He replied with a puzzled, "You mean QUEER?"

"No, a different group."

"Like who?" he asked, confused.

"That's what I'm asking you, Theo. Did you ever overhear him on the phone talking about the bombing or see him with someone you didn't recognize who struck you as, I don't know, sketchy? Anything at all like that?"

"No, but I wasn't with him twenty-four seven. I don't know what he was doing when he was on his own."

I'd only had Freeman run Freddy through the CII—the Criminal Investigation and Identification database kept by California's Department of Justice. After talking to Theo, I decided it was time to expand the search to other databases, the kind that kept track of terrorists.

TWELVE

When I talked to Freeman on the phone the next day, he was skeptical of my theory that Freddy was a terrorist of some kind. He reported that his skip trace had turned up plenty of Freddy Saavedras, but none of them matched our Freddy's description, confirming the name was an alias.

"Why do you think my idea that Freddy's a terrorist is crazy?" I asked.

I heard the flick of his cigarette lighter, followed by a quick inhale and slow exhale. I pictured smoke rings. "I wouldn't say crazy," he said, "but definitely old school."

"Old school?"

"Blowing up buildings went out with bell bottoms and love beads. Last time I heard about something like that in LA was back in '69 when a bunch of Brown Berets tried to burn down the Biltmore when Ronald Reagan was giving a speech."

"The Brown Berets? That takes me back. I never heard about that incident."

"You don't know about the Biltmore Six? They got railroaded into jail." He puffed away on his cigarette. "You think this Freddy is an agent of the revolution? What revolution would that be?"

"Maybe a radical gay group that no one's heard of until now."

"Don't bomb throwers like to take credit for the bombs?"

"Maybe they're waiting for the right moment," I suggested.

"Which would be when?"

I remembered the headline in the *Times* about the new poll showing the quarantine initiative gaining ground.

"Election day, after the voters decide to quarantine at least a quarter of the gay male population. How hard would it be to turn that anger into violent action? I'd be tempted myself."

"Not worth it," Freeman cautioned. "You can't fight the system from a jail cell unless you're Doctor King, and he wasn't doing the kind of time in Birmingham you'd get if you start blowing things up." A long, final nicotine exhale. "Anyway, bombing churches before the votes are cast ain't no way to make friends and influence people."

"The point of a revolutionary action isn't to win friends; it's to precipitate the revolution," I said, paraphrasing a half-remembered college lecture in a class on twentieth-century revolutionary movements. "If you want to radicalize gay people, you need the quarantine initiative to pass."

Freedman chuckled sardonically. "You're really in love with this theory of yours. You really think Freddy's some kind of gay Maoist?"

"I don't know, Freeman," I said, with some asperity. "What I do know is that I need a defense, and the best one I have is to deflect moral responsibility for the bombing from Theo to Freddy. Unless you have a better idea, start checking terrorist databases, and see if anything or anyone pops up."

"Sure," he said, "but you've got your ear to the ground in the gay community. You might ask around yourself while I'm at it."

"Good idea."

"Look, Henry," he said. "Not to burst your bubble, but there's another angle here. What do you know about the victim? Did he have any secrets that made him a target?"

"Daniel Herron? Why do you ask?"

"I looked at the follow-up reports from the bomb squad," he said. "The bomb planted in the building where he died was twice as powerful as the bomb planted at the entrance. What does that mean to you?"

I thought about what Theo had told me, that he believed

Freddy had always intended to kill someone. "The bomber wanted to make sure that if someone was in the building, he wouldn't come out of it alive. But no one knew Herron was there."

"His wife told the cops he counseled people on Thursday night, and if she knew, other people had to know. The people he counseled, for example."

"That's true," I said. 'Herron's secrets? He has a gay son who's HIV positive from a woman who wasn't his wife."

"How do you know that? It sure wasn't in his obit."

I told him how I'd first met Daniel Herron and pointed out that the absence of any mention in the obit of his son suggested another woman. "Of course," I said, "I'm only assuming the boy is gay. He could be straight and hemophiliac."

"Or a junkie. You don't think that's provocative?" Freeman said. "Evangelical with a secret gay son?"

"I'd say more hypocritical than provocative. But I don't see how it's the kind of secret that would've gotten him blown up."

"Don't make assumptions," he said. "Let me look into Pastor Herron's history. Maybe we find a connection between him and Saavedra."

"Okay, but your idea that Herron was targeted isn't inconsistent with Freddy being a terrorist. You said yourself he could've known Herron would be in his office. Maybe he got that tip from an infiltrator in the church."

"You have someone in mind?"

I remembered the security guard Theo said had accosted them when they'd gone to scout the church. A security guard, perfect cover for a spy. I told Freeman about it and suggested he track down the guy.

I ate lunch at my desk while I triaged my cases to clear as much time as possible to devote to Theo. The office was closed at lunch. My new full-time secretary, Emma Austin, locked the door from the reception room to the outside corridor from noon to one. At one, I stepped outside my office and saw she hadn't yet returned so I unlocked the door myself. I opened it and found a woman standing in the hall, evidently waiting to be let in. That wasn't unusual. I often came back to potential clients standing patiently at the door or pacing around the hall in agitation.

This woman, however, didn't look like a potential client. For one thing, she was white. Most of my clients weren't. There was also something antiquated in the way she was put together—a lilac blazer and matching calf-length skirt, white blouse, low heels, stockings, big purse, helmet hair—as if she'd stepped out of a woman's clothing catalogue circa 1958, again not the kind of client who made her way to my office. On the other hand, her lipstick was smudged at the corners and her makeup spotty, as if it had been applied with a hasty or an unsteady hand. Also, from the heavy whiff of mouthwash that didn't quite cover the booze on her breath, I could tell she'd been drinking.

With wary, watery eyes, she asked, "Mr. Rios?"

"Yes, I'm Henry Rios, and you are—"

"Mrs. Daniel Herron."

"What can I do for you, Mrs. Herron?"

She sat across from me, her big handbag in her lap, looking as if she was as dumbfounded to find herself in my office as I was to have her here. My question seemed to focus her.

"You're defending the man who killed my husband."

Her words were confrontational, but her tone was merely inquisitive.

"The man *accused* of killing your husband," I said, emphasizing accused.

She looked surprised. "Oh, you don't think he did it?"

"I can't discuss that with you."

She folded her hands on her bag and we sat in silence. I was about to politely ask her to leave when she blurted out, "Someone helped him."

"I'm sorry?"

"Your . . . client. Someone helped him kill Daniel."

"Who helped him?" I asked.

"Someone in the church."

"You're saying someone in your church conspired with my client to kill your husband?"

She nodded vigorously. "Yes."

"Was it a man named Freddy Saavedra?"

She looked at me blankly. "Who?"

I showed her the photograph of Freddy and Theo taken at the demonstration. I tapped Freddy's image. "This man."

She peered at the photo intently, then reached into her bag and fumbled with its contents before extracting a thick manila folder. She dumped its contents on my desk: a sheaf of typed pages and a stack of eight-by-ten photographs. She tore through the pictures, examining each one briefly before she stopped at one, appraised it carefully, and slid it toward me. I held it up: it was a photograph of Freddy Saavedra arguing with a meter maid who looked like she was about to write him a ticket.

"What is this?"

"I hired a private investigator to follow my husband. He took this photograph at the airport where Daniel was getting on a plane to San Francisco." She handed over the rest of the photographs. "There's another picture of this man somewhere in the pile. Here's the report."

"Do you know this man?" I asked, tapping Saavedra's image again.

"No," she replied firmly. "I've never seen him before, and I don't know why the investigator took his picture, but if you think he was involved . . ." She trailed off into vagueness.

There was definitely something off about Mrs. Daniel Herron. "What makes you think someone at the church had a hand in your husband's death?"

"They're trying to throw me out of my own home!" she exclaimed.

I realized she hadn't just been drinking; she was drunk. Very drunk but, in the way of hard-core alcoholics, able to semi-function even with an amount of liquor in her system that would have knocked out a normal person. She might even have been in a black-out.

"Who are you talking about?" I asked patiently.

"The Overseers. Well, some of them. Bob Metzger. He's the ringleader."

"The ringleader in your husband's death?"

"They wanted to get rid of him, but it takes a unanimous vote; my father made sure of that, oh, how they regretted it but, you see, that's how it was, so they killed him," she babbled.

"Let me see if I understand you," I said. "A dissident group on the governing board was so determined to remove your husband as pastor that they plotted to kill him?"

Her watery eyes brightened for a second. "That's right."

"And you're angry because you've been asked to leave your house?"

"They claim it belongs to the church, but my father built the house. The church, too." She leaned toward me, giving me a blast of Scope mixed with Smirnoff. "It's outrageous! I'm his daughter. I have rights . . . don't I? Legal rights. To the house? You're a lawyer. Don't I have rights?"

"I'm not that kind of lawyer, Mrs. Herron. Your fight with the church is a civil matter." I switched topics to cut off another rant. "Why were you having your husband followed?"

"I thought he was having an affair."

"Was he?"

She grimaced. "No. He had a son by another woman, long before we met and were married. In San Francisco. He'd go there to see them."

The final pieces of Herron's secret life fell into place for me. His son was the child of a woman he'd met in San Francisco in his youth.

"Your husband," I said. "When did he live in San Francisco?"

"What does that have to do with anything?" she snapped, then, abruptly, as drunks do, fell into a reverie. "Dan was a hippie. That's what he told me once. Before he converted, he had long hair and lived in abandoned houses and took drugs and met—

Gwen. She's a nice woman. She's Black! That was a shock. Daddy wouldn't have approved. I suppose that's why he kept her a secret while Daddy was alive and then after he died, Dan didn't want me to know. I wanted to hate her, but—he should have married her. She would have given him the family he wanted." She took a soiled handkerchief from her purse and dabbed her eyes. "You see I can't have children, and Dan—well, I understand now—he needed that family. That boy. He's sick, you know. AIDS. Dan asked Schultz to help get Wyatt some kind of medication and told him it was for his nephew. Daniel doesn't have a nephew. Marie Schultz called me and told me she was sorry her husband couldn't help. That bitch! That's when I hired the investigator."

"What did you do when you found out about the boy and his mother?"

"I didn't know what to do, so I went to Bob. Uncle Bob," she said sardonically. "That's what I called him when I was a little girl. He was my father's best friend. He said he would take care of it."

"You think the way he took care of it was to have your husband killed? Is that how Christians handle their disputes these days?"

"You're mocking me."

"I'm trying to understand why you believe this man— Metzger?—would have taken such a drastic action to eliminate your husband."

"They thought he was too soft."

"Soft? Your husband."

"Not enough of a hater," she said. "Not enough of a man. You see, it's not just a church. It's a kingdom. They wanted a different king, and there was only one way to replace him. Like Shakespeare, you see. One of those plays where powerful nobles plot to get rid of a weak king."

We were again descending into alcoholic gibberish, so I redirected the conversation to more solid ground.

"Why come to me? Why not go to the police?"

"I can't go to the police. They. . . ." she trailed off. "I was arrested."

"For what?"

"Drunk driving," she said in a flat voice.

"Recently?"

She nodded. "The police wouldn't believe me. Do you?" she asked, despairingly.

This was one sad woman. "Mrs. Herron, I'm sorry for your loss. I'm sure you loved your husband very much."

"No, Mr. Rios. I did not love my husband. I hardly knew my husband. I was my father's only child. He had me marry Daniel so Daniel could inherit the church when he died. Now that Daniel is gone, they're throwing me away. You take the report and the photographs. Use them against Bob. I thought he was my friend until he told me I would have to leave my house. The scandal will destroy the church."

"This is all about revenge for you."

She stood up slowly, smoothed her skirt, and adjusted her blazer. "'The Lord is a God who avenges,'" she quoted. "'O God who avenges, shine forth. Rise up, Lord of the earth. Pay back to the proud what they deserve.'"

She left in a gust of booze and indignation. I could have dismissed what she'd said as a drunken rant by a vindictive woman—and most of it was—but she had given me two valuable pieces of information. The photograph of Freddy taken by her investigator and what she'd told me about Daniel Herron's pre-come-to-Jesus life as a hippie in late '60s San Francisco. A place and time of revolutionary ferment.

Maybe I was right that a terrorist group was behind Herron's death but wrong about its identity. Not a secret gay network, but an older one that had nothing to do with gay rights. Maybe Herron had been mixed up with a violent, radical group like the Weathermen who'd claimed credit for twenty-five bombings of government facilities back in the day. Some members of that group had never been caught, were still on the FBI's Most Wanted list. Could he have been one of them and have known the whereabouts of others? Was he going to rat them out now that he'd gone straight? Or had the feds tracked him down and squeezed him to rat out the rest? Was that why he was killed? Was Freddy Saavedra the avenging angel of whatever was left of a revolution that Dan Herron had been about to betray?

I shuffled through the stack of photos Mrs. Herron had left behind, looking for the second one of Freddy Saavedra she said was among them. There it was: Saavedra standing near the gate where Herron was boarding a plane. So Freddy had been following Herron, but when I read the investigator's report, there was no mention of Freddy by any name or a description of the photographs where he was pictured. I picked up the phone.

"Vidor Investigations."

"Freeman, it's Rios. Do you know a PI named Bruce Lindell?"

"Sure. Most of his work is for insurance companies. He takes pictures of guys who said they were injured on the job, cutting down trees or running marathons. Why the interest?"

I gave him a summary of my meeting with Mrs. Herron and the photos of Saavedra she'd passed along to me.

"The thing is," I concluded, "Lindell's report doesn't say anything about why he took those pictures. Could you arrange a meeting with him?"

"I'll call him as soon as we hang up."

"You may be right that the answer to Herron's death is in his past, not Freddy's."

"Told you so," he replied.

The following morning, I picked Freeman up at his office and we drove to our meeting with Bruce Lindell while Freeman sketched out what he'd learned so far about Daniel Herron's early life. It was pretty white bread until he went off to college at San Francisco state in 1965 and dropped out the following year. After that, nothing. The Turn On, Tune In, Drop Out generation hadn't left much of a paper trail, not even a driver's license in Dan Herron's case. His had expired in 1966 and wasn't renewed until 1972 when presumably he was doing God's work and God required a car. Six missing years. The only thing I knew for certain about them was that at some point he got his girlfriend pregnant. Otherwise, he could have been anywhere, doing anything. Selling dope, traveling the world in sandals and a headband, or building bombs in the attic of a San Francisco Victorian to blow up the local selective service depot.

Freeman played devil's advocate.

"If he was a white boy revolutionary," he said, "and did some damage back then, the government would be looking for him, not his comrades."

"Unless," I said, "they were underground, and he knew where they were and was about to snitch."

"After all these years? Why?"

"I don't know. Maybe the feds caught up with him and he cut a deal. Maybe he heard old comrades were about to start blowing up things again and he wanted to stop them now that he's reformed."

Freeman lit a cigarette. We both rolled down our windows.

"I ain't heard of any federal building going up in smoke lately. You?"

"Maybe it was still in the planning stages."

"A lot of maybes," he muttered. "Anyway, this Saavedra, he's a young dude. This sixties stuff would be ancient history to him."

"He could be second-generation," I said.

He laughed. "I think you call those people yuppies."

Miffed, I growled, "Let's see what Lindell has to say, okay?"

Bruce Lindell was a sharp-featured man in a nicely cut suit who had the partner's office in the mid-Wilshire high-rise that housed his agency. He examined the photos of Saavedra I'd given him, looked up, and asked, "Where did you get these?"

"Your client gave them to me," I replied. "Daniel Herron's wife."

"Jessica," he said. "Why?"

"I'm afraid that's privileged."

He narrowed his eyes. "Is she suing me?"

"No, nothing like that. She gave me the photos and your report because she thought they might have some bearing on one of my cases."

He glanced at Freeman, sitting beside me, smirked and said, "You know how you're talking to a lawyer? He opens his mouth and a snake crawls out."

"He's on the level," Freeman said. "I'm working on the case."

"The church bombing," Lindell said flatly.

"How did you—" I began, then shot a look at my investigator. "Freeman?"

"Don't get your panties in a knot, Mr. Rios. Freeman's not my source. I read the papers. I know who you are." He tapped the photos. "So, Jessica Herron gives the file about her husband's secret life to the lawyer defending the guy who's accused of killing him." He pushed an ashtray across his desk to Freeman who'd just lit up a cigarette. "And you want to know about the guy in the picture. You think he's involved in the bombing? I know, I know, you can't say but when this is all over, Freeman, you're going to buy me a steak and tell me the whole story."

"You still like the New York cut at Dan Tana's?" Freeman asked.

"Twenty ounces of grass-fed heaven," Lindell replied.

"The photo," I reminded him.

"I don't know his name, Rios, but I can tell you this. He's a cop."

THIRTEEN

"What! How do you know he's a cop?"

Lindell tapped the photograph of Saavedra with the meter maid. "Because of what happened after I took this. The guy parks in a red zone. She pulls up behind him and gets out her pad. He gets out of the car and goes over to her. They argue for a minute. I take the picture but keep watching. She's starting to write him up when he grabs his wallet, opens it, and shows it to her. They talk for another minute. She closes her pad and takes off. Now, I didn't see what he was carrying, but the only way anyone's going to win an argument with a meter maid is to show her a badge."

"LAPD?" I asked.

"Hell if I know, but it had to be an agency she recognized."

"Why did you notice him in the first place?"

"He was following Herron, too. Saw him parked down the street from Herron's house and when Herron left, so did he. Followed him to the airport and into the terminal. That's where I took the second picture."

"Why didn't you mention any of this to Jessica Herron?"

He shrugged. "I was hired to see if her husband had a side piece. It was no business of mine if the cops were tailing him for something else. I included the photos in case she knew what was going on and wanted me to follow up, but once I delivered my report, that was the end of it." He lay back in his black leather desk chair. "You obviously think the cop was up to something else."

"I appreciate your help, Bruce," I said.

He smiled. "Okay, okay, I understand. Lawyer-client privilege, but here's a tip. You want to know the cop's name?"

"That would be very helpful."

"See here," he said, pointing back at the photo. "The meter maid's cart has a number on it. Find out who's assigned to that cart and show her the picture. I bet she remembers his name."

"Thank you," I said.

"You know I would have figured that out," Freeman said.

Lindell laughed. "Sure, but I saved you the brain cells. Don't forget to call me about that steak."

Freeman and I regrouped in front of Lindell's blocky high-rise. Mid-Wilshire was filled with similar cookie-cutter concrete-and-glass buildings but hidden among them were marvels of Art Deco architecture from the 1920s when the neighborhood had been home to the silent film movie elite. Not far away swan boats had once paddled across the lake in MacArthur Park, which was now a battlefield for warring gangs. Signage in Korean plastered the storefronts on the surrounding streets as a new wave of immigrants claimed the neighborhood. It was a vibrant, if sketchy, section of the city from which the ghosts of the old movie colony had long since departed.

He lit a cigarette, flicked the match to the sidewalk, and said gleefully, "There goes your theory that Saavedra was some kind of radical hit man sent to assassinate Herron."

"Unless Saavedra's working for the feds tracking down old lefties."

"And then he kills him?"

"Who knows!" I said, flummoxed. "Maybe Theo's been lying to me the whole time and Saavedra had nothing to do with the bombing."

"You really think the kid could pull it off without any help? Didn't you say he was a speed freak? You need steady hands and a clear head to build a bomb."

"Hey, I'm open to suggestions if you have one."

"In fact," he said, "now that we know Freddy's a cop, I do have an idea. You remember I was telling you about the Biltmore Six, those Brown Beret dudes?"

"The ones you said tried to burn down the Biltmore when Reagan was speaking."

"After we talked, I went down to the library and looked up the trial because there was something I wasn't remembering, and it bugged me. Turns out, the Berets were infiltrated by *PDID*."

"PDID? What's that?"

"Public Disorder Intelligence Division," Freeman replied. "A unit in LAPD that was supposed to keep track of people conspiring to use violence to overthrow the government. Came out of the red scare in the '50s when people thought there was a Communist under every bed. But instead of investigating actual criminals, the old chief, Davis, started planting agents in all kinds of left-wing groups, whether or not they were violent. Peaceniks, civil rights groups, anyone he thought was a threat to white-bread America." He exhaled a plume of smoke. "And I do mean white."

"Just like the FBI under J. Edgar Hoover."

"They were butt buddies, no offense. Anyway, some of these cops got tired of waiting around for the revolution to start so they tried to talk the groups they had infiltrated into lighting a fuse. Those fires at the Biltmore? They were started by the undercover cop. He talked the Berets into it and threw the first match. Or so the Berets claimed. He testified at the trial it was all them."

"What happened?"

"What do you think happened? The jury believed the cop and convicted the Berets."

"You think Freddy is PDID?"

"PDID was disbanded back in '81 after a lawsuit showed that the cops were spying on city council members, but then it was reorganized in '84 and given a new name. Now it's called the anti-terrorism unit."

"Why was it revived?"

"The department claimed outside terrorist groups were threatening to turn the games into another Munich. Remember that?"

"Yeah, the 1972 Olympics. Palestinian terrorists killed some Israeli athletes. Does the unit still exist?"

"Yeah, and maybe it's up to its old tricks."

"Investigating and discrediting any group that threatens Daryl Gates's vision of LA as a straight, whites-only paradise."

"That's not just the chief," Freeman replied. "Plenty of cops in the rank and file have the same vision. Why do you think I quit?"

"I'd actually like to hear that story sometime, Freeman."

"You'll have to get me drunk," he said. 'And get drunk with me."

"You know I don't drink. Okay, back to Freddy. Let's say LAPD planted an agent provocateur in QUEER. We still have to prove it was Freddy."

"I'll find the meter maid from the airport. What are you going to do?"

"Educate myself," I said, "to see what we're dealing with here."

LAPD's hostility to Blacks, Latinos, and the gay community was common knowledge, but to learn about its intelligence activities, I called a couple of veteran civil rights lawyers who had spent their careers tangling with the department. They confirmed Freeman's account that its spying on citizens went back decades, all the way to the 1920s, but really gathered steam in the '50s under Chief William Parker. A rabid anti-Communist and right-wing demagogue, Parker initiated the PDID. From the beginning its workings were shrouded in secrecy; Parker even claimed its files were his personal property and therefore not subject to subpoena.

One of the lawyers I talked to told me those files included dirt on local politicians and even members of the police commission, which Parker used to protect his position and avoid scrutiny. A subsequent lawsuit brought under the Freedom of Information

Act revealed that Parker had kept files on the local Democratic clubs, the First Unitarian Church, and the ACLU, among others.

Parker was also allied with several radical, right-wing groups of his era, including the John Birch Society and the gun-toting Minutemen. These organizations were not only militantly anti-Communist, but also explicitly racist, anti-immigrant, and often cloaked in fundamentalist Christian ideology. In the 1960s, some of them bombed the homes and offices of liberal activists. PDID not only declined to investigate the attacks, but Parker claimed the victims had engineered the bombings themselves to garner publicity and discredit conservatives.

Parker's successor, Ed Davis, was just as rabidly right-wing. He once called LA, the city he served and protected, "a cesspool of pornography, fruit bars, and bottomless bars, thanks to the United States and California Supreme Courts." Under him, the PDID continued to harass people and organizations the chief deemed subversive rather than investigate actual criminal activity. He began to authorize the use of PDID officers as agent provocateurs in liberal and leftist groups where they tried to foment violent actions.

I heard about one incident from one of the lawyers who had worked on the case. In the late 1960s, a group of middle-class white liberals formed an organization to raise money for the Black Panthers. After several months of harassment that included the rape of a member, they were approached by a man named Jarrett who claimed to be an ex-Green Beret and offered to teach them self-defense. He was, in fact, an undercover LAPD officer. Jarrett agreed to provide the group with Mace for self-protection, but instead he delivered an explosive. LAPD then raided the home of the member to whom Jarrett had delivered the bomb and the member who had paid for the delivery. They were arraigned on federal charges of possession of an explosive. Jarrett claimed they had purchased the bomb to pass along to the Panthers. The defense argued entrapment and the charges were dismissed.

The current chief, Daryl Gates, had come up through the ranks in the Parker and Davis years and was no less a right-wing racist. But he'd been forced to disband PDID after a series of lawsuits exposed the unit's misconduct. The '84 Olympics had given him an excuse to revive it as the ant-terrorism unit. The new unit's activities continued to be conducted in secrecy, its targets unknown and its techniques no doubt as illegal as they had been for the previous forty years.

Gates didn't make Davis's mistake of parading his contempt for gay people in public by calling us names, but his refusal to even consider hiring openly gay and lesbian cops made his personal attitude clear enough. Would his department have sent an agent provocateur to stir up trouble in QUEER? Oh, absolutely.

The phone message at the top of my pile of messages was from Ralph Novotny. I caught him on his way out the door to court.

"Your two weeks is up," he said, curtly. "The death penalty committee meets this afternoon on the Latour case. If you've got something to tell me, now's the time. I have five minutes."

"I need another week."

"No can do."

"I'm on to something, Ralph. Give me another week."

"Sorry, Henry. If the committee recommends death and you come up with something later, we can revisit it. I've got to go. You'll have our decision tomorrow morning. I have to tell you, though, I'm pretty sure it's going to be death."

The next two messages were from Freeman. He picked up on the first ring.

"It's Rios. You have news?"

"I found the meter maid from the airport. She remembered Saavedra, all right, because she's never dealt with an undercover cop before."

"So, Saavedra is a cop," I said, excitedly.

"Yeah," he said, "but his name isn't Saavedra. It's Sumaya. Alfredo Sumaya. Assigned to the anti-terrorism unit."

199

"Get me every detail you can on him that I can throw into a discovery motion," I said. "I need it fast, Freeman. The DA's going to seek the death penalty."

"What's your defense going to be?"

I'd carefully studied the Black Panther case where the defendants had been exonerated, and it had given me a tactic I thought might work for Theo.

"If you find me what I need, entrapment."

Entrapment is a tricky defense. In TV lawyer shows, all you need to prove entrapment is that the undercover cop whispered in the defendant's ear like a little devil perched on his shoulder, "Go ahead, do it." As the texts laid out before me on a long table in the dignified silence of the county law library showed, however, the defense was considerably more complicated. The California Supreme Court had laid out a two-part test to succeed in the defense: *The proper test of entrapment in California is the following: was the conduct of the law enforcement agent likely to induce a normally law-abiding person to commit the offense.* Part one: did the cop's conduct encourage the commission of the crime. Part two: was the conduct so outrageous it would have induced, not my client, Theo Latour with all his psychological tics and emotional problems, but *a reasonable, law-abiding person* to commit the crime.

Regarding the cop's conduct, there were two additional standards. On the one hand, *Entrapment is the conception and planning of an offense by an officer and his procurement of its commission by one who would not have perpetrated it* except *for the trickery, persuasion, or fraud of the officer.* On the other hand, the police were allowed *to provide the opportunity for the commission of a crime including reasonable, though restrained, steps to gain the confidence of the suspects.* In other words, the question was just how far could you lead the horse to water before you were on the hook when the horse drank? Had you grabbed its bridle, dragged it to the stream, and shoved its head in the water (entrapment) or simply pointed in the direction of the stream (not entrapment)?

Plus, words being what they were, and lawyers being who they were, a phrase like "reasonable, though restrained steps" was open to multiple interpretations, some better for the defense, others for the prosecution. Who would decide which interpretation was correct? That would be the least qualified group in the courtroom: the jurors.

There was also a tactical challenge in asserting an entrapment defense in this case: Theo would have to testify. He was the only witness who could describe to the jury the nature of "the trickery, persuasion, or fraud" of Alfredo Sumaya, *a.k.a.* Freddy Saavedra. Then, there was the fact that the so-called "reasonable man" standard in the entrapment instruction really referred to the "reasonable heterosexual white man." Not women, not Latinos, not African-Americans or any other ethnic or racial group and certainly not gay people, each of whom had discrete histories of oppression that left them open to forms of trickery, persuasion, and fraud that wouldn't affect your average straight white guy.

Theo would have to convince the jury that Saavedra had appealed to his rage, shame and self-loathing, not only as a gay man, but as one infected with HIV, to persuade him to blow up a church. I could imagine a bigoted juror thinking Theo *should be* ashamed of, and hate himself for, being a faggot with AIDS, and voting to punish him for that, no matter how outrageous Saavedra's conduct.

Anyway, Theo's testimony would not be enough—even before the prosecutor got a chance to rip him to shreds. I needed corroborating, objective evidence to support Theo's claim that Saavedra had been the moving force in the bombing. Even then, there would be other needles to thread to get an acquittal based on entrapment, not the least of which was that the defense would ultimately force the jury to choose who was responsible for Daniel Herron's death, a police officer or a gay, HIV-infected ex-porn actor.

The day before, while shopping for groceries, I had noticed the headline on the cover of a national magazine in the magazine rack at the checkout stand that blared: NOW NO ONE IS

SAFE FROM AIDS. Beneath the headline were three photographs: a young woman, a young straight couple holding an infant, and a uniformed soldier.

Clearly, I needed a Plan B.

"You'll like this."

Freeman pushed the file across my desk toward me while I pushed the ashtray toward him. He lit up. The folder contained Freeman's one-page typewritten summary and supporting documents.

Freeman's summary consisted of a single paragraph: *Alfredo Sumaya, b. Nov. 12, 1955 in LA. U.S. Army, 1973-1978, explosive ordnance disposal specialist. City College, criminal justice degree, 1980. Joined LAPD 1980, patrol to '83. Assigned to anti-terrorism unit, 1984-present. Single. Residence and whereabouts unknown.*

"He defused bombs in the army," I said, glancing at his army records. "Does that mean he was also trained in how to make them?"

"He had to know what he was looking for," Freeman replied, blowing out a stream of cigarette smoke.

"He went from being a beat cop to the anti-terrorism unit?"

"Some higher-up decided they needed his expertise for the Olympics."

"At what point did he go undercover?"

"You'll have to find that out in discovery."

"You don't know where he is?"

"Standard for undercover cops," he replied. "The department shields them so they don't get made and to avoid retaliation. But, trust me, he's somewhere in the city and the department knows where. Is this enough for you to start?"

"Oh, yeah. This is excellent, but keep on it, okay? See what else you can find out about what he does off the job."

"Sure," he said, stubbing out his cigarette. "I tracked down the last employee who was working at Home Depot where they bought the stuff for the bomb. She recognized the guys in the photo but can't say when she saw them."

"That's something, anyway," I said. "What about the security guard at the church?"

"Yeah, about that. I took two steps on church property and three security guards stopped me and asked me what I wanted. I told them and they, uh, politely directed me to leave."

"Never mind," I said. "I'll subpoena the church's records in discovery and find out the name of the security company and who it employs at Ekklesia."

"You give me that list of names," he said. "I want another crack at those boys."

"*People versus Latour,*" Judge Mayeda intoned. "We're here on the defense's motion to compel discovery." He looked up from his file, puzzled. "It's a little early for this motion isn't it, Mr. Rios? Surely, the People haven't had enough time to respond to your discovery request."

Unlike the full house at Theo's arraignment, Mayeda's courtroom was empty except for Novotny, me, and the court staff. Empty courtrooms are where most of the real work gets done in any criminal case. The pretrial motions, counter-motions, and rulings define the playing field for the trials, if a case even gets that far since most criminal matters plead out, also in empty courtrooms.

Discovery was the defense's opportunity to assess the strength of the prosecution case by forcing the DA to disclose its evidence. It was so crucial to a defendant's right to a fair trial that the Supreme Court had long held the prosecution's failure to disclose key evidence in discovery was grounds for dismissal.

A defendant was required to submit a detailed and specific list of items he or she was seeking and show their relevance to the defense. The requests could run into a hundred pages or more, but the request that had brought us to Mayeda's court was short and to the point. I wanted information regarding a single person,

Officer Alfredo Sumaya a.k.a. Freddy Saavedra. I had served the request on Novotny one week earlier. Two days later I had received a letter from the DA's office categorically rejecting it, no reason given.

When I had asked Novotny before Mayeda came out why he'd turned me down, he made a sour face and muttered, "I'm being stonewalled, too."

"By the cops?"

"Can't say more, Henry. Let's just do this and see what happens."

Now, addressing Mayeda, I said, "Your Honor, this is not a general discovery request but a very limited and specific one involving an individual who will be crucial to the defense, particularly since the prosecutor is seeking the death penalty. The prosecutor has flatly refused to comply with our request without any reason, forcing me to file this motion to compel."

Mayeda flipped some pages in his file. "You want information about a police officer named Alfredo Sumaya. Is this a *Pitchess* motion?"

"No, Your Honor," I said. "I'm not asking the prosecutor to disclose if there have been any excessive force or other citizen complaints against Officer Sumaya—not yet, anyway. All I want to know now is, one, whether he exists, two, whether he works undercover in the anti-terrorism unit and, three, whether he was assigned to infiltrate an organization called QUEER, and the dates of that assignment."

Mayeda stroked his little moustache and asked the prosecutor, "Mr. Novotny, care to respond?"

"Your Honor, in the interests of officer safety, we cannot comply with the request."

Mayeda frowned. "Officer safety? Are you saying if you disclosed this information, Officer Sumaya would be in some kind of danger?"

"That's our position, yes."

"In danger from whom?"

"I can't say, Judge."

Mayeda frowned. "Can't say or won't say?"

"Your Honor," I interrupted, "if the prosecutor continues to reject my discovery request, my next motion will be to dismiss under *Brady*."

The mention of *Brady v. Maryland* raised Mayeda's eyebrows. *Brady* is the Supreme Court case that holds that prosecutors are under a constitutional obligation to disclose any evidence that might tend to show the defendant's innocence; the legal term of art was *exculpatory evidence*. By introducing the principle, I'd kicked up the stakes considerably because the DA's refusal to turn over such evidence required automatic dismissal of the case.

"Are you saying this is potentially exculpatory of your client?"

"Absolutely, Judge."

"Will you make an offer of proof?" Mayeda asked.

"Not in open court."

"All right," Mayeda said, "you and I will discuss this in chambers. We're in recess. Mr. Novotny, stay put."

Mayeda's chambers had an impressive view of the downtown skyline, but was otherwise merely functional. With its wood-paneled walls, fluorescent lights, and institutional carpeting, it could have been the office of a mid-level bureaucrat in the Department of Water and Power. Nor had he added many personal touches beyond the usual framed diplomas—Berkeley undergrad and USC law—and the obligatory plaques handed out like candy by various bar associations; no profession is as self-congratulatory as the law. The exception was a colored woodblock print that hung on the wall opposite the window. It was recognizably Japanese in technique and there was the familiar snow-capped mountain in the background, but in the foreground were a series of barracks-like buildings facing snowy streets.

"An internment camp?" I guessed as we sat down, he behind his uncluttered desk, me in the vinyl-covered chair across from him.

"Heart Mountain in Wyoming," he replied. "My parents met there while their families were interned."

"Heart Mountain," I repeated. "A beautiful name for such a cruel place."

"But not inappropriate, perhaps," he mused. "Heart Mountain was one of the centers of resistance against the draft by young Nisei men."

"Nisei?" I queried.

"It means second-generation and refers to the American-born child of Japanese immigrants. People like me, third generation, are Sansei. A number of Nisei men refused to be drafted until their families were released from the camps. They were arrested, prosecuted, and imprisoned. One of my uncles was among them. The older generations rarely speak of the camps, so I keep this as a reminder."

"A reminder of?" I prodded.

"The fragility of the law. Now, Mr. Rios, tell me why I should order the prosecution to disclose information about this undercover officer."

"Your Honor, my client told me that this officer, going by the name of Freddy Saavedra, came up with the plan to bomb Ekklesia, made the bombs, and told Theo where to plant them. Of course, my client didn't know—and still doesn't know—that Saavedra was a cop. Theo thought he was another gay man with whom Theo became obsessed at a moment when Theo was a heavy drug user and experiencing some rather intense emotional issues, which made him particularly vulnerable to Saavedra's influence. Saavedra used Theo's obsession as psychological leverage to draw Theo into his plot. It's a classic case of entrapment, but to make that argument I need official confirmation that the department deployed Saavedra as an agent provocateur."

Mayeda stroked his moustache in what I now recognized indicated he was thinking; his expression was otherwise unreadable.

I plunged on. "My investigator and I discovered Saavedra's actual identity and were able to obtain his military records showing he was on the bomb squad, which I believe gave him knowledge of how bombs are made. Furthermore, we can show he is currently an LAPD officer assigned to the anti-terrorism unit. I have a dozen witnesses besides my client who can testify that Saavedra infiltrated QUEER. That's all consistent with what my client is telling me."

After a moment, he said, "If true, your allegations against the department are shocking."

"They are not only true, Your Honor, they are consistent with LAPD's long-standing practice of infiltrating what it deems to be radical groups with agent provocateurs." I then gave him a crash course on the PDID.

"This is all rather overwhelming," he said, when I finished. "The government spying on its own people, trying to incriminate them in violent crimes."

"Your woodcut is eloquent proof of the kind of misconduct toward unpopular groups of citizens that the government is capable of."

He frowned. "It's not exactly the same, counsel."

"It's not that different," I countered.

More moustache stroking, and then, "I don't understand why the evidence you've already gathered isn't sufficient for your defense."

My heart sank a bit. Mayeda might be shocked, but he remained a cautious, even timid, jurist. Judges were not immune to political pressures, within the court and outside of it. *People versus Latour* was a high-profile case. Any misstep by Mayeda could result in consequences that ranged from spending the rest of his judicial career in traffic court to removal by the voters when he had to stand for election.

"Entrapment is an affirmative defense," I reminded him, "and the burden of proof is on the defense."

"I'm aware of that," he said, tightly. "But it's a much lesser burden than beyond a reasonable doubt. Preponderance of the evidence, isn't it?"

"That still requires me to prove entrapment was more likely than not. As you said, Judge, my allegations are shocking and, if my client is my only witness to them, a jury might be disinclined to believe them without official confirmation by the police department that it assigned Saavedra—uh, Sumaya—to infiltrate QUEER."

"You can do that through the testimony of the other members of the organization."

"All of whom are gay or lesbian, some of them with criminal records arising from their arrests for acts of civil disobedience. The prosecutor will claim they're biased or lying. My client, who admittedly planted the bombs, would be even easier to attack as lying to save his own skin."

"What about the issue of officer safety that Mr. Novotny raised? If the group discovers someone in their midst is a police officer, they could turn on him."

"No one in QUEER has seen him since the bombing. Unless he's working undercover somewhere else, there is no threat to his safety. The cops are perfectly capable of taking care of their own."

"Well, maybe that's the first thing we need to determine," he said. "Whether this man is still undercover. Let's find out."

"Back on the record," Mayeda said, after he'd seated himself on the dais. "Mr. Novotny, you suggested the officer's safety would be compromised if I granted the defense motion. We need to explore that further."

Novotny got to his feet and said, uncomfortably, "Yes, Your Honor."

"Is Officer Saav—uh, Sumaya, currently working in an undercover capacity?"

Novotny's hands tensed almost, but not quite, into fists. "I can't answer that, Judge."

Mayeda blinked in surprise. "Is that because you don't know or because you won't?"

"I am not at liberty to say anything about this officer, including his current assignment."

"We could go into chambers," Mayeda suggested.

"I'm sorry," Novotny replied. "I would still be unable to answer your question."

"Then why should I believe that granting the motion puts the officer in danger?" Mayeda asked impatiently.

"I make that representation as an officer of the court."

"I don't doubt your integrity, Mr. Novotny, but that is not good enough," Mayeda said. "The defense's offer of proof was quite persuasive. I'm inclined to grant the motion unless you can convince me that doing so would, in fact, compromise the officer's personal safety."

Novotny took a deep breath and exhaled. "I'd like to put this over until Monday to give me time to consult with my office and the police department."

I got to my feet. "I object to any delay. Mr. Novotny had more than enough time to talk to whoever he needed to talk to before today's hearing."

Mayeda said, "This is an important issue, counsel. I don't think giving Mr. Novotny a few more days is going to prejudice the defense. But, Mr. Novotny, on Monday I will expect better answers to my questions."

"Yes, Your Honor."

"This matter is put over to Monday morning. We're in recess."

Outside the courtroom I asked Novotny, "What's going on, Ralph?"

He shook his head wearily. "You really stirred the shit this time, Henry."

"Make me a reasonable offer and all this could go away."

"Any offer would have to be made by someone way above my pay grade," he said. "But I'll let them know."

He started to walk away.

"Tell your bosses I want the murder charge dropped," I called after him.

He waved his hand over his shoulder in what could have been either a gesture of dismissal or understanding.

FOURTEEN

High Power's attorney conference room was in use, so the sheriffs cleared the barber shop just outside the unit, handcuffed Theo to the barber chair, and left us to it. Theo took in his surroundings with a grin, spun in the chair and pointed to a jar of blue liquid on the counter.

"Barbicide," he said. "Is that what barbers drink to kill themselves?"

"I'm pretty sure it's disinfectant. How are you holding up?"

The grin became a tentative smile. "Uh, I'm actually . . . fine."

His jailhouse pallor was unmistakable, but his eyes were clear and beneath the jumpsuit he looked remarkably fit.

When I commented on that, he continued, "I exercise when I'm bored. Sit-ups, push-ups, isometrics. I only eat half the crap they serve us, so I won't get fat. My mom comes to see me almost every day. I get a lot of mail from gay guys who think I'm some kind of hero. I'm completely clean for the first time in my life. I'm reading and doing some writing, too. Telling my story. Maybe if I tell it, it will help some closeted kid make better decisions than I did. Anyway, except for the being locked-up part, I'm really okay, Henry."

His account was unusual, but not unheard of. I'd had a few other clients whose lives on the outside had been so chaotic and desperate that the regimentation of life in custody had given them structure and with it a certain measure of serenity and even purpose. Of course, it was early days for Theo. He might not feel so positive if he got handed a life sentence without possibility of parole. Or death.

"How's your health? Any changes?"

He shook his head. "Not so far."

"Good. I have some news for you, Theo. Freddy Saavedra is an undercover cop named Alfredo Sumaya."

"What!"

I gave him the complete story and showed him the photographs of Saavedra that Bruce Lindell had taken at the airport.

"Holy shit!" he exclaimed, looking at the pictures. "A cop." He handed them back to me. "Is this good for me?"

"It is," I said, and laid out the entrapment defense, though cautioning him that it was, by no means, a slam dunk. "The thing is," I concluded, "if this is our defense, you'll have to testify because you are the only one who can tell the jury how Saavedra induced you to participate in the bombing."

"Okay," he said. "What's the problem?"

"Once I put you on the stand, the DA gets a crack at you. He'll go for broke. He'll try to bring out everything he can about your past to discredit you."

"Like that I was a drug addict? That I did porn and escorted?"

"Yes," I said. "All that. If you really had a jury of your peers made up of other gay people, none of those things would be particularly shocking to them or discrediting to you, but we're going to be dealing with straight people. We can try to minimize the impact by bringing that stuff out on direct and relating it to how you were thrown out of your family as a teenager and had to make your own way."

"What about me being HIV positive?"

"I won't ask about that if you don't want me to."

"No," he said. "You have to. I want the jury to know because it was after I found out that my life fell apart. When I really starting drinking and using, when I got so angry and ashamed and scared. Freddy used that against me."

"All right, maybe the jury should hear about your status." I paused. "I know they'll want to hear remorse."

"That I'm sorry for killing that man? I *am* sorry. I am." He sighed. "I never meant to hurt anyone. I don't even know what he looked like."

I dug through the photographs and found an image of Daniel Herron talking to a couple of older men on the steps of the church. I handed it to Theo. "He's the man on the right."

Theo held the photograph up. "He's a nice-looking man. Was he married? Did he have kids?"

"Married," I said. "He and his wife didn't have children."

Theo didn't need to know about Herron's other family; even the dead are entitled to their privacy.

With a quizzical expression, Theo continued to examine the photograph.

"That's the guy," he said, finally.

"What guy?"

"The old guy on the left? That's the guy who was with the security guard who busted me and Freddy when we went to scout the church the Sunday before we planted the bombs. Who is he?"

I took the photograph and looked at the tall, thin, craggy-faced, white-haired man listening to Herron with a sour expression.

"No idea," I said, slipping the photograph back into my folder, "but I'll have Freeman track him down to testify he saw Freddy at the church that day."

When I got back to the office from the jail, Emma handed me three message slips that she'd paper-clipped together.

"What's this?"

"Someone who wants to talk to you very, very badly," she replied.

I looked at the name. Marc Unger.

The New York Company was a gay bar and restaurant close to the rambling Spanish Mission house Marc shared with his lover, a corporate lawyer named Jacob Miranda, at the crest of a hilly street above the Silverlake reservoir. I'd been to their house for a couple of dinners and while I liked them, they and their crowd were seriously committed drinkers, so I'd politely declined further invitations. Marc was at a corner table exchanging an empty glass for a full one from the handsome, hovering waiter. The waiter's face and the back of Marc's head were reflected in the smoked mirror wall that, along with the tiny pink-lensed follow spots, gave the place a theatrical appearance.

"Marc." I pulled out the barstool and joined him.

He looked up, his eyes heavy-lidded, the smell of expensive booze coming off his breath. He was still wearing his suit, a gray chalk stripe, but he'd loosened the burgundy tie and unbuttoned his top collar button to reveal a tuft of graying chest hair. "You want a drink?"

"I'm fine."

"Oh, right, you don't drink," he remembered. He touched his glass. "This won't bother you?"

"My problem is my drinking, not yours. You wanted to talk to me about the Latour case. What's the city's interest in a criminal case?"

"The same as always," he said, wearily. "Saving the department's bacon. The DA passed along your discovery request for Officer Sumaya. The department is not inclined to give you the information you want."

"I'm pretty sure that's not going to fly with Judge Mayeda. Is the department prepared to defy a court order?"

"I'm here to avoid a standoff." He tasted his drink. "What kind of plea are you looking for?"

"Wait," I said, startled. "You're the city attorney, not the district attorney. You don't have any authority to deal a criminal case."

He rolled his eyes. "Remember what I did with that case in Santa Monica that you were on? I have the authority to do whatever I need to do on behalf of the department to make this go away."

"That was a misdemeanor prosecution," I reminded him. "This is a capital murder case."

213

"What do you want," he asked irritably, "a note from my mom? You want a deal or not?"

"The fact that you're even offering me one is an admission that Sumaya infiltrated QUEER as an agent provocateur and goaded my client into participating in the bombing."

"It's not an admission of anything," he said, flatly. "There will be no admission of any wrongdoing by the department. That's the price of your deal."

He looked tired and half-drunk. I had a feeling this wasn't an easy assignment for him.

"This bothers you, doesn't it?" I asked. "It should. Your client stage-managed a violent attack on a church to swing votes to pass the quarantine initiative by painting gay people as terrorists."

He emptied his drink, held up the glass. The waiter materialized, and Marc grunted, "Same." When he left, Marc said, "The last time I looked the initiative was running behind by three points. Anyway, the sooner your case is resolved, the faster it drops off the public's radar."

"Answer me one question: Did Sumaya know Daniel Herron was going to be at the church when he blew it up?"

"I'm not here to answer any questions. I'm here to settle the case. What do you want?"

The waiter returned, depositing Marc's drink, and looked at me. I shook my head. He left.

"He'll plead to voluntary manslaughter. All the other charges are dismissed."

He stared at me disbelievingly. "Voluntary manslaughter? Three to eleven years for what he did? Are you crazy?"

"What he was entrapped to do."

"That's his story," Marc snapped. "Maybe we'll let Sumaya testify and tell a different story. Who do you think the jury will believe?"

"Let's see, an undercover cop with a background in explosives who was assigned to infiltrate a nonviolent organization and foment violence and who planned and participated in a church bombing that killed an innocent man. That story? The one I'll force out of him on what I promise will be a long, tough cross-examination."

Marc grumbled, "I can't sell manslaughter. He has to plead to murder."

"I'm listening."

"Second-degree murder, fifteen to life. He'd be eligible for parole in as little as five years."

I hadn't expected Marc to agree to manslaughter. Given the publicity surrounding the crime, I figured the DA would need to cover himself by being able to throw around the words "murder" and "life sentence" when, inevitably, people questioned why the case had pled out. He'd have to hope most people didn't look too closely at what he had given up—not only the death penalty or LWOP but even a first-degree murder conviction, which would have carried a minimum sentence of twenty-five years. It was a good deal, the best deal I could have expected. Marc wouldn't be offering it unless whoever he was answering to believed there was a real possibility of an acquittal if I got their cop on the stand.

And that was my dilemma. If I went to trial, maybe I could get an acquittal, but juries are notoriously unpredictable. I'd met Freddy Saavedra, but not Officer Alfredo Sumaya. As Sumaya, he might clean up nicely and present well to the jury. Also, I only had Theo's side of the story, and it is a truth universally acknowledged that all criminal defendants lie to their lawyers about something. I didn't know if Sumaya would reveal details of his relationship with Theo that Theo had lied to me about that would complicate the entrapment defense.

Then there was the near certainty that some jurors, no matter what they said on *voir dire*, would be biased against gays. Finally, the fact remained that a man had been killed—and a clergyman at that. It was only natural that the jurors would want to see someone punished, particularly if the DA brought it as a capital case and emphasized the atrocity of the killing. I'd seen the photos of what was left of Daniel Herron's body and could imagine the DA passing them around to the jurors as the medical examiner testified in full and disturbing detail to the manner and cause of death.

"He has to serve his sentence in Vacaville."

"The prison hospital?" Marc asked, puzzled.

"He's HIV-positive, Marc."

"Jesus," he muttered. "You know placement's up to the Department of Corrections."

"If the judge recommends confinement at Vacaville and the DA concurs because of Freddy's status Corrections won't fight it," I said. "It's in the department's interests to have HIV-positive inmates in one place where they can be cared for and monitored."

He smirked. "You mean they should be quarantined?"

"They're already confined, Marc. It's not the same thing at all. Right now, those inmates are scattered through a system that doesn't even provide condoms—"

"Because butt sex is strictly prohibited in prison," he interjected.

"—much less appropriate medical care," I concluded.

"Write a letter to the editor. Do we have a deal?"

"I need to sell it to my client."

"It's a fucking gift and you know it," he growled.

"I don't imagine he'll object."

He nodded. "How did you figure out Sumaya was undercover?"

"That's privileged. How long before the bombing did you know he was working undercover in QUEER?"

"Privileged."

"Have the cops infiltrated other gay organizations?"

"Also privileged."

"So that's a yes. You're all right with this, Marc? The cops going into our community and trying to discredit the organizations fighting AIDS when no one else gives a shit? You're good with that?"

"Fuck you, Henry. Would you rather have me keeping an eye on the cops or some straight guy who'd sign off on whatever shit they wanted to pull?'

I had to give him that. Marc wasn't closeted or self-loathing or reactionary; he was an out gay man, active in the community and politically progressive. He might not be much of a watchdog on the cops but better any kind of watchdog than a lapdog.

216

"Point taken," I said.

He sighed. "I really wish you drank so we could get drunk together."

I smiled. "You're doing fine without me. You need a lift home?"

"Jacob can come and pour me into his car."

"Give him my regards."

"He wants you to come to dinner. He has a doctor he wants to set you up with. A brain surgeon, no less."

"I'm dating someone," I said.

Marc's eyes widened. "What? You've been holding out on me."

"We just dealt a capital case. My love life didn't seem relevant."

"I have to meet the guy who took you away from me. Come to dinner anyway and bring him. Jacob will call."

"Sure. Good-night, Marc."

I stopped at the entrance, glanced back, and saw him order another drink.

"It's a good deal," I said to Theo and his mother.

"But," she said, "my boy didn't mean to kill anyone."

The three of us sat in the attorney conference room. I'd received special permission to include her in the meeting. It was remarkable how cooperative everyone had become after my conversation with Marc Unger.

I was about to explain to her the felony-murder rule when Theo said, "It's okay, Ma. Henry's right. I planted the bombs at the church, even if I didn't know anyone was there. I didn't make sure the place was empty. I deserve to be punished for that, and fifteen to life is better than death."

"He'd be eligible for parole in as little as five years," I said.

She reached for her son's hand. "I'm the one who should be punished for not standing up for you."

"You're here now," he said.

"You forgive me?" she asked, tearily.

"You know I do. You forgive me for all the worry I caused you?"

"Oh, Theo . . ." She pressed his hand.

He turned to me. "I'll take the deal."

"It's the right thing to do," I said. "Trials are crapshoots. Now at least you know you'll have a future."

"Unless AIDS gets me first."

His mother said, "Don't say that, Theo."

"You'll be at the medical facility," I reminded him, "and your mom and I are both going to be keeping an eye on you."

He nodded. "I appreciate that."

"We'll be back in court next Monday to take your plea. Mrs. Phillips, we need to go."

She grasped his hand in both of hers. "I love you, baby."

"I love you, too, Ma. Don't worry. Everything's going to be okay."

That weekend QUEER threw a fundraiser barbecue for Theo's legal defense fund at Laura Acosta's bungalow in Atwood Village. By the time Josh and I arrived, the nearest street parking was two blocks away. A rainbow of balloons attached to Laura's mailbox marked her house, but the blaring disco music and kids passing joints on the veranda made the same point. We passed through small crowded rooms to the unexpectedly capacious back yard where I caught sight of Kim Phillips.

Theo's mother was clutching a drink with a dazed expression. I tried to imagine the scene through her eyes—the shirtless boys making out on the lawn, bodies twisted together like origami; the spiky-haired, nose-pierced boy in cut-off jeans and a Keith Haring T-shirt; the slender young woman in a sundress patterned with sunflowers, wearing combat boots and with bright pink and purple hair; and Laura Acosta, a striped apron covering her pink guayabera shirt and khakis, standing at an enormous grill, prodding meat with a long fork with one hand and chugging a beer with the other. The warm, still air reeked of grilled beef, beer, and pheromones.

"Kim," I said. "I didn't expect to see you here."

"Theo told me about it," she replied. "This is really something."

"It's a party," I replied. "These people are here to help your son and to have fun while they're doing it. This is my boyfriend, Josh."

"Hi," Josh said, extending a hand. "It's nice to meet you. I've been friends with Theo for a long time."

She took his hand. "You're the one who took him off the streets and let him stay with you."

Josh nodded.

"Thank you," she said. "I hope he didn't get you into too much trouble."

"All that matters now is helping him."

She pressed his hand and released it. To me, she said, "I wanted to thank the person in charge."

I smiled. "If you find that person, let me know."

"What?" she replied, confused.

"Never mind. Let me introduce you to our host."

We made our way to Laura.

"*Hombre!*" she shouted when she saw me. "You made it!"

I squeezed through the throng to reach her. "This is quite a turnout."

"I just hope we have enough food. Tacos for the meat eaters, veggie burgers for the vegetarians plus all kinds of salads, rice, and beans. Yeah, it's a big crowd, and half the people I've never seen before, not at our meetings anyway."

"Laura, this is Kim Phillips, Theo's mom. She wanted to thank you for throwing the fundraiser."

Laura handed me the fork and her beer and embraced the older woman. "I'm glad you're here, Kim."

Nonplussed, Kim murmured, "Um, thank you. I'm glad I'm here, too."

In the same commanding voice she used to quiet the babble at QUEER meetings, Laura shouted, "Hey, everyone, settle down for a minute. I want to introduce you to two important people. This is Henry Rios, Theo's lawyer, and this is Kim, Theo's mom."

Her announcement was greeted by finger snaps and cheers.

219

"Let me take you around and introduce you to Theo's friends," Laura said. "Rios, mind the grill."

"I really don't know how to cook," I said.

She grinned. "And you call yourself a *maricón*." She peered through the bodies, spotted who she was looking for, and called, "Patty, come over here!"

The pink and purple-haired woman in the sunflower dress cut through the crowd.

"Henry, Kim, *mi novia*, Patty. Patty, *el abogado y la madre*. Listen, will you take charge of the grill for a minute so I can take Kim around?"

Patty rolled her eyes and said, "You know I'm a vegetarian."

"*M'ija*, no one's asking you to eat the meat; just make sure it doesn't burn."

I handed the fork to Patty and followed Laura and Kim into the crowd. A firm hand on my shoulder stopped me. I turned. Two men stood before me, the taller of the two still grasping my shoulder. He was a six-foot-something, middle-aged, pink-faced man with thinning, cornstalk blond hair, blue eyes, and decisive features, wearing khakis and a blue Lacoste polo shirt over a religiously exercised body. His companion was a little shorter and at least ten years younger, a handsome, leanly muscular African-American guy with sculpted features and warm eyes in a pink Lacoste polo and carefully pressed white walking shorts. They looked prosperous and out of place in the ragamuffin QUEER crowd; I would have pegged them as Log Cabin Republicans.

"Mr. Rios," the older man said, dropping his hand. "I'm Ed Madden, and this is my partner, Tom Lucas. We wanted to thank you for taking Theo's case. Can you talk about the kind of defense you're planning?"

"Well, actually, I can't. Attorney-client privilege."

"He did it in self-defense," Tom Lucas said abruptly.

"I beg your pardon."

"Killing those bigots is self-defense," he continued. "I only wish he'd thrown the bomb during a church service and taken out more of them."

I glanced at Madden, expecting to see censure but he was nod-ding. When he saw my dismay, he said, "This initiative makes it pretty clear it's us or them."

"We'll defeat them at the ballot, not by blowing up their churches," I said. "Violence doesn't change minds; it only leads to revenge."

"You think if we win that's the end of it?" the younger man demanded. "They're going to keep coming back, year after year, with some new scheme to shove us back into the closet."

"And we'll keep fighting them," I replied.

Lucas said, "Keep fighting them? No one should have to live like that. Just once, Mr. Rios, I'd like to wake up in the morning and not already be furious."

His lover embraced him from behind, arms crossed around the younger man's chest. "We're both HIV positive," Madden said. "Fighting the virus and these bigots—that's asking a lot."

"I know it is."

"My friends die lying in their own shit," Lucas said, in a fury. "Blind, in terrible pain. And these Christians want to lock us up? Hell, yeah, we should kill them. Let them see what it feels like to lose people you love."

His eyes were furious, daring me to contradict him. I didn't know what else to say. Fortunately, Josh grabbed my hand and said to the men, "Will you excuse us? Come on, Henry, you need to eat something."

He dragged me away before I could protest, pulled me beneath an awning that shaded a corner of the patio, and pushed me into a plastic lawn chair.

"Sit," he said, "and don't talk to anyone else."

A moment later, he returned with a plate of food and a glass of iced tea. "Here."

"What's all this? Did you think I needed rescuing?" I asked, balancing the plastic plate on my lap.

"Yes," he said. He pulled up another chair and sat. "Sometimes when you come home from work, you have this look, like you're carrying too many secrets and they're all disturbing. You had that

221

look just now talking to those guys. You can't carry the weight for everyone."

"That's the job," I muttered.

"This isn't work. Relax. Eat. Enjoy the sun."

"You should eat, too."

"I'll get a plate in a minute." His eyes followed Laura and Mrs. Phillips working the crowd. "It's nice that Theo's mom is here."

"They've reconciled." I put down the forkful of beef I'd been about the eat. "You haven't said anything about your family lately."

"I've been talking to my sisters. They've both been working on my dad, but he still won't see me."

"What about your mom?"

"She won't go against him. They're their own little world; they've always been like that. Sam and Selma Mandel versus the universe."

"You're their only son."

"My dad has very traditional ideas about the sexes. Men work and women raise the children. Daughters get married and make grandchildren. Sons get a good education, become professionals, start families of their own."

"One of your sisters is a nurse," I pointed out. "The other one is an elementary school principal."

"Yeah, but they gave him grandkids. I was the disappointment and now I'm more than that. I'm *tref*."

"What does that mean?"

"Literally, food that's not kosher, but my dad uses it to describe anything he considers disgusting. Homosexuals? Definitely *tref*."

"That's appalling."

"I've been giving you a one-sided picture of him," he said. "Once, when I was three or four, we were at a restaurant and a baby started crying, just howling. I was always sensitive, and the baby made me sad and I started crying too. My dad took me outside, squatted down, dried my eyes with his handkerchief, and said, 'Don't cry, Joshie. The baby is not sad or hurt. Crying is how babies talk because they don't have words yet.' Then he kissed me and took me back inside and sat me on his lap for the rest of the meal and fed me from his plate. See, he can be that kind of dad, too."

222

"I hope he can find it in himself to be that kind of dad again. For both your sakes."

"My sisters will wear him down. Persistence is their secret power."

"I love you, you know."

He kissed me. "I love you, too. Henry, do you think this is all happening really fast? We've only known each other a couple of months but I'm basically living with you."

"When you meet in the trenches, and the bullets are flying around you, things speed up. Judgments, decisions, plans. It's life during wartime."

"If things were different," he began, tentatively, "not so crazy, or so scary, would you still want to be with me?"

I looked into his beautiful eyes and said, "I can't imagine any world where I wouldn't want to be with you."

On Sunday evening, I sat at the kitchen table watching Josh chop vegetables for a stir fry while the rice cooker steamed. Cooking, I had discovered, was his secret passion and he was very good at it. I'd never eaten so well. The sun had set but it was not yet night. Still, the room was gloomy, shadows creeping from the corners, the high ceiling fading into darkness. The kitchen was tiled in hand-painted Talavera tiles in green and blue, a big brass light fixture hanging above the island, copper pots and pans hanging from the walls. Ridiculously oversized, like the rest of the place, for two men. I'd been the legal owner of the house for nearly a year, since Larry's death, but I still felt like a squatter. I mentioned this again as Josh sliced mushrooms.

"You could try to make it your place," he suggested. "Buy different furniture, have it repainted?"

"Larry's suits are still hanging in the closet in the master bedroom."

"That's not the bedroom we sleep in?"

"No," I said. "We're in the guest suite." I sighed. "I can't stay here. We can't stay here. It will always be Larry's house to me."

"What are you thinking?"

"We could sell it."

"We?" he asked, smiling.

"We could sell it and buy a place that would be ours."

"You know I don't have money for a house."

"I don't either." I laughed. "But if we sold the place, we could get something smaller with the money. I'd like to stay in this neighborhood. I love it up here in the hills. It's quiet."

"I do too," he said. He pointed his spatula at me. "Are you formally asking me to move in with you?"

I stood up, approached him, and embraced him from behind. "Will you move in with me, Josh?"

He tossed a handful of chopped garlic and ginger into the wok. The oil popped and sizzled.

"Stand back, Henry, and yes, I will."

"That makes me really happy."

Whatever he was about to say was cut off by the phone.

He frowned. "Are you going to answer that?"

Sunday evening calls were never good news.

"I have to. It's probably a client in jail." I picked up the receiver from the wall phone. "Hello . . . Yes, this is Henry Rios . . . Yes, he's my client. . . . What? . . . When? . . . No, don't move him. I'm on my way."

I slammed down the phone.

Alarmed, Josh asked, "Henry? What—"

"Theo's dead. He hanged himself in his cell."

FIFTEEN

The cops had removed Theo's body and shipped it to the medical examiner despite my demand he be left in his cell, exactly as he'd been found, to allow me to inspect the scene. My protests were met with contempt—the sheriffs telling me they were a jail, not a morgue. When I asked whether photographs had been taken for their investigation, I was told there would be no investigation because there was no question about cause of death. The only information they gave—grudgingly—was that Theo had torn a sheet into strips, braided the strips together, and hanged himself.

I left the jail furious at being stonewalled by the sheriffs and incredulous that Theo had killed himself. It didn't take long for the two to gel into suspicion and suspicion to harden into certainty. Theo's conveniently timed suicide terminated his case without any repercussions to the district attorney or the Los Angeles Police Department. The DA wouldn't have to explain why he had plea bargained a notorious capital case to second-degree murder; the threat of exposing LAPD's involvement in the church bombing evaporated with Theo's death; and, in public opinion, Theo's suicide would amount to a virtual confession.

I knew the back story, but without Theo, that's all it would be, unproven allegations against the police department that could not be tested in any public forum. I knew in my heart Theo had not taken his own life—he'd been murdered. I would demand the medical examiner's report and, if necessary, seek a second autopsy from an independent lab. I knew, however, if his death was what I thought it was, I could count on methodical official obstruction, from further stonewalling to evidence tampering. Because what I believed was that Theo had been murdered by his jailers.

I slammed the desk. "I want to see Mr. Unger. Now."

The receptionist, taken aback by my fury, stuttered, "Is, uh . . . do you have an appointment?"

"Tell him it's Henry Rios."

She picked up her phone, pushed a button, and murmured into it, too low for me to hear. She hung up. "He'll be right out."

The windows looked east, toward Chinatown and beyond to an industrial landscape of warehouses and small factories. A gray pall hung in the sky, obscuring the San Gabriel mountains. I tried to compose myself, but I was so wound up I felt a single misstep and I'd be shattered.

"Henry?" With a quizzical expression on his face, Marc approached, hand extended. I ignored it.

"Theo Latour was found dead in his cell just after midnight," I said. "What do you know about that?"

He dropped his hand, and his face tightened. "In my office."

On his desk was a foam container with the remnants of breakfast in it—bits of scrambled egg and bacon, a crust of toast. Beside it was an oversized cup of coffee. He cleared away the food, sat down behind his desk, and said, "Latour is dead? How?"

"The sheriffs say he hanged himself."

"This is the first I'm hearing of it."

"I bet."

His head jerked back. "What is that supposed to mean?"

"Who did you tell in LAPD about the deal we reached and when did you tell them?"

"Communications with my client are privileged."

"Don't try to hide behind privilege. I know you told the cops."

"If you know, why are you asking and where are you going with this?"

"Whoever you told in LAPD didn't think the plea bargain you agreed to gave the department enough protection. They figured the only way to shut it down completely was to kill Theo. Or maybe the DA refused to make the deal and the department had to come up with another way to close the case."

"Are you seriously suggesting the department killed your client? That's insane. In the first place, the jail's run by the sheriff, not LAPD."

"Oh, please. I'm sure the department's helped clean up more than a few of the sheriff's fuck-ups, enough for someone to call in a favor."

"Second," he said, ignoring me, "the police aren't murderers."

"You can say that with a straight face," I said, mockingly. "Your entire practice is defending killer cops."

"Watch your mouth," he said in a low, dangerous voice.

"Theo Letour was killed to prevent a department scandal."

"Your hatred of the police has made you paranoid."

"How many millions did the city have to pay out last year to settle complaints of police brutality?" I shouted.

He shouted back at me, "Your guy killed himself. Period. End of the story. Now, get out. I have work to do."

I got up. "This isn't over."

"I said get out."

There was still the matter of my pending discovery motion in Judge Mayeda's court. When I arrived in the courthouse, Theo's mother was sitting on a bench outside the courtroom. I knew immediately from her hopeful expression that the cops hadn't informed her of her son's death.

"Mr. Rios," she said, rising. "Will Theo be here?"

I took a breath. "We need to talk. There's a conference room at the end of the hall."

227

❧ ❧ ❧

I made it into the courtroom just as the bailiff was calling the court into session. I hurried to the counsel table as Mayeda entered from behind the dais and took his seat high above us. Other than the court staff, the only people in the room were Novotny and me. Theo's mother had left after we talked, to locate Theo's body. The last thing she'd said to me, repeating it over and over, still echoed in my head: "Theo wouldn't kill himself."

"*People versus Latour,*" Mayeda said. "We're here for a disposition on the defense's discovery motion. Mr. Novotny, you'd asked for time to consult your office and the Los Angeles Police Department."

Novotny glanced at me. "Uh, Your Honor, there's been a development in the case. Maybe Mr. Rios—"

"My client is dead, Your Honor."

Mayeda's clerk and the court reporter both abruptly stopped what they had been doing to stare at me. Mayeda's fingers reached to his face automatically to smooth his moustache. After a moment, he asked, "What happened?"

"He was apparently found dead in his cell," I replied.

I felt Novotny's eyes on me, evidently waiting for me to continue, but when I didn't, he spoke up. "He hanged himself, Your Honor."

"That's what I was told," I said. "But I cannot confirm the manner of his death. The sheriffs ignored my request to preserve the scene until I arrived and took no photographs. I was also told they aren't going to conduct an investigation."

"Mr. Rios," Mayeda said, leaning forward. "Are you suggesting he didn't hang himself?"

"I'm saying I have no personal knowledge of the circumstances of my client's death."

Novotny scoffed, "I think we can take the sheriff's word on it."

I turned to him. "Maybe you can." I turned back to the judge. "I want to put something on the record. After Friday's session, I was asked to meet with Marc Unger, the city attorney in charge

228

of the Police Litigation Unit. Mr. Unger told me that, in exchange for withdrawing my discovery motion, the District Attorney would agree to a plea in this case to second-degree murder, dropping all other charges and special circumstance allegations. I conveyed that news to my client who agreed to the plea. He was very happy and relieved, but seven hours later he was dead. With his death, the case is over, and both the discovery motion and the plea agreement mooted."

A long, heavy silence followed my remarks. Eventually, Mayeda turned to Novotny and asked, "Was your office going to make that deal?"

"I believe the district attorney was in discussions with the city attorney."

"Is that a yes?" Mayeda pressed.

"Before I found out that the defendant was dead, my instructions were to request a short continuance to try to work out a plea."

"The plea Mr. Rios talked about?"

"Basically," Novotny said.

"It does seem odd that a defendant who was about to escape death row would kill himself," Mayeda mused. "But then, we can't really know what's in anyone's mind."

Novotny piped up. "He had AIDS."

I turned on him. "You son of a bitch."

"Counsel!" Mayeda snapped. Then, to me, "Is that true, Mr. Rios?"

"Judge, you know better than to ask me to disclose that information. It's both privileged and protected by state law prohibiting disclosure of someone's HIV status."

"Of course," Mayeda said, quickly, but we both knew my response amounted to a yes.

"At the time of his death, my client was in good health, physically and mentally, and he was not suicidal. That much I can say."

For a long moment, no one said anything; then Novotny piped up, "Your Honor, in light of the defendant's suicide," he emphasized the word, "the People move to dismiss all charges."

"Mr. Rios? Any objection?"

"My client did not commit suicide."

Mayeda said, "The People's motion is granted. The case is dismissed."

"Henry?

Josh stood beneath the archway into the living room where I had burrowed into one of the elegant leather lounge chairs that flanked the equally elegant matching sofa arranged in front of the tiled fireplace. A thick treatise on California criminal procedure lay open on my lap. He stepped out of the dimness into the lamplight in a T-shirt and blue briefs, yawning.

"What are you doing up?" I asked.

He pulled up an ottoman to the foot of my chair and sat down. "Me? What about you? It's like, three in the morning."

A lock of sleep-disheveled hair fell across his forehead, and he rubbed the crust from the corner of his eyes. For a moment I could see the small, handsome, friendly, inquisitive little boy he must have been and felt a surge of affection toward him.

I tapped the book in my lap. "Working."

"At this hour? On what?"

"Theo's case."

"What else can you do for him?" he asked softly.

"I don't know. Probably nothing but . . . he didn't kill himself, Josh."

"You said you saw his body and it looked like a hanging."

"He could have been drugged or forced."

"Weren't there other prisoners in the—what do you call it—the ward?"

"Cell block," I said. "He could have been killed somewhere else and brought back to the cell or killed in his cell late at night. Anyway, if you're an inmate and you see the cops kill an inmate, are you going to rat them out? You could be next."

"Even if the police were involved, how can you prove it?"

"I was hoping this book would show me a way to keep the case alive, but so far, nothing."

He picked up the book. "Criminal procedure. What does that mean, exactly?"

"It's the rules for how a criminal case is prosecuted from arrest to appeal. Some of the rules are constitutional, some are ordinary statutes, and some are the product of judicial opinions." I took the book from him, closed it, weighed it in my hands. "The whole damn spiderweb." I set the book aside. "But I can't find anything in it to help me get justice for Theo Latour."

He climbed into my lap and laid his head on my shoulder. I slipped a hand beneath his T-shirt and rubbed slow circles on his back. He mumbled something into my neck.

"What was that?" I asked.

He raised his head and said, "I asked, aren't there other kinds of law?"

"Besides criminal? Sure."

"Could the answer be in one of them?"

He put his head back on my shoulder and I continued to stroke his back as I thought about his question. Thought and thought and thought and then—

"Hey," he murmured, "why did you stop? That felt nice."

"Josh, you're a genius."

"I am? Why?"

"I'll explain later. Let's go to bed. I think I'll be able to sleep now."

Susanna Vane was one of the lawyers I'd called for background information on the history of the LAPD's counter-intelligence operations. She was among the handful of lawyers who had represented plaintiffs in actions against the department—the police misconduct bar. Short, round and sixty-something, she looked like a grandmother, and may well have been, but she was also a charter member of the generation of leftist lawyers—the Bill

Kunstlers and Ramsey Clarks—who had cut their teeth representing members of radical Black and antiwar organizations in the 1960s. Since the mid-'70s she had made a specialty of taking on the cops. From behind wire-rimmed glasses, her gray-blue eyes assessed me as I finished explaining what had brought me to her modest office in Westwood. I'd come to pitch her a wrongful death action against the police and sheriff's departments and the city and county of Los Angeles arising from Theo Latour's death.

"You already know the case," she said when I was done. "Why don't you file the suit yourself?"

"I'm a criminal defense lawyer. You specialize in police misconduct cases; plus, if we go to trial, I'd be a witness."

She nodded. "Testifying to the plea bargain and to Mr. Latour's mental state and demeanor in the hours before he died."

"Yes, that, and the results of my investigation into the department's complicity in the bombing."

"Possible complicity," she replied. "You never got the department to produce official confirmation of Sumaya's undercover assignment."

"Judge Mayeda was on the verge of granting my discovery request before Unger made me the deal and Theo died. Once you file, you can make the same discovery request. Plus, as I understand it, discovery is a lot broader in civil cases than on the criminal side."

"That's true, but even if I get that discovery, it won't mean much without Mr. Latour's testimony that the officer built the bombs and told Latour where to plant them."

"I could testify to what Theo told me about that."

"It's hearsay, Henry."

"It falls under the exception for statements made against the declarant's penal interest," I argued. "Theo admitted he planted the bombs, implicating himself in the crime."

She smiled. "Nice try, but that exception would only get in Mr. Latour's statement against his penal interest, not anything he said about Sumaya's involvement."

"Any judge could see they're inextricably connected."

"Not any judge, but maybe the right judge. I'd say we have a forty-sixty chance of getting past a hearsay objection."

"Even without Theo's statements, the circumstantial evidence I gathered about Sumaya's involvement is pretty strong, and who knows what else you might get out of the cops in discovery, like the names of officers on duty the night Theo died and a list of the inmates in the adjacent cells. Videotapes from the jail, the medical examiner's raw notes. All the things I can't get now that my client's dead."

"They'll fight me tooth and nail."

"I hear you like a little blood on the canvas."

She smiled. "My reputation proceeds me. But, there's another big question. Who's my client?"

"Theo's mother, Kim Phillips. She's agreed to bring the case if you agree to take it."

"I don't suppose she has any money," Susanna said, resignedly.

"There is some," I replied. "About fifteen thousand raised for Theo's defense in the criminal case."

"That won't get us past the first motion to dismiss," she sighed. "Okay, do you have your case file?"

"In a box in the trunk of my car."

"Leave it with my secretary and give me three days to review it; then bring in Mrs. Phillips."

"You'll take the case?"

"A boy the cops killed in his jail cell after setting him up to take the fall for murder? Oh, yes, I'll take the case."

Persuading Susanna Vane to bring a wrongful death action for Theo was only half my strategy of exposing LAPD's complicity in the bombing. The second half had brought me to a modest two-story stucco apartment building, indistinguishable from hundreds of other such buildings in the city, on a palm tree-lined street in Culver City. I rang the bell next to the name tag that identified the resident as "Herron." A second later a buzzer sounded, and I pushed through the double-glass doors into a small entryway that opened up to an enclosed patio. A deserted pool glittered in the late afternoon light. I climbed the stairs to the second floor and knocked at apartment 207.

The woman who answered the door looked nothing like the woman who had come to my office with the implausible story of how her husband had been killed by people in his own church. That woman had looked like the mother in a 1950s sitcom who pushed a vacuum cleaner around a spotless living room in heels and pearls. This woman wore a man's oxford cloth button-down, jeans and flats; her face was bare of makeup, and her hair had been clipped into a short bob. Her bare face projected vulnerability and uncertainty—the face of a real person, not the plastic visage she had presented at our last meeting. She was also sober.

"Mrs. Herron, thank you for seeing me."

"Come in," she said.

The living room was over-furnished with pieces that were too big and too old-fashioned for the modest space. It was as if they'd been salvaged from a shipwreck.

"Sit down, please, Mr. Rios. Would you like coffee?"

"Call me Henry," I said. "I'll have some if you are."

With a trace of a smile, she replied, "I'm Jess. Coffee's all I drink since—" She stopped herself, squared her shoulders a bit and continued. "I owe you an apology."

"For what?"

"I was drunk when I came to see you," she said matter-of-factly. "I've since stopped drinking and as part of my—well, my new leaf, I'm required to—"

"Make amends?" I guessed. "The ninth step."

Surprised, she asked, "You're sober, too?"

"I've got just under three years."

"Ninety-one days," she replied.

"Congratulations. How's that going?"

"Let me get our coffee," she said and excused herself into the kitchen.

On a credenza behind the dining table was a small collection of framed photographs: a black-and-white studio photograph of a couple I assumed were her parents, a wedding picture of her and Daniel Herron, and a picture of a lovely African-American woman and a handsome young man who I took to be her son. I set the photo down and stepped back in the living room just as she entered from the kitchen with a tray holding two mugs of coffee, sugar, cream, and spoons. We both sat and busied ourselves with the coffee for a moment.

"How am I doing?" she said. "Strangely enough for the daughter and wife of a preacher, the hardest part for me has been all the talk in the steps of relying on God. The church ostracized me after Daniel died. I didn't want anything to do with God."

"The God references bothered me, too, in the beginning, since I was basically an atheist."

"But not anymore?" she asked, lifting the mug to her lips.

"No, I'm still basically an atheist."

"How do you deal with the God talk?"

I sipped my coffee and thought about how to frame a sensible answer to a difficult question. "By atheist I mean I don't believe there's an old man sitting on a throne in the sky keeping a list of my virtues and my vices either to torture or reward me when I die. What's kept me going is the kindness, or maybe I should say the love, that I got in the program. That and a sense of my own truth about who I am and what matters to me. When my sponsor coaxed those admissions out of me, he said, well, there's your God, love and self-acceptance. That's enough for me. I don't worry about what anyone else means by God."

"Your sponsor sounds like a wise person."

The warmth of the mug between my hands felt almost like the warmth of Larry's hand grasping mine. "He was."

"Oh, is he—"

"He died last year. Suddenly. A brain aneurysm while he was in Mexico purchasing drugs for people with AIDS."

I hadn't told her I was gay, and now I watched her face as pieces fell into place. "I'm sorry for the loss of your friend."

She assumed Larry was my lover. I almost corrected her, but maybe it was good to leave her with the image of two sober gay men who had made a life together, so I let it go.

"I owe you an apology, too. I wasn't honest with you when you came to see me. I'd met your husband."

"Daniel? How?"

"I've been living at Larry's house since he died. Daniel got Larry's name as someone who could help him get experimental drugs for his son. Daniel called the house and got me. I set up a meeting with another man who has also been active in the drug underground."

"What did he tell you?"

"That his son was infected, and he would do anything to save his life. I told him about the drug trials that, I guess, he tried to get his son into when he called Congressman Schultz."

She absorbed this for a moment. "So, indirectly, you're responsible for me finding out about Daniel's other family because if you hadn't told him about the drug trials and he hadn't called Schultz, his dreadful wife wouldn't have called me."

"I suppose I am. I'm sorry if I contributed to your grief."

"Maybe it was necessary grief. Everything that happened from the moment Daniel called you has led me here. I'm sad about some of it, but not sorry." She wrapped her fingers around her mug, and asked, "Do any of the drugs work? The ones your friends smuggle in?"

"For some people they provide at least some temporary symptom relief, but they're not a cure."

She raised her cup, sipped coffee, set it down, and asked haltingly, "Do you think your friends would let me help them?"

"Bringing in drugs?"

She nodded.

"It's illegal."

She ran a hand through her clipped hair and said, "That God you talked about, the old man in the sky? I'm afraid part of me still believes in him though I may just be picturing my father. Either way, I want to free myself from him. I think one way is to help people that that God condemns. If I can find the humanity in the people I was raised to believe are sinners, maybe I can find my own humanity. Does that make sense?"

I smiled. "You want to join us lepers?"

Over the rim of her mug, she said, "Why not? Jesus washed your feet. He knew something I need to learn."

"What happened to you?" I asked.

"Oh, you mean what was my moment of clarity?"

"If you want to call it that."

"My mother was an alcoholic who spent the last few years of her life in bed while I took care of her—that meant, mostly, supplying her with vodka and taking out the empties. She was quite pathetic. I told myself, I will never be like her. One morning, four months ago, I came to in my bed in a puddle of urine, clutching an empty bottle of vodka. I realized I had become my mother, but with one difference: I had no one to take care of me. No one to change the sheets, get me into the shower, make excuses, listen to my ranting. I felt utterly alone. I considered killing myself because why not, what did I have to live for? But something stronger than self-pity and self-loathing and despair rose up inside of me and said, 'No.' That's all, Henry, a voice cut through the fog and said, 'No. No, you will not die.' It spoke with such authority, such certainty, I knew better than to argue with it. So, I had to figure out a way to stay alive. And here I am. Will your friends let me help them?"

"I'll talk to them, tell them about you, and give them your phone number. I'm sure they'll be in touch."

"Thank you," she replied. "But you didn't come here to talk about any of this. You said something about a lawsuit."

"I hope to persuade you to file a wrongful death action on Daniel's behalf."

"I don't understand. Wasn't your client responsible for Dan's death? You want me to sue him? What would be the point of that? He's dead, too."

"You wouldn't be suing Theo. You'd be going in with his mother in suing the Los Angeles Police Department."

"What?" She was shocked. "The police? Why?"

For the next half hour I told her about Alfredo Sumaya a.k.a. Freddy Saavedra and how he had infiltrated QUEER and engineered the bombing of the church. I explained that, because Sumaya had been working in his capacity as an undercover police officer, the department was civilly liable for his actions up to and including Daniel's death.

"Wait a minute," she said, stopping me. "Are you saying the police department told this Freddy to blow up Ekklesia?"

"I don't know what its exact instructions were to him. That's something we'd have to find out in discovery. I do know he was working in his capacity as a police officer. The department's not only responsible for the consequences of the actions it told him to take, but also the consequences of any actions that were a foreseeable result of those instructions. Maybe his supervisors didn't say, 'Talk these gay people into blowing up a church.' Maybe all they said was, 'Implicate this gay organization in some kind of violent crime to discredit it.' That would be enough to put the department on the hook for any criminal activity Sumaya encouraged and participated in."

"All right, I think I understand, but why me? Why do I need to sue?"

"You're Daniel's surviving spouse. Spouses and children are the people authorized by the law to sue for wrongful death."

"Why do you want to do this now?"

"There's a statute of limitations on these actions. Not for a while yet, but it's better to strike now before the case gets stale." She looked dubious, so I added, "Don't you want the people responsible for Daniel's death to be held accountable?"

"I don't know, Henry. I'm making a new life for myself. I'm not sure I want to be dragged back into the old one."

"You seemed pretty adamant the first time you came to see me," I said. "You believed people in the church were involved in Daniel's death. Do you still?"

With a slight shake of her head, she said, "I was a different person then. Bitter, resentful, and drunk."

"Okay, but that doesn't answer my question. Do you still believe that?"

She spoke slowly, thoughtfully. "There were people in the leadership of the church who would have liked to get rid of Daniel. Those same people benefited from his death. After he died, I had my suspicions but no proof, and after I got sober the suspicions seemed like part of the insanity of alcoholism."

"Do your suspicions seem any crazier to you than the fact that a police officer planned the bombing of Ekklesia?"

She thought about that for a couple of minutes. "Dan and I didn't have a good marriage," she began, crisply. "Or maybe what I mean is we didn't have an honest marriage. Too many things left unsaid on both sides. When I discovered he had a child with another woman, I wanted revenge. I told someone about Dan's affair and the child, and this man told me he'd take care of it. He was one of the people who had wanted to get rid of Dan. After Dan was killed, I wondered if Bob had had anything to do with it. When Bob turned me out of my home for the new pastor, I was furious. I convinced myself he was responsible, but when I got sober, I realized I'd simply been lashing out, at him, at other people. Blaming them for what I'd done to myself."

"Who is Bob?"

"Bob Metzger. He was my father's best friend. He's very prominent in the church's lay leadership."

"I see."

"But what you've just explained to me proves Bob had nothing to do with Dan's death," she said. "It was the police trying to discredit this gay group."

"Even if the church isn't implicated, the police department has to be held to account. Are you willing to join the lawsuit?"

"That kind of lawsuit would attract a lot of attention from the press, wouldn't it?"

"Probably."

"I'm not sure my sobriety could survive the stress of being put under a spotlight," she said. "I have a lot of good days, but I have shaky ones, too, and AA is still pretty new to me. You understand that, don't you, Henry?"

"Of course."

"Let me think about it."

I stood up. "Certainly."

She must have read the disappointment in my tone.

"Give me 'til the end of the week."

I nodded. "If you have any questions before then, call me."

She stood up. "You know, I'm not the only person who could bring the lawsuit."

"You're not?"

"You said spouses and children. Dan has a son. Wyatt."

"The boy in the picture on the credenza? The boy with HIV?"

"The last time I talked to Gwen, his mother, she said his condition was stable. But yes, that boy."

"I'd like to talk to him."

"Let me do that first. I'll tell him and Gwen everything you told me and ask if they want to talk to you."

"Of course," I said. "Thank you. I hope to hear from you soon."

"You will, but I can't promise I'll tell you what you want to hear."

She was at my office on Friday morning and, from the regretful expression with which she greeted me, I guessed her decision. She confirmed it when we sat down in my office.

"I'm sorry, Henry, but, as I said, I don't want to be dragged back into the life I'm trying to leave behind in sobriety."

"Don't you feel some responsibility for nailing your husband's murderers?"

"Was he murdered or was he simply in the wrong place at the wrong time? I mean, do you have proof he was the target of the bombing or was it the church itself? I know that must sound like hair-splitting to you, but it makes a difference to me."

"I can't say for sure Dan was the target," I replied. "That's a question we'd try to answer as we proceeded to trial. I can tell you the bomb planted near his office was twice as powerful as the bomb planted at the entrance."

"That doesn't prove it was intended for him," she said, reasonably.

"No, it doesn't."

"I'm sorry, Henry. My answer is still no."

"Did you have a chance to talk to Daniel's son and his son's mother?"

She nodded. "We talked for a long time, but once I explained why I didn't want to proceed, Gwen said she didn't want Wyatt to have to face the controversy alone. It *will* be controversial."

"Yes, it will. Would it do any good for me to talk to them?"

"I can ask her."

"Thanks." I reached for the folder of photographs that her private investigator had given me. "Before you go, I wondered if you could help me with something."

"Of course. What is it?

I told her Theo's story about how, the week before the bombing, he and Sumaya had cased the church, and had been detained by a security guard and an older man with whom Sumaya had spoken after he sent Theo to wait in their car.

"With Theo gone," I continued, "the only witnesses we have placing Sumaya at the church are the security guard—who we haven't been able to track down yet—and the older man who was with him. Theo identified him in one of the photographs you gave me." I shuffled through the photos. "Could you take a look and tell me if you know who he is, so we can depose him?"

I showed her the photo of Daniel Herron and the man Theo had identified as the older man Sumaya had talked to.

"Do you know this man?" I asked.

She examined it for a long moment, then asked, "This is the man the undercover officer talked to the Sunday before the bombing?"

"That's what Theo told me."

Returning the photograph, she said, "It's Bob Metzger."

"Metzger? The man you suspected of being involved in Dan's death?"

"Yes," she said. She looked at me. "Do you think it's a coincidence that Bob talked to the man who bombed the church five days before it happened?"

"The question, Jess, is whether you do."

"No," she said. "I don't." She took a breath. "I've changed my mind. I'll sue the police department if you'll also include the church."

SIXTEEN

Over the entrance of the civil courthouse muscled male figures carved in a marble frieze held tablets inscribed with the words *Lux et Veritas* and *Lex*: Light, Truth, and the Law. On the steps below, a gaggle of TV, radio, and print reporters had gathered for the press conference where Susanna Vane was announcing the wrongful death actions filed on behalf of the heirs of Theodore Latour and Daniel Herron.

The defendants in Theo's case included the City and County of Los Angeles, the Los Angeles Police Department, the Los Angeles County Sheriff's Department, the mayor, the chief of police, the County Board of Supervisors, and Alfredo Sumaya, as well as unnamed defendants John Does 1 through 10. Named as defendants in the Herron suit were the city, the police department, the mayor, the police chief, Sumaya, and the Church of Ekklesia, its board of directors a.k.a. Council of Overseers, and Does 1 through 20.

The Doe allegations were placeholders for defendants whose identities had not yet been ascertained or for whom there was as yet insufficient evidence to identify them by name. They allowed Susanna to make the broadest discovery requests she could think of to implicate other people and add them as defendants, including Robert Metzger and whoever he had conspired with in the police department to kill Dan Herron. We knew the conspiracy had to involve a much higher-ranking officer than lowly undercover cop Alfredo Sumaya, but we just didn't know who it was yet.

Theo's complaint alleged causes of action for negligent and intentional wrongful death. Meaning: his death was due either to the negligence of the sheriffs to properly monitor him for any signs he was suicidal, assuming it was suicide, or that he had been intentionally killed, presumably by the sheriffs. Daniel's complaint was a single allegation of intentional wrongful death claiming all the defendants, or some combination of them, had murdered him.

The claims were sensational, and the media were out in full force.

Susanna stood before the mics and cameras. Behind her were Kim Phillips and Jessica Herron. Behind them were Gwen and Wyatt Baker; I watched from a little off to the side. Susanna was an old hand at staging these dog and pony shows for the press and adept at squeezing the maximum amount of drama from them. She'd placed the wife of the murdered man and the mother of the man accused of murdering him side by side to show that the families were unified in their belief that the cops were the real culprits in the deaths of Daniel Herron and Theo Latour. Adding to the drama and the mystery were the two figures behind the women—the striking African-American mother and her handsome, teenaged, biracial son. The reporters glanced at them inquisitively—nothing the press liked more than a mystery.

The previous evening we'd all met at Susanna's Carthay Circle home for dinner so she could brief the families on what to expect at the press conference. I'd pulled up to an ivy-covered Craftsman bungalow surrounded by a high stone wall topped with what at first appeared to be some kind of decorative metal work. On closer inspection it was a tight row of razor-sharp, steel spikes. The gate was solid steel and could only be opened from within the house; cameras were mounted at the corners of the house, just below the roof. Apparently, representing victims of police violence was risky business.

A maid admitted me into the house and politely pointed to the pile of shoes in the entry hall next to a row of black canvas slippers. I changed shoes and followed voices into the living room where people were assembled. It was a big room, all chintz and Arts and Crafts furniture, comfortably worn Oriental carpets, and bookshelves where plastic-covered Modern Library editions of great American writers were crammed next to paperback thrillers. Susanna greeted me; introduced me to her husband Rodger, an attorney at the ACLU; put a glass of sparkling water in my hand, and left me to mingle.

I introduced myself to Gwen Baker who was admiring the tiled fireplace at the far end of the room. We'd spoken on the phone but this was our first meeting.

"I wanted to thank you again for joining the lawsuit," I said.

"If the police killed Dan, they have to be held responsible," she replied. "It's funny, though; when I worried about the police and my family, it was Wyatt I feared for." She sipped from her glass of wine. "As a defense lawyer, you must know how the police treat Black boys."

I followed her eyes across the room to the couch where Wyatt was sitting with another young Black man. They were holding hands.

"I do," I said. "Who is that with your son?"

"Gregory," she replied. "His boyfriend. He came down for moral support."

"How is Wyatt doing?" I asked.

"He's on a cocktail of ribavirin and Isoprinosine that's helped stabilize his T-cell count. Once AZT is approved, we'll move him over to it. Dan told me about the ribavirin and Isoprinosine and where I could get them. He said he heard about them from a gay lawyer here in LA. Jess told me you were that lawyer."

I nodded. "Yes, I put him in touch with a friend who's been bringing the drugs up from Mexico."

245

"Thank you," she said warmly, then added, "Wyatt's going to survive this, you know. He absolutely is."

I looked at the two boys, fingers entwined and sharing a youthful smirk at all the old people around them, and hoped she was right.

"... and these families are united in their grief at the deaths of their loved ones," Susanna was saying, "and by their determination that the people responsible for those deaths be held to account no matter who they are. In the complaints filed today, we allege that these tragedies were put into motion when the anti-terrorism unit of the Los Angeles Police Department illegally infiltrated a gay civil rights organization dedicated to peaceful advocacy for gay rights and the rights of people with AIDS. The police department, which has a long history of this kind of misconduct, sent in an undercover officer named Alfredo Sumaya as an agent provocateur with the express purpose of implicating the organization and its members in violent criminal activity. Sumaya, who had military experience of explosives, recruited Theo Latour—a vulnerable and troubled young man—to plant bombs that Sumaya had constructed at a local church called Ekklesia. We allege further that some members of that church were also involved in this bombing conspiracy because it served their purpose of promoting the so-called quarantine initiative that would quarantine people with AIDS by painting gay and lesbian people as violent radicals ..."

At this last statement, the reporters, who had barely contained themselves, now began shouting questions at her. She held up her hand and said, "I'll take questions when I'm done."

We'd gone back and forth on whether to name the church as a defendant. I argued the evidence of conspiracy was still too weak and if we included the church now, we'd be showing our hand prematurely. She pointed out that unless we named the church, we'd have no basis to seek discovery from it to find evidence of the conspiracy. Eventually, she won me over. We needed admissible evidence connecting the church to cops because Theo's statement to me that Sumaya and Metzger had talked the week before the bombing was hearsay. Without this evidence, the church would be dismissed from the suit. If that evidence existed, we could only get it by suing the church now and going after its records and leaders in discovery.

She finished her statement, and the questions began: "Are you claiming the sheriffs killed Latour in his jail cell?" "You're saying the church bombed itself?" "You mean this whole conspiracy was to help pass the quarantine initiative?" The tone of the questioning was incredulous but excited. If the story seemed unbelievable to the press, the reporters also knew it was an attention-grabber that would sell papers and generate TV viewership. Scandal and sensation were the raw meat of the media, and Susanna was throwing them big, bloody chunks of it. Before nightfall it would be a national story, and our version would be the one the public heard first.

"Where is this Officer Sumaya?" a reporter shouted.

Susanna, looking into the cameras, said, "We don't know, but we challenge the Los Angeles Police Department to produce him and let us hear what Officer Sumaya has to say."

When it was over, I drove back with her to her Westwood office, where we'd met that morning, to pick up my car. I'd been amused to discover she drove a black Lincoln Town Car, not the more modest vehicle I would have expected of a leftie lawyer.

"I'm a native New Yorker," she'd explained. "I didn't get my license until I was in my thirties and I'm still a pretty anxious driver, so my husband said I needed to drive a tank and bought me this."

Notwithstanding her claim of nerves, she steered the behemoth with surprising agility in the heavy traffic of the Santa Monica freeway. The city spread out on either side of the road in the sun-smeared, smoggy air—palm trees lifting their shaggy heads over the flats, the hills obscured in the chemical mist.

"You put on quite a show," I remarked.

"It helped that our two main plaintiffs are sympathetic white ladies. If it had only been Gwen and Wyatt, I promise the press would not have shown up like it did."

"What was that about daring the cops to produce Sumaya? You don't really think they will, do you?"

"No, but now every time a reporter talks to the department, the first question they'll ask is where is Sumaya. Eventually, we'll flush him out."

"How will the department respond to the lawsuits?"

"If they're smart, they'll take the standard 'we don't comment on ongoing litigation' line, but the chief's a hothead and an idiot. I'm hoping he'll say something stupid I can use against him." She shifted lanes and chuckled. "I'd like to be a fly on the wall when he has to face the lawyers from the city and the county."

"What do you mean?"

"The mayor and the chief loathe each other, and we've got allies on the City Council and the Board of Supervisors. They'll want answers from the chief and from the sheriff. They'll be pushing for investigations, commissions, what have you." She glanced at me and smiled. "This is as much a political fight as a legal one."

"I'm mostly interested in the legal case. What do we do next?"

"We wait for the defendants to file their answers to complaints and start drafting discovery requests. Civil litigation isn't the same as criminal prosecutions, Henry," she warned. "Your clients have a constitutional right to a speedy trial. That doesn't apply in civil cases. In civil, the name of the game is delay. It's a war of attrition. The defendants have deep pockets; we don't. They'll string this out as long as they can, hoping we'll run out of money and give up. That's why the political pressure is so important. Otherwise, it could be years before we get to trial."

Although I knew this, it was still sobering. Our plaintiffs—Jess, Kim, Gwen and Wyatt—would be fed into the meat grinder of the legal system, answering endless interrogatories, sitting through deposition after deposition, and being run over rough-shod by an aggressive media wanting the next big bombshell. Could they stick it out for years?

The phone intercom buzzed. I flicked on the mic. "Yes, Emma?"

"There's a gentleman here to see you."

Since I'd hired Emma full-time, I'd become familiar with the minute gradations in the voice she used to announce my visitors, which could indicate approval or disapproval and everything else in between. I'd never heard this voice before. It was both circum-spect and inquisitive, and I didn't know what to make of it. I glanced at my calendar.

"I don't see an appointment on the book."

Her voice dropped to a near whisper. "He said he's here on the Latour case. You'll want to see him."

Vouching for a mysterious visitor? Also new.

"Sure," I said. "Send him in."

A thin Black man of average height, formally dressed in a nice navy-blue suit, crisp white shirt and blue tie, with a lean and intelligent face rendered rather professorial by the gold wire-rimmed glasses, let himself into the office and approached my desk. He carried himself with conscious dignity. I stood and extended my hand.

"Henry Rios."

"Caleb Cowell," he replied, shaking my hand in a grip that was assertive without being obnoxious.

"Please sit down, Mr. Cowell. Would you like coffee? Water?"

He shook his head. "You're the man behind the lawsuit against my church," he said. It wasn't a question.

"You need to talk to Susanna Vane about that suit. She's the attorney of record."

"Jessica Herron sent me to you."

I didn't immediately know what that meant. Had she sent him because she didn't want to be badgered by the church or for some other reason? So I asked, "And who sent you to her?"

He blinked, apparently surprised by my aggressive tone.

"I went of my own volition."

"Why?" I pressed.

He sat back in his chair and replied, "I will answer all of your questions if you will answer one of mine."

"Ask away."

"Do you sincerely believe that people in the church were involved in Pastor Herron's murder?"

Here, I thought, was a man who, when he asked a question, however difficult, expected it to be answered truthfully because that's what he would do.

"Yes, I do."

Now it was his turn to press. "Why?"

"A member of your board of Overseers had a conversation with the undercover cop who planned the bombing a few days before the bombs went off. Jess told me the man in question wanted Dan Herron removed from his position as pastor."

"May I ask the name of the Overseer?"

"Robert Metzger."

He took the news impassively.

"You don't seem surprised," I observed.

"Are you a Christian?"

The question startled and irritated me. "How is that relevant to anything?"

"I'd like to know to whom I'm speaking."

"No, I'm not," I said. "Do you speak only to Christians?"

He removed his glasses, cleaned them on a starched handkerchief, and said, "You don't like us. I appreciate your honesty."

"Why are you here, Mr. Cowell? Did the church send you to try to persuade us to drop the suit?"

"No, I'm here because I believe I can help you with the lawsuit, but I needed to know if there was anything to it."

"Metzger's name convinced you?"

"Yes," he said, simply. "He despised Pastor Herron. He wanted to remove him, but that required unanimity among the Overseers and some of us would never have gone along. When Daniel was killed in the bombing, I thought it was a remarkable coincidence it happened as the quarrel between him and Bob was coming to a head."

"What do you mean by that?"

"Bob was going to force a vote of no confidence in Daniel. He lobbied me and Dan's other supporters with threats and promises, but we held firm. There was no possibility that vote would have been unanimous. I thought it equally remarkable that the bombs went off on the one night Daniel was alone at the church and in the building where he had his office."

"You didn't buy the story that the bombing was carried out by a radical gay group?"

"Why our church?" he replied. "Ekklesia is a single, unaffiliated congregation in Los Angeles. If this group wanted to make a political statement, why not attack a national or international denomination? The Catholics, the Southern Baptists, the Mormons? They all have large imposing structures in the city. Bombing one of them would have made headlines around the world. The leaders of those denominations have been far more vocal on the issue of homosexuality than Daniel. Far more supportive of the quarantine initiative. Dan would have avoided the issue altogether had he been able to."

"Why? Didn't he share the prejudices of the pope and the president of the Southern Baptists?"

He frowned. "Those aren't prejudices. Homosexuality is the unnatural use of our God-created bodies, and homosexuals will have to answer to God for it." He spoke this matter-of-factly. "Our church is clear on that, but there were members who felt we weren't getting that message out as aggressively as we should. They pushed Daniel to endorse the quarantine initiative and wanted to devote even more time, money, and manpower to its passage."

"Are you saying he wouldn't have gone along on his own, even though he shared those bigoted beliefs?"

"Name-calling is the lowest form of argument."

"Bigotry dressed up in the Bible is still bigotry."

"To your point," he said coldly, "Pastor Herron was an intelligent man. He realized this quarantine measure would be ineffective in preventing the spread of AIDS and would ally the church with people who truly are bigots and not just against homosexuals."

"Like the Mormons who didn't admit Blacks into their priesthood until the 1970s or the Southern Baptists, a denomination created by slaveholders who claimed the Bible sanctioned slavery?"

"You know your church history," he observed.

"I know the history of hatred," I replied, "and I know that just as the Bible was used to justify the oppression of your people, it's being used to justify the oppression of mine."

"You're gay," he said, surprised, and then, "I suppose I should have guessed by your hostility."

"Yeah, I'm not much for turning the other cheek. You were saying Dan worried about being associated with haters."

"Dan wasn't a hater." His eyes dimmed, and he permitted himself a small, sad smile. "Far from it." He sighed and returned from whatever memory had provoked the smile. "He also worried that involvement in a political issue would deflect the church from its salvific purpose."

"That concern didn't prevent him from publicly supporting the initiative and spending your church's money on it."

"He had to toss Bob and his group a bone."

"Aren't Christian leaders held to a higher standard of conscience than ordinary politicians?"

"The day Daniel was supposed to deliver a sermon announcing his endorsement of the initiative, he preached on love your enemies instead."

"That's nice, but how about, charity begins at home? Dan didn't have the courage to reveal to your community the gay, biracial son he had with a woman he never married. Or maybe that was simple hypocrisy."

"I knew nothing about that until after his death."

"Metzger did," I said. "Jess told him."

"Why?"

"She was angry. She wanted Metzger to punish him. Maybe he did."

"Is that why you think Bob was involved in Daniel's death? To prevent a scandal? That was a youthful indiscretion, long before Daniel's conversion. No one would have held it against him."

"Then why do you think Metzger conspired to kill him? Because it's clear the idea doesn't shock you."

"'No one can serve two masters. Either you will hate the one and love the other, or you will be devoted to the one and despise the other. You cannot serve both and the world.'"

"Even I know that from the Gospels."

"Matthew six, verse twenty-four. This is a perilous time for Christians, we all agree on that, but there's a deep division among us about how to confront that peril. Paul says in Thessalonians that 'the day of the Lord will come as a thief in the night.' Many of us believe that commands us to step away from the world, fortify our communities, and wait for the signs that will herald the end of days. Others want to engage the world on its own terms and enter its political and ideological battles. They think they can Christianize society by electing the right politicians or supporting the right causes. But, like my grandmother used to say, lie down with dogs, get up with fleas. Politics are a cesspool; no one comes out of them clean. If you wade into that swamp, you risk drowning in the very corruption you're fighting against."

"Were those the factions in your church? Daniel wanted to focus on theology and Metzger on politics?"

"Salvation, not theology. Those were the factions. Bob's an important man in the secular world. He's accustomed to power and doesn't understand why everyone doesn't want it. He sees how Christian leaders like Falwell and Robertson helped elect the President. He wants Ekklesia to have the same influence. Daniel understood his role to be pastoral, not political, and as long as he was leader of the church, Bob was stymied."

253

"So Metzger had him assassinated."

"The new pastor is very much in Bob's camp," Cowell said. "His first act was to demand the resignation of every member of the Overseers. He then reappointed Bob and his allies, but not those of us who had supported Dan. We were replaced with Bob's men. One of the new Overseers is someone I think you'll be very interested in."

"Who might that be?"

"A very close friend of Bob's named Raymond Moore, an assistant chief of police in the Los Angeles Police Department."

My pulse jumped. "How do you know about their connection?"

"Bob once invited him to speak to the Overseers about his efforts to evangelize the department."

"Evangelize the department?"

"He talked about setting up Bible studies, furnishing literature, and creating prayer groups."

"While the cops were on the job?"

"The first amendment entitles everyone to practice his faith."

"It also requires the separation of church and state. Cops are public officials. They can practice what they want, off-duty."

"Do you want to argue about the first amendment, or may I finish what I was saying about Raymond Moore?"

"Please do. What else do you know about this assistant chief?"

"I believe," Cowell said, "he's in charge of the anti-terrorism unit."

Susanna was less excited about Cowell's revelation than I'd thought she'd be when I called her and recounted the conversation.

"It's only evidence of connection, not conspiracy," she said.

"Isn't it enough to at least amend the complaint to include Metzger and Moore by name as defendants?"

"We need more, if we're going to get past the inevitable motion to dismiss, than the word of a disgruntled church member who doesn't actually have proof the two men conspired."

I knew she was right. At this point, calling out Metzger and Moore would be little more than a bluff. Still, it was frustrating. "If this were a criminal case, it would be enough to at least haul them in for questioning and rattle their cages."

"We have to jump through a lot more hoops in civil before we get to rattle anyone's cage."

But after I talked to her, I thought there might be one person whose cage I could rattle even with what little I had.

"Thanks for meeting me, Marc."

Marc Unger looked hungover and wary and in need of a drink. Unfortunately for him we weren't at a bar, but at a sandwich shop in the courtyard level of City Hall East where he had his office. The lunchtime crowd of city workers swirled around the little green metal table where we sat with our half-eaten lunches, tuna on wheat for me, pastrami on rye for him. Sparrows clustered near our feet, hoping for a crust of bread or shred of potato chip. I tore off a corner of my sandwich, crumbled it, and tossed it to them.

"Are you fucking Saint Francis now?" he grumbled.

I looked into his bloodshot eyes and saw the dark patches of hair he'd missed while shaving with an unsteady morning-after hand.

"The sushi place sells beer."

He glared at me. "I'm fine, Henry. This is your meeting. What do you want?"

He'd made it clear when I'd called him that he was pissed at me because the plea bargain he'd offered me before Theo's death had made its way into Theo's wrongful death complaint. I'd reminded him that he'd initiated the conversation, had made the offer freely, and hadn't told me it was off the record. He wasn't mollified.

"I want to talk to you about the Herron wrongful death action."

"You're not the attorney of record. Vane is," he said, adding sourly, "the bitch."

"I'll send her your regards," I replied. "She's of record but I'm helping with the investigation. We've turned up some stuff you might want to know about."

He rubbed his eyes. "You're going to give me an advance preview of your case? Why?"

"Because I want the city to settle and let us concentrate on the church."

"What about the Latour complaint?" he said. "You named the city and the department in that one, too."

"A deal on Herron might include dismissal of the city and LAPD from the Latour suit, and we'd go after the sheriffs and the county. It's their jail, after all."

"Hang on." He got up, lumbered across the plaza, and disappeared into the sushi place. A moment later he reappeared with a tall can of Sapporo and sat down. He popped the tab, took a long, grateful drink, wiped his mouth and said, "I'm listening."

"We have evidence that a high-ranking officer in the department and a high-ranking leader at the church conspired to blow up the church."

"What evidence?"

"A witness who can lay out the motive behind the conspiracy and connect the two men."

He blew a raspberry at me, something no one had done since I was in third grade.

"Motive? Connection? Where's your overt act of conspiracy? You got nothing."

"I'm not going to give you our case on a fucking silver platter," I said. "But I will tell you that Raymond Moore is in our crosshairs."

The mention of Moore's name jerked him upright in his chair to full attention "What do you know about Chief Moore?"

"I know he's a fanatical fundamentalist Christian who pushes his religious views on his subordinates in violation of department regulations, not to mention separation of church and state. I know he's not only a member of Ekklesia but, after Herron's death, was appointed to its board of directors. I know he's best friends with a church leader who wanted Herron out. I know he's Alfredo Sumaya's commanding officer. I assume discovery will reveal that he directed Sumaya to infiltrate QUEER and incite them to violence. I can also connect Sumaya to Moore's friend in the church. That's just what I know now before we've filed our first discovery motions or set up our first depositions."

Marc swallowed the information with another gulp of beer. "If you know all that, why haven't you amended the complaint to add him as a defendant?"

"I told you, our real target is the church. You should talk the city into settling, Marc, because when we do amend the complaint to add Moore, you'll be walking into a media buzz saw. I can already see the headlines: LAPD assistant chief implicated in murder conspiracy; department harbors religious fanatics who impose their views on rank and file. You want to be defending that?"

"The department's not responsible for the actions of an officer who wanders off the reservation."

"Agreed. If Moore was freelancing, that's all the more reason to settle the case and get the city off the hook."

He took another drink. "From this moment on," he said, "our conversation is completely off the record."

"Understood."

"I don't know anything about this conspiracy and your allegations seem crazy and/or unprovable." He smiled sourly. "You're probably bluffing."

"You can leave any time."

"Fuck you," he said without heat. "You have enough right about Moore to embarrass the department if you drag him into the lawsuit. Religious fanatic? That doesn't begin to describe him. I've got half-a-dozen internal complaints claiming he promotes guys on the basis of religion and discriminates against non-Christians. Don't get me started on his off-the-cuff comments about Jews. We know he's got a little gang of fellow believers who proselytize on the job, but Gates doesn't seem to think it's a problem."

"The chief part of that gang?"

He shook his head. "He's smart enough not to openly identify as Christian, but his religious beliefs align with Moore's." He tipped the can to his mouth and finished his beer. "Even if you can't prove your cockamamie conspiracy theory, you could still drag a lot of those skeletons out of the closet."

"Sounds like you kind of want me to," I observed.

"I'd love to see Moore go down for murder but only if it doesn't implicate the department." He looked at the empty as if considering whether to get another beer. He crushed the can. "You understand what I'm saying, Henry. The department is dismissed from the case with a clean bill of health, and anything Moore did, he did on his own."

"I don't have a problem with that."

"Hypothetically, what kind of settlement would you be looking for? Don't ask me to break the bank, not with the weak shit you've got."

"You and Susanna can work out the amount of the settlement, but once the city's dismissed from the case, Sumaya testifies that he was directed by Moore to infiltrate QUEER and to work with people in the church to kill Herron."

"You want Officer Sumaya to admit to felony murder?"

"He could testify under immunity so that nothing he says could be used in a criminal prosecution."

"You'd let him walk to get to the church?"

"And Moore. They're the ones who concocted the murder scheme. Sumaya was a foot soldier."

Marc raised a skeptical eyebrow. "He pulled the trigger, Henry. Hell, he built the gun and you're okay with him getting off scot-free?"

"I want justice for Theo and Dan," I said. "That means public admissions that Theo Latour was a pawn in a conspiracy he knew nothing about and that his and Daniel Herron's deaths were murder."

Marc belched softly, stood up, and said, "You've given me a lot to think about. Thanks for lunch."

Election day finally dawned. I stopped on my way to work to cast my ballot. The polling showed the No vote on the quarantine initiative ahead but within the margin of error. That evening Josh and I curled up on the couch in the study with a Mexican takeout and watched the first votes come in. They were bad. The Yes vote surged ahead by seven points but, as it turned out, the first returns were from the state's most conservative counties around the Oregon border and in the central valley. Around ten the urban vote began to come in from the nine counties comprising the San Francisco Bay area and Los Angeles county with its eight million inhabitants. Slowly, the No votes piled up. By midnight, the quarantine initiative had gone to defeat, 49 percent yes to 51 percent no. We wept for joy, but our happiness was tempered by the realization that nearly half the voters had been in favor of the measure.

I switched off the TV while Josh gathered up the leftovers and took them into the kitchen. I followed with plates, cutlery, and glasses. I'd just started washing up when the doorbell rang. Josh said, "I'll get it."

As I put his plate into the dishwasher, I heard a man say, "Hello, Josh."

And then Josh said, "Hi, Freddy."

SEVENTEEN

When I realized who Josh was talking to, my first thought was, *He has a gun.* I dried my hands on my trousers and stepped into the foyer where the two men were standing, Josh warily, the other with a slight, almost embarrassed smile.

"Hello, Henry."

"Hello . . . what do I call you? Alfredo? Sumaya?"

"Freddy," he replied. "That's what everyone in my family calls me, so I used it when I went undercover, easier to remember that way. Saavedra's my mom's maiden name. Are you going to invite me in?"

"That depends on what you want."

He smiled an easy smile. "I could use some legal advice, and you're the only lawyer I trust."

He was wearing jeans, sneakers, and a leather jacket over a black T-shirt; I looked for any gun bulges. As if he knew what I was thinking, he said, "I'm not armed, Henry." With a flirty grin, he added, "Frisk me if you want."

"Wait for me in the living room."

After he left, I said to Josh, "Go to bed."

He looked at me incredulously. "Are you crazy? I'm not leaving you alone with him."

"I believe him when he says he isn't armed."

"That doesn't mean he's not dangerous," Josh said in a fierce whisper.

"You heard what he wants. Legal advice. I'll be fine. Plus, if I am talking to him as a lawyer, you can't be there anyway. There's no attorney-client privilege if another person is in the room."

He shook his head. "I'll be in the kitchen. If things get weird, shout."

"Okay." I gave him a quick kiss

Freddy was sprawled out on the couch, the leather jacket in a shiny heap beside him. I'd only seen Freddy in the flesh a couple of times; my image of him had been formed mostly by Theo's descriptions of a pissed-off, muscle-bound, good-looking macho man but now I saw that image was incomplete. He was muscle-bound and he was good looking: slicked-back black hair, blunt black eyebrows, warm brown eyes. The shape of his face was an oval with high cheekbones, a strong chin, and perfectly symmetrical features, mole above the left side of his lips. His skin was the color of fresh walnuts. His smile was blinding. He moved with a feline grace surprising in such a hard-bodied man. He had old-school animal magnetism, the power to compel you to look at him.

"You got anything to drink?" he asked me.

"Not booze," I said. "You want coffee or a Coke or something?"

He shrugged. "Nah. You don't drink."

"No."

He smiled. "You sober? AA and all that shit?"

"That's right."

"Cool, cool," he said approvingly. "I should probably look into that myself. Where's Josh?"

I'd been standing. Now I took the armchair across from him. "He went to bed."

"He doesn't mind you being alone with me?" he asked, cocking his head to one side with a grin.

"I know you're not gay, Freddy, so knock off the flirting."

He slowly pulled his legs together, sat up. "Don't tell me you weren't checking me out."

I sighed. "For weapons. You want legal advice, answer my question. Where have you been? No one's seen you since the bombing."

"I got reassigned to desk duty out in Devonshire division," he said, laying a hand on the leather jacket. As he spoke, he stroked it as if it were a cat. "After Theo was arrested, they put me on administrative leave. I thought they'd put me back on active duty after he offed himself but then these lawsuits happened, and they hid me in a safe house out in Harbor division."

That explained why the process servers hadn't been able to locate him to serve him with wrongful death actions.

"Why would the department hide you?"

He stopped stroking his coat. "Not to protect me. To protect themselves from me telling someone what I know."

"What do you know?"

He sank back into the couch and frowned. "First off, you need to know the bombs weren't my idea."

"You built them; you told Theo where to plant them."

"Because those were *my* orders," he replied emphatically.

"Orders from who?"

He hesitated and threw me a hard look.

"I'm not law enforcement and you came to me because you trust me, remember? If you've changed your mind, you're free to go. I'm not going to tell anyone you were here."

My bluntness seemed to satisfy him. "Will you be my lawyer then?"

"In the civil suits? Marc Unger in the city attorney's office is your lawyer. Why aren't you talking to him?"

"'Cause he called me up and told me to hire my own lawyer. I asked him why, and he said the city had decided I wasn't acting in the scope of my job. You know what that means?"

"Yes," I said.

"Then maybe you can explain it to me because that *pinche pendejo* sure didn't."

"The city's only obliged to defend you in a civil suit if the things you're accused of doing happened while you were acting in your official capacity as a police officer and you didn't exceed your authority. If you taser an unarmed suspect and he sues you for excessive force, the city has your back. If you kill a guy in an off-duty bar fight and get charged with homicide, you're on your own."

He took this in for a moment. "Unger's saying I did the bombing on my own time?"

"Something like that," I said. I considered the other ramifications of the city's position. "It also means if the DA decides to charge you, there's no guarantee of any kind of immunity defense."

He muttered, "Fuck me." He looked at me. "What kind of charges?"

"If you're charged like Theo was, first-degree murder with special circumstances. A death penalty case."

He sank his head between his hands and rubbed his temples.

"You started by saying you were only following orders," I prodded.

Through outstretched fingers, he mumbled, "Yeah, that's right."

"Whose orders?"

Now he looked up again. "I don't hate gay people."

I offered a tentative, "Okay."

"Seriously, I don't," he insisted, sitting up. "Hanging out with you guys in QUEER, I saw the shit you take, plus the whole AIDS thing getting blamed on you. That ain't fair."

"Okay, you're not a homophobe. What does that have to do with anything?"

"I just want you to understand that what I did to Theo wasn't personal. I liked the little speed freak."

"You were only following orders," I said, not bothering to keep the sarcasm out of my voice.

"Were you in the military, Henry?"

"No," I said, confused by the abrupt change of subject. "I know you were. I've seen your service record."

He nodded. "The first thing you learn in the army is you don't think for yourself. They tell you your life and the lives of your friends depend on following orders. So, if they point to a bunch of people," he pointed at a corner of the room, "and tell you, that's the enemy, take them out. You don't get to go, but, Sarge, some of them are good people." His hand fell back in his lap. "You take them out. The department's like the army." He leaned forward,

263

emphatically. "They send you into Watts and tell you, those Black people are the enemy and you forget about the Black kids you played basketball with during high school or how fucking great Hank Aaron was. The Blacks are the enemy, you treat them accordingly." His voice had become sharp and angry. "They told me, 'These fags, they're the enemy. They're spreading this disease, they're molesting kids, they're doing disgusting things with their bodies and they have to be stopped. You get in there, into this group that has the balls to shove the word *queer* in our face like it was something to be proud of and you fuck them up.'"

"By blowing up a church?"

He fell back onto the couch again and shook his head. "First, they told me, get them to take some swings at the cops at one of their demonstrations, but you know those QUEER guys." He grinned. "They're smart motherfuckers. They tried to provoke the cops to take swings at them. Make the department look bad. So I went back and said, 'They ain't biting.' Then they told me, 'okay, well, get the leaders to plan some kind of violent action,' but they didn't understand." He clenched his fist in remembered frustration. "There's no fucking president of QUEER to incite to violence. People do their own thing and that don't include violence. So, then they say, 'Okay, well if everyone does their own thing, find the weak link and turn him.'"

"Theo," I said.

He nodded. "A fucked-up, submissive speed freak into guys who treated him like shit. He was perfect. Just the right combination of crazy, suggestible, and obsessed."

"Who are these 'they' who were giving you orders?"

"Well, not so much 'they,' I guess, as 'him.' Chief Moore."

"Raymond Moore," I said. "The head of the anti-terrorism unit."

"Now there's a guy," he replied with a smirk, "who really, really hates gays."

"Was he the only one giving you orders? Were there others up or down the chain of command you reported to?"

"No, just Chief Moore. This was his special project. He even had a code name I was supposed to use when I wanted to talk to him. I'd call his office and ask for Eleazer. That's how he knew it was me. I thought his secretary would hang up on me the first time I called, but she didn't bat an eye. Just put me through."

"Did Moore specifically order the bombing?"

He slowly nodded. "He asked me to come to his house one night. When I got there, he introduced me to this old dude, Metzger. They sat me down and explained that getting that quarantine thing passed was a matter of life and death. They talked about the innocent people who would die if the homosexuals were allowed to spread their lifestyle and their disease. The old guy began quoting the Bible about how even God was disgusted by what homosexuals did, and that back in the day they were stoned to death, it was that much of a sin."

I interrupted him. "Are you religious?"

He shrugged. "Catholic. I haven't been to church in a long time, but I know the pope don't like homosexuals any more than Metzger does."

"So then what?"

"They told me it was time for something big to happen to bring people's attention to how much of a threat the homosexuals were. That's when they said I should get someone in QUEER to bomb the church and help them do it." His eyes widened. "I thought they were joking."

"Why?"

"I know what bombs can do. You don't play with that shit. And a church?" He blew out a breath, shook his head. "That's hardcore. But Metzger told me it was his church, and that his church was ready to make the sacrifice if it would get the law passed. They told me damage would be minimal and no one would get hurt, but I had to make sure it looked like gays had done it."

"Moore told you no one would get hurt."

"Metzger said Thursday was the one night nothing goes on at the church and that's when I'd plant the bombs."

"And you said, sure, I'll blow up your church?" I asked, disbelievingly.

"Following orders, Henry."

"Moore and some civilian hatch a plot to bomb a church to swing an election," I said. "Didn't that have the smell of being off the books?"

"No one let me read the book."

I was, by now, pretty skeptical of his claim to have been nothing more than an automaton, blindly carrying out the orders of his superior officers. The department wasn't the army—its officers were entrusted with the power to make their own judgments in critical situations—and Freddy wasn't stupid. He had to have known something this outrageous was both criminal and morally wrong.

"How did you persuade Theo to help you?"

"Theo was into me, way into me. I pretended to be a pissed-off queer radical who wanted to get back at the people who wanted to lock us up in concentration camps. That's all I talked to him about and, you know, like I said, he was suggestible, plus he was HIV positive, so he was already angry. I'd seen the way he'd scream at people at QUEER meetings, not making a lot of sense, just venting. Plus, he was usually speeding, and that shit makes you paranoid. I'd get him all worked up and then I'd fuck him and while I fucked him, I kept at him. Told him we'd be soldiers. It'd be us against the world. Made it sound kind of romantic. I led him to it, step by step, and by the time he knew where I was taking him, he was in too deep to back out."

"You didn't think twice about involving a screwed-up, HIV-positive emotionally troubled drug addict in a major felony that would destroy his life?"

"Hey, I'm sorry about Theo, but the way he was going, it was only a matter of time before speed got him or AIDS did."

"You said you liked him, but you were willing to use him without any feelings about it."

In a hard voice, he replied, "Civilians have feelings, not soldiers, not cops." Then, "Are you going to help me or not?"

266

"What kind of help do you want, exactly?"

"Get me out of the lawsuits and make sure I don't get charged with anything."

"You don't think you have any responsibility here?"

"Not for doing my job. Not for following orders," he insisted. "Scold me all you want, but that's the way it was."

He was shrewd. If the city was trying to cut him loose by arguing he had exceeded the scope of his duty, his only defense was to claim he had followed the orders of a superior in a good faith belief they were legitimate orders reflecting official policy. Then, it wouldn't matter if the orders were invalid or even illegal—that was on his superiors, not him.

Of course, there was the problem of persuading a judge or a jury that any reasonable cop who was directed to blow up a church would have believed that activity fell within the scope of police work. But the defense might at least cancel out Freddy's personal, civil liability for the bombings. As for criminal charges—well, Theo had died with all the original capital charges pending against him. Though he hadn't been found guilty, he hadn't been acquitted either. The cops and the DA could argue he was the perpetrator and, letting political dogs lie, decline to reopen the case based on allegations in a civil suit where there was a lesser burden of proof.

Freddy said, "What do you think?"

"I think you're a liar. You knew damn well when Moore and Metzger brought you in on the scheme to blow up the church, it was a private vendetta, not official police business. You went along with it anyway. Why? I don't know for sure, but the fact you'd wreck Theo Latour's life without a second thought and try to implicate QUEER tells me you're not as okay with gay people as you claim. I don't know if you're a bigot or a psychopath, but I'm damn sure you're not an innocent victim of circumstances."

He threw me a long, hard stare and then he shrugged. "Whatever, dude. Can I get away with it?"

"There's a decent chance," I said, "with the right lawyer. I'm not that person."

267

He stood up, grabbed his coat. "Too bad. I wanted to see that asshole Unger's face when I walked into court with Theo's lawyer. Thanks for the chat, Henry. Now you can go cornhole Josh or whatever it is you guys do." He smiled. "I really don't hate gays. I didn't even mind the sex. No bitch ever gave me head as good as Theo, and his asshole was tighter than a pussy. I guess that proves I'm not a bigot."

As the front door closed behind him, I thought, *Which leaves psychopath.*

In the weeks that followed, the wrongful death actions moved at the glacial pace of most civil suits and got even more complicated when Alfredo Sumaya filed a separate suit against the city and the police department. In it he sought a ruling from the court that the city was required to defend him because all his actions had been at the direction of the department. We filed a massive discovery request. The defendants responded with the first round of motions to dismiss, called demurrers. And then, except when something required my immediate attention, the action slipped into the back of my mind, buried beneath the daily demands of my practice and the happy challenge of merging my life with Josh's.

One morning, I sat down to breakfast and unfolded the *Times.* There, beneath the fold, next to a photograph of Alfredo Sumaya was a headline:

FORMER LAPD OFFICER SOUGHT IN CHURCH BOMBING

Police have issued an arrest warrant for Alfredo Sumaya, 34, a former member of the Los Angeles Police Department's Anti-Terrorism Unit, in connection with the bombing of Ekklesia church last spring. Daniel Herron, the church pastor, was killed in the bombing. Police sources state that Sumaya conspired with Theo Latour to commit the bombing. Latour was charged with first-degree murder, but committed suicide in his jail cell before he could be brought to trial. A wrongful death action filed by Herron's widow and his son allege that Sumaya was operating as an undercover officer at the time of the bombing under the direction of his supervisors at the police department. The complaint alleges that the purpose of the bombing was to discredit a gay activist organization that Sumaya had infiltrated and that Latour belonged to. The city has denied those allegations on behalf of the department. Sumaya had filed his own lawsuit alleging all his actions were within the scope of his duties and was seeking a declaration of immunity from any liability, civil or criminal. Both lawsuits are currently pending, and it is unclear whether this latest development is related to them . . .

Maybe the *Times* was unclear about the connection between the civil suits and this bombshell, but I had my suspicions.

Marc chose another restaurant-bar for our meeting, this one not far from his office on Main Street, but with the same noirish, torch song feel as the New York Company. Apparently when he was drinking Marc liked to imagine himself as a character in a Raymond Chandler novel. This place was called The Twilight Club. Outside, it was a squat, windowless square that could have been a warehouse. Inside, twinkle lights cast a faux-romantic glow over booths padded with red leather, and cocktail waitresses in evening gowns delivered drinks and bar food to equally well-padded men in suits. Although it wasn't a gay bar, its clientele was almost exclusively male. Marc was comfortably settled in a booth with a martini in front of him. A candle burned in a squat orange candle holder on the table, the light flickering across his face.

"Henry, baby," he said when I slid in across from him. So, not his first drink. "You're looking good."

"Thanks, Marc."

The cocktail waitress laid a little napkin in front of me and asked for my order. I said mineral water.

Marc rolled his eyes and told her, "Bring me another one of these, darling. So," he continued as she disappeared into the gloom, "what's on your mind?"

"Why is Alfredo Sumaya being charged now in the church bombing?"

He lifted his drink to his mouth and sipped. Light sparked from his gold cufflink. He set the drink down and said, "Why are you asking me? I'm not the DA."

"Cut the crap. I know who's pulling the strings in this case."

The waitress returned and elaborately placed our drinks before us.

"You're a smart guy, Henry. You must have a theory."

"I do. You told Sumaya that the church bombing was beyond the scope of his duties and that the city wouldn't defend him in the wrongful death actions. That left him dangling out there on his own without any protection from civil or criminal liability. He found himself a lawyer who sued the city to force the city to defend him. In order to destroy the credibility of his lawsuit, the DA charges him with murder and claims he acted alone—well, not alone, but with Theo who's dead and can't defend himself." Marc was grinning like the Cheshire cat, so I knew I was on the right track. I plunged on. "If the criminal case gets to trial first, and Sumaya's convicted, his civil lawsuit goes up in smoke. If he tries to rush through his civil lawsuit, you can argue it should be postponed until after the criminal prosecution because the criminal prosecution will be dispositive of whether he was acting in the scope of his duty." I shook my head. "In other words, you've got his nuts a vise."

"Excellent analysis, counsel," he said. He sipped his drink, and the cufflink flashed again.

"Meanwhile, with everyone focused on Sumaya, Chief Moore and Bob Metzger, who masterminded the bombing, slip into the shadows."

He smirked. "Objection. Assumes facts not in evidence. No proof of who masterminded anything."

"Aren't you worried Sumaya will go to the media and lay out the whole story of how an assistant chief in the police department and a leader of Ekklesia conspired to blow up the church and kill its pastor?"

"Do you think anyone will run that story and risk a slander suit on the word of an accused murderer?" I watched him light a cigarette and sip his cocktail, a self-satisfied expression on his face. "Anyway, he won't talk. He's charged with capital murder. His only hope for a reduced charge is to play ball."

"Are you going to offer him manslaughter because he's a cop?" I asked bitterly.

"He gets the same offer as Latour. Second-degree murder, fifteen to life. He'll take it."

"I wouldn't be so sure," I said, remembering my conversation with him. Freddy didn't strike me as a guy who would take a fall. "And if he does, you're okay with letting a high-ranking police officer who conspired to commit murder off the hook?"

He took a drag from his cigarette and exhaling said, "Chief Moore will be announcing his retirement at the end of the year."

"And Metzger?"

Absently, he pushed the candle away from his side of the table, casting his face into shadow, and said, "Nothing I can do about him."

"Nothing you—wait, is that what this is all about? You working backstage to get your idea of justice?"

"The cop responsible for the bombing goes to jail. The assistant chief who planned it retires. We're preparing a very generous offer to settle the wrongful death actions. You should be happy. Why aren't you?"

"Because it's all bullshit, that's why! You're covering up the real story, that the department and the church joined forces to try to entrap a group of gay activists in a murder to swing an election that would have put a lot of gay men, including my lover, in quarantine camps. The power of the state was used to try to crush a group of its citizens who were peaceably resisting a horrifying plot against them. In America. Is sweeping all that under the carpet your idea of justice?"

"Proposition 54 lost," he said. "It's over, Henry. There's no point in picking over the bones."

"There may not be another initiative, but the bigots will think up something else. They're in for the long haul. There will always be a next time, Marc. That's why it matters that people know the truth about what happened this time."

He finished his drink, dabbed his mouth with his cocktail napkin, and said, "That's your fight. I have other responsibilities." His eyes were sharp and focused despite the booze. "You may think I'm a sellout, but you're a lawyer, too." He slapped his hand on the table, shaking his glass. "You're as much a part of the system as I am. I'm very good at my job, and sometimes part of my job, like part of yours, is choking back the puke and making the deal." He picked up his cigarette. "I'm planning to sit here and drink myself into a coma. Unless you want to stay and watch, I suggest you go home to your cute little twink and fuck his brains out."

EIGHTEEN

We were watching *The Maltese Falcon* when the local news anchor came on at a commercial break and announced: "A series of bombings rocked Los Angeles, claiming three lives, including a high-ranking official in the Los Angeles police department, and destroying a local church. Details at ten."

We looked at each other. Josh hopped off of the couch and returned a moment later with a transistor radio set to the twenty-four-hour news channel while I switched the TV to CNN where the anchor was interviewing some political analyst. The radio newscaster said, "Latest developments on tonight's bombings." I lowered the volume on CNN and Josh turned up the radio.

"Bombs exploded at three locations tonight in Los Angeles, two private residences and a church that had been the site of an earlier bombing, killing three people, including an assistant chief of the Los Angeles Police Department. The victims have been identified as Robert Metzger, 74, an attorney, and Raymond Moore, 60, an assistant chief of police, and his wife, Bridget, 57. The bombs exploded in their residences. A third bomb exploded at Ekklesia Church, which was the site of an earlier bomb attack. While no victims died in that explosion, the damage was extensive. Police have no suspects as yet, but they are treating the explosions as related and possibly the work of a terrorist although no one has claimed responsibility. We will keep you updated as we learn more . . ."

"Freddy," Josh said, clicking the radio off.

I switched off the TV. "He's settling scores."

I guess I was right—he wasn't going to be anyone's fall guy.

"Are you safe?" he asked worriedly.

"Why wouldn't I be?"

"He asked you to represent him and you turned him down."

"I'm not in the same league as Moore and Metzger," I said. "I'll be fine."

"I'll still feel better when the police catch him."

I nodded in agreement, but I didn't really think this was going to end with an arrest.

I turned off Franklin onto Van Ness and then climbed up the hill to home, so lost in thought about the burglary trial I'd started that day I nearly ran into a police barricade at the end of my street. I braked, shut off the engine. The street was sealed off and was swarming with cops in SWAT fatigues. A cop directed me to the curb. I got out of my car, approached him and asked, "What's going on?"

"Police business," he replied, unhelpfully.

"Yeah, I can see that, but I live here," I said, pointing to my house.

"You're at twenty-three twenty-eight?" he asked, ears almost visibly perking up like a dog's.

"Yes."

"Wait here."

He headed toward an ominous-looking black tank-like vehicle marked with the LAPD's SWAT insignia. A moment later, he reappeared with a guy in full paramilitary gear, including the black helmet and full body armor. He had his game face on—hard, cold, and assessing.

"You Henry Rios?" he barked.

"Yes. Who are you?"

"Taylor," he said, biting off the word. "You live at twenty-three twenty-eight?"

"I haven't moved in the two minutes since I last answered that question. Are you going to tell me what this is about?"

His stony expression became even stonier. "Are you a lawyer?"

"Yes."

"You know a man named Alfredo Sumaya?"

"Do you mean, Officer Alfredo Sumaya?" I replied, emphasizing *Officer*. "Yeah, I know him. Why?"

"Is he a client?"

I'd had it with the tough guy bullshit.

"I'm not answering any more questions until you tell me what's happening at my house."

Taylor's expression said, *Fine, asshole*, but what he actually said was "Officers tried to serve an arrest warrant on Sumaya earlier today. There was a shoot-out, one officer down, and he got away. We tracked him to your residence where he's barricaded himself with a hostage."

"A hostage?" I said, heart racing. "Who is it?"

"You tell me," he said with a tiny smirk he quickly extinguished. "Anyone else living with you?"

"My partner, Josh. Josh Mandel."

"Partner?" he asked, perplexed. "What, like a law partner?"

"No, not a business partner. My—" and here it was, the quandary, what word to use with straight people when you couldn't say husband or wife. I ran quickly through the usual euphemisms, but decided I needed to be absolutely clear. "My lover."

A look of disgust flashed across his face.

"Is Josh in there with Sumaya?" I asked.

"If that's who was in the house, then he's the hostage," Taylor replied coolly.

"What does Sumaya want?"

"He wants to talk to you," Taylor said. "Because he says you're his lawyer."

"Let me talk to him."

Taylor said, "Come with me. We'll get him on the line."

"No," I said. "I don't want to call him. I want to go in and talk to him. I want to get him to release Josh."

"That ain't going to happen," Taylor said, sounding briefly human. "We're not letting a civilian walk into a situation where he might be killed."

"Yeah, the liability issue," I said, scornfully. "Don't worry, Officer Taylor. I don't have any family to sue you if he kills me, and besides, I'm not a civilian. I'm his lawyer, and I demand to be allowed to see my client. You want me to sign a release from liability? Whatever it takes but let me into my house."

Taylor considered. "It's your funeral."

"Where's the phone? I want to tell him I'm coming in."

Approaching the front door, key in hand, I was aware of birds singing above the chatter of police radios and the cooling air as evening descended when, behind me, floodlights seared the front of the house, momentarily blinding me in their reflected glare. The air pulsed loudly above me. I looked up. Two LAPD helicopters hovered nearby.

As I reached for the door, Josh cracked it open and said quietly, "Henry?"

"Yes, let me in, slowly, and don't open the door all the way."

I slipped inside. Freddy was standing behind him with a revolver at the back of Josh's head. Jeans and a black T-shirt, same uniform as last time, but lines of tension were etched across the handsome face.

"Hello, Freddy," I said, calmly. "You can put that down. It's just me." I smiled at Josh. "Hello, Josh."

He worked his face into as cheerful an expression as the circumstances allowed and said, "Hi, Henry. And how was your day?"

"Screw the small talk," Freddy growled. "Into the living room."

He herded us into the living room where the TV was on, volume lowered, and a picture running of the cops surrounding my house. I hadn't noticed the TV vans. From the angle of the shot it appeared they were a little down the hill on the other end of the street from where I'd driven up. It was surreal—as if we were in a movie. The living room had its usual, slightly mussed-up appearance, but near the big picture window the floodlights illuminated a little arsenal of firearms. Bad sign. Remembering Freddy's specialty, I wondered if he'd brought a bomb or two.

"Mind if I sit?" I asked, as if it were his house, not mine. He nodded. I sat down in the same chair as the last time. "The cops said you wanted to talk to me, Freddy, so here I am. But before we begin, let Josh go. You only need one of us to keep the cops from storming the place and it should be me. Josh has nothing to do with this situation."

He weighed my words for what seemed an eternity before finally yanking his chin toward Josh. "Get out of here."

"No, no," I said. "We call the cops and tell them he's coming out so that someone with itchy fingers doesn't shoot him."

As Freddy picked up the phone, Josh said, "I'm not leaving."

We both stared at him, me disbelievingly and Freddy with a pissed-off frown.

"Yes, you are," I said.

"Not without you."

"Shut the fuck up," Freddy snapped. "If you don't get out of here, I'll shoot you both. You first, then . . ." He jerked his chin toward me. "Him."

Josh gasped. "Why would you do that?"

"Because, if you haven't noticed, I'm a little stressed and you're getting on my fucking nerves. Besides, Henry's my lawyer and you can't be here for what I have to say to him." He picked up the phone and said, "Sending out the kid. Rios stays."

I wanted to walk Josh to the door, but I also wanted to maintain the illusion of calm, as if this were simply another evening at home and not a police standoff with a nervous ex-cop with a lot of guns and nothing to lose. I remained seated.

"Go on, Josh," I said, smiling. "I'll see you soon."

His lower lip trembled and his eyes were despairing, but he seemed to understand he had to maintain his composure.

"Okay," he whispered. "See you."

At the front door he turned and said, "I love you." I held my breath as he opened the door and light flooded in and didn't release it until he closed the door quietly behind him.

"Why don't you sit down," I said to Freddy.

"Shut up," he replied. He paced the room, revolver at his side. "You should've helped me when I asked you to."

There was a note of pleading in his harsh tone.

"You got yourself a lawyer after we talked," I pointed out. "She filed your lawsuit."

"She dropped me the minute the DA charged me. You wouldn't have done that. You would've fought for me."

"Maybe I can help you now."

"Not likely," he scoffed. "Three dead, plus the cop I wounded. If I wasn't looking at death row before, I am now."

He was right, of course, so I didn't try to bullshit him.

"Why did you kill Moore and Metzger? You could've used your knowledge about them as a bargaining chip with the DA."

"My word against theirs," he said, "and who do you think people are going to believe? A couple of respectable citizens or a psycho cop? That was the choice you gave me, right? Bigot or psycho and I said, I'm not a bigot. But there's another option you forgot. Dupe."

"You were set up."

"Damn right," he said. "You know why they chose me?"

"Your experience with explosives?"

"No, because I'm a spic."

"What do you mean?"

"I'm a spic. Just like you." He lurched forward, grabbed my hand. I was too stunned to pull back. "See, same color. You and me. Brown guys in a white world with funny names from the wrong side of the tracks. Or maybe you didn't grow up poor."

"My father worked construction."

He dropped my hand. "Mine was a janitor at my high school. I dropped out to join the army when I couldn't stand to see him pushing the mop down the hall and pretending he didn't know me so I wouldn't be embarrassed in front of my friends. I always had the stink of a guy with something to prove," he said bitterly. "The bosses smell it on you and take advantage. They know you'll work twice as hard just to prove you're equal to the *gringos*. Go the extra mile for the pat on your back from the *jefe*. You get a reputation as someone who does what he's told, no questions asked, just keep those pats coming. Just like your fucking father, head down, pushing the broom."

"Even if you're told to blow up a church? That's not anyone's idea of police work."

"Anti-terrorism pulls off all kinds of shit that civilians wouldn't consider police work," he replied, casually. "Spies on the mayor and the city council members. Plants drugs on what they call subversives and then busts them. Blow up a church?" He shrugged. "The target wasn't the church; it was QUEER, or that's what they told me. The church was cooperating. What was I supposed to believe? Plus, Moore said he'd protect me from the fallout. I should have known better. I was nothing more to him than the help, like my dad."

"You really didn't know Daniel Herron was going to be at the church that night?"

"I told you I didn't," he said angrily. "He wasn't the target. The church was the target. When I went back to Moore and asked him, what the fuck, he said it was an accident but not to worry; the whole thing would be pinned on Theo."

"You had to know Theo was going to point the finger at you."

"But who was he going to tell? The police?"

"His lawyer," I said. "Me."

"That's why Theo had to go."

"Who killed him?"

"I don't know who killed him, but Moore was behind it."

"Why?"

"Because he was afraid that sweet deal you negotiated with the city attorney was going to raise more questions than it answered. He figured if Theo killed himself before he made the deal, everyone would assume he was guilty and that would be it. It would have been except for those wrongful death actions. That was your doing."

"I didn't file them," I said.

He cast a sour look at me. "Don't bullshit me. You were behind them. You wanted to flush me out."

"I wanted to prove Theo wasn't a murderer."

"Yeah, well, happy now?"

The tension between us had been rising and I was afraid. I looked for a way to defuse it.

"You were set up and you knew no one was going to believe you over Moore and Metzger, so you took care of them in your own way." I took a breath. "You made your point. No one else needs to die."

He smirked. "Are you afraid I'm going to kill you?"

'Of course I am."

"I told you I'm not a psycho," he said, almost hurt. "Here, I'll prove it." He laid the gun on the little table next to my chair and backed away. "Go ahead, make a grab for it. I won't stop you."

"And do what, shoot you? March you out the door to the cops? I won't do the first thing, and I'm pretty sure you won't let me do the second one. Freddy, what do you want from me?"

He sank into the sofa, threw his arm over the back, and stroked it as he'd done with his jacket, as if it were a cat. Did he have a cat? I wondered. A little creature he loved? It was an absurd thought but as I watched his fingers softly stroke the fabric I couldn't shake the image.

"When I die," he said, "they'll close the book on this"—he gestured with his free hand to take in everything that had happened to him—"and I'll be the one, the only one, they blame. They're going to turn me into a monster." He looked at me with his warm, dark eyes. "I need to hear from someone who knows the whole story that he knows I'm not a monster."

"I never said you were a monster," I replied quietly.

"You said I was a psycho."

"You really didn't know Herron was going to be in the building?"

He shook his head. "Why would I die with a lie on my lips? I did not know the man would be there. I did not mean to kill him."

People do lie, even on their deathbeds, and maybe Freddy was lying now, but it seemed urgent for me to say I believed him. If I did, maybe we could both walk out of this room alive.

"I believe you, Freddy."

"No, you don't," he said. "You're just scared, but it's the truth, Rios."

He slowly got to his feet, and, eyes locked on mine, walked toward me. He picked up the revolver. I thought, *he's going to shoot me.* In a moment of blind panic, I grabbed the arms of the chair and lifted myself up to hurl myself at him before he got off the shot. He stepped back, jammed the revolver against his temple and fired. He fell forward on top of me, his hard, heavy body tumbling me to the ground, his eyes peering into mine as the light went out of them.

The door splintered, and the room was filled with shouting as Freddy's body was lifted off of me.

Above me, Taylor, the SWAT guy, yelled, "Rios! Rios! Talk to me."

I opened my mouth to speak and a little blood dribbled into it. It wasn't mine.

I watched the cops roll out yellow crime scene tape across the entrance to my house and wondered what I was supposed to do for clothes when I had to appear in court the next day for trial. I couldn't very well show up in the sweats I was wearing—the cops having confiscated my Freddy-splattered clothes.

Why *had* he come to me? Was it really because he wanted someone to tell him that after everything he'd done, he was still a good guy? Or was it because he thought, hoped, I could pull a rabbit out of my hat of legal tricks and make everything all right?

Or because he didn't want to die alone? One thing was sure. If he was afraid he would be vilified and forgotten, he'd guaranteed that at least one person would be thinking about Alfredo Sumaya for a very long time.

"Henry …" I turned to Josh and pulled him into my arms, holding him tight.

"When I heard the gunshot," he said, tearfully, "I thought he'd killed you."

"I know. I'm sorry I put you through that, but it's over now."

He pulled away, wiped his eyes, turned his head, and said over his shoulder, "Mom? Dad? Come and meet Henry."

"Your parents?" I said in a low, shocked voice.

"I called them to let them know what had happened and that I was okay. They drove out from Encino."

A small, dark-haired woman with a heart-shaped face approached me, arm extended. Behind her was a sour-looking man with thinning hair.

"Henry," she said. "I'm Selma Mandel. Josh told us you exchanged yourself for him when that madman took him hostage."

"He wouldn't have been here in the first place except for you," the man grumbled.

"Sam," she replied sharply. "He saved our son's life." She took my hand. "Thank you."

"Yeah," Sam Mandel said, grudgingly. "Thanks."

Josh asked, "What happens now?"

"I have to go down to Parker Center to make a statement and convince the cops our house is not a crime scene, so they'll let us back in. I don't how long that will take. Why don't you go stay with your parents?"

Smiling wanly, he said, "This is the second time tonight you've tried to get rid of me."

"I don't know how long I'll be in with the cops. You'd just be sitting on an uncomfortable bench in the police station."

"I love you," he said. "I'll wait for you as long as I have to."

Behind us, his father scowled. His mother pretended she hadn't heard. He noticed it.

"Mom, Dad, why don't you go home now? Henry and I will be fine."

His mother started to speak, but his father took her by the arm and led her away.

We sat down on the curb. I put my arm around Josh. He rested his head on my shoulder, and we watched the cops begin to pull away, light bars darkening, sirens winding down, and the helicopters fading into the night sky high above the hard glitter of LA's skyline.

About the Author

Michael Nava is the author of an acclaimed series of seven crime novels featuring gay, Mexican-American criminal defense lawyer Henry Rios. The Rios novels have won seven Lambda Literary awards, and Nava has been named "one of our best" by *The New York Times*. In 2001, he was awarded the Publishing Triangle's Bill Whitehead Lifetime Achievement Award in LGBT Literature. A native Californian and the grandson of Mexican immigrants, he divides his time between San Francisco and Palm Springs.

Learn more about him at
www.michaelnavawriter.com.

Amble Press, an imprint of Bywater Books, publishes fiction and narrative nonfiction by LGBTQ writers, with a primary, though not exclusive, focus on LGBTQ writers of color. For more information on our titles, authors, and mission, please visit our website.

www.amblepressbooks.com

CPSIA information can be obtained
at www.ICGtesting.com
Printed in the USA
JSHW032044110721
16663JS00003B/3